THE
FAMILY

A DOMINIC GREY NOVEL

LAYTON GREEN

This is a work of fiction. Names, characters, organizations, places, and events are either products of the author's imagination or are used fictitiously.

THE FAMILY, A Dominic Grey novel, copyright © 2022, Layton Green. All rights reserved.

No part of this book may be reproduced, or stored in a retrieval system, or transmitted in any form or by any means, electronic, mechanical, photocopying, recording, or otherwise, without express written permission of the publisher.

Published by Sixth Street Press
Cover design by Jeroen ten Berge
Interior by JW Manus

To the Gathering

"There are mysteries that man can only guess at which age by age may only solve in part."

–Bram Stoker

THE SILK ROAD
1011 A.D.

After eleven months of grueling travel across two continents, desperate to find the best prices for his goods, Vasile Ilosvai at last reached the fabled city of Samarkand.

A fever dream of gods and kings and exotic treasure, the walled metropolis sprawled atop a hill so high and broad it resembled a plateau. As Vasile approached the magnificent sight, he slowed his horse to a walk to absorb the view. In the distance, across the windswept plains, snowcapped mountains shimmered beneath an azure sky. By some miracle of human invention—or divine intervention—the inhabitants of this land had managed to transform the parched valley beneath the city into tracts of lush green meadows, pastureland, and orchards brimming with fruit.

The eldest son of a prosperous family, Vasile had prepared an entire year for the journey. He had purchased maps and advice, made arrangements for his family, and learned enough Sogdian to negotiate when he arrived. A score of servants accompanied him, along with an equal number of mercenaries he had hired for protection, and two wagons laden with hides and beeswax from his native land.

All of the cargo had arrived intact. Two of the servants and five of the mercenaries had not. A fortuitous outcome, considering the length and difficulty of the journey. They had fended off bandits on numerous occasions, and would have perished of thirst in the desert if not for the hospitality of Moslem tribesmen. Vasile had known the risks beforehand and felt he had no choice. The invasions of the Magyars had reduced his family holdings, and that of all Dacians, to a shell of what they once had been. The fighting was constant. Able-bodied men were scarce. If something drastic was not done to raise money—such as this journey—Vasile feared his family's land and their beloved ancestral manor would be lost.

Travelers of all sorts shared the road with him: pilgrims and burghers, craftsmen and traders, warriors and wanderers. They came to this crossroads of Europe and Asia from places he had only seen on maps or heard of in wild tales from traveling caravans. Some trudged on two feet bearing great burdens, some arrived on horseback like Vasile and his entourage, some rode on the backs of great plodding beasts called camels.

After taking a moment to celebrate his arrival in quiet contemplation, absently stroking the mane of his exhausted horse, Vasile gave the signal to carry on towards the city wall made of hardened clay that stretched for kilometers around the perimeter of the hill. It was a stupefying sight, a fortification far longer and higher than the battlements of any castle or fortress upon which his eyes had ever lain.

Vasile procured lodging and a stable at a daily rate thrice that of most cities, stamped the dust off his boots, and made his way to the tavern attached to his inn. After a meal of bread, cheese, olives, and a bowl of pomegranate seeds to restore his vitality, Vasile summoned the captain of his mercenary guard and headed into the city to barter. With the proceeds, he planned to purchase a wagon full of exotic wares—silks, spices, and perhaps even the legendary paper made from mulberry bark in the Orient—to sell to the other nobles back home. Perhaps he would even swallow his pride and take his bounty to the royal courts of the hated Magyars. It would please him greatly to charge them double for the price of the goods and recoup some of the damage they had inflicted on his homeland.

Wandering the town, he noticed a stew of pungent aromas. Shishas cooking over open flames, animal dung, aromatic oils and incense, perfumes on the women, carpets heaped with a rainbow of spices from India and the Far East. After the initial shock and wonder, the assault on his olfactory senses began to cloy, and he longed for the smell of pine trees and clear mountain streams.

On his way to the nearest bazaar, he marveled at the size and grandeur of Samarkand. He walked past bathhouses with steam wafting from the central basins, minarets and cupolas, sparkling irrigation canals running like rivers through the city, Turkish dignitaries with long plaited hair, a procession of

Chinese with silkworm cocoons draped over slender poles, and even a copper-skinned princess lounging on a divan carried on the backs of slaves. Frescoes adorned the sides of the buildings, whole blocks carved and painted with elaborate scenes from the history of the region.

The seething bazaar seemed to offer every craft, foodstuff, jewelry, weapon, instrument, and other good ever produced or conceived of by the mind of man. Taken aback by the cacophony of shouting from the vendors, the jarring collision of sounds and smells and cultures, Vasile grimaced and pressed forward into the swarm of merchants, determined to find the highest prices for his wares.

By the end of the third day, Vasile's hopes had soured.

Though he considered himself a savvy trader, he had trouble negotiating in Sogdian, the principal language spoken in the bazaars. Yes, he had studied Sogdian and could speak it, but he could not keep up with the nuance and staccato beat of the dialect in the city, and it put him at a disadvantage. His goods spoke for themselves, but everyone had beeswax, and while his hides were more uncommon, they were not as highly valued as he expected. So far, the prices on offer would barely cover the cost of his trip.

Vasile was the eldest son in his family, a handsome man with a strong jaw and full brown beard, possessor of healthy livestock and bountiful land and a wife who had borne him nine children already, five of whom had survived. Vasile had guided his caravan halfway across the known world, the first of his people to undertake such a journey.

He could not, *would* not, go home empty-handed.

Dejected but unsure how to proceed, he sent his mercenary guard to the inn and wandered the city center, trying to decide on a course of action. Samarkand was a safe place, at least in the crowded neighborhoods, and he would make his way home before dark. He needed time alone to think, to clear his head from the sizzling offal and perfumed air.

He strolled for some time, mulling his options. Afternoon turned to dusk. Candles were lit, prayer vigils begun. Songbirds flitted among the trees in the failing light.

After passing through a tunnel in an inner wall that led to an older section of the city, he wandered into a public square with a gurgling fountain set at the intersection of two canals. The frescoes on the three-story buildings surrounding the plaza were faded, the clay tiles at his feet chipped and worn. A pair of young women in local dress were perched on one end of the fountain, talking in earnest, hands folded primly in their laps. Vasile sat opposite them, his fists balled at his sides, the conversation of the women drowned by the fountain.

Should he carry on to another city, further east? One less saturated with goods and merchants?

Or should he stick to his original plan, trade for the finest silks he could find, and try to reach Venice or even Londyn?

"Hail, traveler."

Startled, Vasile looked up to find a weasel-faced man dressed in woolen trousers and a long-sleeved tunic approaching from one of the narrow lanes that opened onto the courtyard. The man had a cloth bag slung over one shoulder, and the sort of leathery, wrinkled, sun-browned skin endemic to the local traders. His quick brown eyes possessed a hint of desperation.

Maybe mine own eyes, too, reflect such a state.

Vasile started to reply when—even more startling—he realized the stranger had addressed him in Latin. He answered in kind. "You speak the Latium tongue?"

"I speak many languages," the trader said. "I've traveled far and wide, and lived in Rome for many years."

"But why did you presume I spoke it?"

"My assumption is that you're an enlightened man. Your fine dress, the straightness of your bearing. Are you a nobleman?"

"My father is chieftain of our people."

"Yes, I knew it."

"What is it you want to sell me?" Vasile said, irritated by the ingratiating tone. He had just wanted a moment's peace. Did the haggling in this city never stop?

"I also judged your status by the entourage that accompanied you into the city." When Vasile drew back, the trader said, "I watch all who enter. It is my job. My esteemed client—a seller, as you presume—has tasked me with seeking out the most illustrious visitors to the city."

"Have you noticed the maharajahs, princes, and viziers?" Vasile said drily.

"Ah, I misspoke. Illustrious, yes, but of a certain . . . temperament. Someone not so jaded as the other vendors, so consumed with the baubles and petty affairs that accompany the advance of civilization. What I have to offer is most unorthodox, and rare in the extreme. It must go to a special buyer. A very special one, indeed. What my seller is seeking is a warrior. A man of valor and integrity. Someone who will appreciate the unique gifts this merchandise offers and have the courage to use them."

"I've heard enough," Vasile said as he stood. The sun had sunk beneath the buildings, leaving the courtyard in shadow, and he did not like the intensity of the trader's stare. "Ambiguous speech does not entice me."

"Do you not desire something to help you vanquish your enemies?" the trader said softly. "Reclaim that which the Magyars have stolen?"

Vasile stiffened. "How is it you know so much about me?"

"As I said—it is my business to know." The trader took a step forward and spread his hands. "Hear my client out. That is all I ask. A few minutes of your time."

Under normal circumstances, Vasile would have turned his back on this man without another thought. This close to the city center, he did not fear for his safety—he had little of value on his person—so much as he feared wasting his time with a charlatan, a seller of worthless goods.

On the other hand, the trader had touched a nerve with Vasile. *The Magyars*. It was they who had led to his family's decline. They who were the ultimate enemy.

They who had driven him to the ends of the earth.

Vasile had heard of strange and powerful weapons on offer in Samarkand, including an exploding device invented in the Orient. He had not yet seen such miracles, but perhaps they could be used to wage war? Or at least to defend his family's holdings?

Sensing Vasile's indecision, the trader tilted his head to look him in the eye.

"Come," he said, with a cautious smile that exposed a missing tooth. "My client is not far. I promise you, my friend—you will not be disappointed."

He turned his back and began walking through the square. Vasile stood in place for a long moment, his back proudly arched, and then followed.

The trader took Vasile through an open iron gate with arabesque scrollwork that led beyond another wall—how many layers did this city have?— into a quieter section of sinuous narrow lanes and buildings made of oblong bricks that looked older than the square bricks in the rest of the city.

Vasile began to question his decision. "I'll have you know I've nothing of value on my person. Are we close?"

"Oh, yes."

"Is your client in one of the bazaars?"

"He prefers a private, less chaotic environment to showcase his wares. Do not worry, my friend. All will be made clear soon."

"I hope so, or I'll be returning to my inn."

As the sun continued to descend, a chill settled into the air. Vasile drew his fur shawl tighter across his shoulders as they crossed a footbridge over a canal and heard the churn of a water mill nearby.

"Here," the trader said, when they entered a courtyard cast in shadow. Throughout the piazza, short flights of steps led down to different levels of the terraced enclosure. Dry canals and sluice-like openings in the walls led Vasile to believe the courtyard had once housed fountains and cisterns. Crumbling archways afforded glimpses of adjacent enclosures, perhaps the remains of some abandoned pleasure garden.

"Where have you taken me?" Vasile said, crossing his arms as he stood in place.

The trader descended a flight of steps that led to a stone door weathered by the centuries. "My client is just beyond this door."

"Tell him to come out."

"I'm told its best to demonstrate this item out of the public eye. I'm sure you can understand."

This reinforced Vasile's impression that it might be an exploding device of some kind. He grew excited at the thought. "Fine. Can we not meet in the open first?"

"Ah, there is one more thing. My client also has a rare . . . skin condition . . . that forces him to avoid direct light, even at dusk."

"A condition? What do you mean?"

"He is not well. That is all I know."

"He stays in this abandoned place?"

"Oh no. You misunderstand. He prefers to meet his customers here, and will return to his lodging—some of the finest in the city—after dark."

Vasile did not like the sound of this. A man who could not tolerate sunlight? What sort of curse from the gods was this? "If you mean to rob me, as I said, I've nothing with me." He withdrew a foot-long hunting knife out of the scabbard attached to his belt. "Nor will I go quietly."

"Do not fear," the trader said. "Neither I nor my client would ever consider such a base act."

"Tell me now: what is it your client has to offer?"

"I was told only that it's an item of great power which a buyer of breeding and sophistication will appreciate. Take a look. Whatever you decide, I promise to lead you back before nightfall—and the item will surely be sold by the morning."

Vasile shifted on his heels. He supposed he had come this far, and if they meant to rob him in this deserted courtyard, they could have done so already. "I'll step inside, and go no further."

"Thank you. Yes. That will suffice."

If the trader did not speak Latin with such an erudite accent, Vasile would not have proceeded. As it was, desperate to return with something useful, and curious as to the nature of this mysterious offer, Vasile held his hunting knife close to his side as he followed the trader down the steps to the bottom of the courtyard. Up close, he noticed a faint insignia carved into the center of the stone door: a spear planted into the ground on either side of a cave from which the head of a dragon with unusually long fangs was emerging. *What an odd motif.*

The trader pushed on the door and removed a tallow candle from the pouch at his side. He lit the candle with flint and steel, illuminating a large stone-walled chamber filled with slabs of granite either standing upright or stacked into crude enclosures. Vasile had never seen such a thing, and suspected they might be ancient grave markers. He noticed carvings of unfamiliar deities on the gypsum walls. No surprise there; he had seen evidence of strange religions, both new and old, all over Samarkand. He also noticed a very detailed carving of a royal hunt; though on closer inspection, he realized the size of the dogs was enormous, more akin to wolves, and the two hunters carried long spears and trailed behind the pack of canines as if marshaling them on foot. Most disturbing of all, the prey they were chasing through the forest was a human being holding a torch, as if fleeing into the night.

A rat scrabbled somewhere in the darkness. Vasile could not see how far back the gloomy chamber stretched. The air had a musty, unclean odor, as if an animal had died inside.

A hoarse voice spoke to Vasile's left. "Thank you for coming."

Vasile spun to find a tall, stooped figure standing fifteen feet away, between two of the granite slabs. Where had he come from? The figure was so deep in shadow he was barely visible, and Vasile must have failed to notice him. A tattered, full-length cloak hung like a rag off his emaciated frame. Due to the darkness and the depth of the cowl, Vasile could not see his face, though his voice did indeed sound as if it belonged to a very old man who was unwell.

The trader bowed to the cloaked figure and took a step back, giving Vasile the floor.

"I hear you have something of value," Vasile said.

"Value," the cloaked figure rasped. Like the trader, the old man was speaking in Latin. "A relative notion . . . some would consider what I have to offer the most precious gift in the world."

Despite the bizarre choice of words, the use of Latin and the obvious intelligence in the old man's voice helped Vasile relax. This was certainly no common thug. Perhaps it was a nobleman fallen on hard times. If the old man truly had something valuable to offer, even if acquired by dubious means, Vasile might have stumbled into a fortuitous situation. He wished his mercenary guard was with him, though if the situation deteriorated, surely he could defend himself against a frail old man and the trader.

"I'll be the judge of that," Vasile said, "though I admit my curiosity is aroused. I'm told you have something that might help defeat the enemies of my people—is it a new weapon?"

"It is indeed a weapon—and much, much more."

"Arms? A new device of war?"

The figure had his hands clasped behind his back. When he straightened, bringing his hands to the front of his cloak, the threadbare sleeves slid back far enough for Vasile to see that his fingernails were almost as long as his fingers, and drew to a point at the end, as if ten daggers had been affixed to his hands.

Again, what sort of man avoided the light of day and allowed his nails to grow so long? Vasile had heard of mystics from the Far East with unusual bodily characteristics; perhaps he was one of these or had visited the Orient and affected the style.

The old man started to pace back and forth, not in agitation, but slowly and proudly, as if preening before his assembled subjects. "We were once kingmakers. Masters of the night, feared by all who walked the earth. It was *we* who did the hunting. In those times we would never have stooped to such base circumstances . . ." A shiver coursed through the old man, causing him to break off and collect himself.

Vasile was growing impatient. What was the old man rambling about? Or was he simply mad, and wasting Vasile's time? "What is it you have to offer? Let's be on with this. The hour is late."

The old man flicked a pale hand. "Bring it to us."

The soft-spoken command caused the trader to scurry into the darkness. He soon returned bearing a miniature wooden chest secured with iron bands. The chest was small enough for the trader to carry under one arm, so Vasile, a much larger man, should have no problem transporting it—if he decided to purchase it. "Is it an explosive device?" he asked, as the trader set the chest down. "I've heard they can be quite potent. But if so, how is it used in war, and how do I make it in larger quantities? Do you have a method to reveal?"

The cowl of the cloak tipped downward, as if the old man were staring at the chest. "You must promise to bear this straightaway to your homeland. My vassal will give you full instructions, but above all else, you must never expose it to sunlight. Take it someplace dark and damp to fester. It has been . . . fed . . . and will survive the journey. Do you understand?"

Vasile laughed. "Fed? What are you talking about? What price are you seeking? Open this chest immediately. Or are you a court jester, and I the butt of your joke?"

"I forget, we are no longer known . . ." The old man looked off to the side, and a sigh rattled out of his throat. "Of course. You desire a display of the power which the chest can imbue. A demonstration."

Before Vasile could reply, the old man sprang forward with shocking speed and snatched the dagger out of his hands. After stepping back into the shadows, right before Vasile's eyes, the old man gripped the edge of the blade and bent the tip downwards.

"But . . . how is this possible?" Vasile whispered.

The old man stared hungrily at the gash in his hand, watching the crimson liquid pump forth as if mesmerized. Vasile realized it must have been a trick. Somehow, on the walk through the city, the trader must have switched his hunting knife with a false blade, to enable the sleight of hand and intimidate Vasile into making a purchase. The blood on the old man's hand must be that of a pig or a cow, secreted by some further legerdemain in the darkness.

Was he even an old man? Perhaps he was a younger man in disguise, and that accounted for the speed of his movement.

"Where are you from?" the old man asked. "I would know the place where my line will continue."

Vasile snarled. "I hail from Ardeal. A place I would advise such charlatans as yourselves to avoid on pain of death."

"Ardeal," he said slowly, as if tasting the word. "I know of it. Some call it *Partes Transsylvanæ*, 'the place beyond the forest.' Yes, a most fitting home."

"I'll hear no more nonsense," Vasile said, "but I will, before I leave this wretched hole, have my hunting knife returned!"

The old man took a step forward, shuddering as his eyes wrenched away from his blood-covered hand. "You've yet to inquire about the price for this transaction."

Furious at being made a fool, Vasile turned to force answers out of the ferret-faced man who had brought him here, only to find him backing towards the door with an uneasy, almost panicky, look in his eyes. The wretched trader slipped outside and shut the door behind him, leaving Vasile in utter darkness.

No doubt the old man would take the opportunity to slip away through some hidden tunnel. Cursing his own naivete, vowing to track them both down and exact justice, Vasile started to feel his way towards the door just as something jumped on him from behind. He stumbled forward as a foul-smelling cloth covered his mouth and nose, something that stank of mold and rot and the carcass of an animal decomposing in the sun.

Was the old man accompanied by ruffians hiding among the tombs? Did they jump forward with a sack to kidnap me?

Desperate to get away, smothered by the fetid cloth, Vasile reached for his sword with one hand and grasped behind him in desperation with the other, trying to dislodge his attacker. As he fought to get free, he felt a searing pain in the side of his neck, and then his entire body was lifted in the air by someone or something with incredible strength.

The sound of Vasile's screams echoed off the forgotten stone walls.

New York City
Present Day

-1-

"Raise your arms and breathe in through your nose," Dominic Grey said as he demonstrated the meditation technique to eight teenage students kneeling on the sweat-stained tatami mat in front of him. The dojo—a repurposed storage room in the basement of the Washington Heights homeless shelter—had four long rows of mats, a framed yin-yang poster, and Grey's tattered black belt hanging on a wall. "Breathe as deep as you can, deeper, deeper, deeper . . . hold it . . . now drop your arms and exhale."

"I already know how to breathe, yo," said a first-time student named Raya. She was fifteen, homeless like the others, full of spunk and crippling insecurity. "I want to learn to kick ass."

"Hush up."

The rebuke had come from Charlie, an older teen who was Grey's first and most advanced student, the proud possessor of a blue belt.

Unlike other styles, it could take ten years or more to gain a black belt in the art of Japanese Jujitsu. None of the other students had a prayer, at least not yet, of progressing past a white belt.

But that was okay.

Grey didn't give a damn about the color of a belt.

He was going to teach them the right way, the hard way, and at some point, the kids at the shelter had to decide to buy in.

Once that happened, then maybe, just maybe, the lessons they learned in the dojo would spill over into their outside life.

"When Teach says jump," Charlie continued, "you say how high. And trust me, Teach know how to jump."

"It's okay, Charlie," Grey said as Raya rolled her eyes. "It's her first class. We'll give her a break and let her see what we're about. Now let's line up and—"

The door to the dojo burst open. The volunteer chaplain at the shelter, Reverend Dale Hernandez, stood in the doorway. "There's an incident outside. I called the police, but you know how long that can take and . . . you might want to come."

Grey sprang forward, dressed in a black T-shirt and white cotton *gi* pants, not even bothering with his shoes. Though Reverend Hernandez had kept his cool, Grey had heard the urgency in his voice. The reverend had worked at the shelter for years and did not rattle easily.

"Where's the night watchman?" Grey asked as they hurried through the dilapidated brick building. A leaky faucet dripped in the distance, roaches scuttled underfoot, and the hallway smelled of urine.

"He only works four nights a week now. Budget cuts."

With a grimace, Grey pushed through the front door and saw half a dozen gang members—he recognized the colors of the hats and bandanas—clustered around a tall, attractive, slim young woman with long auburn hair and sun-kissed skin. Dressed in designer jeans and a chic brown-leather jacket, she looked as if she had just stepped off the plane from California.

"Stop it!" the woman said, trying to hold on to a camera bag.

One of the gang members, wearing a camouflage tank top despite the chill in the October night air, ripped the bag out of her hands and shoved her away. A beefy man with a moustache and a scar across his cheek caught the woman from behind and held her tight. "No need to struggle, *chica*. We take care of *gente* around here."

"That's enough," Grey said sharply. "Let her go. And give her bag back."

Some of the gang members chortled at the interruption. Grey had seen most of them before, hanging around the shelter, pushing and recruiting.

"The police are on the way," Grey added.

"But they ain't here now, are they?" the man in the tank top said. "We seen you around, *gringo*." He waved his hands in exaggerated circles. "Karate man, right?"

"Get off me!" the woman said, struggling to slip free of the man holding her. He raised her in the air and laughed.

"I won't ask again," Grey said. His eyes swept the crowd, searching for the strongest and weakest members, evaluating, judging distance, thinking through scenarios. He noticed a number of knives and guns, and caught a strong whiff of marijuana. Behind him, he heard a door opening, accompanied by youthful voices. His students must have followed him out. One more thing to worry about.

The man in the tank top stepped forward. "What you gonna do, bro? You barefoot!" The comment induced another round of laughter. "You probably never been in a street fight in yo life. What you gonna teach these kids, huh? They need to come learn from us. We'll give 'em the facts straight up."

Grey walked right towards him, stone-faced, his hands loose at his sides. He stepped on something sharp but didn't look down. When he was steps away, a switchblade popped open in the man's right hand.

"You like this, homey?" he said as Grey kept advancing. "What you gonna teach them about a *knife*?"

When Grey kept advancing, forcing a reaction, the gang member held the blade in front of him and lunged at Grey's midsection. It was an amateur thrust. Grey twisted to the side as the lunge came in, then grabbed onto the wrist holding the knife. At the same time, Grey launched a snap kick to the inside of the man's knee, causing him to crumple as Grey stepped back and corkscrewed the trapped wrist with a *kotogayeshi* wrist lock. Though the knee kick was meant to cause pain, it had also served to divert his opponent's attention, allowing Grey to bend the wrist double and throw the man to the ground as Grey stripped the knife.

The man in the tank top screamed in pain and clutched his wrist as Grey tossed the knife behind him. In close quarter combat, he often preferred the dexterity of his deadly hands to a weapon—especially when he didn't want to hurt anyone. If Grey used the knife the way he knew how to use it, there would be no turning back.

Before the other gang members had a chance to react, Grey kept stalking forward, stepping right to the beefy man holding the auburn-haired woman. The man shoved her aside and drew a gun out of his back pocket, no doubt expecting Grey to back away. Instead Grey became a blur and pounced on him before he had the gun raised, catching him by surprise. Grey gripped the man's hand, pressing the gun against his own chest before he could raise it any higher. "That's enough."

In the corner of Grey's eyes, he saw the other gang members reaching for their weapons. A siren sounded in the distance as Grey continued to speak to the burly man with the scar and the moustache, a few years older than the others and obviously their leader. Grey kept his voice firm but quiet, for the leader's ears alone. "You feel that pressure? I can flip your wrist and shoot you in the heart with your own gun. But let's go with a peaceful solution. The police are on their way. You won't lose face by leaving."

The leader tried to break the grip, but Grey held him fast, using muscles and tendons strengthened by two decades of martial arts, as well as superior leverage on his opponent's wrist. Behind him, Grey could feel weapons pointed at his back, and controlled his surging adrenaline with an effort of will.

"Hey Enrique," someone said, "should I shoot this skinny white boy?"

The sirens drew closer. Grey looked the beefy leader in the eye and saw someone unprepared to escalate the situation and risk getting shot.

Grey, on the other hand, knew the man was looking in Grey's eyes and seeing the exact opposite.

He twisted Enrique's wrist a fraction, enough to let him know he could make good on his threat. "We good here?" Grey said quietly.

Enrique winced as his eyes slipped to the side, as if checking to see if anyone else could hear the conversation. "Yeah," he muttered. "We good."

"I'm going to let you go, but I don't ever want to see you outside this shelter again."

Grey released his hold on Enrique and backed away with his hands up. Someone pressed a gun into Grey's back, and Grey stood very still. For a long moment, he wasn't sure which way the situation would turn.

"Let's go," Enrique said, as tires squealed around the corner. "This shit ain't worth no cage time."

He stuffed his gun into the back of his jeans and slipped into a dark alley adjacent to the shelter. As the other gang members followed him out, Grey exhaled and turned to the woman. "You okay?"

She flashed a weak smile and retrieved her camera bag with shaky hands. "I'm fine. Thanks for stepping in. That was very brave."

"Whoa," Raya said from behind them. "Y'all see that? Teach flipped that guy like a pancake at IHOP."

As a police cruiser rounded the corner, lights flashing, whistles and cheers broke out. Grey turned to see his students gathered by the front door of the shelter. Reverend Dale was with them, his warm brown eyes a bit wider than usual.

"Hey," the woman said. "Your foot's bleeding."

Grey looked down, noticed a trail of blood behind him, and felt a throb in his bare left foot. He must have stepped on broken glass. "Oh," he said. "Yeah. Can I help you? Did you get lost?"

"Are you always this calm after standing down a street gang?"

"I've been working on my anger management."

She eyed him as if trying to decide if he was serious. "I'm looking for someone who might be at the shelter. From the description I was given, I think I might have found him. Are you Dominic Grey?"

"That's right," he said slowly. Not many people knew his name or where to find him. "And you are?"

"Mari Radek."

Grey blinked. "Did you say *Radek*?"

"I'm Viktor's niece, and I need your help. Don't you check your phone, email?"

"I've been away. What's going on?"

She hesitated. "Is there someplace we can talk?"

"Is it urgent?"

"Very."

He compressed his lips and turned to his students. As much as he trusted Charlie, Japanese Jujitsu was not a safe art to practice without an experienced teacher involved. "Class is canceled tonight. Sorry."

"Ah, man, this was just getting good," Raya said. "So what's the lesson? Someone comes at you with a knife, you kick 'em and do that wrist flip thing?"

"The lesson is de-escalate and walk away so you don't get shot in the back."

"Hey Teach," Charlie called out as she walked towards him. "You okay?"

"All good. Can you sweep the mats and lock up for me?"

"You got it. Holler if you need me."

"Thanks," Grey said, with a small smile at how Charlie had transformed in the last year from a brash street kid into a responsible lead student. He turned back to Mari and eyed her stylish outfit. "I know a place close, but you might not like it."

"Try me. Just make sure it has a bar. I could use a stiff drink."

With a shrug, Grey told her to hang on while he returned to the dojo to change clothes. The cuts on his feet were not too deep and could wait until later. He put on his boots and jeans and motorcycle jacket, tucked his helmet under his arm, returned outside, and unchained his restored Kawasaki Avenger from the bike rack in front of the building. "Hop on."

"Um, okay," Mari said. "Do you have another helmet?"

He held out the one under his arm. "Take mine. Or call an Uber."

With another uncertain look, she decided to accept his offer. He hopped on the bike, and she slid on behind him like she'd ridden before.

"Do you know the statistics on head injuries?" she said.

Grey revved the engine.

As he carved the streets of Washington Heights with Mari clutching his waist, Grey wondered what she needed help with, and hoped his employer—and friend—was not the one in trouble. Like Grey, Professor Viktor Radek was supposed to have been on vacation over the past week.

Viktor rarely took time off work. In fact, in the years they had worked together, investigating cult activity and bizarre occurrences around the world, Grey could not remember Viktor spending more than a long weekend away from a case or a research assignment. There was a short stint when Viktor had checked himself into a sanatorium in the Swiss Alps, after a case involving his past had taken him to a very dark place, but that was hardly a vacation.

Grey took Mari to a dive bar near Columbia. Not the type of dive bar that catered to hipsters, but the type of scruffy local joint, hidden in plain sight all over Manhattan, that attracted serious drinkers and loners. The kind of place with a single line of booths across from the bar, dim lighting, a kickass greasy burger, and a bartender who was most definitely not in college. Grey considered it an upgrade from the bars he used to visit, when his younger and angrier self had sought out the edgiest watering holes in town, daring someone to get in his face.

To Mari's credit, as Grey led her inside, she didn't bat an eye at the sticky floor or the scarred wooden booths. On the other hand, when the bartender swung by to take their order, Mari brightly asked if there were any house cocktails.

The bartender had streaks of gray in her ponytail. "Sure. We got Jack and Coke, rum and Coke, and whiskey and Coke."

Mari's mouth opened and then closed. "What about a wine list?"

The bartender tapped the side of her head. "Got it right here. House cab, house merlot, house chardonnay."

"Maybe I'll have a beer," Mari said weakly.

"Good choice. Let me guess: IPA?"

"That'd be great. Anything local is fine."

"I'll take a draft lager," Grey said, as the bartender nodded at him in recognition. "Maybe some food in a bit."

"You got it, hon."

After the bartender left, Mari took off her jacket, revealing toned arms and a blouse with an abstract southwestern design. She leaned her head against the booth and expelled her tension with a long breath.

"Sorry again about tonight," Grey said. "It's a little rough around there. You did good, though. Kept it together."

"I've been in some rough places before."

Grey didn't respond. He knew they had very different definitions of *rough places*.

"I've just never been . . . manhandled . . . like that," she said. "It's not a good feeling."

"No. It's not."

After the bartender dropped off the beers, Mari took a long drink and looked surprised. "It's good."

"Why are you here?" Grey said. "What sort of help do you need?"

"You really don't know? I mean you said you don't check your phone or email, but I didn't take you literally. Oh, wait—are you on a screen sabbatical?"

"I call that a vacation, but yeah, I checked out for a week. Took my bike and went to Maine to just . . . anyway, I got back right before class. Dropped my bag and went straight to the shelter without grabbing my phone. I was running late."

She gave him an odd look, as if he were speaking in a foreign language.

"Mari," Grey said. "What's going on?"

"It's Uncle Viktor. He's disappeared. I'm really worried about him."

Grey felt a chill sweep through him. Viktor had made plenty of enemies over the years. "What do you mean, *disappeared*? He said he was going to his house in the country. Did you check there?"

"He never went. I was visiting him in Prague, and we were supposed to go to Prášily together. But something came up. A new case."

"And I was already gone." Grey swore. "I told him to stay low."

"I don't think he took the case seriously. At least not at first."

"What did it involve? Where did he go? When did you last see him?"

As Mari set her beer down and stared across the table, Grey saw worry and something else, an uneasy expression straddling the line between fear and disbelief, mirrored in her eyes. He had seen a similar look all too often working with Viktor, and he didn't like it one bit.

"I know how this is going to sound," she said, "but my uncle disappeared . . . he disappeared chasing a vampire."

Prague
Eight Days Prior

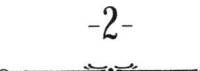

-2-

A grandfather clock in the hall struck the midnight hour.

Professor Viktor Radek, ensconced in a leather armchair in the ground floor study of his Prague townhome, took a sip of Suisse-Couvet absinthe and gazed at the gaslit cobblestone street outside his bay window, a glimpse of history and enigmas and all things lost to the world.

Ah, how he loved the city he called home. No place on Earth—and Viktor had seen many, many places—could match the atmosphere of Prague's Old Town. Viktor was a professor of religious phenomenology and solved unusual cases for a living. To a person like this, someone who often descended like a coal miner with a bobbing headlamp into the darkness of the human soul, someone who sought to unravel the mysteries of the universe like most people worked Sudoku on a plane, the fog-drenched spires and Gothic mystique of Prague were like catnip.

Viktor was in an extraordinarily fine mood that Friday evening. On Monday morning, he was set to visit his lake house near the picturesque village of Prášily for an entire week. In general, he did not care for extended holidays. He loved his life's work, and his mind, if left to cogitate on still waters for too long, became restless and unmoored. He appreciated a relaxing weekend but could not remember his last true holiday.

This time was different. His favorite niece, Mari Radek, had just arrived from Los Angeles. She was sleeping off her jetlag in a guest bedroom upstairs. A documentary filmmaker who had stolen his heart the day she was born to Tomas Radek, Viktor's younger brother, Mari had never visited Viktor by herself. He very much looked forward to spending time with her and showing off the beauty of the Czech countryside.

Viktor admired his niece. She was a wonderful person, passionate about humanitarian causes. Yes, his brother had coddled her too much during her youth in a gated community in Brentwood, but after college, instead of continuing to wallow in privilege, Mari had rejected her father's pleas to join the family commercial real estate empire, moved into a studio apartment about as big as Viktor's thumb, and turned her attention to those less fortunate. Her first film was a gritty but heartwarming chronicle of urban gardeners in Los Angeles seeking to alleviate hunger and malnutrition in impoverished neighborhoods. For her sophomore effort, she wanted to focus on the country of her ancestors. Mari had yet to settle on an angle. First she planned to travel around and speak with the people, an effort in which Viktor was delighted to assist.

He harbored secret hopes she would highlight his country's tradition of handcrafted marionettes, as well as its strange obsession with death. But he was certainly no arbiter of art for the younger generation.

A ring from his cell phone interrupted his reverie. Wondering who might be calling at such a late hour—perhaps his brother, to check on Mari?—Viktor set his absinthe down and rose to get his phone from the kitchen, stretching out to his full seven foot height. He was closing in on sixty, and his knees had begun to ache.

Bah. If that is the most pressing sign of mortality at this age, I count myself lucky.

The caller was Zuzana Andrasko, First Lieutenant with the Prague Police Department. Twenty years ago, when Zuzana had been a new officer investigating a triple homicide, she had attended a lecture Viktor had given on pathological cult behavior, trying to better understand the human psyche. Impressed by his insights, she had stayed in touch over the years, calling upon him for help not just with those rare cases that involved his specialty—cult behavior or mysterious phenomena outside the normal ambit of police work—but whenever she needed a fresh perspective on a tough case.

Normally she invited him to a beer hall after work. If Zuzana was calling after midnight, something serious had occurred.

"Forgive the late hour," she said after he answered. "Were you sleeping?"

"I haven't willingly retired before midnight since I was a boy. The evening hours suit me."

"Of course they do. Listen, Professor, something urgent and . . . rather bizarre . . . has come up. There was a murder in Staré Město."

"That's unusual."

"Unfortunate as well. Tourism is crucial to the city, and we maintain a strong presence in the Old Town. Outside of a drunken brawl that ends poorly, serious crime is rare. Not only do we have a murder . . . but it's a very disturbing one."

"How so?"

"We're still piecing it together, but earlier tonight a young woman was found dead in an alley behind a popular gastropub. Forensics will help confirm, but we're assuming the crime occurred where she was found."

"How did she die?"

"Her neck was broken."

"Could she have fallen at an awkward angle?"

"Sure, but that doesn't account for the partial exsanguination of her body."

Viktor's eyebrows rose. "Where was the wound? Please don't tell me she had fang marks on her neck?"

"The twin bite marks were on her left wrist, piercing the radial artery. The pathologist estimates more than a third of the victim's blood was lost."

He waited a beat to see if she was joking, though knowing Zuzana, she would never make light of a murder. "And these fang marks . . . do they appear to be bestial in nature? Canine? Serpentine?"

"To be honest, we don't know yet. We hardly have an expert on such things. But even if it was an animal, the bite marks were too far apart for a snake, and what sort of animal makes a precise bite with no other observable soft tissue damage, and consumes three pints of blood or more?"

"I . . . don't know."

"Nor do we. I don't know what the hell is going on, but the inference is obvious, and I'm terrified of the negative publicity this will bring. We can't have a vampire impersonator stalking the city, scaring away tourists."

"What makes you think the perpetrator will act again?"

"What makes you think they won't?"

Viktor had stepped back into the study, pacing back and forth across the Persian rug as he absorbed the bizarre account.

"I hate to ask," Zuzana said, "but could you meet me at the crime scene? I want your eyes on this. You might be able to provide a rationale, help stave off the wild claims we both know are coming."

"Do you really need me, in the twenty-first century, to debunk a vampire story?"

"You know the tabloids. You know what will happen."

"My niece arrived earlier tonight. We're touring the city this weekend and leaving for the country on Monday."

"I've no intention of disrupting those plans. If you could just come down here, Viktor, I'd appreciate it. My detectives are unnerved by this one. *I'm* unnerved."

Viktor sighed. "I'm not sure how I can help, but if it will make you feel better, I'll come."

"Thank you." She gave him the name and address of the gastropub and offered to send a car.

"It's a short walk away," he said.

"The murderer is still at large. Let someone pick you up."

"Don't bother. I'll bring my garlic and my holy water."

Under a silver moon lurking among the clouds, the mid-October air seeping into his bones, Viktor tucked his hands into the pockets of his wool overcoat and strode through the labyrinthine streets of Old Town. It was not tourist season. Much of the neighborhood was quiet at this hour. His breath fogged the air as his Italian shoes whisked across the cobblestones, crunching on clusters of fallen leaves. Wood smoke poured from the townhome chimneys, the crisp aroma of the season infused the air.

After four blocks he heard voices and saw blinking lights flashing off a building. He followed the commotion to a brick alley cordoned off by police vehicles. Viktor's nose wrinkled at the odor of stale frying oil wafting through a kitchen vent. Halfway down the alley, just in front of a forensics van, a cluster of law enforcement personnel hovered around a body on the street.

Lieutenant Andrasko, dressed in a beige coat with the emblem of the Prague police on her sleeve, waved Viktor through the blockade on the south side of the alley. The lieutenant had cropped blond hair, a round face, and glacial blue eyes that missed nothing. Though short for a Czech woman, she possessed a domineering presence much larger than her stature. She was known for her quick temper as well as her poise under fire, and Viktor suspected her fascination with the human psyche had originated with her own mercurial nature.

"I appreciate you coming," she said as he met her.

The other officers made way for them, eying Viktor with guarded curiosity. He did not usually deal with rank and file officers, and did not recognize anyone besides the lieutenant.

The harsh glow of a portable spotlight illuminated the bloodless lips and waxen skin of the corpse. Shoulders hunched and heavy brow furrowed, Viktor loomed like some huge bird of prey over the body of the woman splayed on the cobblestones.

She had been young, thin, dark-haired, and blessed with wide Slavic cheekbones. Her lipstick was smudged, and her belted jacket had spread apart to reveal a knee-length jade skirt, a shimmery silver blouse, and a black pearl necklace nestled in her cleavage. The unnatural angle of her head in relation to her neck made Viktor wince.

Finally his eyes latched onto the twin holes in the woman's right wrist, set two inches apart and crusted in newly dried blood.

The lieutenant stood beside him. "On your way over, I was told the bite marks—I refuse to call them fangs—are correlative to the distance between the upper canine teeth for the average human male."

Though not a particularly gruesome wound, the bite possessed a gravitas, a magnetism, which drew Viktor's gaze to the symmetrical punctures. For all of his experience with twisted killers and strange occurrences, he could not suppress a chill that swept down his back. Not because he was concerned about a vampire of legend, but because *someone* had done this. It was an unnatural act for one human being to bite another. Primal, animalistic. And the exsanguination . . . siphoning away the life force of another person was an affront to a society held together by laws and norms and rational behavior.

A line that should not have been crossed.

"Was she violated?" Viktor asked.

"There's no obvious sign of that, other than the smudged lipstick, but we'll find out soon enough."

"Fingerprints?"

"They wouldn't hold up on the body, or even the necklace."

"Interesting the necklace wasn't stolen," Viktor said.

"It's not that valuable, a few thousand koruna at most. But you're right, this wasn't a robbery."

Viktor stroked his clean-shaven chin, absorbing the crime scene. Nothing of value stolen, at least of which they knew, and no sign of a struggle.

An odd crime, even without the disturbing loss of blood.

"First thoughts?" she asked. "Have you ever seen anything like this?"

"In real life? No. And if someone is attempting to mimic the *nosferatu*, or at least the popularized concept of one, then why bite the wrist instead of the neck? I don't suppose it theoretically matters which artery is targeted, but I've never encountered this in the lore. But let us put childish superstition aside, and step back a moment. Who was she? What do we know? Were other clues found nearby?"

"Her name was Daryna Kishka, a twenty-three-year-old au pair from Moldova. We found a work permit in her purse, and sent two officers to her residence in Holešovice to notify the family."

"What else was in the wallet?"

"Cosmetics, a small amount of money, a few more personal items. Forensics will run a thorough scan."

"How did the host parents react?"

"As you can imagine. Shocked, horrified, distraught. The children loved her, and the parents said Daryna was a model employee. Never any trouble. They knew she was out on the town tonight, but claimed they had no idea what might have happened, or who she was with. She left the house alone. There will be a follow-up interview, but we didn't press them further tonight."

"Did Daryna frequent this pub?"

"The bartender has seen her around," the lieutenant said absently as she glanced around the crime scene, her face tight with stress. "We've closed the pub and are interviewing the staff. Listen, we can handle that part of the investigation. I just need to know *why* someone would do such a thing, and whether there's some explanation we might be missing. Something we can give to the press instead of—" she waved a hand across the woman's body—"*this*."

Viktor looked down on the lieutenant. "The interviews *are* the investigation. I assume you do not want me to inform you that a mythological creature crept out of the darkness to drink the blood of this woman, nor would I do such a thing. Your answers, as I believe you already know, will be found in the perverse motivation of a flesh-and-blood human being. Is that not why you really called me here, lieutenant? To provide insight into the depravity of the monsters who walk among us in full daylight?"

Before she could respond, a woman about her same age, dressed in jeans and a white smock, stepped out of the forensics van. The lieutenant gave Viktor a long look and waved the woman over.

"Jana, this is Professor Radek. He consults with me from time to time. Professor, Jana is a crime scene pathologist, and a very good one." She turned to Jana. "You can speak freely."

After a slight hesitation, no doubt wondering what Viktor specialized in, the pathologist looked down at the body. "I've done what I can tonight. I'll issue a full report when the lab results come in, and another after the autopsy."

"Did you find any trace evidence?"

"Plenty," Jana said. "Hair and fibers in multiple locations, and saliva on the wound. Human saliva, I might add."

"Good God," the lieutenant said. "At least we have a shot for a DNA match."

"It's possible, yes. I'm fairly certain there was sexual activity, but I'm not at all certain it was forced. In fact I would guess it wasn't. There are no significant skin abrasions apart from the obvious wounds. Not even minor bruising."

"So what, they had sex, and then he broke her neck and . . . did the rest? Or I suppose the order could be reversed."

"I'll look into this further and update you after the autopsy. I will say that I found certain aspects of the wound quite unusual."

"Of course it's unusual," the lieutenant snapped. "It's bloody hellish."

"Understand these are just preliminary on-scene findings. Pathologists, as you're probably aware, recognize three types of sharp force injuries. Stab wounds, incised wounds, and chop wounds. The twin punctures on the deceased fall closest to stab wounds, where the direction of force applied is generally perpendicular to the surface of the skin, and the wound is typically deeper than it is wide. Without the murder weapon in hand, it's difficult or even impossible to determine for certain the type of instrument used to inflict the wound. That said, we usually have a pretty good idea. I feel confident, due to the circumference or margin of the puncture in relation to the depth, and the tissue bridging inside the wound, that a knife was not used. Or any other sort of typical stab weapon we encounter, such as scissors or box cutters."

"So what did the perp have?"

"As we suspected, I feel confident saying the two puncture wounds are evidence of a bite."

The lieutenant stared hard at Jana. "But you said only human saliva was present."

"Correct."

"Humans don't have fangs, Jana. How do you explain the sharpness of these wounds?"

The pathologist's eyes slipped to the side. "I can't."

"What about an animal?"

Jana shook her head. "Almost an impossibility. There would be bruising or scratches, hair traces, some evidence of the attack of a predator. And the blood loss . . . how to explain that? By the way, vampire bats would not be capable of this, and the fang marks would be much closer in proximity. I checked."

Viktor waved a hand in dismissal. "Do teeth leave identifiable marks or traces?"

"I'm not sure I understand," Jana said.

"On the wound. Can you tell for certain that human teeth were used? As opposed to say, metal teeth? Aluminum teeth?"

"Ah, I see. You're thinking an instrument of some sort was used to pierce the skin, and then—" Jana swallowed, as if hesitant to even voice the thought—"the perpetrator drank the blood of the victim, thus leaving a saliva residue."

"Precisely," Viktor said.

The lieutenant's eyebrows rose with approval, desperate for an alternate explanation.

"It's a good thought," Jana said. "Under normal circumstances, it would be impossible to tell for certain, apart from saliva residue, whether the puncture wounds stemmed from an actual bite. A wooden or other organic tool might leave a trace, but a sharp metal instrument, the likely alternative, would not. Which reminds me: there were no hilt marks on the flesh, which are sometimes present with a knife."

"Any other irregularities?" the lieutenant asked.

"Two. First, the depth of the puncture wounds is quite deep, somewhat more than you might expect from, I don't know, human canines filed to a point."

"What do you make of that?" the lieutenant said.

"I've no idea. As he suggested, perhaps some type of instrument was devised to do this."

"Given the size of the wound," Viktor said, "do you have any idea how long it might take to consume that much blood?"

The pathologist's head seesawed. "Variable, but I estimate at least fifteen minutes. The perforation of the artery would definitely increase the rate."

"A dedicated endeavor," Viktor murmured. "What about the neck wound? Is there anything strange about that?"

"Only the force of application required to break a neck in that manner. It's not as easy as the movies make it seem. Something like that would require, in my opinion, an extremely large male." She eyed Viktor. "Someone your size, or else incredibly strong. Another alternative, I suppose, is the velocity and power of a judo throw, performed by a martial arts expert."

Viktor made a mental note to consult Grey on this when he returned from vacation.

"The second irregularity is the lack of spatter or drip pattern. I would expect less of this with a clean stab wound, but here there was none. Not a trace of blood on the deceased's flesh or clothing."

The lieutenant grimaced. "Implying, once again, a clean bite followed by . . . consumption."

Jana opened her palms and gave a curt nod. The officers close enough to overhear the conversation shuffled side to side and glanced uneasily at the body.

After a long moment with her lips pressed together, the lieutenant turned to Viktor. "Let's go inside. There's someone I want you to talk to."

Viktor did not bother to point out her change of mind. Instead he nodded at the request, and it took him a long moment to divert his gaze from the twin puncture wounds marring the smooth white skin of Daryna's wrist.

New York City

-3-

Grey leveled a hard stare at Mari from across the booth in the dive bar. "What do you mean, Viktor disappeared chasing a vampire? Is this a joke?"

He might have asked her for some ID, except the Radek family resemblance was unmistakable. About three inches shy of Grey's lean six-foot-one, Mari had Viktor's high waist, long legs, wide-spaced eyes, distinguished bearing, and hook-like curve at the tip of her nose. He could see Viktor's face in hers, and, despite her rather innocent foray into one of New York's grittier neighborhoods, Grey could tell by the glint in her eye that she had inherited some of his employer's stubborn resolve.

Not too much, Grey hoped, because Viktor had a habit of ignoring advice that conflicted with his interests, even where his personal safety was concerned.

"A joke?" Mari said. "My uncle's been missing for almost a week."

Grey put a hand to his temple. "Listen, you've been through a lot. Take a deep breath, clear your head, and tell me exactly what's going on. Start at the beginning."

She pursed her lips, and, after a small nod, seemed to calm down. "Eight days ago, I went to visit my uncle in Prague. I'm a documentary filmmaker. I'm planning to shoot my next film in Czechia. Viktor thinks the name change was ridiculous, by the way, and prefers *Czech Republic* in English. Anyway, I was going to tour the country my family is from and see my favorite uncle. Win-win, right? Uncle Viktor and I were supposed to spend the weekend in the city and head to his country house on Monday."

Grey knew that Viktor, the scion of minor Czech nobility, owned a handful of properties. He assumed the Radek fortune extended to Mari's family as well. "He didn't mention you were going with him," Grey said, "but that's not unusual. Viktor rarely discusses his personal life."

"Funny, he said the same thing about you. What is it you do for him? I know you're his partner—"

"I'm his employee."

"I'm just telling you what he said."

"Well, Viktor writes the checks, and I cash them. Draw your own conclusions. Anyway, Viktor rarely teaches anymore, and spends most of his time consulting for police agencies or taking cases for private clients. I help with his investigations whenever he needs me."

"What kind of cases do you investigate? He's never really talked about it. I was going to ask him during my visit, but I never got the chance."

"Viktor has such a wide base of knowledge, and has seen so many bizarre things, that his specialty in pathological cult behavior has morphed into anything . . . out of the ordinary. The strange, the uncanny, the—"

"Supernatural?" she said, putting her elbows on the table and leaning forward.

"Viktor specializes in *debunking* the supernatural," Grey said, though he knew that was not the full story.

Sometimes even Viktor has no easy explanation for the things we've seen.

"How fascinating," Mari said. "I'd love to hear more about your cases and your background—"

"Focus, Mari. What happened to Viktor?"

"I was getting there."

"So do it. Every minute could count."

She steepled her hands against her mouth. "You're right. Okay. It started out normal. The day after I arrived, we toured the city together, and that evening he said he needed to attend to something. I went to a pub near his townhome for dinner. Have you visited him in Prague?"

"Yes."

"So you know he lives right in the center of Old Town. That night he walked to wherever it was he went. When he returned home, we had a glass of wine together, and he seemed . . . absent."

"He gets that way if he's deep in a case, or intrigued by something."

"I asked if something had happened," she said. "He waved it off and said it was just a small matter with the Prague police."

"That's it? Nothing else?"

She shook her head. "Not right then. The next day he canceled our lunch plans. He was very apologetic, but I didn't mind. I had plenty to see and do. That night he took me to a fancy restaurant and asked for a favor. He said something pressing had come up, and asked if I would mind rescheduling our trip to the lake house for the following week. I won't lie, I thought it was a little odd, and my feelings were a tiny bit hurt, but in terms of my schedule, it wasn't a big deal. I just rearranged my itinerary."

"Did you ask him why?"

"Of course. He was evasive and said the police needed his help with some urgent research. By this time, I had an idea what he was helping with. So would you, if you hadn't reverted back to 1950 for the last week."

"I still haven't checked the news. Enlighten me."

"You haven't heard about the Prague Vampire?"

"Um, no."

"You will when you rejoin the modern world. Actually, it's probably no longer news over here. We have plenty of political disasters and celebrity gossip to occupy our time." She took a long drink. "The night I arrived in Prague, a woman was murdered behind a bar in the Old Town, not far from Uncle Viktor's house. Her neck had been snapped, and her body . . . exsanguinated. Drained of blood."

Grey's eyebrows lifted.

"They found a bite mark on her wrist—a human bite mark."

"Jesus."

"As you can imagine, the press and the public went wild, and the police—"

"Called Viktor immediately."

She nodded. "I didn't know for sure until I went to the police myself, but yeah, they called him that night, knowing what was coming."

"Have they arrested anyone?"

"There are no suspects. Or at least that's the story they're feeding the public. I don't buy it."

"Why not?"

"The night after he asked me to reschedule our trip, he packed a small bag and left for the week. At first, I didn't think too much about. I went to a town called Kutna Hora for some research, trying to figure out an angle for my documentary. Viktor even checked in with me from time to time."

"Where did he go?"

"I know he went to Romania, and maybe somewhere else. He wasn't specific, and I'm kicking myself for not finding out more. He always asks about me, and never reveals anything about himself. He's just so sweet, the best uncle you could ask for . . ."

She buried her face in her beer to hide her emotions, and Grey could tell how much she loved her uncle. A mental picture entered Grey's mind of the somber, seven-foot-tall professor bending over to play with Mari as a small child, and it gave him new insight into his friend's character.

"I'm sorry," Grey said. "I was a little harsh earlier."

"No, you're right," she said, firming her jaw. "We need to focus."

"He's probably fine. He's a big boy, a very big boy, and as I said, he tends to get lost in his research."

Mari pressed her lips together. "I want to believe that, but I'm not sure he's fine, Grey. In fact, I'm pretty sure he's not."

"Keep talking."

She closed her eyes and took another calming breath. "As I said, I don't know what happened the night I was with him in Prague. I assumed he was with the police. Then he left, and I haven't seen him since. But the night I returned to Prague from Kutna Hora, I knew he'd been home."

"How?"

"There was a dirty glass of absinthe in the sink—did you know he likes absinthe?"

"Um, affirmative."

"I get the sense he likes it, well, quite a bit. I never knew that before. Anyway, I checked the house, but he wasn't there. There was no note for me. Nothing. And he knew I was coming back late that night."

"So he came back and left the night you got there, without saying a word?"

"Strange behavior for an uncle supposed to be hosting his niece, don't you think?"

"Was his car in the garage?"

"Yes. The week before it was also. I assumed he flew somewhere and took a taxi to the airport."

"Viktor doesn't drive very much," Grey said. "Keep going."

"I tried to call him but he never answered. At this point, I was a little freaked out. I'd been watching the news and just knew Viktor was involved with investigating that weird murder. Three more days passed. Still no word. I got nosy and searched the house. His laptop was gone, but in his study, I found a section with some books missing. Maybe they were missing before, but the section concerned Slavic mythology and folklore. I also found a stack of academic papers in his reading chair, as if he'd been poring through it before he left. The papers all concerned an organization called *Societas Draconistarum*, or the Order of the Dragon."

Grey squinted. "Never heard of it."

"Me either. The Order was a chivalric society in the Middle Ages, founded in 1408 by the King of Hungary. From what I gathered, the Order was modeled after the monastic military orders of the Crusades, such as the Knights Templars or Hospitallers."

"Bringing back the good old days of plunder and oppression."

"I guess. I know this Order of the Dragon was mad exclusive. Only monarchs and high aristocracy could join. It didn't make a huge splash in history, certainly nothing like the Templars. But after the fall of Constantinople, the Order of the Dragon carried on in Eastern and Central Europe, particularly in Hungary, Serbia, and Romania. In fact, during this time period, someone named Vlad II, an illegitimate child who later became ruler of Wallachia, took his name from the society. He called himself Vlad Dracul. Starting to sound familiar?"

"Now you're joking. Dracula?"

"Vlad II was the *father* of Vlad the Impaler, who is thought to be the model for the vampire in Bram Stoker's famous novel. And no, I'm afraid none of this is a joke, though I don't know what it all means."

"Viktor wouldn't care about a fictional character," Grey muttered, "unless he had a very good reason to. Or maybe that stack of research didn't relate to his investigation."

"Do you believe that?"

Grey rubbed at his stubble and rested his fist against the tip of a fine-boned nose left a touch off-center from numerous breaks. "You mentioned potential witnesses. What makes you think that?"

"After I saw his office and couldn't reach him, I went to the police. A lieutenant confirmed my uncle was working with them—"

"What was the lieutenant's name?"

"Andrasko."

"And the witnesses?"

"It isn't much, but I saw a case file spread out on the lieutenant's desk—she was kind enough, since I was Viktor's niece, to invite me back. It was obvious she was working the case in the news. I saw photos of the body and the crime scene on her desk." Mari shuddered. "I also saw a folder marked *witnesses*. It wasn't very thick, but it had multiple tabs."

"So they're looking into people. That's good information. Who was the victim?"

"A Moldovan au pair. Young and very beautiful. She had been in the country for a year. As far as the Czech press is reporting, she was a random victim."

"And you think Viktor might be tracking down a lead, possibly on one of the witnesses?"

"It's the only thing I can think of. Why else would he disappear? Why can't I reach him, Grey? After I contacted the police, I didn't know what else to do. Then I remembered how he talked about you. I thought . . . I thought you should know."

"You thought right," Grey said. He pressed his lips together as he tapped his fingers on the table, processing everything she had told him.

"What are you thinking?"

He finished his beer and signaled for the bill. "That I need to check my phone."

Grey took Mari to his fifth-floor studio loft in Hudson Heights. The exposed-brick loft had a stained concrete floor and a shoji screen separating his sleeping area. Besides his platform bed, the only furniture were some chrome bar stools at the kitchen counter where he ate his meals, a futon, and a pair of overstuffed reading chairs by a window, all of which he had picked up at estate sales. A wall of built-in bookshelves contained a selection of novels, martial arts theory, philosophy, history, and travel guides.

When Grey had first started working with Viktor, he had rented the studio for a year, unsure what the future held. Half a decade later, he was still there. It was longer than he had lived anywhere in his life except for his early teen years when his father was stationed in Tokyo.

Home was a strange concept for a wandering soul like Grey, and he still didn't quite know what it meant, or how he was supposed to act. He didn't know his neighbors or have a lawn to mow. But he had a favorite coffee shop down the street, great takeout, a used bookstore with an excellent foreign literature selection, and what else did one need in life? He liked teaching at the homeless shelter and watching over Charlie, and, since Grey's job with Viktor required frequent travel, New York City was a logical place to base himself.

"Nice view," Mari said, gazing at the puzzle box of apartment buildings and brownstones outside the window. "Though I fail to notice the sort of normal electronic devices that, you know, signal the presence of sentient life. Which makes the fact that you checked out for an entire week more believable."

"It was five days, and I have a laptop. I listen to music and watch things sometimes."

"It's called streaming, Grey."

He strode to the kitchen counter to turn on his cell phone. Once it powered up, he saw a text from Charlie earlier in the day, a text from his landlord informing him there would be some construction near the building, and a voicemail from Viktor, sent four days ago. Grey pressed play and put the phone on speaker.

"Hello Grey, I trust you're enjoying the respite and the New England fall. I hear the leaves are quite colorful this time of year. I wanted you to know I'm headed to Romania for a spot of research. I know, I'm supposed to be taking time off. Something came up, and, well, it's quite a story that I won't get into at the moment. I don't foresee any trouble, but I like to keep you informed of my whereabouts. I'll be staying at the Hotel Platinia in Cluj-Napoca if you need me, and I expect to return to Prague by the end of the week. I'll let you know when I arrive. Take care."

Grey played the message two more times, checking for signs of duress or anything else out of the ordinary. There were two more texts sent in the days following the voicemail. Both texts asked Grey to call as soon as he could. The later text mentioned that Viktor had arrived in Budapest, and included the name of his hotel.

"I've tried the hotel," Mari said. "He checked out days ago, and they have no idea where he went."

After trying to call Viktor with no success—it went straight to voicemail—Grey scrolled through his missed calls, opened his email, and even went down to the foyer to check his snail mail.

Nothing else from Viktor.

"It's odd," Grey said after he returned to his loft and stood by the window with his arms folded, staring at the city lights.

Mari walked up beside him. "What's that?"

"You said he returned to Prague two nights ago?"

"I feel sure of it."

"That's two days after he called and left a message. Even if something happened to him in Prague—and I'm not saying it did—why didn't he reach out again when he arrived?"

"Maybe it slipped his mind."

"Do you often find that things slip your uncle's mind?"

Mari swallowed. "No."

"He gets absorbed in his research, but I'd have expected an email, a quick text, something. He knows I'd worry about him, unless . . ."

Unless something happened to him. Grey balled his fist at his side. *Why hadn't Viktor just gone on vacation?*

Mari looked away. "Do you think it's possible he isn't responding for some reason? Maybe . . . maybe he's doing some undercover research?"

Grey turned to face her. "Sure, it's possible," he said grimly.

Her eyes slipped to the side again.

After this much time had passed, Grey did not believe Viktor was choosing not to answer his phone or respond to Grey or his niece. In Grey's mind, one of two things had happened. Either Viktor had waited too long to reach out for help with whatever he was involved in, and had never gotten the chance—or he *had* reached out, and his efforts were intercepted.

Either way, the outcome was the same.

Grey pulled up the number for Jacques Bertrand on his phone and tried to call him. No answer. Grey left a message to return his call as soon as possible.

"Who was that?" Mari asked.

"Viktor's Interpol contact. If there's someone besides me that Viktor might reach out to, it's Jacques."

"*Interpol?* My uncle?"

"If anything really strange comes across the desk of some local police station, it usually gets to Interpol, and Jacques calls Viktor."

"Oh." She squeezed her eyes shut and pressed her hands to the sides of her face. Grey had the sense she was trying to come to grips with this new side of her uncle. "I've opened a missing person's report in Prague, but nothing's come of it. What should we do? We have to try to find him."

"I agree. I think the next step is to go to Prague and see if we can retrace his steps from that point on. I'll book something tonight and leave first thing in the morning."

"Let's book it right now," she said. "Together."

After purchasing a pair of flights for early the next morning, Grey offered to let Mari crash at his loft, but she had already booked a hotel near Columbia. He drove her over on his bike, then returned to wolf down some ramen, put some antibiotic ointment on the bottom of his foot, and pack a bag for the Czech Republic.

When he finally stopped moving, he stood in the kitchen and ran a hand through the cowlicks in his short dark hair. He and Viktor had been through the fire together. Saved each other's lives time and again. Though about as dissimilar as two people could be, they had become close over the years, a pair of lone wolves who preferred to struggle in silence with their demons but who had learned to lean on each other for support, even if nothing was said.

Grey had no siblings, had buried his mother as a teen, and his father, if he was still alive, was dead to Grey.

Viktor and Charlie were the only family he had.

In tune with his worry, Grey could feel the old rage bubbling forth, the devils inside him clamoring to emerge.

Just take it easy. Losing your head won't help Viktor. Stay calm and rational. Maybe the explanation isn't what you think it is.

Feeling jittery, Grey laid out his tatami mat and performed a Qigong breathing routine until he felt more centered. When he finished, knowing he needed to rest but not tired in the slightest, he nursed a beer by the window for a long time, staring at the sliver of moon in the night sky, wondering what Viktor had stumbled into.

When sleep finally came, Grey dreamt of a pair of dragons creeping through a winter forest at dusk, their mottled green scales absorbing the failing light, and their sharp claws leaving pools of blood where they crunched into the snow.

Prague

-4-

As Viktor and Lieutenant Andrasko left the alley where Daryna was killed, stepping through the back door of a gastropub, Viktor recognized the rough stone walls and long concave ceiling from prior visits. *Setmění*, the popular establishment was called. *Nightfall*. He remembered it as candlelit and full of atmosphere, but the bar had been shut down for the night and emptied of patrons, the glare of fluorescent lights exposing stains on the wooden tables.

A handful of staff with shellshocked faces were rolling silverware at the bar or wiping down tables. Next to a pair of wine barrels in the corner, a police officer was interviewing a woman with a white dress shirt and a clipboard. One of the managers, Viktor presumed.

"We've talked to the staff," the lieutenant said in a low voice. "Plenty of them noticed Daryna in the bar. No one knows her, but two different people said the DJ was trying to chat her up all night. That's him over there."

She pointed to a young man slouched in a booth with his arms crossed, glaring at the seat across from him. He was dressed in ripped jeans and a black T-shirt with a skull on the front. He wore his hat sideways and had a pair of headphones slung around his neck.

"He does not appear pleased to be here," Viktor said.

"I asked him to wait around so I could talk to him myself."

"Is he a person of interest?"

"Let's go find out."

As they slid into the seat opposite the DJ, he slumped even further, and gave them a wary glance. A wispy goatee made his rat-like face seem even longer than it was. "Can we get this over with? I told you I've got another gig tonight."

"What's your name?" the lieutenant asked.

"Patrik."

"Surname?" she said.

He looked uncomfortable at the question. "Svoboda."

"Thank you, Patrik. You understand what happened outside?"

He shook his head and swore softly.

"I'll take that as a *yes*," the lieutenant said. "How well did you know Daryna?"

"Who?"

"The victim."

"Oh. Obviously not that well. I've seen her around town, spoken to her a couple of times."

"About what?"

"What do you mean? About my set, or what she was drinking, or . . . you know."

"I don't know. Were the two of you dating? Were you intimate?"

"I just told you I didn't even know her name." Patrik's gaze whisked to Viktor, as if he were the true interrogator, waiting to pounce. So far Viktor had sat quietly, wrapped in his full-length wool coat, leveling his penetrating stare at the DJ. "Swear to God, I only saw her a few times, when I was doing a set."

"Some of the employees seem to think you were hitting on her."

Patrik fetched a cigarette out of a pack on the table, leaned back, and held the cigarette between his fingertips. "Well yeah. She was sizzling. She liked music, always danced close to my station. Who wouldn't?"

"How did she respond?"

He rolled his eyes. "She said she has a boyfriend. I've never seen her with anyone. Well, there's this one guy she likes to talk to, but she's just a page in his book, if you know what I mean. I guess I'm not her type, though she doesn't have a problem sending her friends over to request a song when they're around."

"Were they around tonight?"

"Not that I noticed. She came in alone, left alone. I saw her slip out during my second set."

"Did she say where she was going?"

"Nope."

"Did she leave with anyone?"

"Nope."

"Was she in a hurry?"

"Yeah, I suppose."

"Did you notice anything else strange?"

Patrik shook his head. "She just grabbed her coat and left."

"This guy she likes to talk to. Was he here tonight?"

"Yeah, for a while."

"What's his name?"

Patrik twirled the cigarette through his fingers. "No idea. Hey, you mind if I light up?"

"We'll be done soon. Tell me about this guy. What does he look like, what do you know about him?"

"I don't know anything about him. He's a good-looking guy, sure. Not the beefcake type, more slim and pretty. An inch or two over six feet, long hair, looks like a wannabe artist. The trust fund type."

"What makes you say that?"

"Those threads he wears . . . he tries to play like he's slumming, but they're all designer. Too new and shiny and just obviously, well, designed. He strikes me as the kind of guy who doesn't own anything normal. He's probably working on a novel or a painting while mommy and daddy pay the bills. I don't like his face, to be honest. It's too smug and smooth. He has a different girl on his arm every night."

"It sounds like you might be a bit jealous."

"That's not why I don't like him. I do okay for myself."

"Have you ever talked to him?"

"Nah, just seen him around. Come to think of it, he was usually at the same places Daryna was. Maybe she was following *him* around."

"When did this guy leave tonight?"

Patrik scratched at his goatee. "I'm not sure. Not long before her."

"The bar doesn't have any cameras," the lieutenant said to Viktor. "And no CCTV outside."

"Unfortunate," Viktor said without taking his gaze off Patrik. "Do you remember anything unusual about him?"

"What do you mean?"

"Something that might help us identify him."

Patrik sniffed and wiped his nose. "He painted his fingernails black. Wore a lot of jewelry, rings, leather necklaces, wrist bands, that sort of thing. The artist vibe, like I said. Kept his hair in a ponytail. Drank red wine instead of beer. I never saw him smile or laugh."

"That's an odd thing to notice."

"I guess it is. I don't know why it came to me. He wasn't all frowns or anything, but you could tell he was going for that mysterious loner vibe. Hey, I guess the chicks dig it, because like I said, there was always someone gorgeous around him. He had these intense blue eyes, too. Kinda reminded me of Jim Morrison. You know, the singer from the Doors? Old school. Not for you I guess. So what, are you thinking he might have . . ." He pawed at his goatee, agitated.

"We don't know," the lieutenant said. "Does he strike you as someone capable of murder?"

"God, I don't know. Is anyone?"

"You mentioned Daryna had a boyfriend. But you never saw them together?"

"I'm pretty sure she was fronting. You can tell when a girl is lying about that, you know? Listen, can I go now? I don't know anything else. I didn't know her at all. And I'm just . . . God, it's just so awful."

Patrik shuddered and rolled the cigarette back and forth between two fingers. The lieutenant took down his contact information and released him. When she and Viktor were alone, she turned and said, "What do you think?"

"That it's very late, and there's too much tragedy in the world."

"I want to talk to this artist guy he mentioned. Does anything about the description strike you?"

"The description of an effete male with artistic tendencies is hardly uncommon. Nor does a penchant for jewelry, red wine, and enigmatic nonchalance hardly warrant a suspicion of the abomination that occurred outside."

"The fact that he never smiles? What if he's a real freak and has some kind of fang implants?"

"Anything is possible," Viktor murmured.

"Okay, okay. I'll stop grasping and try to track him down, ask around at some other bars, see if he shows up on camera somewhere."

"A good idea."

"I'll ask the rest of the staff about him too, as well as the boyfriend. And tomorrow I'll talk to the host family. Would you mind coming with me?"

Viktor hesitated. "I'm sorry, it's not the best time."

The lieutenant's gaze slipped towards the front door. "Understood. Listen, I appreciate you coming out tonight. Let me know if you think of anything that might help, some angle I might have missed."

"Indeed I will," he said. "Good luck."

Viktor returned home and had a nightcap, his mind piqued despite the late hour. He retired to his study, lit a candelabra for ambiance, and uncorked a bottle of 1910 Pernod Fils absinthe. Due to the century long crusade against wormwood in most of the world, a tragedy in Viktor's eyes, vintage absinthe was exceedingly rare and abominably expensive. He wondered if he had the most extensive private collection in the world. It was quite possible.

His throat dry with anticipation, he laid a perforated spoon holding a sugar cube atop a crystal reservoir glass, then trickled cold water over the sugar. The ritual of *La Louche* served not just to dilute the potent alcohol content but to unlock the essential oils and transformative power of the Green Torment, one of the many nicknames for his muse.

When his concoction had the perfect opalescence, a rich but translucent peridot with amber highlights, Viktor relaxed in the stuffed leather chair by the window, surrounded by hardback tomes filling his floor to ceiling bookshelves, most of them rare first editions. He crossed his legs and sipped until he arrived at that relaxed yet strangely lucid realm unlocked by the absinthe. Outside the bay window, shadows pooled on the cobblestones and between the gas lamps set in iron sconces on the sides of the buildings.

Forcing himself to confront the horror of Daryna's death—he had learned from past experience that repressing violent memories only drove them deeper, where they could fester—he shuddered at the tragedy and moved on, the wetness in his eyes acquiring a gleam as he pondered the macabre nature of the crime.

Two fang marks in a woman's wrist.

Exsanguination.

The specter of *nosferatu*, night walker, diseased thing.

Viktor had run across modern "vampires" before. Plenty existed in underground clubs in cities around the world, including Prague itself. In fact, he thought wryly, the atmospheric streets of his beloved hometown attracted more than its fair share of would-be immortals.

The myth of a bloodsucking creature of the night with superhuman powers was a potent one, present throughout history across a wide array of cultures. Surely there was some ancestor myth that bound them all together, but he had researched the lore extensively, and had never found the common origin. *Bah.* Perhaps some giant parasitical creature had existed in prehistoric times, though he doubted it was the progenitor of the vampire bat found in tropical regions of the Americas. The little creature could fit in the palm of a hand and lapped up the blood it needed with a tongue so tiny most of its sleeping victims never woke up.

Whatever the ultimate source of the legend, the reason for its continuing existence was the human psyche, that incubator of infinite possibility, progenitor of pantheons of gods and devils, demons and angels, monsters and heroes, epic tales of valor. Did some of these legendary beings truly exist? A single God, a single Devil?

Viktor didn't know for sure. No one did. But what fascinated him to no end was the sheer kaleidoscopic sprawl, the seemingly unlimited power and reach, of the human imagination. Homo sapiens had brought to life a mindboggling array of philosophies and world religions, developed language and literature, raised cities to the sky and traveled to outer space and produced artistic masterpieces that would make the gods weep whether they existed or not.

Where did all this vision and creativity come from, this self-awareness and depth of thought, this yearning for eternity? Did it derive solely from the evolution of synapses and neurons inside the brain?

Viktor had his doubts. The mind might be a machine, but computers did not program themselves.

In any event, the human psyche could be a terrifying place even without the specter of a bloodsucking fiend. The diseased mind of a serial killer, the horror of a true split personality. Rare psychiatric conditions might have even led or contributed to the vampire myth. Conditions such as Cotard's delusion, whose sufferers believe they are walking corpses, putrefying and drained of blood. Or the laughably named Renfield's syndrome, a compulsion to drink the blood of humans or other mammals.

Viktor had always wondered why this particular monster was the source of such fascination. He supposed he understood the appeal of the modern version, the brooding immortal lurking on the edges of society, offering a chalice of eternal life through a seductive bite, a caress in the night from manicured white hands.

But the true legend of the vampire? The one that had persisted for millennia untold? The timeless belief in a creature that survived by preying on human beings and consuming their life force? Even the thought of such a thing bothered Viktor on the same primal level as stumbling upon a snake in the grass or a tarantula in a bedroll. A kneejerk, elemental response buried deep inside the lizard brain, a revulsion to a force of nature we know instinctively to avoid.

That part of the myth had always struck him as curious.

Worthy of exploration.

Human beings are as fascinated by snakes and giant spiders as they are innately terrified. Mesmerized by specimens kept behind glass in a zoo, unable to look away, entranced by the slithering and the crawling and the death-dealing fangs of the predator.

Was our species once threatened, sometime in the lost hourglass of history, by a vampire-like creature?

Viktor was intrigued by the myth. But other than a bite wound which could easily have an alternate explanation, he had no reason to think Daryna's murder, as awful as it was, had been carried out by anyone or anything other than a depraved or troubled human being.

After savoring the last drop of absinthe, Viktor stared into his empty glass, lost in thought until the gleam in his eyes faded and he succumbed to the sweet lassitude of the night.

The next morning, Viktor greeted Mari with a pot of coffee and his decadent mascarpone French Toast. After a lovely chat on his enclosed rear patio, wrapped in woolen shawls as the autumn sun struggled to break through, he took her sightseeing, waiting patiently as she meandered through the serpentine alleys and fashionable boutiques of Stare Mesto, toured St. Vitus Cathedral and the Royal Garden, and strolled the Charles Bridge at twilight. The city's spires and gargoyles, appearing like wraiths in the velvet mist rising off the water, never failed to move him. He absorbed the view beside his niece, transported to centuries past by the life-size statues and Gothic gates bookending the bridge.

They had a dinner reservation at a French bistro by the river. On the walk to the restaurant, Lieutenant Andrasko called Viktor on his cell. He wanted to ignore her but felt compelled to answer. "Yes?"

"There's been a development. Do you have a minute?"

Viktor glanced at his niece, who was eying a line of chic dresses in the window of a boutique. "We're on our way to dinner, so please be brief."

"I apologize for the intrusion. It turns out there *is* a boyfriend. A drummer in a local band who Daryna had been dating for almost a year. According to her host family, the boyfriend has been on tour for two months. Daryna suspected he was cheating on her. They've been on the rocks, and, more importantly, he was in Italy last night, performing a concert. So obviously not our killer. As for the host parents, the husband, Mr. Petr Anderle, seemed to have had great affection for Daryna. The wife, though she spoke well of her au pair, was clearly jealous of her presence in the home."

Viktor held up a finger and mouthed an apology to his niece.

"Don't worry," Mari said. "The window shopping is extraordinary."

The lieutenant continued, "The real news is that we've managed to interview all of the staff at *Setmění*. One of the bartenders who wasn't working last night is fairly certain he knows the artist guy the DJ mentioned. The bartender doesn't know the guy personally, or even his name, but he thinks he lives in the building across the street from him."

Viktor frowned. "How can he be sure of this, if he wasn't there last night?"

"I sent a sketch artist this morning to the DJ's house. I took the sketch with me when I interviewed the *Setmění* staff. Not only did the bartender I mentioned recognize the guy, he described him in the same way as the DJ, right down to the intense eyes, ponytail, designer clothes, and black fingernails."

"Intriguing," Viktor said. "What else did he say?"

"He's seen the guy come and go outside his apartment, usually with a different woman. I did some checking, and get this. We've had three missing persons reports for young women in the last two months. Not terribly unusual in a city of this size, but in light of everything else . . . I'm taking this guy in. What if he didn't plan to leave Daryna's body in the alley last night? What if he planned to bring her home and gave in to an impulse instead? Or maybe he got interrupted?"

"Nothing I've heard explains the bite marks and blood loss."

"I hate to ask, I know you're on your way to dinner, but could you come with me to pick this guy up, and sit in on the interview? I've got a funny feeling about all of this, a bad one, and I'd like you to be there."

If it had been anyone but Zuzana, Viktor would have denied the request. But he had known the lieutenant for a long time and respected her judgment. The lieutenant knew Viktor was hosting his niece and would not ask unless she truly deemed it important.

After a glance back at Mari, Viktor gave a heavy sigh and agreed to the request.

The lieutenant picked up Viktor in an unmarked blue sedan trailed by a police cruiser. After apologizing to Mari in person, the lieutenant drove Viktor to the north side of Old Town, near the Jewish Quarter. They entered a street lined with timeworn plaster-and-stone buildings with wrought-iron balconies and ivy climbing the walls. He was not as familiar with this part of Stare Mesto.

Near the end of the dead-end street, just before a public green space enclosed by a low wall, they parked on the curb in front of a black SUV with heavily tinted windows.

"That's the one?" Viktor said as he eyed a detached townhome, a rarity in

Old Town. It was a Gothic revival beauty set back from the street by a cobbled walkway. Two of the largest gargoyles he had ever seen were perched atop gutters on the sides of the house.

The lieutenant nodded as she pointed out a taller building across the street. "The bar employee lives in one of those apartments. He thinks our artist guy rents or owns the entire three-floor house, since he's never seen anyone else enter or leave."

"That would dovetail with the DJ's suggestion that a trust fund is involved. That has to be one of the most expensive homes in the city."

The lieutenant and Viktor left the car. The patrol car parked just ahead of them. After ordering the junior officers to stay put unless there was trouble, the lieutenant turned towards the walkway leading to the house. Right after she and Viktor stepped onto the curb, the front door opened.

Viktor paused beside the lieutenant as a man in his mid-thirties and a woman twenty years his senior exited the house. The man was about Grey's height but had a much heftier build. He had full lips and dark hair clipped close to the scalp, a heavy brow, and a boxed beard that accentuated the solidity of his face. He was fashionably dressed in blue slacks and a gray, three-quarter length wool coat with a high collar and a snug fit on his muscular arms. A handsome man of Slavic origin. When he noticed Viktor and the lieutenant, he said something to the older woman too low to hear from afar.

The woman listened but did not respond. Instead she closed the door, pressed a button on the keypad lock, and strode regally down the walkway with a miniature chest tucked under her left arm. Dressed in brown leather boots and a stylish black trench coat belted at the waist, she had long black hair and an expressive mouth. Viktor thought her one of the most attractive women he had ever seen. Both she and the younger man were very pale, bore an obvious family resemblance, and had a cruel glint to their eyes that marred the marble perfection of their features.

Viktor followed the lieutenant's lead, waiting at the edge of the curb as they approached. The older woman, who Viktor guessed was the man's mother, walked imperiously past Viktor and the lieutenant without saying a word, heading straight for the SUV. Her glittering array of gold bracelets, gemstone rings, and a silver choker inset with a teardrop stone Viktor would have sworn was a blue diamond—one of the rarest jewels in the world—suggested wealth. As they passed, Viktor glanced down at the small wooden chest she was carrying. It appeared much older than he would have suspected, like something taken from a pirate ship in the Middle Ages. Wrapped in bands of iron, the coffer had a dull gold latch, and, curiously, a row of tiny holes or indentations along the side.

While Viktor found both the holes and the small size of the chest odd, he would not have thought too much about it had he not glimpsed a faded symbol carved into the side of the container: a dragon with its own tail coiled around its neck.

Viktor recognized the symbol at once. It belonged to the Order of the Dragon, a chivalric order founded in the Fifteenth Century by Sigismund of Luxemburg, the King of Hungary at the time. Though relatively unknown outside of medieval historians, Viktor knew the ranks of the Order had once included Vlad II, the voivode of Wallachia, a minor medieval polity that formed the basis for modern-day Romania. Inspired by his membership in the Order, Vlad had rebranded himself as Vlad Dracul, or Vlad the Dragon.

People with an interest in such matters knew that Vlad II's bloodthirsty son, Vlad the Impaler, was reputed to be the inspiration for Bram Stoker's famous literary creation.

But not many vampire lovers knew that "Dracula" in fact meant "son of Dracul," and that the patronym had started with Vlad II's allegiance to the ancient Order of the Dragon.

"Excuse me," the lieutenant said, as the well-heeled couple continued walking towards the car. Both the man and the woman had a fluid grace to their movements that reminded Viktor of the way Grey walked, like the prowl of a jungle cat. They did not seem to be in a hurry, or bothered in the slightest by the police cruiser parked outside the house.

Who isn't bothered by the police? Viktor thought.

When neither of the two responded, the lieutenant raised her voice. "Excuse me. I'm Lieutenant Andrasko with the Prague Police."

At last the woman turned to face her. The man followed suit, with a hard glint in his eyes that again surprised Viktor. The expression was not the sort of righteous anger affected by guilty criminals when confronted with their crimes, but rather a haughty disdain at the interruption.

"Yes?" the woman said as if speaking to a servant. "Can I help you?"

She spoke with an educated, neutral Czech accent and a cold tone that suggested she had not the slightest interest in helping anyone.

"Do either of you live here?" the lieutenant asked.

"We do not," the woman said. "I have an appointment tonight, so you'll have to excuse—"

"Then who are you?" the lieutenant said. "Why were you inside?"

The woman's eyebrows arched at the interruption. "I'm the landlord. I own the house."

"Does a young man rent from you?"

"Yes. Why do you ask?"

"I need to ask him some questions."

"That might be difficult. He has not paid the month's rent, nor has he responded to our attempts to contact him. We found the house emptied of his personal possessions when we entered tonight."

"Is that his chest?"

"It's mine," she said evenly.

"It's a handsome piece, but if you don't mind me asking, why are you carrying it around?"

"I'm afraid that's my business," the woman said.

Viktor was familiar with most of the old families in Prague, and was certain he had never seen these two before. Of course, plenty of foreigners invested in real estate in the city these days, but they were usually outsiders from Russia, America, and oil-rich countries. These two had Czech accents and features.

So who were they?

Why the odd behavior?

The lieutenant eyed the chest for a moment, no doubt debating whether she had the legal right to seize it. Despite the circumstances, Viktor's knowledge of Czech law told him that she did not, at least not without evidence of a crime.

Viktor wondered what the couple would do if the lieutenant decided otherwise. Something told him they would not comply.

"Your renter is a person of interest in a police matter," the lieutenant said.

"How unfortunate."

"What is his name?"

"Adrian Novák."

One of the most common Czech surnames, Viktor thought.

"I'll need his contact information," the lieutenant said, "and any other personal information you possess. Did he fill out a rental agreement?"

"Unfortunately not. We should probably update our antiquated rental methods. I'm afraid we're very old-fashioned."

"How did he pay rent?"

"He left a cash envelope in the mailbox at the first of every month."

"Who picked up the envelope?"

"I did," the man said, with the same icy tone as the older woman.

The lieutenant stared at them in turn. "Do you know where he worked? How he got his money? I imagine the rent on such a place is not cheap."

"I've no idea," the woman said. "He's never missed a payment before, so we had no reason to inquire. I really must be off, lieutenant. Goodnight."

She turned on a heel and resumed walking. The man followed suit and unlocked the SUV with a key fob.

"Excuse me again," the lieutenant called out. "I'll need your contact information."

"Certainly," the woman said. "You can reach me through my attorneys, Cermak and Overy. Their offices are in *Nové Město*."

The lieutenant looked flustered by the turn of events. "It's likely we'll need to speak again in the morning. I also have a warrant to search this house."

"The door code is 25663. Now *goodnight*."

"One more thing," the lieutenant said as the woman opened the passenger door. "I'm sure you saw the so-called vampire killing on the news today. Just so you understand the seriousness of the matter, that's the crime in which your renter is a person of interest."

Just before the woman stepped inside, she glanced back at the lieutenant, and Viktor thought he saw the hint of a smirk whisk across her pale and haughty visage. "I understand indeed."

-5-

By the time Grey and Mari arrived at Vaclav Havel airport the next evening, rented an eggshell-white Mazda 6, and drove into Prague, the sun had long since set on the spires and red-tiled roofs of Old Town.

Grey had visited Viktor on occasion and knew the way to his townhome. Mari stared anxiously out the window while he drove, as if searching for a glimpse of her uncle in the occluded maze of medieval lanes and cobblestone squares. Grey's eyes slid right by the fairy tale architecture, his thoughts elsewhere.

Leaving New York so abruptly had left him uneasy. He didn't think the gang members who had assaulted Mari would return to the homeless shelter anytime soon, but he had asked Reverend Dale to keep a close eye on the situation, and especially on Charlie. Ever since her kidnapping by a neo-Nazi extremist group, Grey got a pang in his stomach whenever he left town. Charlie had run away from an abusive stepfather years ago and eked out a living by herself on the streets of New York City. She was a survivor. Tough and smart and resourceful.

But she was also brash, impulsive, and did not back down from anyone. Grey had swung by the shelter on his way to the airport, and her brave parting words had made him wince as well as smile.

Viktor's disappeared? Teach, you can't catch no break. I mean he's probably at some resort for rich people, doing rich people things, but don't you worry, I got it covered around here. You do your sensei thing and get him back.

He had warned Charlie—ordered her—not to confront anyone while he was away, and to focus on studying for the GED. When she turned eighteen, she planned to become a New York City police officer.

God, then I really won't be able to sleep.

Worrying about Charlie made him think of his other responsibility, a headstrong professor whose disappearance hung like a specter over Grey and Mari as they drew nearer and nearer to Viktor's townhome. The professor was a grown man who could take care of himself in ways that Charlie could not, but he had also helped put a long list of dangerous criminals behind bars.

Had the professor's past caught up with him? It was something to consider.

Grey's eye caught the twin black towers of Prague's signature Gothic church, the small fleet of spires on the towers thrusting skyward like pitchforks above the golden glow of the Old Town Square. Soon he veered onto a cobblestone street so narrow he worried the Mazda would scrape against one of the luxury sedans parked along the curb. He found a parking space near the end of the street, and they walked back to Viktor's townhome.

As they approached the front door, Grey's eyes swept the gaslit street, wondering where Viktor had gone the night before Mari had returned, and what sort of thoughts his brilliant mind had dwelled upon.

Mari entered a code to unlock the door and disarm the beeping security system. Grey followed her into a foyer with a chandelier, a grandfather clock, and a coffered ceiling inset with decorative tiles.

"The guest rooms are upstairs," she said. "Mine's the first door on the right. You can choose any of the others. Would you like a drink? Something to eat?"

"If there's a beer lying around, I won't say no."

"Help yourself to whatever's in the kitchen."

"Let's meet in the study when you're ready. I'd like to see what Viktor was looking at."

"Sure. I'll just freshen up."

Grey climbed the balustraded staircase and dropped his duffel bag in the bedroom next to Mari's. He barely glanced at the heavy crimson drapes, wood-beamed ceiling, and settee by the window. After finding a Krušovice in the kitchen fridge, he popped the cap, walked down the hall, and pushed through the interior French doors that opened onto Viktor's study.

Though larger than most master bedrooms, the oversize fireplace and built-in mahogany bookshelves lent the study a cozy feel. A glass-doored cabinet stocked with dusty bottles of absinthe took up one corner. Beside the bay window overlooking the street was a leather reading chair that Grey knew his employer favored. Stacks of academic journals and a sea of hardback books occupied the bookshelves, interspersed with knickknacks from Viktor's travels.

Most of the *objets d'art* exhibited Viktor's taste for the macabre, such as a blue-tongued Kali figurine, painted skulls from Mesoamerica, Czech marionettes with leering goblin faces, a mummified cat covered in hieroglyphics, and an African tribal mask that caused a rush of painful memories.

Grey swallowed as he forced his gaze away from the mask. Thinking about Nya and the *N'anga* would only lead him to a lightless place with no doors or windows, no air to breathe.

Focus. Viktor needs you.

"There's the section with the books missing," Mari said as she entered the room, still dressed in the jeans and white cashmere sweater she had worn on the plane. When Grey jumped at the sound of her voice, she said, "I didn't mean to startle you."

That's where letting the past in gets you, Grey.

He waved off the comment and walked over to the bookshelf she was pointing at. A gaping hole in the tightly-packed shelves indicated at least three missing volumes. He read the titles on either side of the empty space. *Slavic Witchcraft and Conjuring. Balkan Lore and Legends.*

After eying similar titles on the long row, Grey moved to the leather reading chair, where someone—presumably Viktor—had left a stack of journals and papers. He picked up the thin bound journal on top. Unfortunately, it was in Czech. Grey spoke Japanese and Spanish, and had a facility for languages, but had never studied a Slavic tongue.

"It's from the University of Prague," Mari said. "*Sigismund of Luxembourg.* He founded the Order of the Dragon."

Grey flipped through the rest of the research. Only one of the papers was in English, an article in the *Yale Historical Review* on trade routes along the Silk Road.

"Most of these concern the Order in some way," Mari said. "I don't know about the Silk Road article."

He held up another of the bound journals. "I recognize a few Romanian titles, but what's this language?"

"Hungarian."

"Do you speak it?"

"Just Czech and English. Hungarian is tough. It's actually Finno-Ugric, and bears no resemblance to its neighbors. Anyway, I made a list of all the titles."

Grey stood back and rubbed at his three-day stubble. "You can summarize the Czech article for me at some point. And we can get a translator for the others if we need. But I don't know . . . this sort of research is Viktor's domain. I have a feeling we could read it a hundred times and it might not get us very far."

"It's better than nothing," she said.

"True. But I doubt it's better than launching an immediate investigation into where he went. Time is essential to a missing person case."

"How do you plan to start?"

Grey glanced outside, his gaze catching the light from the gas lamps pooling on the cobblestones outside the bay window. "I'll start with his friends, contacts, neighbors. See if he mentioned anything to anyone. I left another message with Jacques at the airport, asking him to run a trace on Viktor's credit card."

"Those seem like good avenues," she said quietly. He could tell she was working hard to stay composed. "Grey?"

He didn't turn around. "Yeah?"

"You said Uncle Viktor works to debunk the supernatural."

"And?"

"As far as I know, he's not a religious man. But take a look around. All these books, his profession, the phenomenology of belief . . . do you think he would go to all this trouble if he didn't believe in something?"

When Grey turned to face her, he saw Mari looking off to the side, fingering a slender silver necklace with an ankh pendant attached. "You don't have to believe in something to study it."

"That doesn't make it any less real. Or answer my question."

Her regarded her for a moment. "You'll have to ask your uncle about that."

"You haven't?"

"Not really."

"Why doesn't that surprise me? And what about you? What do you believe in?"

He took a long drink. "The fact that I'm drinking a beer and standing in Viktor's study. Not much else, I'm afraid."

It was her turn to study him. "Liar," she said softly.

"Truth. You're just taking it the wrong way."

"What does that—"

The ring tone on Grey's cell interrupted her. He looked down and saw a blocked number. Worried it might be Viktor, he took the call. "Hello?"

"It's Jacques."

Grey moved swiftly to take the call outside. When Mari tried to follow, he put out a hand to stop her. He had no idea what Jacques had to say and wanted to speak freely.

"About time," Grey said to Jacques. "I'm in Prague."

"I'm fine, thanks. And you?"

"Have you heard from Viktor?"

"If I had, you'd know by now."

Grey put a hand to his temple and took a deep breath. Though a diehard bureaucrat, Jacques was an honest, hardworking Interpol liaison officer who had helped them out of a number of jams over the years. "I'm sorry. What do you know?"

"Not much more than you," Jacques said. "But I might have a lead."

Grey gripped the phone. "Which is?"

"I got your message about tracking his expenses. I thought of that myself, but Viktor uses a Swiss bank that caters to the ultra-wealthy. They have a policy of not releasing records without direct evidence of a crime. Trust me, that's not a route you want to go down. At least not if you're in a hurry."

"I can't say I'm surprised."

"Maybe if we turn something up . . . but let us hope that we do not, and Viktor had his own reasons for disappearing."

"You think he might have gone undercover?"

"It's something he's done on occasion, when he wanted to infiltrate a cult or other dangerous organization. But that was in his younger days, before he had a public profile. Going undercover would be risky for him now, and, in any event, he always left word with someone. Usually me."

"Agreed." Grey had walked down the street far enough to glance through the window of Viktor's study, where Mari was chewing on a nail by one of the bookshelves. "I hate to say it, but I can't believe he would disappear for this long without telling anyone."

"I'm afraid I agree."

"What else do you know?"

"I ordered a CCTV scan for Prague. We've been running facial recognition scans for days and finally got a hit. On October 20, he was seen on a security camera outside a nightclub in Stare Mesto."

Grey tensed. "That's the same night his niece thinks he disappeared. Who was he with?"

"No one. He's seen on multiple streets approaching the club. As best we can tell, he walked there from his home."

"Did he enter the nightclub?"

"It's unclear, but he paused in front of the camera—almost as if he wanted to mark his presence. There are other cameras nearby, and he doesn't show up on any of them. So, unless he went out of his way after that to avoid the cameras, I have to infer he decided to enter the club, and wanted someone to know it."

"Okay," Grey said. "So he was meeting someone who works at the club, or was there for some other reason. Any ideas?"

"Not yet."

"What's the name of the club?"

"Očistec. *Purgatory*, in English."

"Have you told the local police?"

Jacques hesitated. "I was about to inform them, though I have to say I'm quite hungry. I haven't eaten all day. But dinner won't take very long, mind you."

Grey understood. He also realized the purpose of the unlisted number. Jacques was giving him a small window to act on the tip. "I appreciate this."

"Make it count," Jacques said.

As Grey returned inside, searching for the address of the club on his phone, Mari hurried into the foyer to meet him. "Is everything all right?"

"That was our Interpol contact. He might know where Viktor went in Prague the night he returned without telling you."

As Grey studied the photos of the club online, she leaned over his shoulder and said, "Očistec looks swank."

He filled her in on everything Jacques had said. "I'm going to swing by and ask some questions. I'll let you know what I find out."

"I'm coming with you," she said. "Give me five minutes to change."

"Not a good idea." The car keys were still in his pocket, and he reached over to grab his motorcycle jacket off a coat rack.

"Three things," Mari said. "One, you don't speak Czech, and might need me. Two, I know the name of the club, so I'm coming whether you like it or not. Three, are you really going in the same clothes you've been wearing all day?"

He glanced down at his jeans, dark green long-sleeve shirt, and black walking boots. With a shrug, he pocketed his cell phone, slipped on his motorcycle jacket, and reached for the door.

"You can tell from the photos it's a high-end night club, not a dive bar. A single man dressed like you, even if he is good-looking? They probably won't let you in, at least not without a pretty girl on your arm. You won't do Viktor much good standing on the curb."

Grey hesitated. Mari smirked as she turned her back and started walking towards the stairs. "Five minutes," she called out.

When Mari finally appeared, Grey was shifting from foot to foot as he waited outside, eying his watch as his breath fogged the air.

After she pressed a button on the keypad to lock the door, she turned and noticed his agitation. "At ease, soldier."

His retort fell away as he noticed how high the slit was in the bottom of her long-sleeved black dress, and how much tanned cleavage was revealed, and how Mari's jewelry and subtle makeup had transformed her from an attractive young woman to a fashion model out on the town. Her high heels and the clingy fabric of the dress accentuated the svelteness of her limbs. She shrugged into a cropped suede jacket that somehow worked with the dress, clutched a silver handbag in her left hand, and looped her other arm through his as they strode to the Mazda.

"You clean up well," he said.

"I wish I could say the same about you. But I don't really know."

"This is me cleaned up."

She rolled her eyes. "Don't get used to this. It's my movie premiere outfit, if I ever have one."

"I thought you directed a documentary."

She laughed. "That released on YouTube, while I cracked a bottle of champagne with my best friend. It did well enough, got some honorable mentions on the festival circuit, but there wasn't exactly a red carpet."

"Are you proud of the work?"

"Very. But I think it's . . . I won't say immature, but I want to stretch more as a filmmaker. Find that white hot center of the star, if you know what I mean."

Grey didn't say anything, because he liked Mari well enough, and she was Viktor's niece, and he didn't want to tell her that whenever you found the white-hot center of anything in life, it burned you if you got too close.

Purgatory was a mile from Viktor's townhome, just inside *Nové Město*, or New Town. They had driven to save time. When Grey pulled within view of the nightclub, he saw a long line of people waiting to enter, and no street parking in sight. He drove a few blocks away and found space in a public lot.

Mari slipped on her suede jacket as they walked to the club. "How do you plan on finding out if he was there?"

"I'm going to ask around about a seven-foot-tall professor someone had to have noticed, and work backwards."

She gave a slow, agreeing nod. "What if my uncle never went inside?"

"Then we'll deal with that."

As they approached the club, which occupied an entire four-story building on a upscale commercial street, Grey continued walking past the line of hopeful clubgoers dressed in trendy clothing. It was the sort of impossibly chic scene that appealed to him about as much as a colonoscopy. Some of the women shivered in the cool night air, sacrificing body warmth for fashion.

"What's your plan at the door?" Mari asked.

"Tell them I'm a private investigator and hope I don't have to call Jacques."

"Let me give it a shot," she said, unzipping the front of her coat.

Without giving him a chance to respond, she approached a hulking bouncer who looked like a bearded mountain man someone had found splitting logs in the forests of the Czech Republic. His arms were as thick as barrels, and he was almost as tall as Viktor.

Grey followed along behind Mari. The other people in line were glaring at them. The bouncer put out a hand to cut them off, looming over Mari in a threatening manner that made Grey's fingers twitch at his side. She spoke to the bouncer in Czech and showed him something in her wallet while his eyes roamed approvingly—and unabashedly—over her figure. After a moment, he looked at Grey and wagged a finger. Mari said something in response that made him laugh. She pressed her point, and he seemed to relent.

"*Dobrý, dobrý,*" the huge man rumbled, unchaining a velvet rope so they could enter.

Grey hurried to follow Mari through the door to the club before the bouncer changed his mind. They checked their coats by the entrance and wandered into a high-ceilinged dance floor swarming with people. Colored lights strobed the room, and Grey felt the vibrations from the thumping bass of the electronic music.

"What happened back there?" he said, shouting in her ear to be heard. Her jasmine perfume alleviated the sweat-and-pheromone-soaked odor of the dance floor.

"I showed him my Guild card and told him I was a Hollywood director scouting for film settings. Which is more or less true."

"Why was he laughing?"

"He didn't want to let you in, so I told him you were my bodyguard." Amusement flickered in her eyes. "I don't think he was impressed."

Grey shrugged as his eyes swept the club, marking the exit points, on the lookout for anyone watching them enter.

"Follow me," Mari said, laying a hand on his forearm.

"Where to?"

She guided him towards an elevator next to a plunging digital waterfall on a projector screen built into the wall. "While I was changing clothes, I read some online reviews. The club has four levels. There's an absinthe bar at the top."

Grey pushed the button for the elevator. "Nice work."

"There's this new thing called the Internet. It's pretty helpful."

When the elevator arrived and the door slid open, a group of inebriated men in business suits stepped out. The laughter of the young professionals trailed away when they saw Mari. They looked her up and down with raised eyebrows and nudged each other. A blond man with chiseled features and an arrogant smile said something to her in Czech that made Mari snap back. He grinned and stood in front of the elevator, blocking her way inside, until Grey stepped forward and squeezed the tendon behind his elbow. The man yelped and tried to jerk away but Grey kept the hold, pulling him to the side.

After Mari entered the elevator, Grey let the blond man go and backed calmly inside after her. The man cradled his arm like a bird favoring a wounded wing and took an aggressive step towards the elevator. Grey met his eyes with folded arms and a hard stare. The blond man thought better of it and stalked away to join his friends as the door closed.

"I had it under control," Mari said.

"I'm your bodyguard, remember? If anyone's watching, it might have looked odd if I didn't intervene. Plus," he said as the elevator started to rise, "He needs better manners."

She checked her makeup in the mirrored surface of the door. "What do you think Viktor—"

He cleared his throat to cut her off. When she glanced back, he gave a subtle shake of his head. The elevator door opened, and they stepped into a circular, red-themed cocktail lounge with a quieter acid jazz beat.

"We'll talk later," Grey murmured as he glanced around the room. No one seemed to be paying them any attention.

"But aren't you going to ask around about him?"

"That can't be avoided. Recorded conversations in elevators can. We have no idea who we're dealing with yet."

They sidled up to the mahogany bar, which featured three long shelves full of absinthe, plus the usual bar stock. On the wall behind the bar, an artist had painted a post-Impressionistic pastiche featuring a line of famous absinthe drinkers, holding a glass in hand: Van Gogh, Manet, Baudelaire, Oscar Wilde, Hemingway.

The bartender was a heavyset man dressed in a white dress shirt with a purple vest. A short beard reinforced his weak chin, his close-set eyes never seemed to meet anyone's gaze, and his mouth seemed locked in a perpetual downturn.

Grey raised a hand for service as he and Mari squeezed into a bit of space at the end of the bar. "Two absinthes."

"That doesn't help very much," the bartender said in English. He grabbed a cocktail menu and slapped it on the bar.

Grey glanced down and saw a dizzying array of choices on the first page alone. He knew almost nothing about Viktor's preferred drink. With a shrug, Grey chose the first entry, an absinthe from a Czech distillery.

"I'll take the Jade V.S.," Mari said.

After tipping his head in approval, the bartender grabbed the menu and walked off. When he returned, he set a brandy snifter half-filled with absinthe in front of them both, then laid a slotted spoon with a sugar cube on top of each glass. Moving deftly, he placed a vial of chilled water in front of Mari, a larger glass of water in front of Grey, then grabbed a bottle of absinthe off the wall behind him and drizzled it over the sugar cube on Grey's spoon. The bartender whisked the bottle away, lit a match with a cupped hand, set the sugar cube on fire, and dunked it into the glass. The absinthe caught fire, forcing Grey to lean back as flames leaped towards his face.

The bartender poured the glass of water in front of Grey over the absinthe to quell the flames. Without a word, he moved on, serving another pair of customers who had just arrived.

As Grey took an exploratory sip, he caught Mari watching him with an amused grin. "What?" he said, flinching at the harsh taste. How did Viktor drink this swill?

Mari picked up the vial of water and trickled it over her sugar cube until it dissolved, turning the absinthe cloudy. Grey's absinthe was still neon-green.

"Yours taste a bit like gasoline?" she said.

"A bit."

"Czech absinthe is for tourists. Most of it's terrible and doesn't even have the herbs. We started producing it because real absinthe—French or Swiss—is more expensive to make. The Old Town bars will tell you that silly fire ritual is historic, but it started in the '90s and does nothing but scorch the alcohol."

"A little warning would have been nice."

"You seemed to have it under control."

He raised his glass. "I guess there's a sucker born every day."

"Now you'll appreciate the real deal, though anise isn't my flavor profile."

Grey kept sipping so he wouldn't look out of place. When the bartender wandered back over to wipe down the bar after a group of German tourists moved on, Grey said, "You work here most nights?"

The bartender's eyes flicked upward. "Yeah."

"I'm from the States, but I've got a friend in town who knows absinthe. A real aficionado. Seven-foot-tall older guy, wears a lot of dark suits. Maybe you've seen him around?"

"Nope," the bartender said.

"He's kind of hard to miss. He told me he comes in once a week."

"Like you said, it's a popular place."

"His name's Viktor Radek," Grey pressed, "and the thing is, he's gone missing. I'm worried about him. I thought I'd check in with the places he likes to go, see if anyone remembers seeing him the night he disappeared."

"Sorry," the bartender said, with about as much emotion as someone responding to a telemarketer. "I can't help you."

Without looking at Grey or Mari, he tucked the rag into the apron around his waist and moved to the other end of the bar.

"Friendly chap," Mari said.

"He knows Viktor. Or he's at least seen him before."

"You must have heard something I didn't."

Grey kept watching the bartender. "It's what he didn't say. I just told him my friend had disappeared. He didn't even respond. Only someone *trying* not to react does that."

"Maybe he just has no personality. So what now?"

"We wait," Grey said.

"For what?"

"I'm not sure."

Grey kept nursing the absinthe. Though he felt a slight inebriation, it was different than a buzz from alcohol. His mind was piqued but not fuzzy, almost as if it had . . . expanded. Or he was observing the world from a slightly different perspective. He could see why it intrigued Viktor.

For the second round, he followed Mari's lead and ordered a French absinthe. It tasted far better. Pleasant, even.

Once or twice, Grey caught the bartender giving him a sidelong glance, but Grey chose not to interact further at the bar. Instead, he made idle chit chat with Mari to blend in while observing everyone who came and went. Most of the patrons were tourists. No one appeared to be the type of regular who sat at the bar and knew everyone. Not surprising in a club so loud, impersonal, and fast-paced.

The place got even busier as the night wore on. Another bartender arrived, a young Czech woman with short dark hair, a nose ring, and red-rimmed glasses. Her English, though sufficient for taking drink orders, wasn't the best. When Mari got a chance, she asked her the same question about Viktor in Czech. The new bartender claimed not to have seen him either, and Grey didn't detect anything duplicitous in her body language.

Eventually the original bartender untied his apron and set it on a hook behind the bar. At first Grey thought his shift was over, but the bartender made his way towards an alcove-like opening in the rear of the bar that led to the restrooms. Just before disappearing from view, he glanced back at Grey and took his phone out of his pocket.

Grey rose. "Wait here."

"Where are you going?" Mari asked.

"To continue the conversation."

The opening led to a dim hallway with fake palms in giant urns and a line of individual bathrooms labeled gender-neutral. There was no line to get in. Grey leaned against the wall while he waited. More people arrived, but he waved them through until the bartender emerged.

Grey pushed off the wall. "Got a second?"

The bartender frowned and kept walking. "Nope."

Grey stepped in front of him. "That's a bit rude. Especially after I told you my friend has gone missing."

"Look, I said I didn't know him."

"And I think you're lying."

The bartender jerked his head back. "Why the hell would I lie?"

"You tell me," Grey said.

"You need to move."

"We can talk right here, right now, or I can come back tomorrow with a friend from the Prague police department."

Though Grey had already ascertained the bartender was neither a fighter nor a brave man, he didn't flinch at the mention of the police.

"Do what you need to," the bartender said. "Now get out of my way."

Grey sensed a looming presence behind him. As the bartender smirked, Grey turned and saw the giant doorman, his heavy footsteps muzzled by the speakers pumping music overhead. The doorman reached out and grabbed his right arm.

"Let me go," Grey said calmly.

The doorman had a grip like a beartrap. He growled something in Czech that Grey didn't need an interpreter to understand, and jerked Grey forward like he was a misbehaving child. Grey might have complied to avoid a scene, but the doorman was hurting his arm, Grey didn't like being manhandled, and he knew the gig was up.

As the doorman tried to force Grey back into the bar, Grey smacked him in the groin with the back of his free hand. Though not a heavy blow, the doorman reacted to the strike by bending forward, as Grey knew he would. At the same time, Grey grabbed the hand clutching his arm, twisting the fleshy part of the doorman's hand upwards on the pinky side, inverting the wrist in a classic *nikyo* lock that made the doorman roar in pain and sink to his knees to relieve the pressure. It didn't matter if he was five times stronger than Grey; no human being can unravel a proper wrist lock with strength alone. The joint wasn't designed to work that way.

Grey, a master manipulator of joints and tendons and all vulnerable parts of the human anatomy, knew exactly how it worked.

When the doorman tried to regain his feet, Grey applied more pressure, keeping him on the floor. The bartender looked on in shock and fumbled for his phone, then scurried away to make a call. A patron opened one of the bathroom doors, glanced at Grey and the doorman, then fled back into the lounge.

"Get up!" Grey said to the doorman. Applying continuous pressure on the wrist, he brought the giant to his feet, made a motion like casting a fishing rod, and sent the doorman tumbling into the open bathroom. Grey slammed the door and shoved one of the urns beneath the handle, leveraging it closed.

Doubtful the door would hold for long, he hurried back to Mari, who was on her feet with a troubled expression. The male bartender was nowhere in sight.

"What's all the commotion?" she said. "That other—"

"We should probably go."

She blanched and grabbed her purse. They hurried towards the elevator as a loud crash, the sound of a door splintering and a ceramic urn shattering on the floor, emanated from the bathroom hall.

They reached the hallway with the elevator and punched the button, but the elevator was stuck on the second floor. "C'mon," Grey said, pointing at a door with an Emergency Exit sign at the end of the hall.

As they raced for the door, Grey glanced back and saw the doorman storming into the hallway, holding a bottle by the neck. Grey hit the crash bar on the door and took the steps two at a time. Mari stayed right with him. The thump of music increased as they descended.

They bounded down to the ground floor and burst through the one-way door to the outside. It opened onto a smaller street beside the club. Three men in dark suits barred the way forward. While nowhere close to the size of the doorman, the men had earpieces, handguns holstered at their sides, and a far more professional demeanor. The man in the middle was speaking quietly into a microphone on his collar.

What kind of club, Grey wondered, *employs three pro security guards?*

"You can't hold us here," Mari said. "I'm a Czech citizen. We're both Americans." Realizing where they were, she repeated the statement—or so Grey assumed—in Czech.

The men did not respond. When Grey took a step forward, they put their hands on their firearms.

"I advise moving," Grey said. "The police are on their way, and last time I checked, armed detention wasn't legal here."

As Mari started to translate, a slender man in blue slacks tapered at the ankle and a formfitting white sweater stepped around the corner of the building. He was young and suave, with a dimpled chin and coiffed hair. "I don't believe assault and battery of my doorman is legal either," he said in excellent English.

As he approached, he waved a hand and gave a command in Czech. Like trained soldiers, the three guards turned on their heels and left, retreating around the corner that led to the front of the club.

Odd to send away the muscle.

"That's called self-defense," Grey said. "I don't like being grabbed."

The man stopped walking a few feet from Grey. Something about him, an animalistic cunning in his gaze that belied his polished appearance, set Grey on edge.

"Who are you?" the man asked in a measured voice.

"Someone looking for a friend."

"I'm the manager of this club. This friend you're searching for—I hear it's someone named Viktor Radek?"

"That's right."

"I'm sorry he's missing, but I've never heard of him, or seen anyone similar to the description I was given."

"Like I told your bartender," Grey said, "I think you're lying."

The man's eyes narrowed. "Your personal judgments are out of my control. If you tell me how to contact you, I'll be happy to inform you if any of my employees recall any pertinent information."

"Don't worry about it. I'll be in touch."

The manager smirked as his gaze flicked to a camera overhead. As if to say, *don't worry, I'll know who you are soon enough.*

Grey made a mental note to ask Jacques to try to confiscate the security tapes from the night Viktor disappeared, though if the club was complicit in some way, as Grey had come to suspect, he knew the evidence would be erased.

"Perhaps it's better if you were not in touch," the manager said. "In fact, don't ever bother coming back." He took another two steps forward, close enough for Grey to smell his wood-and-citrus cologne, and see a tiny shaving nick on his chin. Uncomfortably close. "Do we understand each other?"

Grey leveled a hard stare at him, but instead of backing down, the man met Grey's eyes with the indolent confidence of a predator, rather than a slight, unarmed bar manager who had just sent away his security team, and had to know that Grey had just manhandled his doorman.

"The feeling's mutual," Grey said, his hands tensing at his sides.

"Let's go," Mari said, looping an arm through his. Grey let her pull him away, but he felt the manager's eyes on his back as they left. When they had passed the line of hopeful entrants to the lounge, and were safely out of earshot, Mari said quietly, "You were right. My uncle was there, and they know it. What now? Do we go to the police?"

"Tomorrow," Grey said, clicking the remote lock as they approached the Mazda. He glanced over his shoulder to ensure no one had followed them. "Right now I'm going to stake out that club and see whose feathers we ruffled."

-6-

Viktor and Lieutenant Andrasko had no choice but to let the haughty raven-haired woman and her companion leave in the SUV. As soon as they drove off, the lieutenant returned to her sedan and ran the license plate.

"It belongs to a rental agency in Prague I've seen before," the lieutenant said once the results came back. "They cater to wealthy clientele and deliver the cars, usually with a driver. I'll lean on them to produce the names."

Viktor was in the passenger seat, thinking about the emblem of the Order of the Dragon on the chest tucked under the woman's arm.

The lieutenant reached for the door handle. "Let's go inside."

"Sure," Viktor murmured.

The two junior officers led the way into the house, using a forensics kit to examine the doors and surfaces for fingerprints and other evidence. With his hands clasped behind his back, Viktor let the lieutenant lead the way.

The old house smelled of lemon-and-ammonia disinfectant. A lifetime of privilege had given Viktor a keen eye for wealth and all its attendant trappings, and he noticed the period furniture throughout the house, some of it quite rare and expensive. A Queen Anne chair here, a Chippendale cabinet there. His eyes rose at the Renaissance oil paintings in pristine condition in the hallways and gathering rooms. The collection could have graced the walls of a museum.

Who rents out a house with such valuable furniture and art?

Answer: no one.

Though the house had solid bones and was in good condition, the cramped floor plan had not been updated in decades. No possessions remained besides the art and furniture, and the house had obviously been cleaned recently, perhaps that same day.

The lieutenant opened all the drawers, checked behind every piece of furniture, searched beneath the couch cushions and inside the cabinets and in every other conceivable space. Viktor found a secret door behind one of the bookshelves, but his hopes were dashed when the opening revealed an empty room with moldy carpet. Another oddity was the lack of windows throughout the house, strange even for older time periods. Heavy drapes that did not allow a scintilla of light to pass through had been drawn across the few windows that did exist. A fact Viktor catalogued with the mounting mysteries.

An hour after they had started the search, one of the junior officers, a red-haired bruiser with burly arms and a cleft chin, approached Viktor and the lieutenant in the living room.

"No prints," the junior officer said, "but plenty of DNA evidence. We found some hairs on a pillow, another on a couch cushion, and saliva on a plastic cup in a bathroom waste bin."

"Send it in," the lieutenant said. "It seems a little sloppy, unless it's from the housekeeper."

"Maybe they had to rush the job."

"Or maybe," Viktor added, "someone isn't worried about DNA." His eyes moved to an archway on the far side of the room which led to a hallway and the central staircase. "I noticed a pull-down door on the third floor. I have a similar one in my house that leads to the attic."

"That was my next destination," the lieutenant said. She turned to the junior officer. "Have you tried it yet?"

"I just came from up there. It's clean except for an empty wine bottle with no prints."

"Did you check for saliva on the stem?" Viktor said.

The junior officer grinned. "Tipped one or two up, have you? I took a sample."

"How long does DNA last in saliva outside the body?"

"Preserved correctly?" the lieutenant said. "Years. On a wine bottle? Hours."

After climbing a wide staircase to the top floor, the lieutenant eyed the pull ring on the hatch door in the ceiling halfway down the hall. "Do you mind?"

Viktor reached up to lower the door, which expanded into a set of rickety folding steps. He led the way, worried at first his weight would collapse the squeaky steps, then had to hunch almost double as he passed through the third-floor ceiling into an attic with hot, trapped air. As the lieutenant followed him up, he pulled a cord attached to a bare light bulb hanging above the stairs. The dim illumination revealed brick walls spotted with age and mildew, wooden floorboards that creaked with every step, and high eaves with cobwebs hanging down like Spanish moss. Wooden support beams spaced throughout the attic made it hard for Viktor to walk upright.

"Not much here," the lieutenant observed, as both their gazes swept the long, empty space stretching the length of the house. Despite the presence of the police officers, the silence and dark corners, along with the bizarre events of the night, made Viktor uneasy.

Who is this family, and how long have they lived here?

"There's the wine bottle," the lieutenant said, as they moved deeper into the attic. She pointed at a recessed dormer window. The empty bottle was lying flat on a wooden bench built into the wall beneath the window. It was one of those architectural oddities common to old houses that Viktor loved.

Unlike the thick drapes concealing the downstairs windows, only a thin gauze curtain obscured the view. After eying the wine bottle, the lieutenant put a leg on the bench, leaning her elbow on her knee to absorb the spires and rooftops of the old city floating in the moonlight. The lights of Charles Bridge and Prague Castle gleamed in the distance, dreamy, ethereal.

"Helluva view," she said.

"Someone else thought so as well," Viktor murmured, eying the wine bottle and imagining their artist suspect lounging by the attic window at night, alone or with a companion, surrounded by cobwebs and shadowy corners, quaffing straight from the bottle as he absorbed the vista and pondered the enigmas of life.

"We'll put the bottle in evidence, just in case," the lieutenant said. As she turned to leave, Viktor sat on the ledge, putting himself in the same position whoever had enjoyed the wine might have occupied. He let his back rest against the wall, observed the view—perhaps the previous occupant had spied his victims on the street?—then looked around the attic. When his eyes roamed upwards, to the wooden beam almost directly overhead, he noticed the edge of a book poking out.

Viktor stood and plucked the book off the beam. Someone shorter than he, though not as short as the lieutenant, could have reached up on their way to or from the window seat and placed the book on the beam. Why someone would have done this, he had no idea, unless his arms had been full. Perhaps the owner of the book only read in the attic, but why not leave the book on the window seat?

With a start, he realized the beam was wide enough for someone to sit on, if they so desired. They would still have a view out of the window—but why not use the window bench?

"What's that?" the lieutenant asked, hurrying back over.

Trying to touch as little of the surface as possible, Viktor held out the thin hardbound tome with gilt-edged leather binding. It looked as old as any book he had seen outside of the archives of a museum, or in the collection of a discerning book collector such as himself. The book was very beautiful, with silver studding on the cover and an enamel clasp securing the pages. Viktor gently undid the clasp and opened the book to the title page, where he saw a shield divided into four fields, one of which contained the crowned, double-tailed Czech lion. No doubt the heraldic symbol of whoever had originally owned the book.

"The title is in Latin," Viktor said as he closed the book. It was too delicate to flip through. "A book of poetry by Johannes Cuspinianus."

"Who the hell is that?"

"If I recall correctly, a minor Venetian scholar from the 15th century. He was known for his political writings, as well as collecting and editing medieval manuscripts. He also served as the prefect of Vienna for some time. I wasn't aware he wrote poetry, but I'm certainly no expert on his life."

She held out a hand. "I'll need to put that into evidence."

He took a few photos and carefully gave her the book. "If you want to preserve it, I wouldn't let anyone touch it besides an archivist. I'm quite certain this is an original. It will be exceedingly delicate. I can refer you to an expert if you like."

"Sure," she said, tucking the book under an arm.

They found nothing else of interest in the house. On the way out, the lieutenant took a call as Viktor headed to the car. He hoped to get home in time to catch Mari still awake. He grew annoyed as the lieutenant stayed on the phone for some time. When she finally joined him, she said, "Have you heard of *The Parlor*? It's a bar and lounge in the Old Town."

"I'm afraid not."

"It's a Goth club that caters to, get this, the local vampire community." When Viktor didn't respond, the lieutenant gave him a sideways glance. "You're not surprised by that?"

"I know they exist."

"Why didn't you say so earlier, at the crime scene?"

"Because a true member of a modern vampire community would abhor the murder of an innocent person just as much as you or I would."

"I'll have to be the judge of that. Anyway, while we were inside the house, one of their managers called the station. He thinks he recognizes the sketch artist's rendition we sent to the Old Town clubs. The manager is positive he's seen this guy in The Parlor on multiple occasions, including two nights ago. I hate to ask, but could you make one more stop tonight?"

Viktor sighed and looked down at his phone. Mari had not yet responded to his first text. He hoped she was out and about, having fun in the city. "Let's go, then," he said.

"I owe you for this."

"Indeed you do. One thing: I need to make a brief stop at my house."

They found the crimson door to the Parlor near the top of a sloping cobblestone lane in the heart of the Old Town. One of those perfectly preserved Prague streets that made the tourists stand and gape, wondering if they had stumbled through a time machine to the Middle Ages.

The lieutenant's eyes flicked to a camera mounted above the wrought iron *Parlor* sign jutting out from the building. "They're checking CCTV in the area to see if we've got him on camera. That is, if our murderous bloodsucker casts a reflection."

Despite the somber circumstances, her comment caused Viktor to chuckle. Amateur scholars of the occult loved to scoff at the idea that vampires do not cast reflections, claiming that particular legend originated with Bram Stoker.

Though vampires made common appearances in Balkan and Slavic folklore, it was true the documented mythology of the region did not extend to invisibility in mirrored surfaces. But that did not mean it didn't exist in the lore. The Slavic "old religions" predated Christianity by many centuries, probably millennia. Records could have been lost or forgotten with the passage of time.

More importantly, limiting vampire, *upir*, and *strigoi* lore to Eastern and Central Europe was a grievous mistake. Legends of fiendish beings who prowled the night searching for human blood were rife in the ancient world, across a wide variety of cultures. Depictions of creatures feasting on human blood had been found on pottery shards in Mesopotamia. Hebrew lore spoke of a leechlike monster called an *alukah* that, according to biblical scholars and a passage in the Sefer Chasidim, was synonymous with a human vampire that lusted after blood.

The bloodsucking *Lamia* of ancient Greece; the *asanbosam* of West Africa; the fearsome *strix* of Roman antiquity; the bloodthirsty ghouls of Arabia; the Australian aboriginal legend of the *yara-ma-yha* that placed suckers on its victims' skin to drain the blood. There was also the shapeshifting *pischacha* of India that prowled cremation grounds and fed on human energy. The bizarre *jianghsi* of Chinese legend were said to have long curved fingernails, moldy fur atop their skin, and a craving for the essence of the living. The *Baobhan Sith* of Scotland. The *ramanga* of Madagascar. The *manananggal* of the Philippines.

Many of these ancient societies also believed mirrored surfaces could hold and even capture the soul of a human being. As photographic technology developed, some indigenous cultures, when encountering a camera for the first time, refused to have their picture taken for this very reason.

Since demonic beings and monsters such as vampires were not believed to possess souls, it was easy to see how a belief concerning their lack of a reflection could have developed and worked its way into the popular consciousness. In fact, Viktor was quite sure Bram Stoker had drawn on other traditions and folklore in existence for untold millennia when fleshing out his arch-fiend.

"Go ahead," Viktor said to the lieutenant. "I'll be in shortly."

"What's wrong? Afraid I'll sully your reputation?"

"Yes, actually. I'd prefer to engage the clientele without the negative association of a police interrogation."

She frowned. "And I'd prefer to conduct the interviews together."

"The vampire community is small and close-knit. They have a justifiable fear of authority, and of being misunderstood."

"You think they might talk to you, but not me?"

"I do."

The lieutenant shifted on her feet, glancing at her watch. "How much do you know about these . . . people?"

"Much more than you."

She opened her mouth and then closed it. "If you really want, I'll wait in the car until you're finished."

"That would be best. You can always conduct an official interrogation afterwards."

The lieutenant backed away with her hands up. "You're the boss with these things. I'll check in with the team while you're inside."

The lieutenant returned to her vehicle. Once she was out of sight, Viktor reached into his pocket and inserted the mouth implants he had retrieved when the lieutenant had swung by his house. He opened the door to The Parlor and saw a doorman perched on a stool in a dimly lit foyer with stone walls. The doorman was dressed all in black, his long hair unbound and reaching halfway down his back. Tattoos swarmed his neck and hands.

Electronic music pulsing with dark ambiance floated through the closed door on the other side of the room. The doorman looked Viktor up and down, noting his stodgy black suit, Italian leather shoes, Swiss watch, and silver cufflinks. "Sorry. We're full tonight."

Viktor's lips parted, revealing a pair of sharpened canines that caused the doorman to hold up his hands.

"My apologies," he continued. "I haven't seen you here before."

Viktor responded with a nod and closed his lips. The prosthetic fangs felt uncomfortable in his mouth. He had not worn them since the late 1990s, when the NYPD had asked him to investigate a serial killer stalking the nascent vampire community in Manhattan. Viktor had hired a member of the community to create a mold for a set of fangs that fit his face. Though subtle in comparison to the depictions of vampires in the movies, sharpened nubs rather than inch-long daggers, the false teeth were quite convincing and, most importantly, a common practice among the community. A set of good prosthetics could give instant credibility in the bars, lounges, and other venues where members of the subculture congregated.

After taking Viktor's cover charge with a handheld scanner, the doorman ushered Viktor through the interior door and into an open room with lacquered Oriental furniture and high walls painted black. The room was dimly lit with standing candelabra bearing real candles. Groups of people congregated at the bar along the far wall or at banquettes covered in red velvet interspersed throughout the room. A waitress in a long-sleeved purple dress carried a wooden platter around, offering tiny silver teacups to the guests. The teacups would contain fresh blood, Viktor knew, either from carefully sourced animals or from human "donors" to the community.

About half the people were dressed in Goth, with all the attendant piercings and eye shadow. The other half resembled normal clubgoers, representing a wide range of age and ethnicity.

From Viktor's prior research, he knew that most serious devotees of modern vampirism claim to experience haematomania, the craving to drink blood, and can suffer from a lack of energy or withdrawal-like symptoms if this need is not met. Only a small amount in relation to a normal diet was required, often a few teaspoons a week.

In addition, some extreme types of porphyria, a poorly understood genetic condition causing abnormalities in heme enzymes, could induce a need for blood infusions due to the body's inability to absorb iron and produce red blood cells. Porphyria can also cause acute sensitivity to sunlight. Vampires being instantly destroyed by sunlight was a Hollywood invention, but the idea that exposure to direct sunlight weakened or harmed vampiric beings, causing them to prefer the cover of night, was rife in folklore and legend.

For the most part, the medical profession did not give any credence to haematomania, and conflated it with blood fetishism. Porphyria was an accepted condition but considered extremely rare and highly unlikely to cause serious "vampiric" symptoms. So, while some modern vampires enjoyed the notoriety and dark romance of the lifestyle, most members of the subculture kept their condition private and considered themselves outcasts to society.

Whatever the true nature of haematomania or other afflictions, as a phenomenologist, it was not Viktor's place to judge. He observed the subjective beliefs of others and catalogued them within his ever-expanding atlas of the human psyche.

His task as an investigator was a different story.

Nearly everyone in the room glanced Viktor's way as he entered. He found an empty banquette and took a seat. Eventually the waitress swung by with the wooden platter. "Would you like one?"

"Of course," Viktor said, making sure to reveal his fangs.

She set one of the silver teacups on the table in front of the banquette. "Something else to drink?"

"Absinthe, please. Pernod if you have it."

When she returned with his order, Viktor took a sip of the chilled blood to establish credibility, forcing himself not to react to the salty, metallic tang.

"All alone tonight?" she asked.

"I'm afraid so."

"We're a friendly group. Let me know if I can get you anything."

"Thank you. There is one thing."

"Sure."

"You're aware of the murder last night?"

Her eyes narrowed. "If you're here to—"

"I'm here to help," he interjected. "I know a follower of the Black Veil would never commit such a heinous act. Unfortunately, the public and the police do *not* know this."

"Who are you?"

"My name is Viktor Radek. I'm a professor and private investigator. I consult with the police at times, but I'm sympathetic to the community."

"You're one of us?"

"At times."

She glared at him. "What does that mean?"

"Don't we all struggle with our true identity?"

After a long moment, she said, "What do you want?"

"As I said, to help." He described the young artistic man seen with the victim on multiple occasions. "He's a person of interest. I know he's been here before. If there's anyone here who knows him, or has talked to him, I'd like to speak with them."

The waitress turned to leave before Viktor could judge her reaction. "If the police and the public think the murderer is one of you," he continued, "the local community might not recover from the stigma."

With her back still turned, the waitress stiffened and walked away. Viktor crossed his legs and calmly prepared his absinthe. Five minutes later, the waitress returned with a younger woman in leather pants and a tight-fitting blouse. A crescent moon hanging on a silver chain was nestled into her bosom. She had long straight hair dyed as black as her clothing, lip piercings, striking cheekbones, and colored contacts that turned her pupils white.

"This is Pavla," the waitress said to Viktor, then turned on her heel and left.

Despite her raw beauty, the woman had a skittish demeanor and a haunted look in her eye that made Viktor think of the victims of domestic abuse in homeless shelters.

"Good evening," he said, then introduced himself as she slid into the banquette across from him. He noted the square cross attached to the bottom of her crescent moon pendant. "You're an admirer of Lilith?"

Pavla's long lashes flicked in surprise. "You recognize her symbol?"

"The first wife of Adam in Jewish tradition, created equal to him in God's eyes and from the same primordial dust. Lilith rebelled from Adam's attempt to assert dominance and fled the garden of Eden. She was considered a demon in Hebrew legend, said to drink the blood of young children, but today she's viewed as a falsely maligned goddess of feminine identity, liberation, and empowerment. She knows the pain of rejection and the oppression of her true nature."

Pavla's right hand strayed to the pendant. "She's a protector as well."

"Is there something you need protection from?" he said quietly.

When she looked away, Viktor folded his hands on the table. "Did the man I'm looking for try to hurt you?

He didn't think she was going to respond, but after pressing her lips together for a long moment, she turned back to him and said, "His name is Adrian."

"Adrian Novák?"

"I don't know his last name. He never said."

"Where did you meet him?"

"Here. About a month ago. Listen . . . please don't use my name. I'm only talking to you because of the murder. If he isn't caught, then everyone will think one of us killed that girl."

"Understood. Thank you. You're doing a brave thing."

"Oh no, I'm not a brave person. I just . . ." she shivered and crossed her arms in her lap, stroking her forearms with her fingertips. "I don't want to end up like her. He *fed* on her."

"Her neck was broken," Viktor said sternly. "That was the cause of death."

She continued as if she hadn't heard him. "Something must have happened. He was interrupted, or he . . . lost control. I sensed it once, the last time I saw him. That he wanted more of me."

Viktor straightened the collar of his shirt and took a drink of absinthe. "Why don't you tell me everything you know about him. It will help us find him and protect you."

Pavla's hands moved to the table, her fingers still intertwined and rubbing against each other like restless snakes. Her eyes, though looking right at Viktor, now seemed distant, reflective. "I've been in the community for a year, but I don't have the . . . craving. I want to, you see. I love the lifestyle, the sense of belonging. I want to be . . . part of it."

She licked her lips while Viktor listened, absently sipping on his absinthe, watching her carefully.

"When he came in the first night, I stared at him. Everyone did. He's a beautiful man, and he has this . . . presence. You want to be around him, as near as you can. I was so flattered when he wandered through the lounge and sat next to me. I smiled at him, shyly, and you know the first thing he said to me?"

Viktor's eyebrows rose.

"He looked right at me and said, 'So you want to be a vampire.'"

"Is that so?" Viktor murmured.

"He said it as a statement, not a question. He had this confidence . . ." she bit her lip and looked away. "Right from the start, I wanted to be with him. To help him, to be his donor."

A donor, Viktor knew, was the terminology among the vampire subculture for people who willingly gave blood to the community. Unlike in the movies, the preferred method of providing fresh blood was using a sterilized scalpel to cut shallow incisions on fleshy parts of the body resistant to scarring. Great care was taken to screen consenting donors for blood-borne disease.

"But he didn't take it like the others," she continued. "He bit me instead."

Viktor frowned. "He bit you?"

She pointed at the entrance to a hallway near the bar. "There are private rooms back there, with scalpels and medical supplies. He took me in the first night we met. Before we did anything, he began to kiss me and stroke my face. He was very gentle, loving. I admit I couldn't resist him. He told me it was going to be different, and was I okay with that? I said I trusted him. And then he took my arm, held it to his mouth, and . . ." She swallowed and held up her left arm for Viktor to see, pushing the sleeve back so the wrist was exposed, revealing two fresh red scars from puncture wounds about an inch apart. Viktor's eyes fixated on the lesions. They were nearly identical to Daryna's wounds.

"He took the vein, not the artery. I barely felt a thing. He didn't feed long, and it was all so . . . sensual."

Her face flushed, as if the memory of the encounter still excited her.

"I don't understand," Viktor said. "We both know prosthetic fangs are for show. They're not designed to puncture or consume. How did he drink?"

"You're not active in the community, are you? Prosthetics have improved a lot. If you have the money, and know the right fangsmith, I've heard you can buy teeth sharp enough to puncture, with hollow tips that allow you to sip."

"Did you see his fangs yourself?"

She nodded. "They were about as long as ours, but much sharper. I could see that when he smiled. They also looked more natural. I mean, prosthetics are really well done, but they still have an artificial quality, a sheen, you can recognize once you've seen enough of them."

"What did you think of all this?"

"I assumed he had extremely high-quality prosthetics I'd never seen before." Her eyes lowered. "What else was I supposed to think?"

"And do you still?"

"Still what?"

"Believe his teeth were prosthetic?"

Her head moved slowly back and forth, causing a prickle on the back of Viktor's neck. "Why not?"

Pavla's eyes flicked nervously around the room. "The third time we met—in here again—I knew I wanted to take the relationship further. We talked for a while out here, and eventually we went into a private room again. I had a few drinks that night."

"Did he drink or eat anything?"

"I never saw him eat, but he drank red wine."

"Okay."

Her hands began fidgeting again. "There's a couch in the private room, on the far wall as you enter. Once we were inside, he went to the couch, and I stayed behind to close the door . . . this is embarrassing . . . took off my shirt. I wanted him to see me, but I don't like to . . . you know . . . with the lights. So I told him to stay there, and I turned the lights off. They're right by the door. As soon as it was dark, he . . ."

She looked away and took a deep breath. Viktor waited in silence as she gathered herself and said, "He lifted me up by my throat with one hand, as if I weighed nothing. Before I had time to think or cry out, he was biting me again, this time on my left wrist. He bit me much harder than before, so hard it hurt. I moaned and he dropped me. When I managed to turn the lights on again, Adrian was backing away and telling me he was sorry."

She pushed her other sleeve back and held out her right wrist. Unlike the twin pinprick scars on the other wrist, the wounds on her right forearm were larger and jagged, as if Adrian's teeth had ripped down her arm as he pulled away.

"When I saw him," she said, "he looked ashamed, but there was also this strange light in his eyes. There was blood on the corners of his lips, and he licked it with his tongue as I put on my clothes and reached for the door. He told me to wait. Against my better judgment, I did. He had this voice, you see . . . I just couldn't seem to say no. Part of me, I have to admit, didn't want to leave. I knew then what he was, and even though it terrified me, and still does . . ." Her voice grew very small and faraway. "Part of me wanted it."

"You mean you wanted him to make you a vampire."

Her voice dropped to a whisper. "When the lights went off in that room, he was on me in an instant. No one can move that fast. The way he lifted me over his head, as if I were a toddler—he isn't a large man. It should have been impossible."

"Sometimes adrenaline gives us extraordinary speed and strength," Viktor said gently. "There's plenty of literature on the topic."

She shook her head slowly. "Not like that. It's pitch dark in those rooms when the lights go out. The way he found me in an instant—his hands didn't fumble, and his teeth were on my wrist in the perfect place. It was like it was daylight for him."

Viktor absorbed her story, wondering just how many drinks she had consumed that night, or whether her vibrant imagination and innermost desires had taken hold of her. "What happened next?"

"I was still by the door. He walked right towards me. I didn't move, didn't know what to do. He came up to me and put his mouth next to mine, so close I could feel his breath. I thought he was going to kiss me or bite me. Instead he said something I'll never forget, not as long as I live. That was three nights ago. It was the last thing he said to me, because I haven't seen him again, and expect I never will."

"Why not?"

"I think he lost control with that other girl. I don't know why, or why it didn't happen before. Maybe it has. But I think he's gone away, someplace where no one will recognize him. And I . . . I think it might happen again."

"What did he say to you?"

For a second, her pretty face contorted, as if she were struggling with some conflicting loyalty. "He whispered in my ear very quietly, right before he walked out of the room." Pavla was staring straight ahead now, speaking in a soft voice, lost in the moment. "'*I can give you the gift,*' he said. '*I can give you life.*'"

Late that night, after Viktor had returned to his townhome and retired to his study, the moonlight glinting on the cobblestones outside his bay window as the city slumbered around him, he couldn't stop thinking about the conversation with Pavla.

I can give you the gift. I can give you life.

Before leaving The Parlor, he had asked Pavla for a physical description of Adrian. Everything she said tracked with the report from the employee of Nightfall who the lieutenant had interviewed. Pavla also mentioned that she had once noticed needle-like scarring on one of Adrian's forearms, similar to that of a heroin or meth addict. Pavla had once been an addict herself and recognized the signs, except she had seen no indication of a blown vein on Adrian. Nor did he exhibit the typical behavior of a user.

She hadn't known what to make of it, and neither did Viktor.

In fact, he didn't know what to think of any of it, except that Adrian was a killer who had cultivated a vampire mythos, presumably to help lure potential victims into his orbit. It was even possible that Adrian had come to believe his own delusion.

The strange charisma Pavla mentioned was typical of cult leaders, sociopaths, and successful politicians. One could argue, of course, they were all one and the same.

As for the heightened strength and sensory abilities, Viktor suspected Adrian was an excellent athlete, and that Pavla's perception that evening had been compromised by inebriation, attraction, and a delusional idealism that fostered her acceptance of the charade.

In other words, she wanted vampires to be real.

Viktor sank deeper into his chair, saddened by the implications. A killer who used prosthetic fangs to drink human blood straight from his victims?

No, that did not bode well for the public's perception of the vampire community.

Though strange, the case might not have interested Viktor further—at least not enough to impinge on his plans with his niece—were it not for a final detail Pavla had mentioned.

When describing Adrian's clothing and personal effects, just before Viktor had left, she had recalled him wearing a silver ring with an unusual carving on the wooden face: a dragon with its tail coiled around its own neck.

The same symbol on the miniature chest the woman had carried out of the townhome earlier in the night.

After a long sip of absinthe, Viktor rose to study his bookshelves. He reached up and pulled out a modest tome published in Florence over a century ago. The title was

STORIA DEGLI ORDINI MONASTICI
HISTORY OF THE MONASTIC ORDERS

He consulted the index and flipped through the book until he found the page describing the insignia to be carried or exhibited by the members of the Order of the Dragon.

> . . . we and the faithful barons and magnates of our kingdom shall bear and have, and do choose and agree to wear and bear, in the manner of society, the sign or effigy of the Dragon incurved into the form of a circle, its tail winding around its neck, divided through the middle of its back along its length from the top of its head right to the tip of its tail, with blood forming a red cross flowing out into the interior of the cleft by a white crack, untouched by blood, just as and in the same way that those who fight under the banner of the glorious martyr St George are accustomed to bear a red cross on a white field . . .

When Viktor had pressed Pavla about the carving on Adrian's ring, she had described the same image, the effigy of the coiled dragon, with one key difference: except for a cross on the back of the dragon, Pavla had seen two silver spears arranged in a cross-like pattern.

Viktor had seen the exact same image on the antique wooden chest tucked under the woman's arm. At the time, he had not found it odd that the cross on the back of the dragon was formed by two intersecting spears, because he wasn't an expert in the symbology of the Order of the Dragon. But he definitely remembered that detail, even with a quick glimpse in the darkness.

And he remembered for certain the spears forming the cross were silver instead of red.

What did this mean? Why did the symbol track so closely to the Order of the Dragon, but with two variations?

There was obviously a connection between the killer and the two people Viktor had seen leaving the house. But a connection of what sort?

Were the man and the woman Viktor had seen participants in the ruse Adrian was using to beguile his victims?

Concerned friends or family members trying to cover up his crimes?

Viktor returned to his bookshelves. There was another itch he had to scratch.

This time it was not so simple as pulling out a book. He consulted a number of reference materials and obscure tomes to follow the breadcrumb trail of knowledge in his sights: tracing the original source of the book of poetry by Johannes Cuspinianus which Viktor had found in the attic of Adrian's residence.

He was not certain the answer lay within his own library, or had survived the passage of centuries. Many centuries ago, before the widespread adoption of the printing press, the vast majority of books were transcribed by hand in monasteries. For a minor author such as Johannes, a few copies at most would have been made. Even fewer would have survived.

Two hours later, just as the gold-red light of dawn appeared outside his bay window, he at last found a reference to the obscure poetry of the Austrian scholar. As far as he could tell, only one library in the world had ever possessed a copy of this book, and the name of the library caused Viktor to set his absinthe down and walk to the window, where he stared above the pitched roofline of Prague in the direction of the aristocratic old house he had visited earlier in the night.

Near the end of the fifteenth century, a book of poetry by Johannes Cuspinianus had been catalogued in the collection of Matthias Corvinus, the king of Hungary from 1458 to 1490. Matthias was a beloved, almost legendary figure in Hungarian history. He had been very well educated, a known bibliophile and patron of the arts. At the time, his *Bibliotheca Corviniana*, the royal library which he had scoured the world to stock with rare volumes, was one of the largest and most prestigious collections of literature in all of Europe. The Greek classicists in the collection alone inspired awe: Aeschylus, Aristotle, Hesiod, Homer, Plutarch, Sophocles, and many others, so many that a visitor to the library had once said they defied enumeration.

The library declined after the death of Matthias. When the Turks invaded Hungary in 1526, the books in the library, along with the royal archives and other priceless treasures, were destroyed by the Ottomans or smuggled out of the country. Very few works survived. Painted on the title pages of most of those that did was a symbol emblematic of King Matthias's royal arms, a shield divided into four fields. One of the fields displayed the same silver lion on a red background which still graces the modern-day Czech coat of arms.

The same crowned, double-tailed Bohemian lion Viktor had seen painted in excruciating detail on the title page of the poetry anthology written by Johannes Cuspinianus.

Unless a world-class forger had gone to great lengths to duplicate an authentic book plate, leather binding, enamel clasp, and silver-studded cover for an extremely obscure tome over five hundred years old, then Viktor felt quite certain the book he had found in that house had once belonged to the lost library of Matthias Corvinus.

It was an extraordinary find under any circumstance. But in this particular situation, coupled with another historical fact of which Viktor was aware, the knowledge sat heavily in his stomach, like a piece of greasy, hard-to-digest meat.

Matthias Corvinus, beloved King of Hungary at the height of the Magyar Empire, had enjoyed a long association with another historical figure, one who had lived in exile in Hungary for many years and who no doubt had access to the library.

That person was Vlad the Impaler, an historical figure known to the world by his famous patronym, Vlad Dracula.

A fellow member, like Matthias Corvinus, of the Order of the Dragon.

-7-

Mari did not want to be left behind, until Grey explained that he might be sitting in his car for hours staking out Purgatory, and another couple of hours following the bar manager around town. Not to mention the potential for violence or police trouble.

But Grey did not plan on getting caught. He had undergone surveillance training during his stint with Marine Recon before he became a diplomatic security agent. Both of those careers had ended prematurely—and poorly—after Grey clashed with authority figures whose code of ethics differed from his own.

Joining was not his strong suit.

After dropping Mari at Viktor's place, Grey grabbed a navy blue hoodie from his duffel bag and a pair of birdwatching binoculars he found in a kitchen drawer. He returned to the nightclub, drove around the block, scoped an apartment building with a rooftop view of the entrance, and parked the Mazda nearby. Grey climbed to the top of the fire escape behind the apartment building, used a window ledge to clamber onto the pitched roof, found a position that overlooked the club, and wedged himself behind a stone waterspout with a leering demonic face.

The binoculars afforded him a good view of both the front and side entrances. His earlier reconnaissance had revealed an alley behind the club, but it did not seem like the sort of exit a well-dressed manager would use.

During the wait, Grey busied himself with memorizing the surrounding streets on Google maps. At 3:35 a.m., with the club still in full swing, the manager walked out the side door, accompanied by one of the armed security guards. Grey flattened against the wall and watched them approach a cherry red Porsche 911. As soon as Grey saw the security guard reach for the door, Grey flew across the roof and down the fire escape. With a map of the streets in his head, he floored the Mazda's accelerator and raced towards an intersection that linked up to the street on which the 911 had been parked.

As Grey turned left onto a busy avenue, he heard the purr of a throaty engine and saw the Porsche making a right turn two blocks ahead. With his quarry in his sights, and the security guard obeying the speed limit, Grey had no problem following the Porsche across the Charles Bridge, passing Malá Strana and Prague Castle on the right. Grey stayed a block behind them and blended in with the taxis and other vehicles prowling the streets of Prague after hours.

Not long past the bridge, the Porsche entered a toney neighborhood with modernist homes sprinkled among embassies and grand apartment buildings. The Porsche pulled up to the curb in front of a detached white townhome with a flat roof. A brown Renault was parked on the street. Grey passed the house and watched in the rearview as the manager walked to the front door, bent down as if entering a security code, and disappeared inside. The security guard stayed in the car.

Grey turned left at the next intersection, parked the car, hurried back to the bar manager's street, and found a copse of spruce trees to hide inside while he peered through the binoculars. Five minutes later, the bar manager emerged wearing a different pair of slacks and a sleek lambskin jacket. He locked the front door and hopped back inside the Porsche.

Grey had a snap decision to make. While he had planned to follow the manager around town, Grey now had a golden opportunity to explore his house—if he could get inside.

After the 911 drove off, Grey walked past the property, probing for seams. He had to assume the house had a security system, which he was not prepared to disarm, but private residences had other means of ingress that homeowners often ignored. AC units that could be removed, leaving a hole in the window. Chimneys wide enough to shimmy down. Crawl spaces that could be breached, giving access to the floorboards.

The bar manager's townhome looked secure to Grey except for one thing: a garage door at the bottom of the sloped driveway with a line of small, decorative glass squares along the top of the door.

Grey pulled up his hood over his head, skirted the outdoor cameras trained on the lawn as best he could, and approached the garage door by jumping off a retaining wall.

These days, he knew many home security systems utilized WIFI sensors attached to doors and windows. Homeowners considered their garage doors impregnable and did not bother to install sensors on them. Nor did they turn on their indoor motion sensors unless leaving town for the night.

Grey was banking on both of these assumptions.

He donned a pair of surgical gloves and used his pocketknife to pry off the piece of hard plastic around the perimeter of the central piece of ornamental glass along the top of the garage door. Easy enough. After some prying, he managed to ease out the pane of glass and set it on the driveway. He did not feel guilty about breaking and entering. These people knew something about Viktor.

They had opened the door to their own house.

He stood on his toes, shone his light inside the opening, and saw what he was looking for: a manual release cord hanging from the ceiling. Grey carried a trash can over, hopped on top of it, and thrust his arm inside the small pane. He just managed to grasp the release cord and give it a tug. The mechanism popped, and the bottom of the door lifted a few inches off the ground, digging painfully into Grey's arm.

Bingo.

He eased his arm out, replaced the trash can, lifted the garage door the rest of the way up, and ducked inside. After closing the door, he used his phone to find an overhead light and flicked it on, revealing a single-car garage with a tool bench and a Porsche sign hanging on the back wall.

A door with a deadbolt led to the interior of the house. Grey extracted a set of emergency lock picking tools, a tension wrench and rake, from the heel of his left boot. It took him a minute to solve the deadbolt, and then he pushed the door inward, cringing as he waited for an alarm to sound or someone inside to cry out.

Nothing.

No one.

As he had suspected, the bar manager had not bothered to connect the alarm system—if there was one—to the door leading to the garage.

Grey found a light by the door and flicked it on, revealing a windowless room with a king-size bed and a set of sliding doors that opened onto a large bathroom. A master bedroom, by all appearances. Though who puts a master bedroom in a finished basement with no windows?

Stranger things awaited.

Along with a nightstand and a wooden armoire and a desk with file folders stacked neatly on top, a wine fridge stood in the center of the wall across from the bed. Through the glass door, instead of racks of fine wine, he saw custom shelves laden with test tubes filled with a crimson liquid that Grey did not think had anything to do with fermented grapes.

He opened the glass door. Cold air rushed out, much colder than a typical wine fridge. None of the stoppered vials were marked. They all appeared identical. He opened one, sniffed it, and caught a faint metallic odor. Blood. After hesitating, he returned the vial, closed the door, and stood in front of the wine fridge for a long moment, uneasy, recalling what Mari had told him about Viktor.

He disappeared chasing a vampire.

Unsure what to make of the fridge—was the bar manager a hemophiliac?—Grey turned away and searched the bedroom. The armoire was full of stylish clothes and shoes that fit the manager's style. In the top drawer of the bedside table, Grey found an assortment of male jewelry, two bottles of cologne, a money clip stuffed with bills, and a passport. He opened the passport, saw a head shot of the bar manager, and read the name.

Anton Speluncescu.

Grey took a photo and returned the passport to the drawer. He searched the papers on the desk and in the file cabinet underneath it. Everything was in Czech, but he noticed *Očistec* on the cover of numerous folders, as well as receipts, stock orders, and invoices for the club. He took a few more pictures and moved on.

At the foot of the bed was an antique trunk wrapped with iron bands. The lid was secured with a steel plate and a sophisticated keypad lock. Oddly, the chest had a line of puncture holes along the rim, just below the lid. Grey shone his light inside. He couldn't see anything, but when he put his face right next to the chest, he caught a foul odor that reminded him of decaying roadkill.

He knocked on the top of the chest. The ancient wood felt as solid as the hull of a pirate ship. He took another picture and left it alone, unsure how to open it without destroying it.

Feeling more and more unnerved by the bizarre contents of the home, Grey wandered up the stairs and explored the two main floors, which were decorated with modern Scandinavian furniture. The living room and the guest bedrooms had an austere, unlived feel to them. In the kitchen, he found a stocked pantry, which comforted Grey more than he liked.

What, did you think the owner of the house only drank blood?

Pull it together, Grey.

Except for a wall safe that he had no way to crack, he found nothing else of interest. He had taken his time searching the house and sensed it was time to leave. He passed through the kitchen on the way to the stairs when he saw headlights swing onto the street, and heard the roar of the Porsche's muscular engine.

Grey had waited too long. The Porsche would pull into the driveway and cut off his escape route. Not only that, the manager would see the missing pane of glass at once.

Grey flicked off his cell phone light and stood poised by the pantry, ready to dart out the front door as soon as he heard the garage door open.

But the Porsche didn't pull into the driveway. Instead it stopped alongside the curb in front of the house, and both the bar manager and the security guard stepped out. The guard left the door to the Porsche open, said something to the bar manager, and walked towards the brown Renault still parked on the street.

Why didn't the security guard pull into the garage?

Because the bar manager doesn't want anyone inside his creepy house.

The brown Renault drove off. The bar manager started to open the door of the Porsche when, all of a sudden, he raised up and faced the house, tilted his head in the air, and sniffed the air like an animal, his head moving higher as if catching a scent.

Unsure what was happening, Grey moved deeper into the shadows of the kitchen, slipping further behind the pantry until he could just barely see through the window.

The house was completely dark. No way anyone on the street could see him.

After sniffing the air, the bar manager's tongue darted out of his mouth and then ran lazily along the edge of his upper lip. Grey thought he could see the tips of two fanglike canines beneath the gums, sharpened or filed to needle-like points, but he couldn't be sure in the darkness. *I fought a man once who filed his teeth. Anyone can do it. It doesn't mean a thing.*

Plus I saw the bar manager's mouth earlier and would have noticed such a thing. My imagination is playing tricks on me.

The bar manager stared at the house for a long moment, in the general direction of the kitchen. Grey kept watching but didn't move a muscle. The bar manager seemed to know someone was in the house. Grey didn't know how, but he did.

Did I trip the security system after all? Is there a hidden camera inside?

The manager started walking towards the front door. Grey had to get out. He raced to the guest bathroom on the ground floor, which had a window overlooking the narrow strip of land separating the neighboring townhome.

The front door opened. Grey's adrenaline spiked as he unlocked the bathroom window and pushed it open. The window was quite small. He had to squeeze through. When he was halfway out, with his legs dangling above the toilet, he thought he heard footsteps in the hallway. Worrying he would be trapped, fear surged through him, an unreasonable sort of panic laced with a dread of the unknown, a lurking fear of the dark and nameless things that he had not felt for some time.

He got his legs through the window and dropped to the grass beneath it. A motion sensor light flicked on, illuminating the narrow space between the townhomes. Not bothering to close the window, Grey raced into the neighbor's back garden and hopped a six-foot fence that led to another property. A dog barked in the distance. Grey kept going, weaving through the neighborhood until he felt safe enough to return to the street.

As he fled into the darkness, planning to circle around to the Mazda at some point, he couldn't stop thinking about the wine fridge full of blood, the foul smell emanating from that wooden chest, and, most of all, the unnatural way the bar manager had cocked his head to sniff at the air, as if he could smell Grey inside the house from fifty feet away.

-8-

"What do you expect me to make of all this?" Lieutenant Andrasko asked. She was sitting across from Viktor at his favorite spot for cappuccino, the Municipal House Cafe, the morning after Viktor had visited the Parlor.

He had just described the disturbing connections linking Daryna's alleged murderer to the Order of the Dragon and the strange couple they had seen leaving the house in Old Town.

"I don't know," Viktor replied. He took a sip of his beverage and cupped his hands around the mug. "I'm not even sure what I think."

"Don't tell me you're starting to believe this kid avoids sunlight and garlic, drinks blood, and can turn into a bat."

Viktor waved a hand, not even bothering to respond.

"We've had some developments," the lieutenant said, knocking back her double espresso before rubbing at a red-rimmed eye.

"You must sleep less than I do."

"Sleep? I'm a lieutenant working a high-profile homicide. So we won't have DNA results for at least a couple more days. As I feared, the rental agency won't give out the names of their clients. Even if they did, the agency does not require documentation or proof of identity. A false name could have been given. I applied for an emergency order, but unless our mystery couple become active suspects, we might be out of luck."

"It would be odd, if they indeed live in Prague and have generational wealth, for me not to recognize them." Viktor shrugged his massive shoulders. "But we don't know where they really live, or if they truly have means. Maybe the woman was lying, and the house isn't hers. I assume you've checked the property records?"

"It belongs to a private holding company in the Cook Islands."

"Whatever privacy laws the car rental agency can lean on, they'll be as sturdy as wet paper compared to the Cook Islands. The name of the trust?"

"Continental Holdings AB."

He took another sip. "Spectacularly unhelpful."

"Agreed," the lieutenant said, then leaned forward on her elbows. "But we might have caught a break."

Viktor's eyebrows rose as the lieutenant ordered another espresso, along with a chocolate croissant, from a passing waiter.

"When I returned to the station last night," the lieutenant continued, "I met with our sketch artist again. She drew the man and the woman we saw leaving the house. You can't run a sketch through a database, but I sent it around the municipality anyway, and to Europol on a whim. This morning, to my surprise, someone at Europol got back to me. One of their agents, an organized crime guy on loan from Albania, thinks he recognized the man we saw. He's a Romanian national named Cezar Speluncescu."

"Latin," Viktor murmured. "Just like Adrian."

The lieutenant blinked. "What?"

"Romanian isn't a Slavic tongue. There's plenty of Slavic influence, but Romanian derives from Vulgar Latin, and is the only Romance language in Eastern Europe. The history of the region is a long and convoluted one, but during the resistance to the Magyars—the Hungarians—Romanized names that were difficult to translate to Hungarian became popular. As were names that reflected the region's Dacian heritage, despite the fact that Dacians resisted Roman rule."

"That's way more information than I needed."

"Cezar Speluncescu, roughly translated, means 'ruler of the cave.' Speluncescu is an unusual patronym. I don't believe I've heard it before. In any event, what do we know about our modern-day emperor?"

"Europol believes the Speluncescus control a number of criminal enterprises in Central and Eastern Europe."

"What kind of criminal enterprises?"

"Something we call the Red Market."

"I'm unfamiliar with that term."

She looked him in the eye. "It's shorthand for the illegal sale and smuggling of human body parts, particularly blood and organs."

Viktor lowered his cappuccino. "I see."

"According to the Europol agent, the Speluncescu family is as notorious in certain circles as they are secretive. I've never heard of them, and don't know much else at this stage. Europol is sending a full report later today, though the agent warned me it would be thin."

"If they live in Prague, why haven't you heard of them?"

"I don't think they do. The agent said there was no evidence of activity in the Czech Republic, other than a nightclub owned by the family called Purgatory. I know of it, but other than the usual nonsense that goes on in places like that, we've never had trouble. Certainly nothing involving the organ trade. I'd bet my pension the family keeps it aboveboard and uses it to launder money."

Viktor steepled his fingers. "So the Speluncescus own a nightclub and likely a house here, and I detected a Czech accent in the woman's voice—yet the last names and nationalities are Romanian. How sure is this agent that Cezar Speluncescu is the same man we saw?"

"He wasn't sure, but *I* am." She took a small stack of photos out of a manila folder lying on the table. The first photo depicted the same ruggedly handsome, well-built man they had seen leaving the house in Old Town. "This is Cezar Speluncescu. The agent sent these over."

"Undoubtedly one and the same." Viktor leaned back in his seat and tapped his index fingers together. "A good development. And the woman? The murder suspect? Are they part of this family?"

The lieutenant moved the photo aside to reveal the one underneath it, a grainy photo of a strikingly attractive woman in her late teens or early twenties. "It's the same woman, don't you think?"

"She's so young here, but the resemblance is strong . . . the same hair, cheekbones, angular nose, eye spacing. Yes, I believe it's her."

The lieutenant tapped the photo. "That's Cezar's mother. This is the only photo we have on file, from her university days at the Sorbonne forty years ago. Her name is Dumitra."

"The goddess of the harvest," Viktor said. "Roman once again. And the Sorbonne means she's highly educated."

"Her husband died of a heart attack when he was only forty-two. Both her parents passed years ago. Dumitra lives in Bucharest, and while Cezar has been spotted across central and eastern Europe, the agent doesn't know where he lives now. He said they both roam about like rich ghosts."

"And our young artist?"

The lieutenant revealed the third photo, a headshot of a fine-boned young man wearing a graduation cap-and-gown with a stole that matched his intense green eyes.

"Our suspect's true name is not Adrian, but Florin Speluncescu. He's 23 years old. I assume you want to opine on the esoteric meaning of the name?"

"If I recall, it's the diminutive of *fiore*, Latin for *flower*."

"I was expecting something more grandiose."

"Maybe that's why he changed it." Viktor stared at the photo. Though the young man fit the descriptions they had been given, he was even slighter than Viktor had imagined, almost gaunt, and his eyes burned with a fierce, introspective intelligence. So different from his older brother, a strapping man full of confidence and swagger. Now Viktor understood why Pavla was so surprised when Florin had lifted her off her feet with one hand.

How did *this frail recent graduate accomplish such a feat?*

The lieutenant revealed the fourth and final photo. "That's the middle brother, Anton. He manages Purgatory, the nightclub in Prague. I'm told there are some cousins as well, but as far as we know, that's the immediate family."

"So they came for the youngest son," Viktor said. "To extract him from justice."

The lieutenant's face was grim as she replaced the photos in the manila folder. "It looks that way. There's no record of any of them leaving or entering the country. We'll keep an eye on the house, but I have the feeling we won't be seeing them in Prague again. At least not for some time."

"The cap and gown . . . did Florin attend university under his own name?"

"Yes, according to the records."

"Where?"

The lieutenant crossed her legs and met Viktor's eyes as she took a sip of carbonated water from a teacup that accompanied the espresso. "Romania. Cluj-Napoca. He graduated two years ago."

"Cluj-Napoca?" Viktor said, recalling the book he had found. "That's the birthplace of Matthias Corvinus."

There was a devious, knowing glimmer in the lieutenant's eyes. "Is that right?"

Viktor clasped his hands atop the table. "What are the next steps in the investigation?"

"I'll interview Anton, then continue searching for the suspect and try to manage the press."

"But you think Florin has left the country?"

"I do. I'll involve Interpol, but with this family's history, my instincts tell me they'll stash him somewhere we can't reach."

Viktor tapped his index fingers against the backs of his hands and noted the lieutenant still had that strange glimmer in her eyes. "You think a better way to find Florin is through his family, don't you?"

"The thought crossed my mind," she said.

"With a family as secretive and powerful as you believe the Speluncescus to be, they would most likely have an ancestral estate or something like it, far from prying eyes. Somewhere they can escape to with impunity."

"My thoughts exactly."

"If I were a jaded man, lieutenant," Viktor said evenly, "which I happen to be, I might suspect you're trying to lead me somewhere."

"I have a nagging suspicion you've developed an interest in this case. Interpol can look into the family's criminal holdings, but the best way to find Florin, as you suggested, might be to find his true home. My instincts also tell me that location will have something to do with the chest his mother was carrying, the book you found, and how they connect to the family history."

Viktor met her gaze. "I do not disagree."

"It also comes to mind that you might be the one person with the knowledge and ability to unearth the origins of such a family, and connect the dots from the past to the present. In fact, I believe in this strongly enough that I would like to engage your services to do just that."

Viktor looked off to the side, thinking of Mari and the unfortunate timing of the case, as well as the obvious perils it presented. He would like to involve

Dominic Grey, and planned to do just that as soon as he returned from vacation. Unfortunately, Grey liked to go off the grid when he took days off—especially when Viktor was supposed to be safe and secure at his lake house.

"I accept," he said, "and I'll ensure my fee is one the department can manage."

"I'd like to keep this off the books for now, as I would not want any . . . curious ears . . . within the department to get wind of such a thing. That could make your task more dangerous than it already is."

He waved a hand. "Pay me when you can."

"I thought you might say that." She leaned forward across the table. "I truly appreciate your help, but I want you to understand this is not a family to trifle with. Find out who they are, but only on paper. Do not engage them or their associates in any way. If you find something, we'll take it from there. Do we understand each other?"

Viktor calmly raised his cappuccino to his lips. "Of course."

-9-

The morning after Grey's nighttime reconnaissance, at the request of Lieutenant Zuzana Andrasko, Grey and Mari appeared at a police station not far from Viktor's townhome.

When they arrived at eight a.m., a junior officer led them to a conference room with a kitchenette from the Soviet era, linoleum flooring streaked with grime, and an interior window that overlooked a hallway. The junior officer spoke halting English but managed to convey, on his way out, that the lieutenant would arrive soon, and they should help themselves to the refreshments.

The smell of burnt caramel emanated from a coffee pot simmering on a burner. Mari eyed the geriatric coffee maker as if it were diseased. She took a glass of water to the long conference table as Grey poured a cup of the stale brew. He liked good coffee as well, but after his late-night escapade and the early call from the lieutenant, he couldn't afford to be picky.

"We're out of milk," the lieutenant said briskly, sweeping into the room wearing grey slacks and an unbuttoned police jacket, carrying a laptop in one hand and a travel mug in the other. A compact, middle-aged woman with a short blond haircut as no-nonsense as her demeanor, Grey got an immediate vibe of competency from her.

"I take it black," Grey said as he sat beside Mari.

The lieutenant set the laptop on the table and took a seat across from her visitors. Mari's arms were folded protectively across her chest, subdued in the way that most civilians are by police authority. The lieutenant seemed to take that in—and the fact that Grey was not.

Grey assumed the lieutenant had summoned them to discuss the case, but she stared right at him and said, "Where were you last night?"

He calmly returned the stare. "Out and about."

"Two things. One, I do not at all appreciate someone—I assume Interpol, since that's who gave me the info as well—tipping you off before we arrived.

This is my jurisdiction, and my investigation, and you compromised it by making a scene at the nightclub."

"All I did was ask questions. They sent their muscle after me."

"It's a private club. He asked you politely to leave first."

Grey laughed. "Is that what they told you?"

"Be that as it may, you knew what you were doing there, and also when you broke a window in Anton Speluncescu's garage after you left the club."

Grey leaned back in his chair, crossed his legs, and took a sip of coffee. He did not want to lie to her, but neither did he want to incriminate himself. He had no idea where her loyalties lay, or how she knew where he had gone the night before. Probably she had just guessed. In the seat beside him, he could see the tension in Mari's hands, now folded atop the table.

The lieutenant continued, "The bar manager—Anton—reported seeing an intruder fitting your general description snooping around outside his house. He knows your name and told us about the incident at the club."

Grey was surprised the bar manager had reported the minor crime, since Grey was convinced the manager had something to hide.

"He said no one got in the house, but we did fingerprint his garage, which could get you in very hot water."

Still Grey kept his cool. He had been careful and did not expect any evidence to surface.

"If we find something," the lieutenant said, "Anton could make noise. Purgatory brings in a lot of money."

"But he won't, because we both know he had something to do with Viktor's disappearance."

"He already *has*. Anton donates generously to the mayoral campaign. The superintendent called this morning and wants me to detain you. How we finish this conversation will determine whether I do."

Grey didn't show it, but he was starting to think he shouldn't have been so brash the night before.

But then I wouldn't have seen what I did.

"He's just trying to find my uncle," Mari said. "I asked Grey to come to

Prague. However much this club owner donates, I guarantee—I *know*—my uncle has done far more for the city."

"Your uncle is the only reason I have some leeway here," the lieutenant said, "but I still have to do my job." She looked right at Grey again. "I'm going to brief you on some things, and then I highly suggest you leave the country as soon as possible. If you don't, and any evidence connecting you to the break-in manifests, I'll be forced to arrest you. Viktor has told me about you before. You don't strike me as the type of guy who would be deterred by a basement door, or even a security system. Nor would I discount the possibility that someone might have planted some evidence against you."

"Anton—" Grey began, but she cut him off.

"Will be investigated by *me*. You're not to intervene a moment longer, either of you. Am I clear on that?"

Grey could sense Mari waiting for him to respond. Left with no choice, he gave his assent with a reluctant nod. He couldn't risk an arrest at this crucial juncture.

Yet Lieutenant Andrasko was clever, and he sensed something else might be in play.

"I'm glad we understand each other," the lieutenant said. "I promise you I'll do everything I can from my end."

"You better," Mari said. "I'm wondering if you're too afraid of this *businessman* to investigate him properly."

Grey chuckled to himself. *I guess she got over that healthy fear of the police.*

"Yes," the lieutenant said. "You're Viktor's niece." As Mari's face tightened, the lieutenant rose to close the blinds on the window. "That conversation wasn't for show, but it's best if the rest of this remains private." She opened the laptop and positioned it in the middle of the table so they could see it. "I want to tell you what I've learned from Europol about this case."

During Grey's career as a special agent with Diplomatic Security, he had used the services of both Interpol and Europol on numerous occasions. Interpol, with whom Viktor often accepted referrals through Jacques, was an organization that facilitated the flow of information among police agencies worldwide. Their officers were bureaucrats who pored through records and databases and issued international alerts. They did not put boots on the ground.

Europol was a similar organization that tended to focus on cross-border investigations of dangerous criminal groups in the EU. They employed full-time staff at their headquarters in the Hague, as well as liaison officers from member states.

"I don't understand," Grey said. "Why is Europol involved with a local murder?"

The lieutenant rose again to refill her coffee. When she returned to her seat, she took off her jacket and draped it over her chair. "The name of the manager you met is Anton Speluncescu. The club is owned by a private conglomerate led by his mother, Dumitra Speluncescu. In addition to the legal business interests of the Speluncescus in Eastern and Central Europe, Europol informs me the family is heavily involved in the red market."

"The what?" Mari asked.

"Traffickers in body parts," Grey said grimly, remembering his confrontation with a sinister diplomat from Lagos who kept a gurney and gleaming tools of vivisection in a hidden room in his basement in Harare, a torture chamber that reeked of fear and formaldehyde. Grey would have died in that room if Viktor had not intervened. "Organs, blood, bones, you name it. Anything and everything involving the human body that can be sold for profit. And nearly all of it can."

She shuddered. "How very awful."

"The global market is enormous," the lieutenant said. "Billions."

At once Grey recalled the refrigerator full of blood he had seen in Anton's bedroom. At least there was a rational explanation for that—though why keep so many unmarked vials in his bedroom?

Surely there were more secure—and less personal—places to store their product?

The lieutenant gave them the rundown on the family, including the older brother, Cezar, and the youngest, Florin, who the lieutenant suspected had murdered and exsanguinated the young woman in Old Town. As Grey absorbed the report, as well as the historical connections Viktor had uncovered, Grey's wheels spun as he tried to fit it all together. "Why didn't Jacques tell me about this when he sent me to the nightclub?"

"He hadn't connected the dots. So far, no one in the family has slipped up. We know they're involved in the red market, they have their hands all over it, but Europol hasn't pinned a thing on them. Anton is the only member of the family in the public eye, and his record is as clean as a dealership floor. The club, Purgatory, has no serious citations. I feel lucky I caught someone at Europol who knows the family's reputation."

"How did the agent make the connection?" Grey asked.

"Before Viktor disappeared, he and I encountered a man and a woman leaving a house in Prague where we believed Florin—who went by *Adrian Novák* in Prague—was living. My contact tells me Viktor and I had an extremely rare sighting of Cezar and Dumitra Speluncescu. Except for Anton, we have no known photos of the family after college graduation."

"They get a solid education before they join the family business?" Grey said.

"Apparently so. Dictators and crime lords around the world send their kids to school in America, Paris, London."

"I suppose that's true."

"Anyway, after leaving school, Florin seems to have been floating around Prague. Maybe he was bucking the trend and wanted to do his own thing."

"Like snapping the necks of Moldovan women and draining their blood?"

The lieutenant took a sip of coffee.

"So in addition to investigating a murder," Grey continued, "Viktor might have run afoul of a family protecting one of their own."

"That's how I see it."

"Did Viktor know about the true family business?"

"Not right at the start. Before he left Prague, yes."

Grey swore. "Then why the hell did he go off without me? Why did you let him?"

"You speak as if I, or anyone else, has control over Viktor Radek. He was only supposed to research the family's history. Find a way to track them down."

"Which you encouraged."

"Viktor is a professional investigator," the lieutenant said evenly. "With decades of experience."

Mari shifted in her seat. "Why didn't he contact you the night he disappeared? Tell you he was in town, and where he was going?"

"He did. The night he arrived, I was working a case, but he left a voicemail telling me had returned to Prague and found some things of interest. We scheduled a meeting for the following morning. He never showed, and I haven't heard from him since."

"And yet he wasn't officially missing for days?" Mari said in disbelief. "Why didn't you say anything?"

"*Officially*," the lieutenant said. "Listen, when your uncle left Prague the first time, he told me almost nothing. I know he was going to Cluj-Napoca, then I didn't hear from him for days. But he returned, so when he missed our meeting, I didn't panic at first. I thought he might have gone off again. Yes, it was unusual not to call me and cancel, and don't think I wasn't worried, or haven't been looking for him. I didn't want to alarm *you*. That said, I trust Viktor, and he knows how to take care of himself. But the more I learn about this family, the more nervous I get. This morning Europol told me it thinks the Speluncescus use local intermediaries to harvest blood and body parts from rural villagers. They approach the poorest of the poor, usually single mothers, and offer a year's wages in exchange for kidneys, eyes, you name it."

One of Mari's hands slipped to her mouth. Grey watched with hooded eyes, saddened but no longer shocked by the level of depravity to which human beings could sink.

The lieutenant continued, "They pay a pittance up front and renege on the rest. It's typical in the business. You can guess what happens to anyone who complains or tries to involve the police."

"What about the organized crime in these countries where they operate?" Grey asked. "Albania, Ukraine, Macedonia? They're nasty customers. Why do they allow it?"

"The Speluncescus have carved out their own territory when it comes to the red market. I'm told the local gangs avoid them."

"Why?" Grey said bluntly.

The lieutenant pressed her lips together and tapped the fingers of her left hand on the table. "I'm also told the Speluncescus have . . . reputation . . . as a family not to cross. There are stories floating around. Enemies who were found drained of blood in alleys, flayed alive, their organs and tongues removed." She grimaced. "Other stories about Cezar and his mother appearing only at night, avoiding crosses and garlic, and disappearing into the mist."

Grey stared at her. "You're joking."

"I wish I was. I'm not sure what to make of it. Europol hasn't bothered with it because it's only rumors at this point, and the victims were all hardened criminals."

After a moment, Grey murmured, "They're using the vampire myth to keep them away. Safeguarding their product with local legend. Viktor and I have seen it before, in the drug trade."

The lieutenant cocked her head. "Interesting angle. I suppose I could buy it, in those places."

"It's smart business. I bet the Speluncescus keep their market share low enough not to truly anger anyone, and they've taken a page out of the drug cartel playbook by making sure their reputation is terrifying enough to make anyone think twice about crossing them."

Mari rubbed her arms as if she had a sudden chill. "You're telling me my uncle is caught up in this? That these monsters kidnapped him, or . . . is there even a chance he's still alive?"

Grey and the lieutenant exchanged a grim look. "Your uncle is a very resourceful man," the lieutenant said.

"That's not very comforting," she said in a near-whisper.

"Maybe they plan to blackmail him. Listen: until we know otherwise, we assume he's alive. Okay?"

Mari looked small and very lost as she gave an agreeing nod.

"Something else," Grey said, wagging a finger. "If this was just about the murder of the young woman, and they already had Florin out of the country, why bother with Viktor? Maybe they want to erase some evidence he uncovered about Florin—but that isn't why Viktor left the country. He left to dig up dirt on the family. I doubt that during this process he would have uncovered anything incriminating on a crime in Prague."

The lieutenant's eyebrows lifted. "It's a good point. A really good point."

"Viktor's a fairly high-profile target, with connections in law enforcement. They wouldn't risk kidnapping him without a good reason." Grey paused, thinking it through. "I think we have to assume he found something. Something the Speluncescus don't want to see the light of day."

"If that's true," the lieutenant said, "Viktor's too smart to keep it to himself. I know we had a meeting scheduled, but don't you think he would have kept a record of what he found somewhere? Or told someone?"

"I do," Grey said. "And I think it might be keeping him alive."

Mari thrust her palms on the table, excited, but then her eyes dimmed. "They'd want to make sure he didn't tell anyone or hide the evidence," she said quietly, as if she understood full well what that meant.

That if Viktor was keeping something from these people, and he was still alive, he might wish he were dead.

"It gives us hope," Grey said, "but we need to *move*." He rose and started to pace. "So what now? It sounds like if we find Cezar or Dumitra, we find Viktor."

"Agreed," the lieutenant said. "Anton may or may not know something, but from everything I'm told, he's not in charge. He's off-limits to you anyway, maybe me as well. Leaning on him without evidence will get us nowhere and raise the family's guard."

"Give him space," Grey said. "Put a mole inside the club, bug his house, see where he goes."

"All of which would have been easier before your little adventure."

Grey ignored the comment. "Is there anything else?"

The lieutenant opened the laptop and showed them photos of the members of the Speluncescu family. After that, she brought up an image of a drab concrete building that looked Stalinist to Grey.

"This is a hospital in Skopje, Macedonia." The lieutenant's eyes found his from across the table. "Europol believes human organs have a way of disappearing inside, and ending up in the hands of the Speluncescus."

Grey compressed his lips as Mari stared daggers at the screen.

"You think they took my uncle there?" Mari said. She swallowed and looked down at the table. "To . . . make him talk?"

"I don't know," the lieutenant said. "Don't think about that."

"Then what? You think Cezar or Dumitra might be there?"

"I doubt that."

"So what's the point?" Mari said in a shrill voice.

"It's a potential link," Grey said. "Does Europol have anyone inside the hospital?"

"Not anymore. They had an undercover nurse in the maternity ward last year, investigating reports of newborn infants disappearing. A month into the assignment, the nurse slipped off the rooftop deck of her apartment and fell to her death."

Grey's jaw tightened, and Mari slumped in her seat.

"Skopje is an absolute backwater," the lieutenant said, "and the intel is dicey, so Europol hasn't followed up. Listen, I don't think you should get within a hundred miles of these people. The rumors about Cezar are particularly bad. But I've seen your background and I have a feeling you're going to look for Viktor no matter what I say."

"You're right about that."

"I'm desperate here, so, well . . ." the lieutenant closed the laptop. "That's that."

"You don't seem too worried about my nighttime activities when it's not in your jurisdiction."

"And?"

Grey gave her a tight-lipped smile. "Is there anything else?"

"You tell me." The lieutenant folded her hands atop the table and gave him an insinuating look, which he took as an invitation to discuss, in a roundabout way, his visit to Anton's house.

Without admitting to anything, he described the refrigerator full of blood and the old wooden chest. But he kept the strange behavior of Anton to himself, the sniffing of the air like an animal, the flick of his tongue across his lips, the glimpse of pointed teeth, and the way he seemed to know Grey was inside.

Why Grey kept these things to himself, he wasn't sure, except they seemed ludicrous to discuss out loud. Even in his own mind, he had begun to question whether he had seen what he thought he had.

Cluj-Napoca, Romania

-10-

Viktor had not been to Cluj for over a decade, but for a long spell of his academic career, he had visited the city twice a year as a guest lecturer. The ancestral home of Matthias Corvinus was one of the largest cities in Romania and home to plenty of businesses, but Cluj was a college town at heart. Its universities attracted the best students in the country, who often stayed after graduation to become professors, artists, and entrepreneurs.

Cluj was also the capital and beating heart of Transylvania, a mountainous principality in central Romania with a global reputation that far outstripped its modest size. Whenever Viktor traveled in the region, absorbing the ruined castles and gloomy forests and the brooding, impossibly craggy peaks that rose like sword thrusts above the valleys and constricted mountain passes, he could see how Bram Stoker's own visits had inspired his Gothic tale.

Nor did Viktor fail to recognize that his current visit, an attempt to track down a murderer imitating a vampire, stemmed from the ongoing legacy of that novel.

Or did the blame lie instead with the powerful myths and legends, so prevalent in the region, that had seeded the Irish writer's imagination in the first place?

Was Viktor chasing folk tales, or were the folk tales chasing him?

At the airport, he stepped into a private car his travel agent had arranged with Hotel Platinia. Though not on par with the five-star luxury to which Viktor was accustomed, the hotel was upscale for Romania, had a lovely restaurant with an Italian chef, and lay within walking distance of the areas Viktor needed to visit.

On the way, Viktor sent a text to Grey, disclosing his location and asking him to call when he had a chance. Viktor did not expect a quick reply. Grey would certainly get back to him if he checked his phone, but Viktor had his doubts that would occur anytime soon. Days, even.

So be it. Viktor had made the decision to take the case and had survived on his own for years before he met Grey. As long as he concentrated on research, he did not expect trouble.

Then again, when one poked a nest of hornets, no matter how careful the touch, one had to accept the consequences.

Viktor felt terrible about disappointing his niece. He had also disappointed himself. For months he had been looking forward to spending time with Mari, and hoped they could pick up where they left off when he returned. Viktor did not fault the ethics of his decision to help the lieutenant solve Daryna's murder. It was a worthy cause that would benefit from Viktor's unique insight. But deep down, he knew his fascination with the bizarre elements of the case, a potential link to the Order of the Dragon and a missing piece of history, had led to his decision as much as the ethical concerns.

Do prdele. You have to learn when to say no, Viktor. Not to the police but to yourself.

As the private car wove through the concrete high-rises and uninspired glass buildings marking the city center, Viktor turned his thoughts to his dual purpose for visiting Cluj. The focus of his visit was Dr. Belá Fessler, a professor of history of Hungarian descent at Babes-Bolyai University, the largest college in Romania. Dr. Fessler had published most of the only peer-reviewed articles on the Order of the Dragon that Viktor could find. While Viktor had never run across the historian in professional circles, Dr. Fessler had studied at the best schools on the continent and had an excellent reputation among Viktor's colleagues at Charles University in Prague. Viktor had unearthed precious little information on The Order of the Dragon himself, and hoped Dr. Fessler could solve the mysteries at hand or help point Viktor in the right direction.

The historian was not available until the evening. That was fine. Viktor had a different fact-finding mission for the daytime hours, since Babes-Bolyai University was also the alma mater of Florin Speluncescu.

After a wash in his hotel suite, Viktor made time for a caffè macchiato at the espresso bar in the lobby, a quick pick-me-up instead of his usual late-morning cappuccino.

The macchiato was first-rate. He tipped the barista in kind and started the ten-minute walk to the university, which reminded him why Cluj had always been his favorite city in Romania.

It was said that the beauty of Bucharest, the capital of the country, had once rivaled the best cities in Europe. Many called it the "Paris of the East." Viktor wished he had seen Bucharest in its heyday, before the bombings of World War II had leveled most of its historical center. The loathsome Nicolae Ceaușescu had added insult to injury by using brutalist Soviet architecture as inspiration for the rebuild. Modern-day Bucharest was a shell of its former self, and a city Viktor did not enjoy visiting.

Cluj-Napoca also suffered from urban sprawl, and was not a stunning city by any stretch of the imagination. But the parts of Cluj were greater than the whole. The city came to life in the courtyards and bohemian cafes stuffing the historic center, where live musicians serenaded passerby on the street corners, university pubs sponsored spirited debates and impromptu poetry readings, and the *joie de vivre* of the student population enlivened a country where optimism was often in short supply. As long as one knew the areas to avoid, Cluj was a place to stroll deep in thought until one stumbled in serendipity upon the perfect leaf-strewn square, hunched over a good book on a park bench as an ancient clock tower in the distance chimed the hour.

With no time to wander, Viktor spent the day flashing his Interpol badge to administrators and professors who might have come into contact with Florin. The youngest Speluncescu had attended the university. That was not in question. The records confirmed his attendance.

Beyond that, he learned very little. The handful of professors who remembered Florin agreed that he avoided teacher contact and had never spoken in class unless called upon. Not too unusual for a college kid. While a good-looking and well-spoken student, Florin, by all accounts, had seemed painfully shy and withdrawn. No one knew anything about his personal life. He had not played any sports or belonged to any clubs. He studied hard and made excellent grades, graduating with honors in the top ten percent of his class. Viktor was intrigued to discover that Florin had studied literature with a focus on the English Romantics.

Perhaps he left school and reinvented himself as one of the mysterious dashing figures he so loved to read about.

When Viktor scored a meeting with Florin's advisor in the Literature department, Dr. Maria Petrescu, he learned two facts of potential importance: that Florin had a girlfriend during his junior year, and when they had broken up the following summer, Florin was so distraught he had overdosed on pills and landed in the emergency room.

After Dr. Petrescu learned of the breakdown from Florin's girlfriend, the professor had visited Florin at his apartment. Rather shame-facedly, he claimed he was fine and had a momentary lapse of judgment. Dr. Petrescu did not believe him but there was little else she could do. She contacted the family member on record—an uncle living in Prague, she believed—but did not remember his response. Once the semester began, Florin had seemed fine and performed well in school.

Another break came when Viktor asked Dr. Petrescu if she remembered the name of Florin's girlfriend.

The professor gave him a name, Amza Horvath, and something even better. During school, Amza had worked at a café near the university to help fund her education. Apparently, she still had the job, and had waited on Dr. Petrescu just the other day.

In the late afternoon, when Viktor entered Ritual, a café on the first floor of a handsome baroque building, he encountered an exhibit of oil paintings with saturated hues that resembled technicolor. At the center of each painting was an androgynous face bearing the solemn, haunting features of a Roman bust. Instead of hair, a crown of technology adorned the heads of each figure, frizzy coiled wires and Medusa-esque cables and TVs on the ends of antennas. The quality of the artwork was quite good. Viktor approached one and saw the initials of the artist, A.H., in the lower right corner.

There were other collections as well. The art hanging on the staid mahogany walls gave the café a slick aesthetic, an old-World coffee shop with a postmodern vibe.

People from all walks populated the café. Before taking a seat, Viktor observed the scene and noticed two servers: a bearded man in his thirties and a young woman with a face so striking it took him aback. She had full lips with an alluring curve, skin as smooth as the spot of cream in Viktor's coffee that morning, straight dark hair parted in the middle above a high forehead, and wide Asiatic gray eyes. A mixture of features that could only occur in a region with a stew of ethnicities such as Romania. Viktor was not one to stare at younger women—he found such behavior untoward, and preferred maturity in a lover—but he could appreciate her beauty and had to force himself not to gape as she approached his table.

"Romanian, English, French, or German?" she asked, holding out an array of menus.

He replied in fluent but heavily accented Romanian. "I'm Czech, but any of the above will do."

"English it is," she said with a warm smile and a slight accent. "I need to practice."

"How's the cappuccino?"

"A specialty of the house."

"And the food?" he asked, perusing the plastic menu. "I could use a morsel."

"The baguettes are made fresh every morning. I like the goat cheese and arugula."

"Done," he said, returning the menu. He pointed at the exhibit he had seen when he walked in. "I'm curious about those paintings. They're quite fetching. Do you happen to know the artist?"

"She's right in front of you."

His eyebrows lifted. "I'm very impressed. It reminds me of technicolor."

"That's an astute comment, and certainly the inspiration. I use a similar dye technique with photographs, then gloss them with enamel paints. Are you an artist?"

"Bah. I like to collect, though I tread lightly in the world of modern art.

I like to think I know good work when I see it, and that's about all. Unless I completely miss my mark, you have real talent."

She blushed and took his menu. "Thank you. Maybe someone will buy one someday."

On her way back to the kitchen, the other waiter called her by name, and Viktor knew for sure he had found the right person. Amza returned with his cappuccino, and he sipped in silence while he observed her at work. She seemed bright, industrious, and personable. He could see why Florin had fallen for her.

She returned with the baguette. "Would you like anything else at the moment?"

He met her eyes. "At some point, Amza, I'd like to ask you some questions about someone in your past."

Her face became guarded in a wounded way, as if disappointed that yet another customer who seemed nice had decided to hit on her. "How do you know my name?"

"The other server called it out. More germane to our conversation, Dr. Petrescu gave it to me."

"Oh," she said, less on her guard at the mention of the professor. "She did? Why? What is this about?"

"Florin Speluncescu."

A dark cloud settled over Amza's eyes. "Florin? I haven't seen him since graduation."

"I'm sorry to dredge up bad memories."

"They're not all bad."

"Ah. Yes." Viktor lowered his voice to ensure no one overheard him, in case Amza found the conversation embarrassing. "You seem like a nice person, and an honest one. I'll be as forthright with you as I can. I live in Prague and help the local police with certain investigations. I'm sorry to say Florin is a suspect in a recent incident—"

"It's that girl, isn't it? The one they found with her . . . the bite wounds . . ."

Viktor compressed his lips, wondering why she had come to that conclusion so quickly. "Yes."

Amza's hand clapped over her mouth. She murmured something in Romanian too low and fast for him to understand, though he heard the principal emotion loud and clear.

Fear.

"I just have a few questions about Florin," he said. "I'd be happy to return after your shift."

"Finish your baguette. Then I'll take a break and we can go outside."

Viktor did as she requested, paid the bill, bought a painting, and left a very large tip.

When Amza met him on the busy brick street outside the café, Viktor noticed her hands shaking as she untied her apron and lit a cigarette.

"I don't smoke anymore," she said as a city bus plastered with advertisements sped by. "I had to borrow one."

"I'm sorry to be a bad influence."

"And thank you for the tip and buying my art. That was unnecessary."

The sun had sunk below the buildings. A cold wind stirred a pile of leaves and debris in the gutter near Viktor's feet. "Should we go inside? You look cold."

"I'm fine." After a long drag, she said, "He's a good person. He would never kill anyone, especially . . . like that."

"I assume you knew him as well as anyone."

"Perhaps. At least during school. Though contrary to what everyone thought at the time, we were never a couple."

"You were just friends?"

"I know Florin wanted very much for us to be . . . something else. I did too. He was smart and kind and thoughtful and loved the arts, all the qualities I look for. He was deeper than the other guys too, always seeing to the true heart of things, always making art out of life. We met the first day of British Poetry class our third year and had a, how do say in English, a connection, from day one. But it just wasn't, he never gave me—gave us—a chance. He wanted it too much, right from the start. He was infatuated with me, so I never had a chance to fall in love with him. Does that make any sense?"

Her words caused Viktor to remember his own past, and the girl his best friend Darius had wanted in the same way.

So instead, Eve had become the love of Viktor's life, and the awkward love triangle had led to tragic consequences. "Love can't find a foothold on an uneven surface," he said. "Nor does it flourish from need."

She nodded as she stared into the distance.

"Do you know where he is?" he said. "Where he might have gone?"

"I have absolutely no idea."

"Where is he from?"

"As strange as it sounds, I don't know that either. We never talked about his family or his past. Well," she said with an uneasy look in her eye, "almost never."

"What do you mean?"

She took another long drag. "The night I told him it wasn't going to happen for us, and that I only wanted to be friends—" She stopped talking to press her lips together, suppressing an emotion. "I don't know if you know this, but he overdosed on sleeping pills that night."

"Dr. Petrescu mentioned it."

She fiddled with the collar of her white dress shirt. "Earlier in the night, when I confessed my feelings, he said something very strange. He was emotional when he said it, distraught, but on his way out the door he said his family had a secret. A secret he would have soon, and when he did, I wouldn't be able to resist him."

"What a strange thing to say."

"It disturbed me. As if he was going to do something to himself or . . ." She began sucking down the cigarette, finishing it off and lighting another with the smoldering tip of the old one. "I saw something," she said in a voice a touch throatier than before. "Something I don't understand."

"I happen to be quite good at unraveling unexplainable mysteries."

"I'm not even sure what I saw. I mean, I think I'm sure but . . . how is it possible?"

"Why don't you talk me through it?"

She held the cigarette to the side and took her bottom lip between her teeth. "They kept him in the hospital for a full day. I checked on him three times and was there when they released him. He refused to speak to me and said he never wanted to see me again. Later that evening, I went to his home. He lived in an old house all by himself. That alone was strange for a student. I always got the feeling his family had lots of money. Florin is classy and never talked about it. Anyway, I just wanted to lay eyes on him, you know. I cared about him. He was my best friend. I wanted to know he wasn't going to overdose again. Well, there was this bay window on the first floor he liked to sit beside and drink wine while he read. It was on the side of the house overlooking an overgrown park. Very private. I knew he wouldn't answer the door, so I snuck into the park until I had a view of the window. I saw Florin but he wasn't reading. He was standing in the middle of the room talking to someone."

"A woman?"

Her lips pressed tight as her head swung back and forth. "A man. Someone older and much bigger than Florin. A real brute of a guy, though he had on nice clothes. Even from a distance, I could see the resemblance in their profile, their posture. They had to be close relatives."

"What were they doing?"

"Arguing. That much I could tell. It got so intense the older guy slapped him. I was shocked. Florin stumbled backwards holding his cheek and then started forward like he was going to fight him. At some point they had turned, so I was looking at Florin's back and the other guy's face. That's when it happened."

She touched her hands to her cheeks and was so silent for so long Viktor had to nudge her. "Amza?"

She shuddered and said, "When Florin came at him, the other guy opened his mouth, and he had . . . he had *fangs*. He was standing right under a light, and I could see them even from a distance. They had to be an inch long, and he opened his mouth like he was about to use them. Like he was some sort of animal. They could have been fake, of course, but Florin stumbled backwards as if the guy had hit him."

Viktor swallowed.

After a moment, she said, "I'm Romani, you know."

"I guessed as much."

"I don't believe in the legends. I don't believe in *strigoi* and *moroi* and the power of a grandmother's curse. I'm a med student now. I believe in science."

"But you believe in mysticism and the power of art as well," Viktor said softly. "That's why you paint what you do."

"I believe in the union of it all. Reality is multidimensional and so are we. But I don't believe in monsters. So I don't know what it was that I saw that night."

Viktor took a moment to absorb the incredible thing he had just heard. "Do you think they could see you?"

"I was hiding behind a bush. It was also very dark. A new moon. They were so preoccupied with each other that no, I'm positive neither one noticed me. I didn't give them the chance either. I was so freaked out I left the park and ran home. I called Florin at once. He answered and sounded fine but hung up on me. To this day I feel like a coward for not knocking on the door instead of running away."

That act probably saved your life.

Amza stubbed out her cigarette, stuck the butt in her pocket, and crossed her arms against her chest in a protective manner. "I saw Florin the next day. He looked normal. No injuries. I was so relieved I tried to hug him, but he pushed me away. He asked me if I loved him yet. I said no. He said he'd be back for me one day, and that I wouldn't even recognize him. Those were the last words we said to each other."

They stood in silence as pedestrians and traffic flowed around them.

"No matter what happened to Florin," she said, "I know he could never kill anyone. I just know it. But if I were investigating a murder that involved him in any way," she shivered as she held her arms even tighter, "I'd find out who that other man was."

Viktor opened his coat and took out a small collection of photos from a plastic sheath in his inside pocket. Lieutenant Andrasko had given them to him before he left Prague. He found the one he wanted and showed it Amza. "Is this the man you saw?"

She gave a sharp intake of breath and took a step back. "You know him?"

"As you suspected, he's Florin's older brother. I have no reason to think he'll come here, but if you see him, stay far away."

Her face paled, and she gripped Viktor by the arm. "Take care of Florin. He couldn't have done that, I know it."

"I promise I'll do what I can." Viktor handed her a business card. "If you think of anywhere he might have gone, a special place or a family gathering spot he might have mentioned to you, it's of the utmost importance to let me know."

She nodded and said, "There's one more thing. Part of the reason Florin gave me an ultimatum was because I started seeing another guy. Adrian and I are still together. You don't think this man, Florin's brother, would come after Adrian for some reason after all these years, do you?"

In response to her question, Viktor was at a rare loss for words, because all he could hear was the name of her boyfriend repeating inside his head.

A name Florin had adopted as his own.

Skopje, North Macedonia

On the same day Grey met with Lieutenant Andrasko, he flew to Macedonia and deboarded at Skopje International Airport, a glass-and-concrete rectangle squatting in a valley surrounded by dry and barren hills. Preferring not to use a credit card, Grey took out three hundred dollars' worth of Macedonian denars at an ATM, and took a cab into town instead of renting a car.

The pleasant medley of undulating hills, pastureland, and orange-roofed houses on the outskirts of the city surprised Grey. It seemed at odds with his impression of an impoverished nation still suffering from ethnic tensions and the scars of conflict. In truth, he knew little about North Macedonia—a former part of Yugoslavia renamed by the international community to distinguish it from the Greek region of Macedonia—except what he had read on the flight, and his remembrance of the Balkan Wars.

But the bloom faded off the rose as the taxi wound through the concrete eyesores ringing the city center and he saw the trash and graffiti in the streets, dismal gray suburbs choking on the smog-filled air. A picture-perfect postcard of the wreckage left behind by the Soviet Union.

Yet Grey knew, as with people, that an ugly façade often hid the beauty underneath. In his experience, the remoteness of a backwater location was often in inverse proportion to the warmth of its populace and the opportunity for interesting, off-the-wall experiences.

The proximity to Bulgaria, across the border to the east, brought back vivid memories of a former case. A lover he had left behind, a friend who had betrayed him, a research center hidden deep in the Egyptian desert, and a strange elixir that, to this day, made him ponder now and again the nature of immortality. His thoughts on the matter hadn't changed in the handful of years that had passed.

He was in no rush to die, and had no idea what awaited on the other side of the curtain, but to him, the looming specter of death gave life meaning. Eternal anything was a curse. The people he had known who clamored the loudest for life everlasting seemed to get restless on a rainy afternoon.

That train of thought led his mind to wander to creatures of legend who lived for centuries and stalked villages and deserted city streets after the sun went down, fangs bared and white faces gleaming, searching for the necks of victims in the pale moonlight.

With an annoyed shake of his head, Grey refocused his attention on the scenery. He liked to orient himself as best he could in a new city. On the plane, he had studied maps of Skopje, a city of half a million residents. The cab driver spoke too little English to be of any help, but Grey had given him the address for a city hospital that employed a surgeon rumored to be involved with the red market.

They entered the city center. After most of the buildings were destroyed in the earthquake of 1963, the city was rebuilt with grim Soviet architecture, then underwent a facelift during the "Skopje 2014" nationalist restoration project. Grey had read about the absurdities of this project, but the eyewitness evidence was making his jaw drop.

The most glaring example was the goliath, sword-wielding statue of Alexander the Great straddling a horse atop a hundred-foot tall mushroom-shaped pedestal rising out of a fountain in Macedonia Square. Everywhere he looked, he saw gilded, oversize statues of heroes and historical figures. Megafountains and rotundas slapped haphazardly among the streets. Corridors of bizarre, faux neoclassical monuments and high-rises that looked assembled in a factory in China. A reproduction of a wooden pirate ship moored inexplicably along the side of a river. The center of Skopje evoked a tacky millionaire's home with Doric columns and sphinxes guarding the driveway—except the cringe-inducing architecture occurred on a citywide scale.

Even more surreal, many of the monuments and buildings had been paint-bombed by vandals in a kaleidoscope of colors, giving the city a wild, postmodern, Dr. Seuss meets replica-ancient-Macedonia vibe.

It made Grey chuckle. At least it was different.

The taxi driver was waving a hand at the monuments and speaking in a derisive tone. Grey heard "denars" once or twice and understood the gist of the rant: why build this misguided ode to the past when people are going hungry in the slums?

Because the politicians want to distract the populace from the present, that's why.

Grey jerked his gaze away from the spectacle and focused on his mission. He still had not decided how to approach Dr. Bogdan Ristov, chief of nephrology at City Hospital of Skopje. On impulse, before leaving Prague, Grey had taken Viktor's Interpol badge off his bedside table. The badge might come in handy, and Grey had debated threatening Dr. Ristov with police trouble if he didn't cooperate.

But Grey had almost shelved that course of action. He did not worry so much about the consequences of impersonating an Interpol agent. If caught, he could bribe his way out of Skopje, and Jacques would probably help him out of a jam, given the circumstances.

And in terms of impeding any active police efforts, Grey had been told Europol was no longer investigating Dr. Ristov. Their cover had been blown, and no leads had surfaced to implicate him—or anyone else—in the death of the Europol agent who had fallen from her balcony.

Still, Lieutenant Andrasko had told Grey about Dr. Ristov's involvement in confidence. Grey did not want to jeopardize her relationship with Europol. Besides, given the fate of the last agent, Dr. Ristov did not sound like someone who lived in fear of being caught.

He sounded like someone who had paid off the right people and operated with impunity in his little corner of the world.

The taxi pulled up in front of a tall but narrow concrete building that loomed above the street like a misplaced door. Grey gave the driver a handsome tip and stepped into the brisk evening air. The sun had almost completed its descent, leaving the cloud-spotted sky awash with deep purple hues and streaks of red. He caught the scent of orange and cinnamon wafting from a street cart selling "hot wine"—whatever in the world that was.

Not many pedestrians were on the street. Grey stuck a hand nonchalantly in the pocket of his motorcycle jacket and strolled through the revolving front door of the hospital. Inside, staff and visitors and patients in wheelchairs bustled about a large, white-walled, antiseptic lobby that was brighter and cleaner than Grey had expected.

It was easy to blend with the crowd. Grey wandered around the large space, reading the signs above the corridors. He was looking for a word in Cyrillic, *nefrologija*, a Slavic cognate he had looked up beforehand.

He located the Macedonian word above a hallway opposite the front door. Grey followed the twists and turns to an elevator bank in the center of the building. No one paid him any attention. His worn jeans, scuffed motorcycle jacket, lean profile, dark hair, and stubble were not out of place among the men in the city. Just another visitor to the kidney ward.

It got dicey when he reached a nurse's station and one of the receptionists took note of his presence. Grey spied a waiting room through a glass door, went inside, and picked up a magazine. He stayed put until the receptionist turned her back to engage in conversation with another visitor. Hoping she had forgotten about him, Grey slipped out of the waiting room and down a hallway.

Still no one accosted him as he strode past a long line of closed doors. When a nurse exited one of the rooms with a rolling cart full of medical equipment, Grey got a glimpse of patients squeezed three to a room with no privacy or windows. The deeper he went, the grimier and more unkempt he found the interior of the hospital.

At the end of the hall was a door marked *Staff Only*. Near the door was a folding chair set up outside one of the patient rooms. Grey sat in the chair to wait. When he heard footsteps approaching, he slumped and pretended to be half-asleep.

A nurse passed him without a glance and pushed through the staff door. Deciding it was too risky to follow, he waited twenty minutes for a female doctor to exit the door from the other side. After she passed by, walking briskly down the hall, Grey leaped silently to his feet and caught the door just before it swooshed shut. He slipped through and let it close. On the other side, he saw a corridor with faded blue linoleum and doors with nameplates inscribed with another Cyrillic cognate. *Doktor*.

At this juncture, Grey needed a little luck to stay unnoticed, and he got it. No one else wandered the hallway before he passed a T-intersection and found, halfway down the next hall in the nephrology department, a door with Dr. Ristov's name on it.

Even better, the door was unlocked.

Grey slipped in without knocking. No one was inside. With a sigh of relief—he could pick a quick lock, but now he didn't have to worry—Grey's eyes swept the contents of the room.

Diplomas on the wall. Photos of two teenage daughters on the desk but no evidence of a wife. Plastic models of the kidney on one shelf, a neat line of gilt-edged medical tomes on another. A tidy desk full of papers and folders that Grey couldn't read. He debated taking photos of these, but did not get the sense they contained anything incriminating. They were too exposed and mundane.

He found the keys to a Mercedes in the pocket of a wool overcoat hanging on the door. Grey dipped his finger into the cup of coffee on the desk. Lukewarm. He had a high suspicion his quarry was still inside the hospital.

The laptop was password protected. No safe or hidden drawers he could find. Grey finished his search and stood behind the door, on the side with the hinges, listening for the sound of approaching footsteps as he recalled Lieutenant Andrasko's briefing on Dr. Ristov.

A lifelong resident of Skopje, part of the ethnic majority, Dr. Ristov had come of age in the Socialist Republic of Macedonia. His parents were government officials in the bureaucracy and enjoyed all the privileges that entailed. They even had enough money to send Bogdan to medical school at Imperial College in London. Dr. Ristov appeared to have every advantage in life, and yet he still decided to become a key figure in the burgeoning illicit organ trade. Surgeons in the country made very little compared to those in wealthy nations, so Grey assumed Bogdan had decided to supplement his income. The surgeon's position in the food chain was simple and entailed little risk.

Grey had also read up on the red market. Not that long ago, all manner of body parts could be bought and sold like any other good: blood for transfusions, bones and skeletons for research, organ tissue for black magic potions in certain areas of the world. But the market was tiny. Outside of fringe religious communities and medical schools, the demand for human body parts was not much of a problem.

That changed with advances in technology. Once kidneys, lungs, and other organs could be transplanted to improve and extend the lives of wealthy patients, criminal enterprises took full advantage of the lack of regulation. Supply and demand exploded. In the second half of the twentieth century, as the public grew aware of the growing human rights abuses, nations passed laws *en masse* to put a stop to the practice. It was illegal to purchase human tissue in Macedonia, even from willing donors.

But like most countries, it was also illegal to disclose the identity of those donors.

Which meant the source of human body parts procured on the red market was more obscured than ever.

Criminals quickly realized they could procure valuable organs—usually through coercion, force, or pursuant to a contract no one could force them to uphold—and sell them up the food chain with no repercussion. Once the hospitals had them, no questions were asked. No questions *could* be asked. Privacy laws made it nearly impossible for authorities to stop the practice, and these loopholes created a global market in human flesh more robust and profitable than ever. Kidneys and partial livers from healthy donors could sell for upwards of a hundred thousand U.S. dollars.

In Macedonia, similar to other impoverished nations, the organ gangs liked to approach desperate targets with an offer too good to pass up. *Sell us a kidney for five thousand U.S. dollars. We'll pay you a portion up front and the rest when it's finished. You can feed your family for a year with this money, or send your children to school, or pay for a medical procedure. You have two kidneys. You only need one. What is there to lose?*

The gangs would pay the initial fee—a fourth or less of the actual price—and bring the patients to someone like Dr. Ristov. Under the guise of performing a needed surgery, perhaps a kidney donation for a relative, he would perform the procedure and fill out the paperwork and send the poor victim back to whatever slum or village they had come from.

No follow up medical care.

No more of the money that was promised.

No way for the authorities—those who were not bribed—to trace the identities of the "donors."

International authorities knew Dr. Ristov was a key middleman but could do little to stop it, especially after the death of the agent that was sent. North Macedonia was notorious for bribery and exploitation, as were most of the places where the red market thrived.

Footsteps in the hall.

Grey tensed, just as he had the first two times, but this time they did not continue past the door.

This time they stopped.

When the door opened, Grey remained very still as a heavyset man in hospital scrubs hurried into the room. The man shut the door behind him without looking and sat behind his desk. Only then did he notice Grey stepping quietly into the center of the room.

After a shocked exclamation, Dr. Ristov rose and snapped a command in Macedonian. He had drooping eyelids and an unkempt salt-and-pepper beard that covered his round face like a doormat. His eyes, shrewd and untrusting, did not match the gaze of someone dedicated to improving the lives of others.

Those were eyes, Grey thought, used to wading into the muck of violence and human misery.

Eyes that reflected a soul on loan to the highest bidder.

"I know you speak English," Grey said. He had already checked the room for hidden cameras, security intercoms, and weapons. "You studied in London."

Instead of flinching, Dr. Ristov bristled and pointed a finger at Grey. "Who are you? What are you doing in my office?"

Grey stood right in front of the desk and crossed his arms. "Classy enterprise you have here."

"Excuse me?"

"How many innocent people have you gutted? How many died of post-op infections after you sewed them back up and stuck them on an overnight bus with no meds? How many couldn't work again or had complications they had no money to treat? Not to mention the fee they never received for selling their kidneys, or the kids and orphans you cut up to buy yourself a condo in Malta."

"I have no idea what you're talking about. Do you know who I am?"

"I know exactly who you are."

"Leave my office at once."

Dr. Ristov took out his cell phone and started to scroll. With a casual movement, Grey reached into his pocket and withdrew a scalpel he had found in the top left drawer of Dr. Ristov's desk. "Put that phone away."

When Dr Ristov saw what Grey was holding, he set the phone down but still did not seem intimidated. He sneered and said, "Who are you? CIA? Europol? I've done nothing wrong."

"All that matters is that I know what you do, and you have something I want."

"I don't think so."

"I want Cezar Speluncescu."

At the mention of the name, Dr. Ristov lost a bit of color. Showing fear for the first time during the conversation, he pushed air through his throat, a disbelieving laugh that he cut off half-formed. "Who?" he said, though he was looking at Grey with an expression that said, *You're either insane or very, very foolish.*

Grey had already decided this venal man would be moved by one of two things: violence or money. "Tell me how to find him, and we're good here. Refuse, and I'll stuff your mouth with your shirt to stifle your screams, then take one of your own kidneys with this scalpel. Right here in this room, right now. Then I'll ask again."

Dr. Ristov paled further and stared at Grey with his mouth half open, as if trying to wrap his head around the seriousness of Grey's intent.

Grey ran a thumb along the stem of the scalpel and started to walk around the desk. "I'm not much of a surgeon, so I can't promise a clean procedure. So what will it be, doc? Lose a kidney, maybe both, or give me what I want? However you decide, I'll walk out this door and disappear the same way I got in."

"Okay," Dr. Ristov said. He put his hands up and fell back into his chair as Grey loomed over him. "You win."

"I want an address and a phone number and everything else you have. If they don't work, I'll come back for you."

"You don't understand. I can't give you any of that. I swear it. No one can.

Or at least no one I know of. They don't *want* me to know." Grey raised the scalpel, causing Dr. Ristov to cringe. "Just wait! Believe me, I've never even met him. I just . . . know of him. I know he comes to Skopje on occasion and . . ."

"And takes his cut?"

Dr. Ristov swallowed. "Something like that."

"Then you know how to contact him. Don't tell me you don't. You're too important to the operation."

Dr. Ristov looked away and pawed at his beard. Grey knew he was thinking of a way to weasel out of the situation. Not wanting to give him time to think, Grey took a quick step forward and grabbed him by his hair. Grey jerked his head back and touched the scalpel to his neck. "Time's up, doc."

The shock and violence of the sudden movement caused Dr. Ristov to tense up and straighten his fingers. "Fahri Bajram," he whispered.

"Who's that?"

"A middleman. Between me and the person you want. I've never been any closer, you have to believe me."

"Fahri's in Skopje?"

"Yes. A middleman, like I said. That's his job."

"Set up a meeting for tonight. Tell him you're the one who's coming. I'll do the rest."

"I don't think I can—"

"You're going to do it right now, while I'm watching."

Grey nicked the surgeon's neck, causing a line of blood to appear, then stepped back enough to allow Dr. Ristov to move. Dr. Ristov touched his neck, wiped his bloody fingers on his scrubs, and eyed the scalpel as if it were a pit viper. With a shaky hand, he pulled up the contact on his cell phone for the name he had mentioned. Grey loomed over him to watch.

"Make it someplace public, where he's used to meeting," Grey said.

"It will have to be near the Turkish Quarter. That's where he lives. He'll be suspicious otherwise"

"Fine. What does he look like?"

"Very short, bald, pudgy, a scar above his left eye. He does not like the cold. With this weather expect him to wear a white fur coat and a fez hat."

"Before you hit send, I'd think very carefully about what you say." Grey reached over and picked up the photo of the two girls atop the desk. As he did this, Dr. Ristov's face caved, and Grey knew he had found his leverage. He stuck the photo in the pocket of his jacket. "Don't try to set me up, or do anything other than what I've asked."

The doctor's face mottled with rage and fear, but he choked back his emotions and continued typing on the cell phone. After he pressed send, Grey stood over him until a reply from Fahri came through, less than a minute later.

"It's done," Dr. Ristov said. "Midnight at the Stone Bridge. It's a landmark in the middle of the city. That's typical for him."

"I know it. Which side of the bridge?"

"In the middle."

Grey grabbed the cell phone and pocketed it. "You can tell them someone stole your phone and you had no part in this." After he strode to the door and opened it, still gripping the scalpel, he turned and patted the jacket pocket with the photograph of the girls. "Behave yourself and you'll never see me again."

Dr. Ristov sat rigid in his seat, his face as tight as a steel cord. Grey closed the door and returned swiftly the same way he had come. No one bothered him. After leaving the hospital, he dropped the scalpel and the photo of the two girls in the first trash can he saw.

As night deepened, Grey familiarized himself with the area around the Stone Bridge. A sturdy piece of architecture built on Roman foundations during the Ottoman Period, the lovely pedestrian footbridge stretched seven hundred feet across the Vardar River, connecting Macedonia Square to the older parts of the city.

Grey did not like meeting Dr. Ristov's contact at such a late hour in an unfamiliar city. At least the Stone Bridge was a public thoroughfare in the heart of Skopje. If Grey had been set up, it was a poor choice for an ambush.

His plan was to insinuate that he wanted to do business with Cezar and talk his way into a face-to-face meeting. If that failed, he would read the situation and either try to threaten Fahri to divulge Cezar's location or, more likely, back away and follow the middleman home. None of these options thrilled Grey, but he was a step closer to Cezar and Viktor, and he would just have to make it work.

Satisfied he could disappear into the city from either side of the bridge, he left the behemoth monuments of Macedonia Square behind and walked across the bridge to the other side of the city. Soon he entered the Old Bazaar, a maze of cobblestone alleys, mosques, street vendors, markets, and quaint shops in the Turkish Quarter. Minarets tinged with moonlight floated above the rooftops. The ramparts of a ruined fortress dominated a hilltop just north of the bridge. The area had a surfeit of charm that Grey could hardly believe co-existed with the garish pomposity of downtown Skopje.

He ate dinner on a street full of restored two-story buildings with cream-colored walls and handsome wood trim. The restaurant had menus in English and plenty of foreigners, the most he had seen in the city. Mostly Westerners, and a handful of Chinese. The waitresses wore red-and-white frocks with colorful embroidery that Grey assumed were traditional folk costumes. He would have preferred a more authentic spot, but he was starving and did not want to be noticed. On a recommendation from the waiter, he ordered stuffed cabbage rolls and a golden pastry filled with meat and leeks. Longing to order a local beer and kick his feet up, he opted for water and a Coke to stay alert for the meeting.

The food was quite good. After dinner, he sipped on a Turkish coffee as black as oil and thought about doctors who snatched babies from maternity wards and robbed people with no hope of their kidneys.

Grey had searched the contacts in Dr. Ristov's phone and found no entry for any of the Speluncescus. He also translated the text message to the middleman to make sure Dr. Ristov was telling the truth. After Grey left Skopje, he would send the phone to Lieutenant Andrasko. He debated calling her and asking her to search for information on Fahri Bajram on the sly, but that would probably require a Europol inquiry. Better to let this play out and see where it led.

At 11:30 p.m., Grey left the restaurant and made his way back to the bridge, his eyes roving the streets, searching for incongruities.

Nothing caught his eye. No one was following him. As he passed the Holocaust Museum and approached the river, he saw that a thick fog on the water obscured most of the Stone Bridge from view. His pace slowed as he neared the reconstructed guardhouse at the river's edge. He did not see anyone coming or going and had underestimated how deserted the bridge would be at midnight on a cold October Sunday.

Wisps of clouds trailed like fingers across the moon. Grey blew on his hands to warm them. He studied his surroundings a final time before striding onto the bridge and passing through a veil of mist. It felt like entering a dream dimension. Soft lighting along the sides of the bridge might have provided good visibility on a clear night, but the greasy stew of fog and dim artificial illumination did little to aid him. After ten yards he could not see the city or the water or even the stones beneath his feet.

There was no one else on the bridge. When he reached the center, five minutes early, he stood with his back to one of the raised sides, still and ready, listening for the sound of footsteps. If no one appeared by midnight, he would walk to the other side and back again.

The minutes ticked by. The air was still, the city quiet all around him. The faint stench of effluence rose off the water. Just as Grey started to check the time on his cell phone, a man emerged out of the fog so close to Grey it made him jump, barely ten feet away.

Grey's hands tensed at his sides. *How had he approached so quietly? I should have heard him.*

The man did not meet the description of a short, pudgy man that Grey had been given. In fact, quite the opposite. Not only was this man tall and ruggedly handsome and dressed in a full-length woolen coat with a fashionable silk scarf draped around his neck, but his face, especially the penetrating eyes and heavy brow and arrogant curve to his mouth, was one Grey recognized from his briefing with Lieutenant Andrasko.

"Greetings," Cezar Speluncescu said. "I hear you're looking for me."

Prague

-12-

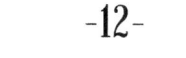

At Café Louvre, a former haunt of both Kafka and Einstein, Mari could not bring herself to finish the decadent Viennese coffee she had ordered. Her stomach was roiling as she watched another harrowing news exposé describing the worldwide bazaar for human body parts. The "red market" as the lieutenant had termed it.

After the incident at the nightclub, Dominic Grey had strongly suggested she return to Los Angeles or stay very close to Viktor's townhome. Itching to help the investigation but unsure what to do, Mari had started researching the previous day, as soon as Grey had left for Skopje, and continued through most of the night and into the morning, shocked and disgusted by what she had uncovered. When the video finished, she removed her headphones and slumped in her seat with tears in the corners of her eyes, numbed by the level of depravity it took to treat human beings as Legos to be torn apart and sold piece by piece to wealthy buyers.

Most people, herself included, knew the red market existed to some degree. She had heard a story in the news now and then. But she had no idea of the extent of the problem, or the impact on the affected communities.

She had not known about the third-world villages full of women with jagged scars below their rib cages, where the fields had fallowed or the fisheries had dried up and the only way to survive the next month was to sell your own kidney.

Nor did she know about the professional organ farms operating out of Brazilian favelas and Indonesian resettlements and African shantytowns.

Or the refugee camps where human traffickers came like lions to a savanna and snatched victims in broad daylight.

Or the orphanages in impoverished countries who raised children like dairy cows for their body parts.

Or the persistent rumors about prisons in China that pumped prisoners with narcotics so government doctors could remove a grocery list of organs while their hearts were still beating.

The wealthier nations played an equal part in the transactions. They just sat on the opposite end of the negotiating table. Central and Eastern Europe was a particularly fertile market due to its EU connections. To Mari's dismay, she learned that criminal gangs in Hungary and the Czech Republic sourced victims from poorer countries in the region, like Ukraine and Moldova and Romania, and sold their "products" to Western buyers.

She found no mention of the Speluncescus. This did not surprise her, though Mari wondered if there wasn't something more to uncover. Rumors or stories journalists had stumbled across without a source verifiable enough to use for an official story. Drumming her fingers on the table, she thought about her own profession. Like good investigative journalists, documentary filmmakers sometimes went places the authorities could not or would not go.

Feeling as if her uncle was slipping further away by the minute, she started researching the authors, reporters, and filmmakers who had tackled the red market. In a few hours she had a solid list of names. She sent an email to each person with contact information online, introducing herself and praising their work and asking two simple questions.

Did you ever come across the Speluncescu family in your research?
If so, would you be willing to talk off the record?

She was hopeful about one person in particular, Erik Mittelman, a Canadian video journalist based in Bucharest. Or he was based there a decade ago when he had filmed an exposé on Romanian orphanages called *The Abattoir of Souls*. Though not focused on the red market, the documentary had described a dystopian conveyor belt that ran from some of the children's homes straight to the arms of human traffickers.

Mittelson had covered the entire region in depth. Mari really wanted to talk to him, but he did not have contact information online, and had not published an article in a decade. In fact, after a little digging, she realized *The Abbatoir of Souls* was the last piece he had published, and he seemed to have disappeared after that.

The lieutenant had said that Dumitra Speluncescu lived in Bucharest.

A prickle of goosebumps crept down Mari's spine.

Her eyes slunk around the café as if expecting to find someone watching her. She swallowed and then scoured the web for Erik's contact info. She even wrote the news organization that had published the story. Finally she rattled off some inquiries to her L.A contacts.

Satisfied she had done all she could, Mari steepled her fingers against her mouth and blew out a long breath. The tinkle of glassware and the smell of roasting coffee had started to cloy. She no longer wanted to be sitting in a cozy café with tourist-priced drinks. Not when those *things* she had just researched existed in the world.

She put her laptop in her shoulder bag and rose to leave, grimly satisfied that at least one positive development had come from her morning research.

Now she had a subject for her documentary.

Mari had rarely been so pensive as she walked the cobblestone streets and passed through the Old Town square in the afternoon. She sat on the steps of a monument and immersed herself in the majesty of the architecture, the Kinský palace and the quirky astronomical clock and the twin Gothic towers of the Church of our Lady before Týn, towering over the square like something out of a Brothers Grimm story.

She did not yet know what to make of Dominic Grey. She had never met anyone like him, so unconcerned with the normal things in life and so . . . intense . . . about others.

One thing she knew for sure: she wished he had not left town.

She chose not to dwell on the sinister, downright creepy events surrounding the disappearance of her uncle. Even the shadows cast in broad daylight in the nooks and crannies of Prague's old buildings seemed to spook her now. She had not enjoyed spending the night alone in Viktor's house, surrounded by macabre travel mementos and a library full of books on the occult.

The problem was, Mari was quite spiritual in a New Age kind of way. She believed the universe was alive in some unknowable manner and that something *else* existed somewhere beyond the natural world, or perhaps encompassed it, though she had no idea what that might be. Viktor had long ago convinced her of the inexplicable powers of the human mind. She went even further than he did. She believed in ESP and psychics and déjà vu and, well, a little bit of everything.

And thus, while she told herself she did not believe in vampires, a little voice in the back of her mind clapped back.

It whispered to her in the dead silence of the night behind the closed doors of her uncle's townhome, from the gaping mouths of the masks in Viktor's study whose frozen gazes seemed to track her as she passed.

Why not, Mari?

If you allow for the possibility of everything, then why not that?

Because vampires aren't real, she told herself. *Some things just aren't . . . possible.*

Oh no?

And just what exactly is this thing called reality?

Is it the world we see in our everyday lives, or is it quantum entanglement and deep-sea creatures with alien features and virus DNA frozen in ice for millions of years? What is normal but the abnormal rendered commonplace through familiarity? What is the line between our darkest dreams and the waking world, Mari?

Or is there a line at all?

By the time she returned to Viktor's townhome and checked her email, a barrage of negative responses to her inquiries had hit her inbox. On the bright side, one of her mentors had written back and claimed to have once met Eric Mittelman. This mentor, Arlene Keller, a family friend and successful TV producer who knew everyone in Hollywood and had advised Mari on her first documentary, thought Erik had married a Czech woman and settled in Prague. Arlene had no idea why Erik no longer published or where he currently worked. She had not talked to him in years.

But she had his old email.

Mari wrote Erik and asked the same questions about the Speluncescus. If Erik was in Prague, maybe they could meet up. An hour later, he had not responded, but at least the email address had not bounced.

Restless, she did an hour of yoga, took a long shower, walked to the closest market, and picked up the ingredients for a peanut stir fry. As she cooked, she dwelled on what she had not told her uncle when he had asked about home. She had not lied to him, but she had not disclosed the full truth about her strained relationship with her parents.

Mari was born and raised in Brentwood, a wealthy suburb of Los Angeles. Her family's pool was bigger than most homes. The landscaping fees would be rent in some zip codes. Unlike Viktor, who used his inheritance to fund his intellectual pursuits, Mari's father was a commercial real estate investor who had parlayed his portion of the Radek fortune into even vaster sums of money. Her father cared deeply about money and status. He hosted dinner parties throughout Mari's childhood for celebrities and power brokers and politicians. To her father's great delight, Mari's two older brothers had followed in the old man's footsteps.

Mari had not.

All her life, though she never made waves or spoke of her ambitions, she knew she wanted to take a different path. She admired the career of her favorite uncle, whose eccentric life her father scoffed at behind Viktor's back. Mari did not know what she wanted, but she knew it wasn't country clubs and plastic surgery and a life measured by a checklist of acquisitions.

Her first act of rebellion was attending the University of Santa Cruz against her father's wishes. UCLA and Pepperdine, more prestigious schools close to home, had both accepted her. But she had to get away. She had to breathe. So she went north and studied among the redwoods, devoted herself to the countless causes *en vogue* among the progressive student body. She chose to study film, which further enraged her father.

You can't support yourself making films, he had told her. *Even if you had the talent, you're not dedicated enough to make it.*

Her father's words cut deep, but at the time, Mari did not disagree. She didn't have the ego to be an actress or a producer. She didn't have the imagination for writing or directing fiction. To be honest, she had chosen film because she liked movies and didn't know what else to do. The path of least resistance. Along the way, she realized she did want to tell stories—didn't everyone to some degree?—but she didn't know what to say or how to say it.

The uncomfortable truth was that she didn't have very much to give. She knew all the cool things to wear and do and see. She was hip and wanted to change the world but didn't know what that meant. It was a theoretical thing to her, like raising a family or growing old. She had read about injustice and seen the homeless camps in L.A. but had never experienced anything remotely similar herself.

After graduation, despite her troubles at home, Mari was flush with the optimism of the young. Like her peers, she expected to make her mark and cast a magic spell on life, wriggle her tanned fingers in the air and bend reality to her will.

She decided on a career path: documentaries. It seemed like a great idea. She could tell *other* people's stories.

When she told her father of her ambitions, he demanded she let go of her dreams and go to grad school, study finance, and enter the family business.

Or he was going to cut her off.

Mari's mother was a socialite who never questioned her husband and valued everything Mari did not. Both parents had always treated her brothers differently. Encouraged them to achieve at every turn. Never asked when they were getting married or why their outfits were so revealing.

Mari ignored her father's edict and used her modest life's savings to finance her documentary. It received some critical acclaim but lost money.

Her father cut her off just like he said he would.

Mari's magic spell had sputtered and died.

When she arrived in Prague to see Viktor, she had her film gear and enough money in the bank to live on the cheap for six months. The future was a black hole drawing her closer and closer to its orbit.

Mari did not let the world see her problems. If nothing else, her life of privilege had taught her this.

So for now, it was easy to push aside her angst about her future. She had an uncle in desperate need of help, and Mari's father had been wrong about one critical thing.

When Mari was focused on a project she loved, she *did* have dedication.

Planet-conquering amounts of it.

With Viktor's life on the line, she had channeled her focus like never before, and opened the floodgates to her natural optimism.

She had a feeling she would need it.

When Mari checked her email after dinner, she was thrilled to find a reply from Erik Mittelman. Her excitement faded as she read the short note.

> I'm sorry to say I no longer work in the field, and I've never heard that name.
>
> Best,
>
> Erik

Dejected, Mari cleaned the kitchen and carried a glass of wine to the couch. Though happy she had found a passionate topic for her documentary, her uncle was missing and she didn't know what to do.

A glance at her phone revealed another round of negative replies. She decided to unclog her Inbox and saw some bills she had to pay—cell phone, gym, credit cards that were getting scary, a streaming service she never watched and needed to cancel. A few friends had written to see how she was doing, and there was an email from someone named Frank Smith, with an odd subject line that made her pause before she marked it as Spam.

A Response To Your Inquiry

The name *Frank Smith* didn't ring a bell, but she had sent off a lot of messages earlier in the day. Just to be sure, she opened the email, her pulse quickening when she realized who had sent it.

> Meet me at St. Cyril at noon tomorrow. Come alone and sit on the third pew from the front.
>
> Erik.

That was it. No explanation for the bizarre request or the pseudonym.

Do you really need an explanation? Mari asked herself as her gaze stole to the window, all of a sudden feeling exposed to the darkened streets and things that go bump in the night.

Because I think you know full well why he did that.

Cluj-Napoca, Romania

-13-

On the way to consult with Dr. Belá Fessler, professor of history at Babes-Bolyai University, Viktor passed by the Matthias Corvinus Monument in front of St. Michael's church in Unity Square. The bronze statue depicting the beloved king of Hungary sat astride a horse, long hair cascading to his shoulders, flanked by generals waving the flags of vanquished enemies. Cluj-Napoca and Transylvania were of course no longer subject to Hungarian rulers, or Dacian ones for that matter, though many of the residents had a patriotic affinity to those bygone sovereigns of the troubled region. A few blocks to the east, Viktor knew, was a statue of Avram Iancu, who fought to keep the Hungarians *out* of Transylvania.

The handsome effigy of the Raven King—*corvus* meaning *raven* in Latin—caused Viktor to reflect as he passed through the plaza. From where did the Speluncescu family hail? What monarch or voivode or boyar had once claimed their allegiance? How were they connected to the Order of the Dragon?

As he crossed Strada Napoca, a quaint thoroughfare lined with shops and pubs and galleries, his thoughts turned to the modern descendants of the Speluncescu clan. From his conversation with Amza outside the café, he had learned that after leaving Prague, jilted and heartbroken, Florin had adopted the name—Adrian—of the man Amza had chosen instead of him.

Not only that, but Florin had become an entirely new person. A playboy artiste with a dark side, a seducer who cultivated the mythos of the vampire.

Was he trying to become someone he thought his muse would prefer? Or had something else happened? What family secret had he mentioned to Amza? How did Cezar acquire fangs and why did he bare them at Florin that night? Was he angry at his little brother for showing weakness and putting the family at risk? Did Cezar bite his brother that night?

Do prdele, Viktor, what nonsense has come over you?

With a grim shake of his head, he focused on his meeting with the historian.

The only way through this morass was to strive for truth and not succumb to fairy tales. There was something deeply strange about this family, that much was certain, but Viktor was determined to get to the bottom of it.

The university was less than four blocks away. Now and again Viktor looked over his shoulder, cataloguing the faces on the street as Grey had taught him, searching for incongruities or patterns of behavior. Viktor did not consider himself possessed of any talent when it came to subterfuge, but it was a basic precaution he could take. He noticed some people leaving Unity Square at the same time as he did, but this was to be expected. It was a busy area. So far, no one seemed suspicious.

At the next intersection, he passed a wrinkled old woman in a black shawl and a patchwork skirt selling bulbs of garlic hanging from wooden poles. She gave him a toothy grin as he passed, curling a finger to draw him over, muttering something in Romanian he could not quite catch. By the sour reek of the garlic Viktor could tell it had passed its prime.

When he glanced over his shoulder again, he saw something that disturbed him. One of the men who had left Unity Square close in time to Viktor, a lean man in his forties wearing a shearling denim jacket and a scarf worn loosely around his neck, crossed the street ten yards before reaching the intersection where the old woman was standing. He had moved to the other side of Strada Napoca for no apparent reason, right in the middle of traffic.

Why did he cross the street?

Was it to avoid the loops of garlic strung on the pole the woman is holding?

Again Viktor berated himself. This case was getting under his skin like no case had in years.

People ignore crosswalks in Romania all the time. There were a thousand reasons that man might have crossed the street. Meeting a friend, going to a store halfway down from the intersection, deciding all of a sudden to pop into his favorite bar.

Except when Viktor looked over his shoulder a short while later, the same man was still walking down the other side of the street, keeping the same distance between them.

No shops, no friends, no bars.

Viktor tried to get a better look at him without drawing undue attention to himself. Under the halo of a streetlamp, he glimpsed a weathered face with a hint of stubble, short brown hair, fluffy sideburns that reached his jawline, and a furrowed brow. A local man intent upon the purpose of his walk, perhaps headed home to his family. His hands were shoved into his pockets, and he did not appear to be paying Viktor or anyone else any attention. He plowed forward against the wind, keeping pace with Viktor despite the man's shorter stride. A detail Viktor chalked up to their difference in age.

Minutes later, when Viktor stepped off the street and onto a paved walkway running through the manicured quad of the university, he looked back again and saw no sign of the man in the denim jacket.

Viktor walked deeper into the campus. The sounds and smells of the city faded, replaced by a low hum of insects and the scent of fresh pine. That part of the campus was not well-lit. He supposed classes were over for the day and most of the professors had gone home. Viktor picked up his pace, not liking the solitude of his surroundings.

By the time he reached his destination, the faculty building that housed Dr. Fessler's office, almost deserted by this time, Viktor found himself throwing open the door of the building and hurrying inside like a child rushing to find a light switch in the dark.

Dr. Fessler's rather beady eyes, as did those of most people, widened when confronted for the first time with Viktor's broad-shouldered, seven-foot frame.

"Please come in," Dr. Fessler said with a posh, affable English accent he had no doubt acquired during his time at Cambridge. Sage-infused incense perfumed the office. A Bach concerto played softly in the background. "Coffee? Tea?"

A tall glass of absinthe? Maybe the whole bottle?

"Some water if you have it," Viktor said.

"But of course."

As Dr. Fessler rummaged in a wine fridge against the wall behind his desk, Viktor glanced around the office, noting the tidy stacks of research and the framed diplomas showcasing the professor's expertise in Eastern and Central

European history. There were two photos: one of Dr. Fessler crossing the finish line of a footrace in a sweat-soaked yellow jersey, and another of a miniature German Schnauzer lounging on a day bed.

After an introduction typical of academics, a quick regurgitation of resumes and fellowships and mutual contacts, Viktor settled into a stiff wooden chair across from Dr. Fessler's desk. The historian had an uneven mouth and a boyish, clean-shaven face. A thicket of curly white hair was delineated within such careful boundaries that it brought to mind a box hedge.

"I daresay there isn't an academic in Europe who doesn't follow the exploits of Professor Viktor Radek to some degree," Dr. Fessler said. "Some of us, like myself, read every single one of your fascinating papers. Not to mention the accounts in the press of your more famous cases."

"Is that so?"

"You've a most facile mind, professor. And a very brave constitution."

Viktor gave a wry smile, remembering the way he had scurried inside the building. "Let us say my curiosity at times outweighs my trepidation."

"And modest as well," Dr. Fessler said, leaning back in his chair and then bringing his hands together with a sharp clap. "So how can I help with the Order of the Dragon? A most fascinating topic. I have to ask whether your inquiry is academic or regarding one of your . . . cases?"

Viktor had given Dr. Fessler very little information in the request he had sent. When Viktor described the true nature of the inquiry, the search for Daryna's murderer, Dr. Fessler blanched.

"I've seen this on the news. Exsanguination . . . murder . . . are we in any danger here?"

"In your office? I don't have any reason to suspect so." Viktor felt a twinge of guilt when he thought about the man in the shearling coat.

Fear of a man who crossed the street in front of a woman selling garlic is not a rational definition of danger.

"Meaning that elsewhere might be . . . my God, it's a wee bit different when the package lands on your own doorstep. I'm afraid I'm not nearly as brave as you." Dr. Fessler gave a self-effacing chuckle. "Or brave at all."

"I understand. I can seek counsel elsewhere if you prefer. It wouldn't be the first time."

The historian seemed taken aback by Viktor's matter-of-fact reply. After inhaling and looking down at his hands, he said, "No, no. If I can help, I should. And I will. I shall. I'm not handling this very well, am I?"

"Bravery is a natural instinct of which I possess very little myself. Courage is a decision to act in the face of fear, which you've just demonstrated. So I believe you're handling this very well indeed."

Dr. Fessler's face lifted to regard Viktor's. "Thank you for saying that. I suppose I've wasted enough of your time already. How may I help you?"

Without mentioning the Speluncescus, Viktor described the book he had found inside the old house in Prague, and the mysterious wooden chest with the symbol of the coiled dragon he had seen Dumitra carrying. After he finished, Dr. Fessler tapped the fingers of his left hand, which bore a sizeable silver ring, on the desk. "Do you have photos of these items?"

Viktor took out his cell phone and showed him the photos of the book of poetry by Johannes Cuspinianus. The historian enlarged the images so he could peer closer. "Yes. Yes, indeed! The lion, the binding, the enamel clasp, it's all there. I'd have to examine it in person to be certain, but it appears to be an authentic work from the *Bibliotheca Corviniana*. A previously unknown volume at that."

"I'm not a Corvinus scholar, but I am a collector of rare books. I can state with some certainty that the craftsmanship is indicative of the time period. The Prague police are in the process of obtaining an accurate date."

"I do hope they're careful."

"I instructed them on who to consult."

After studying the photo for another spell, Dr. Fessler looked up. "This is a remarkable find, but I doubt I can postulate on the chain of ownership. Too much uncertainty surrounds the dissolution of the library."

"I'm aware of this in general, but can you elaborate?"

"The library began to decline as soon as Matthias died. His successors simply did not have the desire, or the force of will and charisma, to maintain the collection. You have to understand that for the time period, Matthias's focus on the humanities was very unusual in the region. He admired the Florentines and the Venetians and worked hard to emulate them. He was a tireless champion of the arts. His library was admired across Europe. It was a beautiful achievement. Unfortunately, his successors did not share his vision, and debts of the crown forced the sale of many works. Others were lost to neglect or vermin."

"My understanding was the library was destroyed in the Ottoman wars."

"A common misperception, though I suppose it bears some truth. When Suleiman the Magnificent sacked Pest and Buda in 1526, he burnt almost everything *except* the royal palace where the *Bibliotheca Corvinus* was housed. That said, there's strong evidence his army plundered the collection and scattered it across Europe and the Ottoman Empire. So, yes, the Turks were largely to blame. Some of the volumes turned up in Constantinople years later, only to disappear again. Such a tragedy. Perhaps not quite on the level of the Library of Alexandria or Nalanda, but not far behind. So much lost knowledge."

"How many volumes survived?"

"A few hundred, in large part due to the efforts of foreign scholars in the centuries after Matthias's death who knew of the collection and were aghast at the destruction."

"I see the difficulty in tracing the origin of the book," Viktor said.

"It will be doubly hard with the work of a minor figure such as Cuspinianus. I might say impossible."

"If you had to opine, how do you think the book ended up in that house in Prague?"

"Given the excellent condition, my first inclination would be that it was sold to a nobleman or a prominent family for penuries of the crown soon after the death of Matthias. Or a distant ancestor might have stumbled upon it in a bookshop in Constantinople or Venice, stuck it in a library, and forgotten about it. It's possible, I'd say likely, the current owners have no idea of the true origin."

"If the book was sold to a family by the state, what are the chances of tracing the family name?"

"Almost nil. As I said, I've seen every known reference to surviving works of the *Bibliotheca Corviniana*."

Viktor compressed his lips, disappointed by the outcome. "If you don't mind, I'd like to arrange for the book to be sent to you for study."

"I would like that very much."

Viktor took a sheet of paper out of his pocket, an illustration that represented his best approximation of the image of the coiled dragon carved on the miniature chest Dumitra had carried out of the house. After letting the historian study it, Viktor said, "Another witness saw a ring with the same motif, though she claims the cross on the back of the dragon was formed by two silver spears. I remember the same detail with the carving on the chest. What do you make of that?"

Dr. Fessler rubbed his narrow chin. "While the ouroboros is a universal image, this particular variation, the cross on the back and the unique shape of the dragon, is specific to the Order. But you know this of course."

"And the spears?"

"Quite frankly, I don't know. I've never seen that motif before. They seem rather incongruous to the nature of the cross, do they not?"

"So do knights and swords and murderous Crusades."

"I suppose that's right. As you probably know, the Order of the Dragon was a chivalric order along the lines of the Knights Templars and Hospitallers."

"A clear push by Sigismund to keep the Ottomans out of Europe by uniting the kings and noblemen close to the border."

"Yes, though maybe not so clear as you think. I harbor doubts as to the true origin of the Order. Not so much the *why* as the *who*."

"What do you mean?"

Dr. Fessler waved a hand. "Sigismund was not a popular ruler, or a very charming man. I've never felt the rallying cry of the Order bore his signature, so to speak."

"You think it was someone else's idea? An advisor, perhaps?"

"Something like that. Nothing of the sort is in the histories. But that's the problem with the Order of the Dragon. It existed in a specific place and time for a discrete purpose and then seemed to disappear from history. We have a handful of artifacts that were handed out to the members, a few lines in the history books. So many questions remain. While the other chivalric orders worked hard to expand their footprint, the Order of the Dragon was a private club from the beginning. Even today, precious few know about it, other than—"

"Someone who has studied Vlad the Impaler and Matthias Corvinus."

Dr. Fessler blinked. "You've done your homework."

"Yes, though as you say, there's a dearth of research on the topic. I found little information other than the agreement of most scholars that both men were members."

"By the time Matthias took the crown, the Order was in decline. Its real prominence came from the previous generation. Did you know both their fathers were members too?"

"I knew about Vlad II, of course, because his patronym derived directly from the Order."

"Vlad II was a first-class member, as was John Hunyadi, Matthias's father. The life stories of both men were eerily similar, and could have spawned a Shakespearian tragedy. Both underwent a meteoric rise from obscurity in Transylvania, a backwater of the empire, to become very powerful men. Both came into the orbit of Sigismund, the Holy Roman Emperor, at around the same time. Both joined the Order of the Dragon, thus dedicating much of their lives to keeping the Turks out of Transylvania. Both suffered ignominious endings: Vlad II was beheaded in battle, and John Hunyadi died of the plague."

"Intriguing," Viktor said. "Especially as most historical attention goes to their sons."

"Yes, yes, indeed. Where were we? Ah, yes. My guess is you want to know if the ancestors of the family who own the book and the miniature chest were perhaps members of the Order of the Dragon?"

"Precisely."

"It might help to know the name."

After hesitating, Viktor told him, though he kept the details of the case to himself.

Dr. Fessler leaned back in his chair and crossed his legs. "I'm aware of all the known members of the Order, and *Speluncescu* is unfamiliar to me. That said, as I've mentioned, the Order suffers from a lack of historicity. We don't have reliable records of the full roster." He wagged a finger. "Perhaps the Speluncescu family name changed over time. If so, *that* we might be able to trace."

"How many members do we know about?"

"Sigismund brought in twenty-one in the beginning. A handful more were added in later years, plus foreign allies who did not swear an oath of fealty. I'm quite certain other members existed of which modern scholars are unaware. Conquering armies at the time tended not to leave historical records, or much of anything, in their wake."

"That's a smaller group than I realized." Viktor leaned back in his chair, frustrated with the lack of progress.

"I'd love to get my hands on that chest and the ring," Dr. Fessler continued. "Those items, along with the book, raise some intriguing questions." He tapped a finger against his lips. "There's someone to whom I'd like to refer you at CEU. Do you know Professor Agnes Szekely?"

"I've heard the name."

"She's even more knowledgeable than I about the Order of the Dragon, especially the heraldic angle. If those crossed spears belong to a family crest, she'll know the one."

"Then I'd love to talk with her," Viktor said.

"I'll write her in the morning."

"Thank you."

As Viktor stood to leave, Dr. Fessler rose with him and said, almost shyly, "I doubt this is of any interest to you, but I thought I'd mention it just in case you might want . . . it's such a strange case that . . . well, you see, I'm a collector too. I've had a lifelong appreciation for, a fascination with, really, the works of Abraham Stoker. One work in particular, of course, being the one everyone around the world is familiar with. Oh my goodness, how I'm blathering."

Viktor squinted at him. "Are you trying to tell me you're a Dracula scholar?"

"Yes, I suppose I am, though I'm more of an expert on the life of the author. I don't live too far from here. I'd be happy to walk over with you, prepare us both an evening drink, and show you my collection. It's been featured in a few magazines. There's also a theory I have which might interest you, though I admit it's one of pure speculation. An indulgence of mine. I've never tried to publish it because, as you know, our profession tends to frown on frivolous pursuits by serious scholars."

"What sort of theory?"

"It involves the rather sudden emergence of the aristocratic version of the undead in nineteenth century literature. Contrary to popular thought, Bram Stoker was not the first author to use the motif."

Viktor had read extensively on the vampire mythology in cultures throughout history, but the vampire figure in fiction was a topic with which, outside of Bram Stoker's seminal work, he was only passingly familiar. He waffled, not too keen on dallying with popular culture.

On the other hand, the best fiction was an excellent mirror to society, including its folklore and legends. The Speluncescu family, and Florin in particular, drew upon the myth to seduce their victims and control their criminal empire. Perhaps Viktor would learn something that might aid the investigation in some way. Plus, he had no other plans for the night, the hour had grown late, and Dr. Fessler's other suggestion sounded very attractive indeed. "Why not?" he said as he shrugged into his coat. "Let's have a drink and discuss the most famous bloodsucker of all time."

Skopje, North Macedonia

-14-

As Cezar Speluncescu stepped out of the dense fog blanketing the Stone Bridge, arriving as if by magic, Grey did not cringe in terror or run away, which he knew Cezar expected him to do.

This is how they run their operation.

They establish the myth and control you with fear.

"Nice trick," Grey said, taking a step to his right, away from the side of the bridge. He did not want his back pinned against the wall. "How long did it take you to tiptoe over here?"

Cezar circled to his right, keeping Grey in front of him. "I assure you I arrived in the same manner you did." Crisp British diction underlaid his Slavic accent.

"Or wait, let me guess. You flew here in bat form."

"Perhaps your hearing isn't as keen as you think it is."

Despite himself, Grey found himself trying to catch a glimpse of Cezar's teeth. A memory of Anton Speluncescu sniffing the air in the darkness like an animal flashed in Grey's mind, tugging at the corners of his rationality. With a grimace, he pushed the image away.

"Human senses are quite limited," Cezar continued, as if latching on to Grey's discomfort. "Compared to those of true predators."

We'll see who the true predator is. "I guess Dr. Ristov drank the Kool-Aid. He's so terrified of crossing you he sold out his own daughters."

"Dr. Ristov is a cautious man. A wise man."

"Dr. Ristov steals organs from single mothers trying to feed their families. He's a stone-cold sociopath like you."

Cezar eyed Grey for a long moment after the remark, then tucked his hands into his pockets and took a step closer, causing Grey to shift his weight to the balls of his feet. He noticed that Cezar's arms filled out the tailored sleeves of his coat, and his jaw was more solid than in the photos, almost simian. The Czech man stopped walking five feet from Grey as the mist thickened and enveloped them in a cocoon that seemed too small for the two of them, as if the metamorphosis about to occur would only release one of them back into the world.

Grey kept his hands loose and ready at his sides, watching for the slightest sign of movement. *Two mistakes, pal. You just put yourself within my reach, and you took your own hands out of the fight.*

Grey didn't even care if Cezar had a weapon in his pocket. At that distance, Grey could close on him before he could use it.

"You're not curious as to why I'm here?" Cezar asked. "Why we're having this conversation? Most men would have asked me by now."

"I don't care why you came. Where's Viktor?"

"You're not afraid of this bridge? The limited egress and your own lack of weapons? No, a man with your sort of background might not be."

"This bridge is too public for an attack. You're not afraid I'm wearing a wire? Or that someone's watching from a distance?"

"An attack?" Cezar said quietly. "I came simply to give some advice to someone I know came alone to Skopje, and who has no allies in the city."

"How do I get my friend back?"

Cezar cocked his head for a moment, in the same manner as his brother, which caused a chill to sweep down Grey's spine. He knew Cezar probably had men on either side of the bridge, but once again he wondered why the Speluncescu family had such confidence in their physical abilities.

"You're a man of action," Cezar said. "I respect that. But you can't win a fight with my family."

All of a sudden, Grey realized why Cezar had come to meet him in person, and why Viktor was probably still alive, at least for the time being.

The one thing the Speluncescu family seemed to fear, or at least abhor, was publicity. The secrecy that fueled the mythology swirling around them kept their enemies in the dark, and in check. It helped the family business stay off the radar of law enforcement. He guessed Cezar had come to either pay him off or scare him away, and that Viktor was being kept as insurance until the storm surrounding the murders in Prague blew over.

There were flaws in this theory, but Grey chose to ignore them for the moment. "I'm going to ask a third and final time," he said. "Where is Viktor Radek?"

"You're a poor listener. I'm afraid the lesson isn't getting through."

"I was never the best student," Grey said, his eyes canvassing Cezar's body, keeping up the banter as Grey picked out the target of his first strike as soon as Cezar reached for his weapon. Or maybe he had more people creeping through the fog as they talked. "You'll have to spell out the lesson for me."

"It's quite simple. If you continue to interrupt our business, or if I'm forced to waste more of my valuable time with another visit, then your employer is going to have a companion in the darkness."

Grey did not know what he meant by that last statement, but Cezar had emphasized *the darkness* in an odd manner, as if it were a tangible thing, alive in some way. "Wherever he is in theory, of course," Grey said. "Since you don't know."

In response to the sarcastic remark, Cezar took his hands out of his pockets and turned his back on Grey. "I suppose the lesson will have to be taught another way."

Grey had no idea why Cezar had turned around, unless he wanted to signal to someone through the fog. Surely Cezar had allies on either side of the bridge. Grey watched him carefully, especially his hands.

When the Czech man turned back to face him, Grey's thoughts and plans evaporated like a snuffed candle, and all he could think about were the inch-and-a-half long fangs revealed in the top of Cezar's mouth as his lips pulled back in a snarl. Fangs with cruel pointed ends as sharp as daggers, and that jutted out of the gum line just above Cezar's natural teeth. Grey should have noticed them before and did not know how this was possible, unless Cezar had stuck them in when he turned his back.

Such an obvious, almost comical, ruse seemed beneath a man like Cezar.

Yet the alternative was unthinkable.

"That must have been some surgery," Grey said as he slowly circled the larger man to keep him off-balance.

Cezar turned with him, his eyes gleaming as if imbued with a sudden feral energy. A guttural low growl issued from his throat. All of a sudden, his mouth opened wide and he sprang forward faster than Grey had anticipated.

So fast Grey could not believe it.

Grey's snap kick to the groin connected, but Cezar closed on him so fast that Grey's kick had little power behind it. Cezar ignored the kick and grabbed onto Grey's shirt with both hands, yanking Grey close as his face buried into Grey's neck, the fangs sinking into his flesh like a knife through warm caramel.

Grey gasped and jerked back, caught off-guard by the speed and savagery of the attack. Cezar held him tight and stepped forward, carrying Grey with him, pressing his back against the side of the bridge with incredible strength. Grey tried to shove him away but it felt like trying to move a parked car. For the first time in a very long time, Grey's mind went blank during a fight. No matter how much training martial artists or soldiers receive, they will never be prepared for that first street fight or tour of duty. The only thing that can prepare a warrior for live combat is live combat. That was why jujitsu schools were so brutal, to approximate an actual fight as closely as possible. In the old days—in Grey's day—some students picked street fights with actual thugs, because if death or injury was not on the line, the experience just wasn't the same.

Grey knew all this intimately because he had lost count of the times he had been in street fights, combat, and life or death situations. Though he still experienced a surge of adrenaline that hollowed out his stomach—he lived in fear of the day when this no longer happened—Grey had learned how to manage that debilitating swell of panic that accompanied the adrenaline. He knew how to focus in the center of the storm and channel it during battle.

But this time was different. None of Grey's experience or decades of training had prepared him to face a predator that had latched onto his neck with the speed and strength of Cezar Speluncescu. The abnormality of the attack, the sheer unnaturalness of it, caused Grey to freeze in the worst possible moment. By the time Grey recovered his wits, Cezar's teeth had sunk deep, and Grey could feel the blood spilling down his neck and onto his hands.

Fighting back against the horror, Grey finally cleared his mind and allowed his training and instincts to take over. All of his limbs were still free. He moved his left hand to the top of Cezar's hand, put his right hand on Cezar's left shoulder, and snaked his right leg through the middle of Cezar's legs and vined their ankles together.

Cezar did not seem to notice any of this. His head was buried in Grey's shoulder, drinking from him like an animal. Grey blinked away the pain, grabbed a fistful of hair on the back of Cezar's head, and jerked straight back. At the same time, he thrust back with his right foot, lifting Cezar's left leg off the ground. Grey pushed as hard as he could with his right hand on Cezar's shoulder. All of this together served to unbalance the larger man on his left side, and despite Cezar's preternatural strength, Grey used the leverage to shove him backwards and cause him to fall.

Normally Grey would have pressed the attack and tried to end the fight. But with his blood loss, and Cezar still uninjured, he did not like his chances. Grey had once fought a genetically altered opponent named Klaus atop Stone Mountain in Georgia, but from the opening salvo of the fight with Cezar, Grey thought the Czech man's speed, strength, and reflexes exceeded even those of the German warrior. Had the Speluncescu family gained access to a similar technology?

It didn't matter. Grey had to retreat. After Cezar fell to the ground, Grey turned to run towards Macedonia Square. After his first step, he felt a hand grab his ankle, causing Grey to trip. As he fell, he turned his head to the side and slapped his forearms on the ground, narrowly avoiding smashing his face on the stones.

Cezar dragged him backwards by the ankle. With a heave, Grey twisted his torso and lashed out with his other foot from his back, going for a knockout blow to the temple. Cezar blocked the blow and pounced on him, straddling Grey as his fangs went for the jugular again. Grey raised his arm just in time to ward off the blow. Cezar bit deep into Grey's forearm, sending fresh waves of pain coursing through him.

Cezar grabbed Grey by the face as Grey bucked beneath him, desperate to keep him away from his neck. Fighting from the ground was familiar territory to Grey, and he could dislodge almost any opponent within moments from any position. But Cezar was so much stronger and more agile than anyone Grey had faced that all of Grey's efforts failed.

Cezar's fangs inched closer and closer to Grey's neck as the two men fought. Grey could smell the wintergreen of Cezar's mouthwash. He used every trick he knew to keep Cezar at bay, but Grey's arms quivered with exhaustion and blood loss, and he was running out of time.

A scream pierced the silence of the night, followed by a young woman's voice shrieking in English. "Oh my God! There's blood everywhere!"

Grey jerked his head to the side and saw a group of young people who looked Western, probably from an NGO or a corporation with an office in Skopje, standing twenty feet away in the fog. Most of them were holding a bottle or can of beer.

With a deep-throated snarl, Cezar dug something out of Grey's pocket and leaped off of him. After giving Grey a final baleful look, Cezar darted into the fog in the opposite direction from the newcomers. With a start, Grey realized that in his last glimpse of Cezar's face, his fangs were no longer visible.

Someone shouted at Cezar to stop as one of the young women raced over to Grey, bending down to ask if he was okay with alcohol-soaked breath. He was disoriented and his breathing felt rapid and shallow. As his vision began to recede, he croaked out a reply, telling her not to take him to City Hospital, then turned his head in the direction Cezar had disappeared. With his last breath before he lost consciousness, he threw a question into the union of darkness and wraithlike mist obscuring the bridge.

"What are you?" Grey whispered.

-15-

The day after Mari had received the mysterious email from Erik Mittelman, she took a seat just before noon in a red-cushioned pew on the left-hand side of Saints Cyril and Methodius Cathedral. The beautiful church with the blue-and-gold patterned ceiling was in New Town, the youngest of the five medieval cities that form the historic center of Prague. New Town was founded in 1348. The fact that "new" in Prague correlates to something that occurred in the fourteenth century was one of a million reasons why she loved this city.

As she waited, Mari thought about the clandestine precautions Erik Mittelman had taken in anticipation of this meeting, and his abrupt decision to abandon his profession.

What had he stumbled upon in Bucharest all those years ago?

This train of thought led her to ponder her own work. She wanted to vow right then and there never to be intimidated or abandon a project in which she believed. But that was a dangerous road to go down.

What did she know about true peril, about the impossible choices people sometimes had to make? She had glimpsed the same question reflected in Dominic Grey's hard green eyes when they had first met, when she claimed to have visited her fair share of dodgy places.

Have you really, Mari? His level stare had intimated. *Are you sure about that?*

Not counting the homeless camps in L.A. and San Francisco, and a rowdy trip to Tijuana, she knew she had seen very little of the world. And she was wise enough to understand that she would never truly know herself until put to the fire—and that she may not like what she found when the flames melted away the privileged outer shell and revealed her inner core.

But something inside her needed to know.

Who are you, Mari?

What are you made of?

Noon came and went. Fifteen minutes later, she turned to peer down the aisle but only saw a pair of elderly women praying five rows behind her. She did not think either of those squat figures could be Erik in disguise. She had seen photos online of him, a Jewish man about her height with a dimpled smile and curly brown locks framing a narrow face.

Another quarter hour passed. Feeling nervous, Mari checked her email for the umpteenth time to see if he had written her. Still nothing.

Had someone intercepted their communication? Were they watching her right now?

She had given him enough time. Frustrated, she decided to leave, hoping he had gotten tied up with something, and that nothing more sinister had happened.

On her way out, a man with cropped gray hair stepped out from behind a massive pillar in the foyer of the cathedral, startling her. She realized it was Erik at the same time he touched her elbow and said, "Follow me."

Without waiting for a reply, almost as if trying to distance himself from her, Erik headed outside. She followed behind and saw him descend the main church steps and disappear inside a separate door on the street that led to the crypt. After chewing on her bottom lip, she followed him through the door and hurried down a gloomy stone staircase. There was an attendant at the bottom, which relieved her. Mari paid the small fee and walked into a tiny exhibition space with glass cases. She gathered the memorial had something to do with Czech paratroopers and World War II.

Erik was slipping through another door at the far end. She followed him through the small and curved entryway, which had the feel of a bunker. The door led to the actual crypt but only opened in one direction, forcing her to continue once she entered. That made her nervous all over again.

Mari took a deep breath and made the plunge. The crypt was dimly lit and smelled of dry stone. It consisted of a single vaulted corridor honeycombed with empty cubbyholes which she assumed had once held bodies or coffins. Busts of soldiers were spaced along the walls, attached to standing plaques with flowers at the base. Erik was standing near one of these in the middle of the crypt. No one else was inside.

The lack of people unnerved Mari, but she had the feeling the solitude was exactly why Erik had chosen this location.

What is he afraid of?

"Thanks for meeting me," she said, doing her best to sound casual, or at least not terrified. "I didn't recognize you at first."

Erik gave a bitter smile and passed a hand nervously over his scalp. His face was craggier, much older and timeworn than in the photos. "My wife prefers short hair. The premature gray . . . how did you get my email?"

"From a producer. A family friend."

Erik gave an understanding nod in solidarity with her reluctance to divulge her source. "It's fine. I never let it go . . . just because, I guess." He swallowed as he peered around the crypt. "I knew this moment would come. I've been dreading it with all of my being, yet I've also . . . it's eating me up."

Despite the chilly underground air, a light sheen of perspiration dampened Mari's palms. "What is?"

"Keeping it inside. I haven't talked about what really happened in Bucharest with *any*one. Not even my wife. I told her I switched to banking because I wanted to be more financially stable for our family. That's a valid reason, but it's not why I stopped doing what I love. I stopped because I was goddamn terrified. And still am."

Stay calm, Mari. Be professional. "Terrified of who? The Speluncescus?"

Ever since they had started speaking, Erik's eyes had not stopped roving the shadowy spaces around them. He finally focused on her. "Before I speak further, I want to know why you're here. Please be honest. If I think you're holding something back, or lying in any way, I'll walk. And if you think I won't believe something you have to say . . ." A grim smile creased his lips. "Try me. First, let me guess—you're here because of the recent murder in Old Town."

Her confirmation of his suspicion caused his face to slowly crumble.

Pressing further before he changed his mind about the meeting, Mari told him about her uncle's disappearance, and most of what she knew about the ongoing investigation, confidentiality be damned. Viktor's life was on the line.

As Erik listened to her story, his face grew pale, and his left thumb started to rub against the inside of his fingers. When she finished, he closed his eyes and exhaled a deep, shuddering breath.

"Do you know something that could help my uncle?" Mari said. "Please, if there's anything . . ."

"I don't. I'm sorry."

"Then why are we here?" she snapped.

"You asked me about the Speluncescus. Not your uncle."

"Oh. Yes. I did. Sorry."

"It's okay," he said gently. "I understand, and I'm truly sorry to hear what happened. I can't help you with that, but maybe I can . . . shed some light . . . on what you're dealing with. Not that I really know," he muttered.

"I'll take whatever help you can give. I can tell this is hard for you."

His thumb rubbed faster. "You have no idea."

"Are the Speluncescus why you changed professions?"

"One of them was. Or at least I think . . . maybe I'll just tell you what happened, and let you form your own opinion."

"However you want to do it." Her eyes slid around the crypt. "I have to ask: why are we meeting down here? I understand you don't want us to be seen together, but isn't this place a bit . . . secluded?"

"You're worried we'd be trapped if anyone did find us. Yes, I considered that." Erik regarded her in silence for a moment before his eyes moved to a large wooden cross hanging on the wall by the bunker door. "Along with the privacy, this crypt is closer to the original sacred ground this church was built on. I'm not religious, but let's just say I'm hedging my bets."

"Oh," she said in a small voice.

Erik again ran a hand through his hair. "It's been a long time. You'll have to bear with me. I should provide some context first."

"Take as long as you need."

"I only have my lunch hour, but I work a block from . . ." He trailed off as if realizing he had not wanted to divulge that information. "I work close," he mumbled. "Let's start with this: how much do you know about the red market? Or do you even know the term?"

"I researched it yesterday, and watched your piece last night. It was brave work. I'm a documentarian, and it inspired me."

His eyes flew to meet hers, and he spoke with such force it took her aback.

"You can't mention my name in public or in your work. Ever. Not to anyone. Swear to me right now or I walk. Swear it on your life."

"I swear," Mari whispered. "On my life."

He held her gaze for a long moment before shaking his head. At first she thought he was going to leave anyway, but his mouth formed a self-effacing grin and he said, "I'm a coward by nature. That's kept me alive, but it came at a high price. Every night when I go to sleep, I see the faces of those children and wonder what else I could have done."

A look of quiet devastation overcame him, the memory of something she could tell had gnawed at him for years and left him as barren and hollowed-out as the discarded husk of a wasp's nest.

"How can you call yourself a coward?" she said. "Your work was amazing."

"Reporting on something is not the same as living it. Since you're familiar with the subject, I'll keep that part brief. As you know, I was based in Romania for a year while I worked on my investigation. I knew about the orphanages—the world knew it too and still does—but until you witness it firsthand, talk to those poor children and smell the stench of their filthy living conditions and hear the caretakers talk about them like they're animals kept in a pen . . . until you see the bruises covering the childrens' bodies and watch them clamber for your attention, desperate for any form of human contact, the barest hint of the love they never received . . . no story can ever convey how deeply it affected me."

"Why are the orphanages so bad there?"

"They're bad in most places. But yeah, Romania might win the prize. Ceaușescu banned abortions and contraceptives to keep the population from shrinking. He even forced women to report for regular gynecological exams to detect early pregnancies. The result was predictable. No one could afford these children. Tens of thousands of unwanted kids flooded the streets and orphanages. The government coupled this policy with propaganda marketing the orphanages as a viable alternative to a normal family. Nothing could be further from the truth. Not all of the orphanages were corrupt, but most of them were, and I don't think I need to spell out what happens in those places, or how a disturbing number of human beings tend to act like monsters when they gain control over other human beings, and how that behavior seems to spread like a cancer, especially within institutions."

Mari bit her lip and nodded.

"Most of these children," he continued, "ended up in prison or homeless when they left the orphanages. The vast majority had mental health problems stemming from a lack of love and simple human touch. The constant smell of urine and the silence, Mari. That's what got me the most. The damnable silence these children lived inside their entire childhood. That should never happen to a human being." Erik put his hands over his face for a long moment. "Do you know how much a human body is worth these days? About fifty million, if taken apart and sold piece by piece, organ by organ, chemical by chemical."

"My God. That much?"

"The realities of harvesting and transportation drive that number down, and figure about a tenth of that price on the street, but you get the idea. In the West, to the right buyer, a heart alone can go for a million. Global profits in human trafficking—the parent company of the red market—are about 150 billion per year."

She clapped a hand to her mouth. "I knew it was substantial, but not that huge."

"Drugs and weapons have their source industries, their poppy fields and munitions factories. Human trafficking has third world villages and urban slums. No investment needed. But orphanages are the easiest target of all, provided the people who run them can be bought. The children in orphanages have no recourse, no one to turn to when they're sold into slavery or taken to red market hospitals for operations."

Mari looked away. "I just don't understand how anyone . . ."

"Neither do I. And however bad you think it is, the reality is even worse. Once I learned about the pipeline from the orphanages to the red market, I started nosing around Bucharest. I made contacts at the local orphanages and even did a few undercover gigs, posing as a buyer."

"Hardly the acts of a coward."

He looked off to the side. "I got deep inside the business. Real deep. So deep I began to realize I could bring some of the orphanages down. Maybe even a whole pipeline or two. Eventually I heard a rumor about a private orphanage on the outskirts of the city where kids just disappeared. A child or two every month. I won't get into the details about where I first heard it, it would turn your stomach, but when I started asking around, no one wanted to talk. I finally uncovered the name of the owner, Dumitra Speluncescu, but whenever I mentioned her name to my sources, they would clam up and get a wild look in their eyes that unnerved the hell out of me. These were hardened criminals, mind you. People who bartered children for profit." He took a deep breath and tilted his face towards the ceiling. "That's the first time I've said that name out loud in a decade."

"What did they say about her?"

Erik lowered his eyes to meet hers. "That she was a *strigoi*. A vampire."

Mari felt a chill creep down her spine. "Did you . . . did you believe them?"

"Hell no. I'm not superstitious in the slightest—or I wasn't then—and after all, this is Romania. The old beliefs are alive and well. Did you hear about the dead villager whose relatives were convinced he had become a vampire? A group of people dug up his body from the cemetery, cut out his heart and burned it, sprinkled the rest of his body with garlic and staked it, then drank the ashes of his heart with a glass of water."

"Jesus."

"Sounds like something out of the seventeenth century, or a Hammer movie, doesn't it? That happened in a Romanian village in 2004. The only people who were surprised were the ones who saw it on the international news. So no. I didn't believe them. I thought Dumitra Speluncescu, whoever she was, had done a good job convincing the Bucharest underworld that she was a creature of the undead. Anyway, I was determined to find out more about this orphanage. When I couldn't get anyone to tell me how to reach Dumitra, I took matters into my own hands. I speak German, so I posed as a buyer from Berlin—a pedophile—and made inquiries in person at the orphanage she owned, using the disgusting lingo I'd learned, letting it be known I was in the market. A piece of undercover work that I still can't shower away. But I found my connection. My inquiries led to a groundskeeper who I was told snatched children out of their beds at night and carried them away. No one seemed to know what happened to them next. I assumed Dumitra and the director of the orphanage knew—they had to, right?—and that maybe the ultimate buyer was a public figure whose identity everyone was protecting. A politician, businessman, someone big."

"Did you ever find out where they went? Or who was being protected?"

"I don't think they went anywhere. The only guess I have is . . . unthinkable. You can draw your own conclusions when I'm done. So I approached this groundskeeper with the same spiel I'd been using. I told him I wanted a steady supply. I figured that would get the attention of the director or Dumitra. My plan was to get them both on the record and go public, first with the story and then to the authorities with everything I'd uncovered."

He began to pace again, his fingers twitching and his eyes roving the darkened corners of the crypt. Mari thought she had never seen anyone who needed a drink quite so badly.

"I thought this would be it. My career would be set. I might get a book deal, a movie, an invite to the talk shows. Most of all, I'd do some good in the world, and take down a major player in the red market. It would barely make a dent in the grand scheme, but what does? At least it would be something *I* did."

She stayed quiet and listened as his eyes went distant in remembrance.

"The night after I met with the groundskeeper," he continued, "I was sitting in my top-floor studio in Bucharest. I'll never forget the details. I was drinking Canadian Club whiskey with a splash of Coke. The kitchen smelled of the canned tuna I'd used in a casserole for dinner. It was summer in Bucharest and there was no AC, so I was shirtless and had opened a window to deal with the heat. The rental apartment was ancient but it had charm and a view of downtown. I was doodling with an outline for my story, nervous but excited about the next meeting with the groundskeeper. When my glass was empty—I still remember the damn mosquito buzzing around my head—I rose from the table and turned towards the kitchen. A tall older woman with dark, waist length hair and a face like a model's, dressed all in black, was standing right in the middle of my apartment. I dropped my whiskey glass. It shattered on the floor. I'd been working with my back to the door and the window, but I lived on the twelfth floor. I would have heard someone come in. How did she get there? When I asked who she was, she said I already knew. And I suppose I did."

"Dumitra?" Mari asked in a small voice.

"She never said. But who else? Before I could reply, she—" Erik shuddered and wrung his hands together. "She moved across the room so fast I could barely follow. It was late and I was drunk but not that drunk and I'm telling you, no human being can move like that. She flowed like water and the next thing I knew she was standing behind me with her lips next to my ear. I can still smell the cloves in her perfume. She took the side of my head in her hand and pushed it gently to the side. I hate to admit it, but she was very beautiful and it was almost . . . well, there was no *almost*. It was erotic. Her other hand took my arm and stroked it as she spoke in my ear. 'Erik,' she said. 'I can't let you continue your investigation. You may publish your article, but you will leave out my orphanage and the others I name, and anyone associated with them.' She named a handful of orphanages while I stood there like a dumb ox, transfixed. I should have been fighting or running away or screaming but I could only stand there and listen. To this day, I'm unsure why. I was terrified, yes, but it was more than that. I felt *compelled*. Her fingers kept stroking my arm and her voice was so soft and . . ." he shuddered again. "No, I have to be honest. She didn't hypnotize me, I was just too weak and afraid to resist. If I had, I know to this day I'd be dead, but so be it. I probably should be."

He fell quiet, lost in the memory for so long that Mari had to prompt him to continue. Her head was spinning from the story, but she wanted to keep him in the moment. "What happened then?"

When he resumed speaking, his voice sounded almost confused, as if still bedazzled by whatever strange influence Dumitra possessed over him. "Her tongue ran lightly up and down my neck. After that, I felt something sharp prick my skin. When I recoiled, she drew away, and I saw her teeth for the first time. Her fangs. My God, they were so long, so white . . . so perfect and deadly . . . she was still holding my arm, and before I could react, she lifted it up and latched onto it like some kind of leech or parasite. She bit me, Mari. She fucking bit me and drank my blood. I started to scream but her other hand clamped over my mouth. She pushed me to my back on the floor as if I weighed nothing. That shouldn't be possible. She was as slender as a reed and had to be pushing fifty years. She crawled on top of me, and I laid there on my back as she fed, sure I was going to die. I'll never forget the feeling. I simply resigned myself to my death. I'm not a fighter but I could have done . . . something. But then she stopped. She dropped my arm and left me on the floor while she told me she knew I'd be a good boy and do what she asked. And that if I didn't, no matter where I lived in the world or how far away I ran, she'd return to finish what she started."

As Mari watched with a stunned expression, Erik pulled back the sleeve of his shirt to reveal two faint, pinprick white scars set two inches apart on his left wrist. Mari stared down at the scars with a terrible fascination.

"I told my wife a dog bit me," he said in a faraway voice. "I lost a pint of blood that day."

"Have you ever felt, you know, different?"

His lips creased in a grim smile. "You mean like a vampire? No. I have no idea if she was such a thing or, if so, how it really works. I don't know anything except I remain convinced to this day that Dumitra Speluncescu is not a normal human being, and that if I ever mention her name in public, or reveal something she warned me not to, she'll do exactly what she promised."

He shuddered again. By the look of sheer trauma on his face, Mari had no doubt he believed everything he had just told her. She had to work hard to keep her thoughts clear and focused.

Erik's voice turned wooden as he pushed his sleeve back into place. "I don't think she let me live to be merciful. I think she let me publish my piece to hurt her business rivals. Or maybe to draw attention away from herself. The orphanages I named in my story were terrible offenders, and needed to go down, but the worst ones of all, and especially hers . . . they're places of pure evil, Mari. And that woman, or whatever she is, is the devil incarnate."

She laid a hand on his arm. "You're very brave for telling me all of this. I don't care what you say."

A harsh laugh escaped him. "She's destroying children, and doing God knows what else. I've sat on this knowledge for all these years because I'm too afraid to speak up. Brave? I think not."

"No one would have believed you. You went undercover and almost died and still published the piece."

He shook his head. "I'm—I was—a journalist. I had a duty to the truth and to justice. I failed in that duty in the worst possible way. I'm not a brave man, not when it comes to risking my own life. I learned this in Bucharest. But here," he said, digging into his coat and handing her a folded piece of Moleskine paper. "It's taken me a decade to do this one simple act, and maybe you're a better person than I am."

Cluj-Napoca, Romania

-16-

A light rain began to fall on Viktor's evening walk to Dr. Fessler's home. The Romanian historian pulled out an umbrella and kept up a steady chatter on the way, discussing everything from the price of gasoline to the difficulty of young scholars vying for tenure to the fine points of medieval politics in the Romanian principalities.

Viktor ignored the drizzle, refused Dr. Fessler's offer to share the umbrella, and listened with half an ear. Most of his focus was on the lamplit lanes of Cluj, keeping a sharp lookout for a sign that someone might be following them, or the quick drawing of a blind from one of the three-story townhomes looming over the street.

The hour was not late, just before eight p.m. The mixed-use district they had entered had plenty of streetlamps and people on the street. While Viktor knew the Speluncescus would not appreciate anyone looking into their affairs—that risk was real—he did not worry about a physical attack in the middle of the city. But he did suffer from a creeping disquiet this case had engendered in him, an irrational dread of dark city streets and tree branches scraping against windows that he could not seem to shake. It disturbed him. He was the clear-minded professor, the debunker of charlatans and sham phenomena. Yes, he had a healthy respect for the unexplained powers of the mind, and had seen things for which he had no rational explanation over the course of his career.

But undead creatures that prowled the night and stole the blood of the living did not exist. Despite the odd affectations of the Speluncescus, Viktor had seen nothing on this case to convince him otherwise. The chest and the ring and the book from the lost library all presented intriguing historical mysteries he was itching to solve—and nothing more.

Viktor and Dr. Fessler turned onto a quiet brick street with parked cars and scooters lining the curb. A tunnel of townhomes pressed together on both sides.

The homes had exquisite Gothic features, angular arches and steeply pitched roofs and delicate vergeboard on the gables. Dr. Fessler had said he lived close to the university, but they had been walking for fifteen minutes. Viktor did not like the solitude and had to suppress an urge to lash out in annoyance.

"Here we are," Dr. Fessler said as they approached a townhome with dormer windows and a forest-green roof. Flowerpots with autumnal blooms brightened the windowsills.

"A beautiful home," Viktor murmured.

Dr. Fessler beamed with pride and unlocked the door. After a final glance around the empty street, Viktor brushed the rain off his coat and followed him inside. The antique furniture and mahogany paneling evoked a bygone era. Though a bit stuffy and cluttered for Viktor's taste, it was obvious much care had been given to decorating the interior of the townhome.

Dr. Fessler offered Viktor a hand towel and led him to a spiral staircase that wound to the upper stories. "The collection is in the attic. "Why don't you take a look while I see to the drinks. Any requests?"

"I prefer absinthe if you have it."

"I have almost everything except that."

"Red wine, perhaps?"

"This I have in abundance. Any grape in particular?"

"I'm partial to Bordeaux and Piemonte, but anything will do."

Dr. Fessler clapped his hands. "Done."

As the host left down the hall, Viktor hung his coat on a hook, used the towel to wipe his face, and climbed three flights of stairs to the attic. He flicked the lights to reveal a sizeable space with sloping walls. The room bore a faint smell of paraffin. While Viktor was not the sort to gape, when he absorbed the contents of the wood-floored attic, his eyebrows slowly lifted.

Modesty was not the defining character trait that came to mind when Viktor thought of Dr. Fessler, but the historian had underestimated the size and sheer audacity of his collection. Track lighting placed at artful angles illuminated a room brimming with memorabilia related to Bram Stoker and his infamous creation. Throughout the room, at least twenty signed movie posters from different eras hung on the walls and from slender wires attached to the ceiling.

Lake of Dracula, Son of Dracula, Brides of Dracula, the Return of Dracula. Viktor did not keep up with popular culture and had no idea so many films of the immortal count had been made.

A life-size coffin rested beneath a window on the far wall. The lid of the coffin was propped open, revealing a wax effigy of Dracula sleeping in the velvet-lined interior, dribbles of fake blood spotting the corners of his lips. On the wall to Viktor's left was a glass case full of hardbound books. He took a closer look and saw many different editions of *Dracula*, along with other works from Bram Stoker's oeuvre. *The Primrose Path, The Jewel of Seven Stars, The Lair of the White Worm*. From browsing the spines and the volumes displayed with the cover out, Viktor could tell the books were in immaculate condition.

Other memorabilia, such as movie props and bric-a-brac from Stoker's estate, were artfully displayed on stands and pedestals with placards describing their origin. Viktor clasped his hands behind his back and wandered the room, impressed by the display, noting some of the highlights.

One of the original Underwood typewriters Bram Stoker had used to write *Dracula*.

Framed newspaper articles from London reporting how the publication of the novel had capitalized on the vampire hysteria in Eastern Europe.

An authentic vampire hunting kit said to belong to a Dominican friar in 18th century Bucharest.

In the center of the room was a miniature replica of the ruins of Whitby Abbey. According to the placard, the ruins looming over the blustery seaside town in England that Stoker had chosen as the setting for the scene where Dracula arrives by boat at the headland, assumes the shape of a large black dog, and darts up 199 steps to a graveyard.

Viktor wandered over to the coffin and gazed out of the sole window, down onto a street corner marked by the bare branches of a plane tree. As the rain slashed against the windows, he felt something cold and clammy brush his wrist. Startled, he jumped back as a pale hand reached out of the coffin. Viktor's heart thumped wildly as the torso of the caped figure rose to a sitting position and the head swiveled to stare at Viktor, the eyes glowing with a crimson light.

"*Do prdele!*" Viktor swore as the hands of the wax effigy returned to their crossed position against its chest, and the torso lowered back into the coffin.

"I apologize for that," Dr. Fessler said, again startling Viktor. He whipped around to find the historian walking across the room with two drinks in hand and a grin teasing the corners of his lips.

"One would think I would not be so susceptible to parlor tricks," Viktor said.

"Oh, your reaction was quite subdued. Most people scream their bloody heads off."

Viktor waved a hand across the room. "This is quite the collection. I'm impressed."

Dr. Fessler gave a half bow. "Did you see this book?" he asked, walking towards a glass case that sat atop a waist-high pedestal in a corner of the room. The case housed a mustard-colored hardback with *Dracula by Bram Stoker* written in blood-red font on the cover. Beside the book was a clamshell box bound in black morocco with a leather onlay depiction of the Count's castle. "The prize of my collection. First edition of course."

"It's a beautiful piece," Viktor said with all sincerity. As a collector himself, he could appreciate the mint condition of both the hardbound tome and the period box that had once housed it. "I don't suppose it's signed?"

"By Stoker *and* Bela Lugosi."

"My my," Viktor murmured, estimating the price of such a work at tens of thousands of American dollars. Maybe more, depending on how many were in existence.

"The castle in Transylvania, yes?" the historian posed as a question, still looking down at the leather onlay box cover. "Legendary home of Count Dracula?"

"I assume so."

"There is no doubt Transylvania is the setting for the first part of the novel. Stoker tells us as much, and modern scholars assume that Stoker based Dracula's residence on Bran castle. It's the only location in Romania that reasonably fits the description of a castle 'on the very edge of a terrific precipice' above a chasm where the rivers 'wind in deep gorges through the forest.' But Stoker never visited Romania, or Eastern Europe at all. He might have based the description on an illustration of Bran Castle he saw in a book we know he owned, but I'm one of the minority who believe he used Slains Castle in Scotland—a place he actually visited—as inspiration."

Viktor's eyes roamed the room, his eyes settling on a disturbing bronze bust of a vampire with batlike ears and a demonic face. "You mentioned a theory?"

"Yes of course. I apologize, I was getting there in my roundabout way. Even more than the location of the castle, you'd be hard-pressed to find a historian, or anyone, who believes the ruthless Vlad the Impaler was *not* the inspiration for the fictional Count Dracula. Am I right?"

"I'm no literary historian, but it seems a reasonable assumption."

Dr. Fessler spread his palms. "Call me the nonbeliever. After decades of studying Stoker's life and his source material for the novel, I've come to believe the idea for the count came from somewhere else entirely."

Viktor took his first drink of wine. "Excellent, thank you. A Barolo, if I'm not mistaken?"

"Well-spotted." Viktor gave the full-bodied wine a gentle swirl as the historian raised his own glass to his lips and approached the gruesome bronze bust. "I saw you eying Count Orlok from *Nosferatu*. The movie borrows so heavily from Stoker's work that a court in the early twentieth century ordered all copies of the film destroyed. Thankfully some prints survived, and now it's one of the best-known horror movies of all time. One of my personal favorites. But I digress. While Murnau did borrow heavily from Stoker, his depiction of the vampire itself, as you can see from the bronze bust before you, returned to that of the mindless creatures haunting the folktales of Eastern Europe." Dr. Fessler wagged a finger. "The *upir*, the first name of which we're aware for *vampire* in the region, is a term that arose in the middle of the eleventh century A.D. It's believed to mean 'the thing at the feast or sacrifice.' The *upir* was the furthest cry from a suave aristocrat one can possibly imagine. They were bloated, foul-smelling, clawed, fanged, filthy beasts who stumbled through the night like wild animals plagued with a terrible disease, desperate to satisfy their unnatural cravings."

"A vivid description," Viktor said drily, "and an accurate portrayal, though the legends are not unique to Transylvania."

Dr. Fessler nodded in a slow, chastised manner. "I forget to whom I'm speaking. Of course you'd be well-versed in the actual traditions."

"Though the basic legend arose in a startling range of cultures, the form of the vampire varies quite a bit, from batlike creatures to wispy revenants to the more humanoid depiction you just described in Eastern and Central Europe."

"One wonders why that may be."

"One does," Viktor said, "though not too deeply."

Dr. Fessler chuckled. "Of course, of course. Then again, I've read your commentary on the kernel of truth in all legends, and how you often trust that kernel more than so-called facts and accepted history. It made quite an impression on me."

"Touché."

"History is the political narrative of the victor, to paraphrase what you once said, while legends and the collective memory of a culture are the building blocks of the genuine record."

"The spice that flavors the stew," Viktor murmured, remembering his own words.

"A journal essay discussing, if I recall, the commonality of the flood narratives and the potential for scientific research based on creation stories."

Viktor's gaze rested on the coffin. "It's true I believe legends which have stood the test of time harbor elements of truth. It's also true the neocortex has endowed humankind with remarkable powers of imagination."

"Abraham Stoker felt the same. In fact, he liked to seed his fiction liberally with both facts and truth. One only need to examine the full name of the true hero of the novel—*Abraham* von Helsing—to discover this."

"That's not much of a cover-up."

"Did you know that Dracula's ship full of dead crew and crates of earth that floated ashore in Whitby Harbor was based on a similar mysterious—and very real—occurrence in the same location a few years prior? The name of the actual vessel was the *Dmitri*; in the novel it was the *Demeter*. Rescue workers in Whitby claimed to have seen a large black dog flee the hull of the *Dmitri* and climb the steps from Tate Sands beach to the cemetery outside St. Mary's church. Sound familiar? That scene is repeated almost verbatim in the novel.

Even more astonishing: did you know that Stoker originally wished to publish Dracula as nonfiction?"

Viktor took another sip. "Now *that* is hard to believe."

"The publisher forced Stoker to cut the first 101 pages—never found, by the way—as well as the original preface claiming the author was convinced of the veracity of the events presented in the book."

"A marketing gimmick, surely."

"We'll never know. At the very least, the unpublished preface, in which Stoker claims that many of the characters are real, and which we do still have, raises eyebrows. I could point you to innumerable places in the story that bear parallels to real life. Stoker once boldly told a reporter that the account of vampiric shenanigans at Count Dracula's castle was a blend of mystery and fact. Imagine such a thing! Remember that Stoker was not famous at the time, and trying to pass off a novel as nonfiction was a . . . curious . . . choice. Then again, half of Europe at the time believed vampires were real. Whole villages were abandoned based on rumors of infiltration by the undead. I promised you a theory, so here it comes. Contrary to popular belief, I do not believe Stoker modeled his villain on Vlad the Impaler. There is no direct evidence of this. Yes, the book mentions a 'Voivode Dracula' of Transylvania, the 'land beyond the forest,' who fought against the Turks. That would seem a rather obvious parallel. But there were a good many historical voivodes from the house of Drăculești, and no direct evidence in Stoker's note that he had chosen Vlad the Impaler specifically, or even researched him. On the other hand, Stoker made a note in his papers that *Dracula* means *devil* in Wallachian, a separate principality from Transylvania. I believe Stoker chose the name *Dracula* for its connotations, and *not* to denote a particular person. Think about it: Vlad III was hardly a debonair aristocrat. That inspiration might have come from the actor, Sir Henry Irving, to whom Stoker was a personal assistant for much of his life. Perhaps most curious of all, consider what I alluded to earlier tonight: the concept of a seductive, well-bred vampire was such a departure from the norm, such a radical reimagining of the myth, that one wonders how it ever took hold in the first place. Did you know Stoker's Dracula was not the first literary vampire of its kind?"

"I believe it was predated by Sheridan LeFanu's *Camilla*? Which I confess I've never read."

The historian wagged a finger. "Not even *Camilla*. The honor of the first work to mark the transition of the vampire from slavering beast to creature of seductive refinement was *The Vampyre* by John Polidori."

"I'm unaware of that title," Viktor said.

"Not many are, outside of vampire enthusiasts and Gothic scholars. Polidori was a personal physician to Lord Byron who traveled widely in Europe. In fact, both Polidori and Lord Byron were on holiday with Mary Shelley when she first conceived of *Frankenstein*. What if Polidori, in his travels to the frontiers of Europe, stumbled upon a figure who passed himself off as a vampire? You've heard of Lady Báthory?"

"The Hungarian noblewoman and serial killer said to bathe in the blood of her victims."

"When I heard the news about the case in Prague, I couldn't help but think of the parallel to my own theory. Is it that hard to imagine some common-born rogue or minor nobleman wandering around eighteenth-century Romania, capitalizing on the myth so prevalent in his day, using the terror of the populace to his or her own nefarious ends?" Dr. Fessler grinned, seeming very pleased with himself. "Or perhaps Polidori stumbled upon a descendant of the House of Drăculeşti who he suspected really *was* one of the undead. Maybe all the Drăculeşti voivodes were vampires. Why should Vlad III be the only one? Bram never explained the origin of the count's unnatural affliction. Where did it come from, and why not pass it on to his descendants? Why indeed are the vampire legends so prevalent and potent in Eastern Europe? My theory is one of pure conjecture, but the central question is valid: why *did* the vampire as aristocrat emerge from seemingly out of nowhere?"

"It's a fair question," Viktor mused.

"Was it a feat of imagination alone, or does the legend possess a seed of that elusive truth? Would you care for another glass?"

Viktor wandered to the window and noticed the rain had slackened. "I really must be going."

"I understand. I hope I didn't bore you too much."

"On the contrary, I'm impressed by your passion and knowledge."

"I have a car, but it's parked at my sister's house. Shall I call a cab?"

Viktor peered down at the empty street below the window, deciding to err on the side of caution. "Sure."

Dr. Fessler made the call and spoke quickly in Romanian. After a short conversation, he held the phone away from his face and said to Viktor, "It will be thirty minutes before they arrive. I apologize. Shall we try another company?"

Viktor estimated the walk to the hotel would take less than twenty minutes, barely a mile, and most of it through the well-lit city center. *The hour is not even late. I'm jumping at my own shadow.* "I'll walk after all," he said. "I like to stretch my legs before bed."

After seeing Viktor to the front door, Dr. Fessler said, "It was a true pleasure, Professor."

"Likewise. If you think of anything that might be of interest to the case, something I might have overlooked, do pass it on."

"Of course, of course."

"Oh, and please do make an introduction with Dr. Szekely. I'd like to talk with her about the heraldic angle as soon as possible."

After the door to the townhome closed, Viktor stood on the street outside and glanced in both directions, feeling ill at ease despite his internal admonitions to relax. No one else was out. The moon was high, and the smell of wet leaves made the air feel heavy. Viktor fastened his double-breasted wool coat and strode quickly towards the university.

When he reached the next intersection, he saw the tall streetlamps in the distance marking the border of the campus. It would be quicker to cut through the grounds of the university but also more solitary, unless a group of students was out.

Bah. Since when does my peace of mind require the presence of college students?

With a snarl, Viktor shoved his hands into the pockets of his coat and hunched his blacksmith shoulders. Just before he plowed forward into the night, he looked back once again, a final glance at the darkened row of townhomes on Dr. Fessler's street—and saw a man less than a hundred yards away, walking steadily towards Viktor.

A man wearing a scarf and a shearling jacket.

-17-

Grey woke to dim fluorescent lighting and a chemical odor that failed to mask the reek of disease and human waste. The smell recalled a vivid childhood memory, when Grey had visited his grandfather in a state-run nursing home in New Jersey. Grey had never forgotten the stench of urine and decaying flesh in his grandfather's room and in the hallway.

A flimsy white curtain surrounded his cot on three sides. An IV ran from his arm to a pole with a bag of blood hanging from it. He turned his head and noticed a line extending from the IV tower to a bank of medical equipment that looked as if it was made in the 1950s.

A bandage covered the spot on Grey's forearm where Cezar had bitten him. Grey reached up and felt another bandage on the left side of his neck. A sudden uneasy thought made him look down to ensure there was no binding covering one of his kidneys or another organ.

Besides the two bite wounds, everything else seemed intact. He felt reasonably well-rested, though his throat was parched.

Every now and then a moan of pain broke the silence, he assumed from another patient. Before he could decide what to do, his IV machine emitted a long beep that caused a woman with curly blond hair to push aside the curtain and step into the room. She had intelligent blue eyes, a smattering of freckles, and a mousy chin that imparted a coquettish sort of beauty. Instead of a blouse with a plunging neckline and a moss green leather jacket, her outfit when she had rushed to Grey's aid on the bridge, she was wearing hospital scrubs and a pair of tennis shoes.

"Good timing," she said with an Irish accent, checking the medical equipment with a practiced touch. "And good morning."

Grey sat up. "What time is it?"

"Just after nine. You slept through the night."

He had a jumbled memory of someone attending to his wounds and attaching the IV to his arm. "Where am I?"

"Not City Hospital. You can relax, Mr. Grey."

He tensed. "How do you know my name?"

"Because when doctors stumble upon strange men in the middle of the night, bleeding to death on the street, they tend to look for identification when they take them to the hospital. You really should keep an emergency contact in your wallet. Everyone should. At least you had your blood type. That's smart."

He started to speak again but his throat felt coated with gravel. He coughed and swallowed to produce saliva. The woman slipped outside the curtain and reappeared with a bottle of water.

Grey drank the entire bottle. "Thanks. You're a doctor?"

"You had the good fortune of being found by a group of rather snockered members of Doctors Without Borders." Her face turned grave. "If that hadn't been the case, you mightn't have made it. What in the world happened back there? Did that guy have an animal with him? Who was he?"

Grey averted his eyes. "Something like that."

"I haven't notified the police yet. Should I?"

"No."

"Are you with the government? Military? You have that look."

"No."

She put her hands up. "Okay, I don't have to know, especially in Skopje. Though I would like to ask what you have against City Hospital? It's a wee bit more sanitary than this place."

He flexed his fingers and rolled his neck. "Is there any reason I can't leave?"

"Um, maybe because you should be monitored after replacing two liters of blood?"

"Will it make a difference at this point?"

"I'd think any allergies would have shown up, but there can be other complications. Not to mention possible signs of disease from whatever bit you. A trained dog with sharpened teeth, I assume? Thus the specific bites to major arteries? I gave you an antibiotic in the IV, but the animal could have rabies or another virus. It's best to stick around for at least a few hours."

"I'll take my chances. I'm also starving." He eased off the bed with his back to her and realized he was standing in his boxer briefs. From her slight intake of breath, he guessed she had seen the *irezumi* tattoo sprawled across his back, intertwined with a patchwork of faded scars and burns from the tips of his father's cigarettes.

Someone had folded the rest of his clothes and set them on a plastic chair beside the bed. He reached for his pants and saw her gaze slip to the muscled ridges in his stomach. "I'll let you dress," she said, and stepped out again.

Grey checked the pocket of his jeans and motorcycle jacket. Everything seemed intact, except Dr. Ristov's phone was missing. Grey swore as he remembered Cezar digging in Grey's pocket after the fight. Grey had wanted to send the phone to Interpol.

When he swept the curtain aside, he realized his makeshift cubicle was one of many spread out in a large room with painted concrete walls and fluorescent tube lights. A nurse striding across the room saw him but said nothing.

"Do you have a smaller bandage for my neck?" Grey asked his guardian angel when he stepped into the Spartan, gray-walled waiting area outside the room.

She reached into a medical bag at her side, took out a vial of antibiotic ointment and a packet of bandages, and pressed both items into his hand. She also gave him a piece of paper with her name and number on it. Dr. Cara O'Dwyer. "Call me if you need anything or experience any strange symptoms."

Like turning into a vampire?

He nodded and laid a hand on her arm. "Thank you. For everything."

"Of course. It's my job. Are you sure I can't convince you to stay a bit longer?"

"I'll be fine."

As he moved away, she said, a touch nervously, "Do you live in Skopje? I'm in the country for a while. You can also call me . . . some other time."

He returned the promise in her eyes with regret and genuine attraction of his own. A different day, a different situation. "I'm leaving tonight."

"Well then. You take care of yourself, Dominic Grey. Stay away from violent men and dress those wounds twice a day."

He responded with an assurance that he knew would only apply to the latter.

After Grey left the hospital, which he realized was not far from the Stone Bridge and Alexander Square, he returned to the same touristy restaurant as the night before and ordered the largest breakfast on the menu. Fried eggs, bread, sliced tomatoes, feta, sausages in some type of sticky sauce: he devoured it all as if working to regenerate more of the lifeblood Cezar Speluncescu had tried to drain from him.

A shudder coursed through him as he relived the fight for his life on that foggy bridge. What the hell had happened up there? How could Cezar move that fast? Where did his unnatural strength come from? Again Grey asked himself: what the hell was he dealing with?

The obvious choice, the one the Speluncescu family wanted everyone to believe, was an option Grey refused to entertain.

While hunched over a café Americano after breakfast, doing his best to focus on reality instead of fantasy, Grey debated whether to leave Skopje that evening. Though he had no desire to stick around, in fact it was dangerous for his health, Grey wasn't sure where to go next. He sensed Cezar had moved on, but he needed to rule that out before he ran blindly to a new destination.

Even if he stayed for a night or two, he knew he couldn't see Cara, as much as the prospect enticed him. He couldn't place her in danger. The world needed its saints alive and healthy.

He knew of one person who might have an answer to his questions. Someone whom Grey had a strong desire to visit so they could have a little chit chat about the incident on the bridge.

Later that night, just after eleven p.m. in a wealthy suburb of Skopje, Dr. Bogdan Ristov opened the door to his upstairs study and turned on the lights. For the second time in as many days, he was greeted by the cold hard stare of Dominic Grey.

"Shut the door and take a seat," Grey said from a few steps away.

After freezing like a startled deer, Dr. Ristov's eyes flicked to the hallway as if judging his chance of escape.

"Don't think," Grey said quietly as he unfolded his arms to reveal a fixed blade knife he had picked up in the Turkish Quarter earlier in the day. "Do."

Dr. Ristov blanched. "My bodyguard—"

"Has no idea I'm here, and will never reach you in time. Your cameras are easy to circumvent too. I suggest an upgrade on both."

After hesitating a moment longer, Dr. Ristov closed the door and took a seat in the leather office chair behind his mahogany desk.

"I'll give you the benefit of the doubt with your daughters," Grey said. "You probably thought Cezar would kill me."

"What are you talking about?"

"Don't bother." After breakfast, Grey had purchased a thin black scarf that would not look out of place in the chilly Skopje weather. He lowered the scarf to reveal the blood-encrusted puncture wounds on his neck. "You know exactly what I mean."

At the sight of the twin wounds, Dr. Ristov seemed to disappear into his chair. "Are you . . ."

"A vampire? Maybe. I don't know, and it's irrelevant to this discussion."

Dr. Ristov's voice was hoarse. "I don't have any control over him, I swear."

"But you let him know him where I'd be. I told you what would happen if you crossed me."

"Please don't hurt my daughters."

"I'm not pond scum like you. But if you don't tell me where I can find Cezar, right this damn second, I *am* going to hurt *you*."

"You're not listening. I told you. *I don't know how to find him.*"

As Grey took a step forward, Dr. Ristov's hand moved slyly towards the top drawer of the desk. "Why risk your life when you could line your pockets instead? I can make you a rich man."

"Refer back to the *pond scum* comment."

Dr. Ristov sneered as he pulled a Glock 17 out of the drawer. "No one cares about them, you know. These filthy peasants with no hope. They're nothing but a plague, a drain on our resources. I'm doing the country a service."

In the long wait for the doctor to arrive, Grey had debated the morality of simply killing him. The filth he had just spouted only increased Grey's desire. Rarely had he loathed a human being this much, and killing him would put a dent in an abominable practice plaguing the lives of poor and downtrodden

Macedonians. A small dent, but a dent nonetheless, and small dents added up to larger ones.

Killing Dr. Ristov would save innocent lives.

But the balance of those lives hung in the future and not the present.

A different justification.

What it came down to, Grey supposed, was not whether killing Dr. Ristov would make the world a better place.

At first blush, that was easy.

That was truth.

Except maybe it wasn't. Grey had given a lot of thought to the cycle of violence afflicting humanity and how to alleviate it. As much as this well-fed ghoul with the trimmed fingernails deserved punishment for his crimes, maybe cold-blooded murder was not the path to a better world.

The best barometer of his own actions, Grey had always felt, was not his righteous anger or the law of the land. It was whether he could close his eyes at night and live with himself.

And he had lost enough sleep in his lifetime.

The next sequence of events happened as he had imagined it would. Grey sprang forward, causing Dr. Ristov to stand, point the Glock at Grey's face, and pull the trigger.

Click.

Click click click click click click click click.

"I was really hoping you would do that," Grey said. When he had entered the office, his first act was to search it for weapons. He had found the gun, removed the bullets, and replaced the Glock for just this very reason.

Because trying to kill him *was* a present action.

Dr. Ristov shrieked and threw the empty gun at Grey's head. Grey leaned to the side to avoid it, then caught Dr. Ristov by his shirt as he tried to run away.

Grey jerked him back in the seat. "Put your right hand on the table."

"What?"

Grey raised the knife. "Do it now."

With a whimper, Dr. Ristov raised his eyes to meet Grey's, disbelieving. Grey pointed the tip of the knife at his eye.

"Don't," Dr. Ristov said as he lifted a shaky hand and set it on the desk.

"Palm down," Grey said.

Dr. Ristov started to breathe heavily as he slowly flipped over his hand.

"Bite down on your arm."

"Why?"

"So you'll stay quiet and I don't have to kill you."

A bead of sweat dripped off Dr. Ristov's forehead, and he had a dazed stare in his eyes. "Cezar will come back for you. Let me go and I'll do what I can. Try to call him off. I swear it."

Grey placed the edge of the knife against the doctor's throat and pressed hard enough to draw blood. "You have to the count of three. I'm already at one."

Dr. Ristov's eyes flew around the room as if seeking a desperate, last-second salvation. Grey pressed even harder, and the doctor clamped his teeth over his doughy forearm just before Grey reversed the knife and slammed the hilt down on the brittle bones comprising the back of his hand.

Dr. Ristov bucked like a wild stallion, his roar muffled by the flesh of his own arm. For a moment Grey thought he might pass out, but instead the doctor leaned back in his chair, gulping in deep breaths, moaning as he cradled his ruined hand.

"I hope you never lift a scalpel again," Grey said.

Dr. Ristov rocked back and forth in the chair, repeating a phrase in his own language over and over.

Grey snapped a finger in his face. "Pay attention. We're almost done here. Where's Cezar?"

"I don't know."

Grey reversed the knife again and held the blade lengthwise across his throat. "Last chance."

"I don't *know*," Dr. Ristov said, his voice rising to a hysterical whine. "Are you stupid? Deaf? You've taken my profession, what else can you do to me? Cezar doesn't tell us where he lives, where he goes. I do what he says and not the other way around. I was told he left Skopje this morning and that's it. There is nothing more to say. Maybe he went to America, maybe to Antarctica. *I don't know*. Kill me if you must, break all the bones in my body, but my answer to that question won't and can't change."

Grey heard the truth in his voice as one of his daughters called out from downstairs. "*Tato?*"

Frustrated by the lack of information, both ashamed and grimly satisfied by his own actions, Grey gave the surgeon a final threatening stare before he climbed out the same window through which he had entered.

Resigned to staying in a cheap hotel for the night, Grey took a taxi to Čaršija, a charming hillside neighborhood with winding cobblestone streets, an authentic Turkish bazaar, and the oldest buildings in the city. Filled with teahouses and mosques and restaurants, the streets were still lively enough for Grey to wander in anonymity while he thought. He was not yet tired and did not feel like holing up in a cramped room with stale air. It was risky to roam the streets, but at the moment he just didn't give a damn.

The encounter with Dr. Ristov had left him feeling greasy, unwashed on the inside. For years Grey had struggled to believe in that spark of goodness among men, and monsters like Cezar Speluncescu and Dr. Bogdan Ristov did not help Grey's faith.

As the night deepened, Grey found himself keeping to the lighted sections of the town, staying close to open establishments and within the orbit of drunken tourists and edgy locals roaming the neighborhood. Normally Grey would have strayed to the shadows, keeping to the perimeter of human activity, a lone wolf observing the flock.

Was Cezar out there somewhere, smiling in the darkness? Watching Grey at this very moment?

Did he have minions, more people who were . . . afflicted . . . like him and his brothers?

Were the murky corners of this town festering with glistening fangs and pale white hands and men who sniffed the air like animals?

Grey's phone rang. Startled by the late call, annoyed at how jumpy he was, he looked down and saw that it was Mari. Grey stepped under the awning of a closed restaurant to take the call. A rowdy British pub was right across the street.

"Grey? You're okay?"

"I'm fine. You're up late."

"I couldn't sleep." After a pause, she said, "I . . . I'm glad you're okay. Some things happened. I was worried and have a lot to tell you. How's it going there?"

"Not too well. I found Cezar, but I think he popped in to say hello and left town."

"My uncle?"

"They have him all right. I don't know where."

A sob escaped Mari. Over the next half an hour, they exchanged abbreviated accounts of their activities since they had parted. Mari listened in shock as Grey described his encounter with Cezar. He did not want to terrify her, but she needed to know what they were dealing with.

"Jesus," she said. "I can't believe . . ."

"Me either. I don't know what's going on. Just stay out of harm's way and let me deal with it. I don't mean to be overbearing, but I just . . . the danger is very real, Mari."

"I know," she said quietly, and relayed an incredible tale to Grey that a former journalist had told her in the crypt of a church in Prague.

A tale that, after the events of the last twenty-four hours, did not seem as impossible to Grey as it once would have.

At the end of her story, she told him what Erik had written on a piece of paper he had given her: the name of the orphanage in Bucharest owned by Dumitra Speluncescu, and the identity of the groundskeeper who had facilitated the kidnapping of children for her.

"The orphanage has changed names a couple of times," Mari said. "It's why I didn't call you earlier. I spent the day trying to research it. But the one I just gave you is current."

"Does Dumitra still own it?"

"I don't know. Her name isn't listed, but we know she works through shells. Plus it's Romania. She could just pay to keep her name off."

"What about the groundskeeper?"

"I got his name but it's a dead end. There aren't any records I could find. I'm sorry."

"Don't be. That's great work, Mari."

"I'm doing my best, and it's not enough. I feel him slipping away, Grey."

"I promise you we'll find him," he said, wondering if that would be the second promise to a woman that night he couldn't keep.

"Thanks for saying that," she said in a small voice. "What are you going to do next?"

Grey checked his watch. It was almost one a.m. "Get a few hours of sleep and take the first flight to Bucharest."

-18-

When Viktor looked back and saw the man in the shearling jacket walking down the street outside Dr. Fessler's house, Viktor's hands felt clammy, and blood began to pound in his ears.

He had no doubt it was the same man he had noticed earlier that night. Even from forty yards away, a puddle of light from a streetlamp illuminated the same lean and weathered face, bushy sideburns, and camel-colored scarf slung around his neck.

The second appearance of the same man that night—someone obviously following Viktor around town—made an earlier question rise to the forefront of his thoughts.

Why *had* the man crossed the road to avoid the old woman selling garlic?

Viktor told himself the answer remained the same: another calculated ploy by the Speluncescus to twist his mind and make him believe the unbelievable.

Viktor was standing at an intersection near the edge of the university campus. He could not retreat to Dr. Fessler's townhome without passing the man in the shearling coat. In fact, the wild thought entered his mind that maybe Dr. Fessler had played a part in this. How *had* the Speluncescus found Viktor so quickly? Dr. Fessler was obsessed with vampire lore—was it possible he was part of their network? The name *Renfield* sprang into Viktor's head. With a snarl, he pushed it away. *It's only a novel.*

A decision had to be made. The fastest way to his hotel was via the paved walkway that cut through the campus. But he saw no pedestrians in that direction. He had no idea who this man was—he had not called out or made a threatening gesture—but he was obviously following Viktor, and he did not want to be caught alone with him. Viktor did not even have his kris, the wavy Indonesian dagger he liked to carry on dangerous cases. He had no protection other than his imposing size and a cell phone he could use to call for help.

Neither of which, he knew, would help him in the immediacy of an attack from a trained adversary two decades his junior.

A thick layer of clouds veiled the night sky and snuffed the light of the moon. A light rain began to fall again.

Viktor hunched his shoulders and started walking.

He chose to stay on the street and circumvent the university. It was a longer route to his hotel, but he knew the route and would not have to consult a map. More importantly, there would be more people.

Viktor hurried down the avenue to his left, walking three full blocks with the campus on his right, glancing over his shoulder every few steps. The man in the shearling coat kept pace with him but did not gain ground.

What is he playing at? Is he herding me somewhere? Am I walking right into a trap?

Viktor kept a constant eye out for a cab. Both the traffic and the number of pedestrians increased as he passed the next intersection and veered towards the city center, making him feel less exposed, able to duck into one of the open bars or restaurants if the man behind him made a move. Instead his pursuer kept a steady forward pace, staying right with Viktor when he used his long stride to walk faster. The implacable nature of the pursuit began to grate on Viktor's nerves almost as much as if the man had started to chase him. It felt as if Viktor was the prey for a predator who was in no great rush, someone who knew he could take his time and await the perfect moment to close in for the kill.

At last Viktor spotted the lights of his hotel in the distance, less than two blocks away. He did not break into a run—he had too much pride for that unless absolutely necessary—but he carried forward as quickly as his stride would allow. He had rarely felt so relieved as the moment when the doorman opened the glass door to his hotel and welcomed Viktor back.

On the way inside, Viktor turned and noticed the man in the shearling coat standing on the sidewalk across the street beneath a streetlamp, staring at Viktor with a steady, emotionless expression. Buoyed by the safety of the hotel, Viktor held the man's gaze for a long moment, wondering if he would dare to come any closer. Instead the man turned and walked leisurely down the street in the opposite direction.

If the man had wanted to catch Viktor, he could have. The professor also suspected the man had already known the hotel where Viktor was staying. The man had found him earlier in the day and at Dr. Fessler's house. He seemed to know all of Viktor's plans.

A point had been made, a warning delivered.

The pertinent question, Viktor knew, was how many more he would receive.

Rattled by the events of the night, fingers twitching for a glass of absinthe, Viktor settled for a steaming shower and a Perrier from the minibar. He supposed he could send the concierge to a liquor store but decided he could survive the night without the help of his muse.

After pulling the curtains and double-checking the chain lock on the door to his suite, he retired to the sofa and tried to call Grey again.

Still no answer.

He texted Grey to call him as soon as possible. Viktor wanted to contact Mari and apologize for the extended delay, but he dared not involve her, not even with a quick call. He debated ordering her back to the United States, but she was too old for paternalistic edicts. He also had the suspicion that if he tried such a tactic, or hinted at the danger he was in, it could backfire, and she would insist on becoming involved.

Instead he took a more circuitous route to protect her. He needed to call Lieutenant Andrasko anyway, to check on developments with the case or with the Speluncescus.

He glanced at his watch. Eleven p.m. Unless the lieutenant had collapsed from exhaustion, he suspected she was awake and working. He tried her number. She answered on the second ring.

"It's late," she said. "Is everything okay?"

"I'm in no immediate danger, but I would not classify the situation as *okay*."

He briefed her on his conversations at the university and with Dr. Fessler. He also told her about the man who had followed him home, leaving out the episode with the old woman selling garlic. Viktor found this too . . . speculative . . . to mention to the lieutenant.

"That's troubling," she said. "How did they know where you were?"

"I've no idea."

"They're telling you what they think about your involvement," she said. "Come home, Viktor. It's getting too dangerous."

"I'll take more precautions going forward."

"Why won't you listen? You're on your own out there."

"As I was for many years," he said evenly.

"The Speluncescus are obviously concerned with your investigation. That's beneficial to the case and bad for your personal safety. What are you getting close to? Is it just their criminal empire?"

"Those are the same questions I'm asking."

"There's been an interesting development. Do you remember the disappearances of young women in Prague I mentioned?"

"Indeed."

"Last night, someone called in a tip about strange noises coming from the apartment of a street sweeper in Nové Město. We put a tail on him and caught him bringing a drugged woman home after his shift. Purses and undergarments from two of the missing girls showed up in his apartment. He hasn't confessed but the evidence is clear."

"Does that impact the case against Florin?"

"It got me thinking, and I have a new theory. Or an alternate one. From everything we know about Florin—and your recent interviews seem to agree—he is not the murderous type. Oh, sure he could have done it. I have no problem with that. People snap and you never really know what's inside them. But what if he *didn't* do it?"

"Does the evidence not point strongly to his involvement?"

"Sometimes the evidence is misleading. Who else is involved with this case who might have killed someone in such a horrific manner? Someone who might better fit the profile?"

Viktor did not have to think long. "His brother. Cezar."

"Exactly. Europol is convinced he's a hardened criminal, and we've both met the man. Who's a better fit for the crime, Cezar Speluncescu, or his sensitive little brother?"

"Is there any evidence he was in the city at the time?"

"No, but we have no idea *where* he was. So why not there, with his brothers?"

"But why? It doesn't fit the family profile. They don't like publicity."

"I have a theory about that too. What if Cezar came to teach his little brother a lesson? What if the Speluncescus didn't like how Florin was behaving? As you just said, they operate in the exact opposite manner. The family hides who they are, or excuse me, what they would like others to believe they are. But Florin flaunted it. Went around the city like a vampire movie star. Maybe a very powerful object lesson was delivered."

"But the lesson was interrupted," Viktor said, running with the theory. "Maybe Cezar was forced to leave Daryna in the alley. When you started digging, the family couldn't risk the exposure, so they took Florin out of the city."

"Or killed him," the lieutenant said quietly.

"Yes. Or killed him."

"Either way, Daryna's murderer is still out there. We're at a bit of a loss on our end, and the pressure is mounting. The news gets more lurid by the day. Tourism is taking a hit, and the mayor wants answers. You won't believe this, but there's even a vampire hunter who arrived from London and announced his presence to the tabloids."

"Oh, I can believe it."

"We took your advice and tracked down all the known fangsmiths—I can't believe I just used that word—in Prague, as well as in Paris and New York. There aren't that many. We showed them photos of all the Speluncescus, and no one remembers creating fangs for any of them. We've increased patrols in Old Town, and I'm sorry to say there's been incidents involving the vampire community. Attacks on innocent people. Someone threw a pipe bomb into the Parlor and caused extensive damage."

"People fear what they don't understand," Viktor said. "I'm afraid little has changed from the medieval societies who saw deformities as the mark of the devil and put witches to the bonfire."

"I'm afraid you're right. Keep me informed, Viktor. And for the love of God, don't take unnecessary risks."

The next morning, Viktor received an email from Dr. Agnes Szekely, Professor of Medieval Studies at the Budapest campus of Central European University. His research revealed she was a highly credentialed scholar who published on a regular basis in the most prestigious journals in her field. Viktor agreed with Dr. Fessler that she appeared to be a source of deeper knowledge on the Order of the Dragon.

Professor Szekely wrote that she would be happy to talk to Viktor on short notice, either by phone or web cam or in person.

Viktor had half a mind to rent a driver for the day and go to Sighisoara, the childhood home of Vlad the Impaler. A scenic little town in the heart of Transylvania which Viktor had visited before, Sighisoara was less than three hours' drive from Cluj. He had a wild notion to short-circuit his research by scouring Sighisoara's cemeteries and ancient buildings for the emblem of the crossed spears, then work to establish a tie, if he found the emblem, between the modern Speluncescus and the infamous Drăculești family. Perhaps the crossed spears were a forgotten family crest of the Drăculeștis, or important to them in some way.

While an attractive theory, he had no basis for it. First off, Sigismund's establishment of the Order of the Dragon predated the rise of the House of Drăculești. Why would Vlad II, Vlad the Impaler, or another descendant alter the symbol of the Order of the Dragon? Perhaps as a slap in the face to Christianity? Contrary to the popular mythology, the Vlads had no problem taking up the cross to defend their homeland against the infidel Turks. Indeed, that was the sole purpose of the Order of the Dragon.

Also, if the Speluncescus were related to the Drăculeștis and wished to perpetuate the vampire myth, why change their name? On the other hand, it fit with their modus operandi of avoiding the limelight.

He decided to stay the course and consult the expert.

After debating a Zoom call from the safety of his hotel, Viktor decided to get on a plane to Budapest. He preferred to meet in person, the flight was very short, and he might need to make a side trip to one of the museums that housed some of the remaining relics from the Order of the Dragon.

Most of all, he didn't want to stay in Cluj-Napoca or Romania a second longer. The man in the shearling coat, and presumably the Speluncescus, knew Viktor was in Cluj. He would feel better as soon as he left the borders of Romania, especially the dark and ancient forests of Transylvania.

Viktor wrote Professor Szekely, set up a meeting for that evening, made travel arrangements to Budapest, and packed his bag. As he pressed the number for the concierge, he couldn't stop thinking about something Dr. Fessler had said about the origin of the vampire legend.

Where did it come from, and why are the legends so prevalent and so potent in Eastern Europe?

Why indeed, Viktor wondered.

Bucharest, Romania

-19-

After leaving Skopje in the early morning, Grey flew to Bucharest, changed into a polo shirt and sport coat he bought at the airport, rented a motorcycle, and wound through the smog-and-diesel choked streets of the inner city. He crossed the city and entered a depressing suburb full of asthmatic Soviet cars, matchbox houses behind security walls made of corrugated iron, wires strung haphazardly overhead, laundry hanging out of windows, and old women selling vegetables and skinned chickens on street corners.

Eventually warehouses and then light industry replaced the houses. Beneath a gloomy afternoon sky, just as plots of vegetables and pastureland began to appear, he pulled up to a four-story concrete building that, except for the lack of guards, could easily have passed for a prison.

A faded coat of beige paint on the exterior. Bars on the windows. Tall barbed-wire fencing around the rear of the property meant not to deter outsiders, but to keep its unfortunate occupants from escaping.

Patches of scrub grass dotted the muddy grounds. While it was late afternoon on a mild day, Grey detected no signs of life inside or out, as if the building were abandoned instead of an orphanage housing upwards of four hundred children. They might as well have hung a sign out front that said, "Abandon all hope, ye who enter here."

Though Grey had been young, he remembered when the eyes of the world were riveted in horror on Romania's state-run orphanages after the fall of Ceauşescu. Grey did not remember the details but had done a little homework on the flight from Skopje. The accounts from the journalists and medical workers who had first entered the orphanages had made him feel numb, ashamed to be a human being. Starving, naked children banging their bowls for food in communal mess halls. Emaciated toddlers sitting in their own urine and feces, with no one to pick them up when they cried. Lightless rooms with no heat in the harsh Romanian winters, growth-stunted children lurking about like ghouls, bereft of human love and contact, their mental and emotional deficiencies even more acute than the physical ones. Rocking back and forth or hitting their heads in an effort to self-stimulate.

Grey parked the bike and approached the orphanage on an uneven cobblestone path with weeds spilling out of the borders. By all accounts, conditions had improved in Romania since the 1990s, but there were still orphanages and desperate poverty and yawning societal ills. He did not know what to expect other than misery, especially at an orphanage once—and maybe still—owned by Dumitra Speluncescu.

More than most, Grey understood a glimmer of the hardships these kids had undergone. Raised by an abusive father, Grey had left home as a teenager after his mother died from cancer. Not long after her death, Grey's father had come home drunk yet again, a nightly occurrence, ready to take out his frustrations with the world and his own inadequacies on his son.

Without the calming presence of his mother as an intermediary, Grey, swollen like a blood-filled tick with loathing for his father, had snapped. They had fought. Grey's father was much bigger, a former Marine, and a tough old bastard. But he was piss drunk and not a jujitsu prodigy like his son. After leaving his father moaning on the floor in a pool of his own blood, Grey walked out of the door and never went back.

Grey had never trusted an authority figure again. He had issues with blind orders from his first day in basic training to the day he refused to release sniper fire from a dusty hilltop into a crowd of villagers.

Maybe that crowd was full of terrorists like his commander had said.

But Grey couldn't pull that trigger.

Over the years, to come to grips with his own past and better understand what Charlie and the other students at the Washington Heights homeless shelter were going through, Grey had studied up a bit on child homelessness. Exposés on Romanian orphanages had led to important psychological studies on early development in humans and other primates. The studies reached the same conclusion: the earlier that children were orphaned, the worse they fared. A mind-numbing percentage of infants separated from their caregivers before their second birthdays suffered from psychological disorders and emotional trauma as adults. They often lacked empathy and the ability to love and trust others. Their tiny brains, instead of forming healthy connections of neurons, withered and atrophied like plants trying to grow in a closet with no light.

After Grey's mother died, he had lived on the streets or in seedy motels for years, fighting on the underground circuit and training with the most grueling martial arts schools he could find, wandering from city to city across Asia and then Europe, a lost soul in search of something he could never quite find. He had it rough. He knew what it was like to be alone and hate the holidays and feel like the entire world was against you.

Yet Grey's mother had been a stable presence throughout his childhood. His brain and his body had not been stunted from birth by a lack of human touch and affection. His research had taught him how lucky he was in comparison to others.

Working to corral his frustration with the world, Grey focused on the present and tried the door to the orphanage. Unlocked. He stepped inside and found himself in a dimly lit foyer that smelled like used gym socks left in a bag for weeks.

A trio of hallways with concrete flooring led deeper into the building. Grey heard a scream in the distance, followed by a harsh shout and a banging sound. Visions of workers abusing children dressed in rags danced in his head.

Grey opened the door to the administrative office on the left side of the foyer. The middle-aged woman behind the desk looked startled to see him. She set her pen down and said something in Romanian.

Grey kept his voice as polite as possible. "I'm sorry, do you speak English?"

"A little," she said.

"I'm here to inquire about adopting a child."

"You have appointment?"

"No."

"This is not possible. Need papers. Procedures. Big process."

Grey pretended not to understand and kept repeating his request. Another employee emerged from a cubicle in the back and reinforced to Grey in halting

English that it was not possible to adopt a child in person. Grey waved his arms, spoke very fast, and asked to see someone in charge. The two staff workers grew more and more flustered. Grey gave them a glimpse of his passport and began to plead in a firm but non-aggressive manner. He refused to leave and kept repeating his request.

The woman behind the desk raised her voice and pointed at the door. Grey stood firm. She picked up the receiver to a rotary analog phone and made a call. He was worried she would call security or even the authorities but after a moment, she stood and said, in a curt voice, "Follow please."

Now obedient, Grey padded along behind her, hoping his instincts about the director would prove correct.

That the person on the other end of the line had heard Grey's request and sniffed an opportunity.

The woman took him down the hallway that ran beside the front office, a better lit corridor that smelled of lemon antiseptic. The first door on the left had a plaque beside it that read DIRECTOR ALBESCU. She opened the door and ushered Grey through with an impatient wave.

"Thank you," he said.

She spun on her heel and returned down the hallway, her footsteps echoing on the concrete.

During the Ceaușescu regime, the worst abuses had taken place in the *Cămin Spital Pentru Copii Deficienți* orphanages for disabled children. Direct translation: Home Hospitals for Irrecoverable Children.

Who labels a child *irrecoverable*?

According to Mari, the orphanage Grey was standing in was one of these types. Even though Nicolai Ceaușescu and his wife were executed by a firing squad, almost no one associated with the orphanages had been prosecuted for crimes against children. In fact, many of the workers had kept their jobs—including the silver-haired man with an aquiline nose sitting behind the polished mahogany desk, watching Grey with an oily smile that broke the spell of his dignified bearing. A gold signet ring gleamed on his left index finger.

Grey offered a hand. The director stood to accept, then returned to his comfortable leather chair. Romantic black-and-white photos of Bucharest hung on the wall beside folksy knickknacks such as hand-painted plates and embroidered tea towels.

The director folded his hands atop the desk and spoke in English. "I hear you wish to adopt a child."

Grey took a seat on the other side of the desk. "Very much so."

"Where are you from?"

"New York."

"A wonderful city. I haven't visited in years. Have you filled out an adoption application? If you've traveled all this way, I'm sure you realize there are proper channels for adoption in this country?"

The director had a thick accent but spoke with excellent grammar. Grey met his gaze for a long moment. "These channels are unavailable to me," he said evenly, dropping the pretense of a prospective parent.

Children with disabilities or of Roma descent—the ones sent to *Cămin Spital Pentru Copii Deficienți*—were unwanted by Romanians. While there would still be some red tape for an American wishing to adopt such a child, Grey could not imagine it would be that difficult. Trying to speed up the process in an illegal manner would not be worth the risk.

Thus the director had to suspect there was only one reason why someone might walk into an orphanage like his and try to circumvent the adoptions laws.

Because that type of someone was the last person on Earth who should be around a child.

"You must know this is an impossible request," the director said.

Grey smiled. "I believe every impossible thing has a price."

Pretending to be a monster took every ounce of self-control Grey possessed, and, like even the simplest act of violence, chipped away a tiny little piece of his soul.

The director sat back in his chair and clasped his hands in his lap. Grey wondered if he had miscalculated and the director was about to call the police. But instead of reaching for the phone, the director unlocked his fingers and began to rub the top of his signet ring with his left thumb.

"Name your price," Grey said, sensing an opening. "I'll do anything." He wanted to seem like a desperate customer instead of a shrewd businessman. Someone the director could manipulate.

After a long moment, the director's eyes flicked to the closed door. "Write down what I tell you," he said as he pushed a pen and a pad of sticky notes across the desk, "and never come here again."

The sun had sunk beneath the skyline of Bucharest by the time Grey grabbed some fast food off the highway, made his way all the way across the city, ditched the Polo and sport coat for a black long-sleeve shirt and motorcycle jacket, and approached a nightclub on the edge of a slum. The club occupied the bottom floor of a ten-story concrete building with chunks of concrete missing, as if hit by mortar shells and never repaired. A sign above the black-painted door proclaimed the name of the establishment, *Roz*, in garish neon letters.

Director Albescu had provided Grey with three pieces of information: an address, a time, and a name. Grey was staring at the address, and he had arrived an hour before nine p.m., the meeting time with the person the director had given him.

A name which happened to be the same one Mari had uncovered. A groundskeeper who had once facilitated the kidnapping of children for Dumitra Speluncescu.

Grey parked his rental bike, a red Honda Africa Twin with white chrome, a block from the club. He walked back, arriving early on purpose so he could scope out the scene. He let the doorman frisk him, paid ten *leus* to get in, and stepped into an open space the size of a small warehouse.

The lighting was very dim except for a violet glow illuminating the stage in the center of the room, where two naked women gyrated around a pair of poles and with each other. Boisterous working class men were seated on benches below the stage or at tables with folding chairs spread throughout the room. The interior had very little decoration other than a corner bar and a gold curtain along one wall. Ceiling speakers pumped in banal Europop. The air was stale, the floor sticky, and he caught a faint odor of sour milk.

Depressing.

As he waited, he catalogued the features of the room and the faces of the patrons. No one suspicious jumped out at him. He suspected the location of the meeting was chosen to weed out honest people seeking an actual adoption. He doubted John Smith from small-town USA would be comfortable sitting in a strip club in a Bucharest slum to negotiate the addition of a new family member.

Grey ordered a beer and tipped the dancers now and again to ensure no one took undue notice of him. After every three songs, the dancers worked the room while a new pair of women stepped out from behind the gold curtain and took the stage.

Just after nine p.m., a wiry man with thinning hair and a sloping forehead walked in smoking a cigarette. Like the other patrons, his clothing was nondescript, work boots and dark slacks and a gray wool coat a touch short at the sleeves. The newcomer exchanged a laugh with the doorman, nodded at the barman, and took a look around the club. When he saw Grey, he approached his table, his left foot dragging behind him as he walked.

"You are meeting someone?" he said to Grey in harshly accented English. Up close, Grey could see acne scars pitting his face, and noticed his fingernails were dirty and unkempt.

"Petru Lupei," Grey said. "Is that you?"

The man jabbed a finger at his chest and grinned. One of his teeth was chipped. The rest were crooked and nicotine-stained. Grey guessed his age in the early fifties, but smoking and hard living had taken their toll, and he might have been younger.

Petru's gaze wandered to the stage, his eyes glowing with lust. On the way to the nightclub, remembering how the journalist Mari had met was targeted by the Speluncescus, Grey worried Director Albescu might have set him up. But as he watched this simpleton sitting across the table leering at the women onstage, Grey's fears in this regard were mostly quieted. His greater worry was trusting himself to keep his cool as he engaged with this piece of trash who ferried orphans to organ traffickers and pedophiles.

"The director sent me," Grey said. "He told me you could help."

Petru's gaze snapped over to Grey, and he wagged a finger in Grey's face. "No no no. No speak of him. Do business with me."

"Sure," Grey said, resisting the urge to snatch the finger out of the air and break it in half. "My apologies."

A simpleton indeed, Grey thought as he pretended to be cowed. Petru takes all the risk while the director sits in his comfortable office with his gold signet ring.

The bartender walked over to hand Petru a beer, then said something that caused Petru to cackle and glance at Grey. After the bartender left, Petru resumed staring at the stage and spoke to Grey out of the side of his mouth. "What do you want? Male, female, other?"

Grey swallowed. "Female."

"How old? More young, more money."

Grey was glad Petru was looking at the stage, because Grey knew his revulsion for this process showed in his eyes. "A teen," Grey mumbled.

Petru nodded sagely. "Is good. Easy order. Blond, brunette? Short, tall?"

"First available."

Petru's skinny head swiveled to regard Grey. His leer returned, and he patted Grey on the hand. "A hungry man. *Da*, I understand. I help you. The price is two thousand leus. You pay this?"

Grey did a quick calculation in his head. Five hundred U.S. dollars.

The black-market price for a young girl.

After doing his best to look concerned by the fee, yet nonetheless willing to pay, Grey said, "I can do that."

"One week, you come back here. Same time. Alone. We meet. You pay. I give you girl."

Grey didn't want to ponder how he was supposed to take a human trafficking victim out of the city and then the country, not to mention the nightclub, or what this vile man thought Grey would do with her after that. "Agreed. I'll see you in a week with your money."

"*Da*, is good. Cash only. One more thing." Petru gripped Grey's arm and dug his filthy nails into his skin. "Who are you?"

Grey had expected this question and prepared for it. Though surprised Director Albescu had never asked for his name, Grey reasoned the director wanted as little to do with the transaction as possible.

Except, of course, pocketing the lion's share of the fee.

Grey showed Petru a fake driver's license he carried in his wallet. John Lionel Ramsdale was a deceased insurance salesman from Omaha, Nebraska, given new life in the datasphere—with Grey's photo superimposed—by a hacker from Los Angeles who a mercenary acquaintance of Grey's had once recommended. Over the years, Grey had run into enough situations in need of false credentials that he had decided to acquire a permanent one.

"No passport, John?"

"Not that I carry around the streets of Bucharest at night."

Petru removed his hand from Grey's arm to inspect the driver's license, and took a photo of both sides. "We make sure you are who you say."

"Understood."

With a grunt, Petru left the table and moved to the bench seating beneath the stage. Grey stayed long enough to finish his beer and left. He doubted the director would do anything other than a rudimentary records check on the driver's license. In any event, Grey would not be returning in a week. Grey had only showed up at the nightclub to allay suspicion and buy himself time. He planned to search Petru's home and follow him around town, see if he could connect the dots to one of the Speluncescus or someone close to them.

Down the street, Grey found a seedy bar with a second-floor window that overlooked the front of club Roz. The rough men in the bar gave him sidelong glances which Grey either ignored, or, if they lasted long enough, returned with an even harder stare. Thankfully no one started any trouble as he nursed a beer by the window and waited for Petru to leave.

An hour and a half later, the pockmarked Romanian shuffled out of the strip club with his arm around a young woman with purple hair, a denim jacket with sequins, and fishnet stockings. Grey had already paid his tab. He left the bar and followed the pair down the street towards the slum. Plenty of people were out and about, and by the way Petru was clutching the young woman to his side and lurching about as if drunk, Grey had little worry of being noticed.

Petru turned down a side street filled with potholes. The shabby neighborhood consisted mostly of duplexes with tarpaper roofs, broken windows, and trash strewn about the yards. At the next intersection, the housing units gave way to a dystopian warren of concrete apartment buildings in various stages of disrepair.

Petru veered onto an overgrown walkway fronting a duplex with a sagging roof and barred windows. Grey stood behind a van and watched Petru unlock the door to the left side of the duplex, then disappear inside with the woman.

Reasoning these two weren't going anywhere for a while, Grey jogged back to retrieve his motorcycle and parked a block from the duplex, swerving around the deep potholes in the road.

Decision time.

Grey assumed Petru wouldn't leave again that night, but Grey didn't want to miss an opportunity to search the house. He resigned himself to a long wait. Before he took more forceful measures, he wanted to see what secrets he could find in the duplex. That said, he wasn't sure he wanted to peel back the layers on the life of a human trafficker.

Grey walked to a corner with a view of Petru's home. Clouds obscured the moon again. No sign of a streetlamp. All the duplexes looked shuttered. So did the apartment buildings in the distance. It was eerie. Grey wondered if the whole neighborhood was condemned and Petru was squatting. That didn't account for the handful of cars on the street, but on closer inspection, every single one of them had a flat tire or a huge dent in the side.

A dog barking nearby led to a chorus of howls that raised the hair on Grey's arms. Packs of stray dogs roamed the streets of many towns in Romania, including Bucharest. That was an enemy he did not want to fight. He needed to get off the street. After studying his environment for another moment, he started walking towards Petru's house, checking every car door on the way, keeping an eye out for someone watching from a window. He scored on the third vehicle he tried, a dark blue Peugeot missing a front fender.

Food wrappers and smelly clothes were piled on the backseat. Grey grimaced, shoved it all to the floor, hunkered down on the cloth seat, and waited.

The howling grew louder. Soon a pack of mangy dogs loped by, stopping to sniff Grey's car before moving on. Every now and then someone hurried past and disappeared into the ring of lightless apartment buildings.

The events of the day had left Grey feeling filthy and hollowed out. He would have paid large sums of money for a hot shower and a good meal. With no caffeine or sugar to help him stay awake, he kept dozing off despite his best efforts. He slept lightly and did not think he had missed anything, but when the sun rose and cast a feeble light on the blighted neighborhood, exposing more of its warts, Grey could not say for sure that Petru had not left. With a grimace, Grey ignored his dry throat and stayed the course.

An hour later, the woman with the purple hair walked out of the front door, and Grey got a glimpse of Petru. He patted the woman on the rump as she left, which caused her to giggle. Petru disappeared inside again. As soon as the woman turned her back to the house and started walking down the street, her face soured as if she had suddenly fallen ill. She clutched her purse tight to her chest and disappeared in the direction of the club.

Two more hours passed. Grey was forced to urinate in a plastic bottle he found under the seat. Would Petru never leave?

After noon came and went, Grey surmised Petru had stayed up all night with the woman and was sleeping extra late. The other houses on the street did in fact seem abandoned, though whenever someone passed by on the way to the apartment buildings, Grey rolled over and pretended he was sleeping.

Dizzy with thirst and hunger, he decided to take a risk. He slipped out of the car, hurried to the intersection, and looked around. To his left, he spied people on the street two blocks away. He jogged over and saw a street vendor selling hot dogs and sodas. He returned to the car with his bounty, devoured two hot dogs, and guzzled a Coke. A five-star meal in his famished state.

It was a good thing he fueled up, because Petru didn't leave the house for another five hours. Just as Grey debated giving up his stake-out, cramped and miserable in the back seat of the Peugeot, an engine rumbled to life. Though Grey couldn't be sure, he thought the noise had come from a sliver of broken blacktop leading behind Petru's duplex. Grey had not investigated further, fearing he would be seen through a back window.

The engine coughed and gurgled as it picked up. When Grey saw the vehicle squeezing through the driveway of the duplex with Petru in the driver's seat, Grey's stomach clenched, and his fists balled at his side.

It was a geriatric, yellow-and-black American school bus with square headlights that looked as if it had not been in service since the 1950s.

Good God. Someone put this man in charge of transporting children?

Or does he just drive around and pick up strays?

Grey had planned to enter Petru's house as soon as he left. Seeing the school bus made him rethink that decision.

As the bus passed by Grey, turned left at the intersection, and sputtered away, Grey hesitated a moment longer. He knew where Petru lived now, and could search the house anytime, even if he had to stake out the property again.

His gut told him to follow the bus. More importantly, his heart couldn't bear the thought of letting that man anywhere near children when Grey had a chance to intervene.

Maybe the bus was Petru's only transportation and he was going to the store or out to meet a friend.

And maybe he wasn't.

Grey opened the door of the Peugeot and raced to get his bike.

During the long wait in the car, Grey had used his cell phone to familiarize himself with the surrounding streets. He caught up with the school bus as it was turning onto the avenue leading to downtown.

Following the bus through Bucharest was a simple matter. Petru had never seen the rental motorcycle, and Grey had a helmet on. The streets were clogged with two-wheeled vehicles, and with riders wearing black leather jackets similar to Grey's. The school bus chugged along like a heavy smoker struggling to climb a hill, the carburetor sputtering as it worked to accelerate after every stop light or lull in traffic.

When the bus veered onto the ring road winding around the city center, Grey had a suspicion as to the destination. His intuition was confirmed as the bus exited onto the same highway on the south side of town that Grey had taken the previous day. Twenty minutes later, the bus pulled in front of the orphanage Grey had visited, where a group of children waited in line by the curb. The children all wore the same uniform: white shirts, black pants or skirts, and a red scarf tied around their necks. Unlike normal school children, there was no laughing or playing. A stern woman stood with crossed arms at each end of the line to ensure order.

Petru wasn't even banned from the orphanage, Grey realized in shock.

They had just moved him from groundskeeper to bus driver.

Grey kept going and parked within view of the school bus. After the bus collected the children and returned the way it had come, Grey resumed tailing it.

This time, instead of taking the ring road, the bus entered the diesel-choked chaos of central Bucharest. After passing a mind-numbing series of tall, gray, blighted apartment towers, the historic core of the city emerged. Grey still saw plenty of Communist-era buildings smudged with grime and pollution, but the eyesores were alleviated by the graceful cupolas of Orthodox churches, Belle Epoque mansions, and pedestrians ambling through verdant parks.

The school bus passed alongside the largest building Grey had ever seen, a block-long monstrosity that seemed to embody the hubris of Ceausescu's Orwellian fever dream. By this time Grey guessed the children were on a field trip. Maybe he had misjudged things, and there was no ill intent involved, at least not on this day. He would stick around to make sure, then race back to Petru's house and search it while the children attended their event or museum.

After veering onto *Strada Vasile Parvan* for a kilometer, the bus turned left onto a busy tree-lined avenue flanked with commerce and apartment buildings. It came to a stop along the side of the road to disgorge the occupants. Grey parked a safe distance back and watched the children and their wardens cross the street at a stop light and continue down a pedestrian pathway. A large sign at the entrance to the pathway read *Opera Națională București*. The National Opera.

Twilight had fallen. The children must be attending an evening performance. If Petru had stayed with the bus, or walked down the street for some dinner, Grey would have raced back to the duplex.

But Petru had stayed with the children. He was limping along behind the warden at the rear of the line, hands shoved in his pockets, dressed in a felt cap and a shabby brown coat.

That felt off to Grey. Why was a bus driver attending the opera? Maybe he was just walking them to the door. Grey left his helmet with the bike and followed discretely behind on foot, navigating the pedestrian pathway and watching the children walk through the lovely trio of high arched porticos fronting the opera house.

Petru went right with them.

Grey had a sudden twinge in his stomach. He checked his watch: 6:38 p.m. The performance must start at seven. After blowing on his hands to warm them after the chilly ride, Grey approached the opera house, keeping a close eye out for Petru.

Five minutes before seven, giving the children plenty of time to take their seats, Grey slipped inside the marble-floored lobby and bought a ticket. He felt grossly underdressed and exposed when he entered the grand circular theater. The lights had not yet fallen. An usher checked Grey's ticket and led him to the upper level.

He had a seat near the center of the first row of the balcony. Grey lowered his head to shield his face from view as he made his way past the other patrons.

After taking a seat, Grey spotted the children from the orphanage in the front left of the opera house. The group took up an entire section. Petru was with them. He was still wearing his coat, as if he had a chill or did not plan on staying very long.

Soon the classical orchestra struck the first chord, and the sweeping red curtain hiding the stage began to retract. Grey had not even looked to see what was playing. He had never attended a live opera before.

Everything looked normal with the children. He began to relax until, just before the lights dimmed, he glimpsed someone familiar watching the opera from a private VIP box on the side of the theater just above the children. The person he saw, a slim older woman with long dark hair, was dressed in a black evening gown with a diamond choker that sparkled all the way across the room.

Grey caught his breath. He could not be absolutely sure from that distance, but from the photos he had seen, together with the attendance of Petru at the event and the proximity of the VIP box to the children, Grey had a very strong suspicion he was looking at Dumitra Speluncescu.

Budapest, Hungary

-20-

By five p.m. of the same day Viktor had left Cluj-Napoca and flown four hundred miles west to Budapest, he had checked into a five-star hotel with a view of the magnificent Hungarian Parliament, freshened up in his room, sent the concierge to procure a bottle of absinthe on Honvéd Avenue, made time for a late lunch at the Michelin-starred restaurant at the hotel, reread his notes on the Order of the Dragon while he dined, and topped off the afternoon with a cappuccino on a terrace above the Danube. In less than an hour he was scheduled to meet with Dr. Agnes Szekely, Professor of Medieval Studies at the Budapest campus of Central European University.

Though Viktor aimed to keep a low profile, clandestine behavior was not his forte. He would do his best to avoid travel at night and isolated places, and he did not think anyone had followed him to the hotel. With any luck, he would leave Budapest in the morning and return to the relative safety of his home city.

As he gazed down at the water, the hypnotic current of the Danube, one of the great rivers of Europe and a former border of the Roman Empire, made him think of the mesmeric powers attributed to Bram Stoker's infamous count.

Dr. Fessler was right. The sudden transition of the vampire in literature and the eyes of the public was strange. Not only had the repulsive graveyard ghouls of the past transformed seemingly overnight into debonair counts, but the new version of the *wampyr* could influence the actions of men and women with the power of their stare alone.

Do prdele, Viktor admonished himself, vowing not to waste another moment of mental energy on such fantastical ruminations.

Let us see what Dr. Szekely has to say about these crossed spears. Every family comes from somewhere. Not even the Speluncescus can hide from history.

The meeting had been set for six p.m. at the National Széchényi Library. In her correspondence, Dr. Szekely had mentioned she wanted to show Viktor some items from the national archives.

Part of the sprawling Buda Castle complex, the library was just down the river from Viktor's hotel, but the taxi ride took thirty minutes during rush hour. Viktor never failed to marvel at the size and grandeur of the Hungarian Capital. The massive neo-gothic and art-nouveau buildings lining the Danube were a buffet of architectural wonders. While he loved to visit Budapest, and found the hotels and restaurants as first-rate as any in the world, the city did not possess the allure and intimate charm of Prague.

Then again, what city did?

The taxi wound through the tourist infested streets of Várnegyed, or Castle Hill. Buda Castle—ancient residence of Hungarian kings, including Matthias Corvinus—was located on the southern tip of the hill, along with the library and a host of museums. The first stone of the castle had been laid in the thirteenth century, but the site had been razed and rebuilt a number of times over the years.

As Viktor left the taxi and walked across an expansive brick courtyard, he mused that comparing the National Széchényi Library to the average public archive was akin to equating the American Pentagon to a local police station. Housing over eight million items in a five-story building, the library easily contained the most extensive collection of Hungarian literature in the world, including thirty-five codices from the *Bibliotheca Corviniana*.

After passing through a stately archway and into the main entry hall, Viktor spied Dr. Szekely waiting for him near a registration desk. She was a birdlike woman dressed all in black, with a bob haircut streaked with gray and a penetrating gaze that matched the intensity of Viktor's own. For some reason, perhaps because he was a child of the Sixties as well, he could imagine her smoking a slender Capri cigarette and discoursing on civil rights with a room full of intellectuals.

She waved him around the line at the desk. "You are Professor Radek, yes?" she said in English, for which Viktor was grateful. Though he spoke passable Hungarian, it was a very difficult language.

"I am. Thank you for agreeing to meet me on such short notice."

"I'm always happy to support a fellow academic. Though since you haven't taught in some time, and this is not your area of expertise, I must imagine the inquiry involves one of your private cases."

Due to the threat from the Speluncescus, especially the troubling appearance of the man in the shearling coat, Viktor had decided not to disclose the true nature of his inquiry to Dr. Szekely. He had limited his correspondence to mentioning the book of poetry he suspected belonged to the *Bibliotheca Corviniana*, along with the carving on the miniature wooden chest which Dumitra Speluncescu had carried out of the house in Prague.

"I see you've done your own research," he said.

"Just a logical deduction." She curled a finger for him to follow, then turned and began walking. "Why don't we visit the archives while we chat?"

Despite the length of his stride, Viktor found himself hurrying to keep up with this no-nonsense woman as she led him towards a grand marble staircase that a pair of elephants could have navigated side by side. The top of Dr. Szekely's head barely reached Viktor's chest, but she seemed as unmoved by his great height as she was by his credentials.

The next floor up contained walls of glass cases marking the Manuscripts Reading Room and Early Printed Books Archive. As they strolled through the room, Dr. Szekely said, "I have some items on reserve, but may I see the evidence you mentioned?"

On a drafting table in an unoccupied corner of the room, for the second time in as many days, Viktor revealed the photos of the book of poetry by Johannes Cuspinianus, along with his illustration of the carving on Dumitra's chest that resembled the emblem of the Order of the Dragon.

The creases around Dr. Szekely's eyes deepened as she studied the images. "The book does appear to be from the *Corviniana* collection, which I'm sure Professor Fessler confirmed. Remarkable. In a moment, I'll show you a codex with a nearly identical cover."

"I would like that."

She turned to the illustration, hovering above it like a raven peering down from the branch of a tree. "This serpent coiled into an ouroboros is another matter. I've never seen its like."

"You're not convinced it's from the Order of the Dragon? I know my drawing isn't perfect, but I saw the symbol in person, and the parallels seem obvious."

"Except the cross on the serpent's back is formed by two silver spears instead of the typical wooden motif," she said without looking up. "A rather important detail, no?"

"A detail I assumed was of secondary importance to the shape of the dragon."

"Mmm. You know as well as I the danger of assumption. You're correct of course about the similarities, which do imply a relation, but I've never seen this particular motif before, either from the Order or on any heraldic items. That is . . . most curious." She finally looked up. "May I ask where you got this? You mentioned a chest—to whom does it belong? Where did it come from?"

"To be honest, that's what I'm trying to discover." He hesitated, weighing the possible threat to Dr. Szekely simply by mentioning a family name. "If you don't mind, let's focus on the iconography for now." He didn't want to unnerve her by finishing with *for your own protection.*

She gave him a sharp look. "As you wish." After another long moment observing the illustration, she mused, "The crudity of the spear . . . the tapered end without an obvious headpiece, as if carved instead of assembled . . . is that something you remember for certain? Or just the way you drew it?"

"That's how it appeared. Does that mean something?"

"It resembles the older, more archaic versions of the spear. A pointed end carved directly from the shaft—though with wood and not silver, of course. I assume the silver is an aesthetic detail." She tapped a finger against her mouth. "It could certainly be a heraldic symbol, in fact I have a strong feeling it is, but I don't believe the origin is Eastern or Central European. It appears almost . . . Hunnic. Though it could be older. Much older."

"The Huns had coats of arms?"

She chuckled. "Just spears. Some Hungarian families like to proudly trace their lineage to the Huns, as if a relation to warring clans of patriarchal tribesmen was something of which to boast. But I was speaking not to the heraldic symbols themselves, which were likely adopted at a later time, but of the iconography from which they derive."

Hunnic, she had said. Viktor recalled something he had read on one of the placards in Dr. Fessler's attic.

In Stoker's novel, Count Dracula was a Transylvanian nobleman who claimed to be a direct descendant of Attila the Hun.

"What time period are we discussing?" Viktor asked.

"The oldest surviving heraldic emblems are the Germanic equestrian seals of the latter half of the twelfth century. Heraldry developed somewhat earlier, during the chivalric tournaments at the start of the High Middle Ages. As with all iconography, these seals and symbols did not arise out of nowhere. They were based on earlier visual imagery such as coin insignias, field banners, and animal motifs. The familiar lions, eagles, wolves, and of course dragons. We've traced the development of some European coats of arms directly to Scythian art forms as far back as the 7th century *BCE*."

Viktor's eyebrows rose. "Intriguing."

"Especially when you consider the archaeological records we've found, as opposed to what might actually exist, are likely the tip of the iceberg. From where did the Scythian art forms arise? And the ones before that? I read just the other day how a recent find in New Mexico pushed back the timeline for human habitation in the Americas by ten thousand years. That's almost *double* the previous estimate. Remarkable. As a heraldic scholar, I feel certain I can tell you how heraldry developed during the course of the Middle Ages, but I'm just as certain we're in the dark concerning the true origin." She waved a hand. "I realize this is far more information than you require."

"On the contrary," he murmured, thinking that he and Dr. Szekely might share similar philosophies of world history, and could have an interesting discussion one day.

"As for the Order of the Dragon," she said, "the founding documents are quite clear that the Red Cross of Saint George directly inspired the emblem. So the inclusion of the spears on the chest you saw . . . I suppose it's possible it could be a random occurrence without historical significance. An artistic rendition of the cross."

"But if it's not random?"

She shrugged. "Then I suppose it's a mystery."

"What if we assumed the motif on the chest was an emblem or coat of arms belonging to a particular family? Is it possible there's one you haven't seen?"

"Yes, yes, of course. I'm certain there are thousands of undocumented heraldic symbols for minor families, as well as those lost to the ravages of time and war. However, the cross is a problem. Not crossed spears per se—that is not uncommon—but their use within a symbol belonging to the Christian milieu."

Viktor had researched the origins of the cross and its derivations extensively, from the ankh in Egypt to a representation of Tammuz in Chaldea, from the Hindu swastika to burial rites in the Bronze Age. No one knew the ultimate origin of the symbol. Petroglyphic cross-shaped incisions had appeared in European caves as far back as the Upper Paleolithic period. "The cross was a common icon to a multitude of pagan cultures predating Christianity."

"I'm aware of this," she said. "As I said, it's the time period that's the problem."

"I don't quite follow."

"We're talking about medieval Europe. It was a total society. Of religion, that is. Any family with enough money and power to possess heraldic icons would never risk offending the church by taking liberties with its most powerful symbol."

"I see," he said. "Yes, that makes sense. But is it possible the dragon with the cross-shaped spears came from somewhere else? And inspired the emblem of the Order of the Dragon?"

"Yes, it could well have derived from another heraldic symbol or iconography lost to history. Crossed spears on a seal or a coat of arms. Maybe the shape on the chest you saw, the fashioning of the cross, is unique to that piece."

Except Florin Speluncescu wore it on his ring as well.

Still, the train of thought excited him. "Dr. Fessler mentioned a theory concerning the true origins of the Order of the Dragon. He didn't believe Sigismund developed it on his own. What if the crossed spears *did* come from a family emblem—the true progenitor of the Order?" He wagged a finger. "The Order of the Dragon was committed to Christianity, at least on paper. Maybe the crossed spears on the back of the dragon was an early model for the emblem of the Order. A prototype that was rejected because, as you say, it would have raised eyebrows."

As she considered his comment, her eyes narrowed shrewdly. "Come with me," she said, leading him back to the stairs. "Before we view the codices, let's move in a different direction."

They climbed to the next floor and entered a stately reading room surrounded by seemingly endless rows of bookshelves. Just before they turned down one of the long aisles, Viktor glanced back and caught a young woman standing by a bookshelf who looked quickly away. She was very pale and striking, blessed with full red lips and fine boned features, her wavy hair caught in a braid. With her knee-high leather boots and tight-fitting black dress, she did not look like a librarian on duty, nor did women that attractive stare at Viktor these days. For some reason, she looked somewhat familiar, though he felt sure they had never met. With a start, he realized she resembled another raven-haired woman he had seen recently, though a few decades of age separated the two.

Yes, the young woman bore a strong resemblance to Dumitra Speluncescu.

Surely thousands of women in Budapest have those sharp cheekbones and almond-shaped eyes?

Maybe, but are they quite that *beautiful?*

Viktor watched the young woman pull a book off the shelf and peruse the back cover. He pulled his gaze away as Professor Szekely kept walking through the aisles until she reached a corridor that ran along the back side of the room. She crossed the corridor, opened a door that required a special access card, and led him to a private chamber reserved for staff and scholars. The long marble tables in the middle of the room were unoccupied but bore evidence of recent use: open books, notepads, pens, coffee cups.

Professor Szekely approached one of the glass cases along the wall and pulled out a slender clothbound tome. Viktor translated the title in his mind.

Heraldic Symbols of the Order of the Dragon.

"This book is only available in Hungarian. As far as I'm aware, it's the only copy." She slipped on a pair of surgical gloves from her pocket, carefully turned a few pages, and showed him a familiar list of names and titles.

THE FAMILY

"The original twenty-one members of the Order," Viktor said.

"I've come across the known coats of arms for most of the founding members, but not all."

"What about later members, such as the houses of Drăculești and Hunyadi? Is there anything similar to crossed spears?"

That penetrating stare of hers found his eyes again. "No," she said slowly.

"And the founding members with whom you're not as familiar? What if Dr. Fessler is right, and one of them influenced Sigismund?"

"I do not disagree with the theory. In fact, knowing Sigismund, I think it's rather likely. Mmm. If I were to guess which founding members had advocated the hardest to develop the Order, it would be one of the three Transylvanian voivodes. They were closest to the Turkish border, and had the most to gain from an alliance." She ran her finger alongside the names without touching them, reading them in order. "Stiborius Stiboricz, Jacobus Laczk de Zantho, Nicolaus de Chak."

"Do we have their coats of arms?"

"I believe so. It's been a long time since I've checked." She met his gaze. "But we're about to."

As she flipped to the index, he asked, "Did one of those three have the ear of Sigismund?"

"Not that I'm aware. But records are scant in that regard. One name that's always stood out to me," she said, as she found the reference she wanted and began turning pages again, "is Nicolaus de Chak. He's a mysterious figure we know little about. His family were traders who made their fortune on the Silk Road and rose to prominence in the eleventh century, long before Nicolaus was born. Some of the family intermingled with the Drăculeștis, but the Chaks declined in importance and disappeared altogether in the late nineteenth century, when the last of the the family emigrated to Bohemia."

Viktor's hands felt clammy when he heard that last bit. Bohemia was the historical name for much of the Czech Republic. "Bohemia?" he echoed. "Why there?"

"I don't know. I'd have to look . . ." She trailed off and, with a frown, held the book open and showed him the page she had found. At first, he didn't notice anything odd, but then he realized what had caught her attention—a missing page revealed by a neat incision clipped right next to the spine. "That's the page where the de Chak coat of arms should be," she said. "This is abominable. I'll have to notify the archivist."

Viktor swallowed as he looked down at the tear in the manuscript. "Can we find the de Chak coat of arms somewhere else?"

"Not that I know of. It's such a minor family." She closed the book and looked up at Viktor with a grim expression. "Maybe it's time you tell me what this is really about."

He let out a deep breath, remembering the young woman he had seen in the reading room. "I think it's best if I took my leave. Your help was very much appreciated. If there's anything else you can think of concerning the de Chaks or the crossed spears, please let me know."

"I've already thought of something."

"Oh?"

"But I want to know what this concerns first. I doubt a scholarly opinion could put me in danger, but if that's the case, then so be it. Knowledge is not always without risk."

Viktor hesitated, then asked Dr. Szekely to wait. He returned to the reading room and peered around a corner of a bookshelf, feeling somewhat foolish until he noticed the young woman in black still lingering in the same place he had seen her. She had a book in her hands but did not appear to be reading, as if holding it just in case she was observed.

And how very pale she was.

To his left, Viktor noticed a window not in her line of sight. He hurried over to it, peered down, and saw that it overlooked the courtyard through which he had entered the library.

Leaning against the wall of a side wing was a man in a shearling jacket.

Viktor drew a sharp breath and returned to the private room across the hall. "I don't suppose you know another way out of the library?"

Dr. Szekely blinked. After a long moment, she said, "You don't appear to be joking."

"I wish I was. There are two people nearby who do not, let us say, have my best interests at heart."

"Can you call the police? A security guard?"

"I'm not sure what to tell them. And once I leave the library, the threat will remain. It's better if I'm not followed at all."

A look of dismay swept her face, replaced by a firm jaw and narrowed eyes. "I do happen to know an excellent way out of the library, as well as the castle complex. We can use the hallway outside this door, and we don't have to reenter the main archive."

"I hate to bring this on you. What if you—"

"I'm already involved. I'll see you to safety and we can go our separate ways. That is, after you do some explaining. Now come," she said, once again moving at a brisk pace towards the door.

Not used to being led by the ear, Viktor felt as if he had lost control of the situation as they entered the hallway outside the door. Dr. Szekely took off the gloves and led him to the right, in a direction reserved for the staff. "Where are we going?" he asked in a low voice.

"To the labyrinth beneath the castle. There's an entrance in the basement of the library, and the tunnels can take you almost anywhere in old Buda. I used to be a tour guide and know the routes."

"The labyrinth?" he said as she used her access card to enter a concrete stairwell. "I'm not sure we should be entering an underground passage right now."

She flicked on a fluorescent light. "If you want to leave the library without being seen, it's the only way. Unless you think someone has anticipated this?"

"I doubt it but—"

"Then we'll walk a few streets over and surface as soon as you like. It won't take that long, and it's not straightforward down there, in case you're thinking of leaving me behind. I'll need to lead you." A gleam entered her eyes. "Besides, I'm an old woman and miss the excitement of, how do you say it in English, my checkered past."

Viktor hesitated. He did not like the plan one bit. But he did not see a better way, and if she knew the route as well as she promised, then he supposed it could work, and he could see her safely home. After that, it was time for him to return to Prague as swiftly as he could, and wait for Grey before proceeding.

"Okay," he said. "Thank you, and lead on."

Bucharest, Romania

-21-

The goose bumps on Grey's skin induced by the beautiful arias were of a different sort from the feeling of spider legs creeping down the back of his neck as he observed the silhouette of Dumitra Speluncescu in her private booth from across the opera house.

During the first half of the opera, he detected nothing unusual in her behavior. The other seat in the booth was unoccupied, and she watched the show intently, applauding with the rest of the crowd after a spectacular performance and at the end of each act. So far, neither Petru nor any of the children had left their seats. Grey could only imagine what would befall one of the orphans if they embarrassed the stone-faced wardens sitting rigidly at the ends of the rows.

At intermission, the wardens rose and led the children through the nearest exit, presumably to use the restrooms. Petru went with them, and Grey counted the children as they left. Thirty-three. Not wanting to be seen, he buried his face in his program and kept an eye on Dumitra. Ever since the curtain had fallen, she had been talking on her cell phone, her long black hair covering the left side of her face.

Eventually a bell chimed for the audience to return to their seats. As the children began filing in, the wardens shooing them down the rows, Grey performed a head count. Twenty-nine, thirty, thirty-one, thirty-two . . .

No more children returned to the theater. Where was the last child?

Grey did a quick recount to ensure he hadn't missed one, but got the same number. With a start, he also noticed Petru had yet to return. Grey swung his gaze around but saw no sign of the lame-footed bus driver anywhere in the theater. The seat in which he had been sitting, the last row of the section with the orphans, had one of the warden's coats draped over it.

Just before the lights winked out and the curtain parted, Grey glanced up at the private booth where Dumitra had been sitting for the entire performance.

Empty.

The twinge of anxiety Grey had felt from the moment he had seen her became a pinball of fear bouncing and spinning in his gut. Under the cover of darkness, he hurried down the row, bumping knees and stumbling over feet, apologizing as he went, hoping none of the wardens noticed the commotion. If the worst outcome had not already occurred, he needed to preserve every element of surprise he could.

Grey took the stairs three at a time and emerged in a dark hallway with track lighting along the floor. An usher said something to him in Romanian. "Restroom," Grey muttered, then hurried into the grand foyer at the end of the hall.

Still no sign of Dumitra, Petru, or a missing child. Grey hurried through the main entrance, emerged into the night, and saw a chilling sight: Petru limping slowly down the lamplit pedestrian footpath, heading for the street.

Alone.

Grey strained to peer into the darkness off the path. Nothing. No one. Hardly able to believe a child had been snatched from right under his nose, Grey returned inside and ignored the stares of the staff, wondering who else was beholden to Dumitra.

He found a hallway which led to the section of the theater in which the children were sitting. As soon as he was out of sight of the foyer, he raced down the sloping corridor, passing two entrances to the theater. A booming tenor muffled the sound of his footsteps.

The dim red outline of an emergency exit awaited at the end of the hall. Grey hated to stop moving but took a moment to think through his options. If Dumitra had taken the child outside and left in a vehicle, there was little Grey could do about it now. His best bet in that scenario was to track Petru down and force him to reveal her location, though Grey doubted Dumitra would confide in Petru in this way.

On second thought, Dumitra would not want to be seen in public with a child not her own. That was too risky. She would have used a more clandestine method to take the orphan to a waiting vehicle. Maybe there was a hidden exit from the opera house? Somewhere Dumitra had a vehicle and a driver waiting? If this was true, Grey might have a window of opportunity to catch them.

His gaze whisked to the Emergency Exit sign again. A side entrance to the opera would be a much better place to escape with a child than the front door. He ran to the emergency exit and paused with his hand on the crash bar. If an alarm sounded, interrupting the opera, Dumitra would be on high alert.

But he was running out of options.

Holding his breath, he pushed the door open and cringed. It opened onto an unlit concrete stairwell with another exit sign above a door on the opposite wall. No alarm rang. This relieved him, though maybe Dumitra had disabled the alarm.

He stepped into the stairwell and eased the door shut behind him, using his cell phone for illumination so he didn't have to risk a light. The stairs led down into the darkness.

Again Grey hesitated. If he did have a chance to find the missing child, it was fading fast, and he had to make the right choice here. Logic told him Dumitra had left through the side door and driven the child away. If so, as much as it pained him, the child was likely out of his reach. He also feared pressing his luck with an alarm.

On the other hand, where did these stairs lead? To an underground garage or another exit further from the public eye? Knowing Ceaușescu and his paranoid delusions, he had probably built underground escape routes from all his favorite haunts.

He chose the stairs. After racing down a flight, he found himself in another stairwell with a metal door. He tried the handle. Unlocked. The door opened onto a large room strewn with theater props. He listened for a moment. No sounds other than the pounding of his own pulse.

Growing more nervous by the second, he shut the door and returned to the landing. The stairs continued down another level, ending at a rough concrete floor and a wooden door reinforced with iron bands.

This time the door was locked. Grey did not think Dumitra was down here. He thought he had missed his chance and she had fled into the night with an innocent child. But he couldn't give up. He extracted the lock picking tools he carried at all times, a miniature rake and tension wrench, from the heel of his left boot. It took him less than a minute to solve the deadbolt, pocket his tools, turn off his cell light, and ease open the door.

As Grey took a silent step forward, he heard male voices floating down the long dark hallway behind the door. Grey tensed and opened the door another foot, just wide enough to slip through, glad he had killed his light. He eased the door shut behind him and stood very still in the darkness. Up ahead, about thirty yards away, he saw two men facing each other in a halo of light at an intersection, smoking and waving their hands as they talked. The voices were too distant for Grey to understand.

The trace of an unusual smell was present in the hallway. It took him a moment to recognize it, but when his brain reached into his sensory memory and drew out the ever-so-faint aroma of clove and citrus, as if a woman had just passed by and her perfume still lingered, Grey flexed his hands at his sides, preparing for action as adrenaline dumped into his system.

The men at the other end of the hall kept talking, oblivious to Grey's presence. They did not sound nervous or worried. *What the hell is going on? Why are they guarding that intersection? Why haven't they left with Dumitra?*

The brick hallway had chipped mortar and a rounded ceiling, reminiscent of an old subway tunnel. The air was moist and cool. Cobwebs hung in tatters from the ceiling.

Grey did not think too hard about what he had to do. He reached into his pocket and palmed his lock picking tools in his left hand, then kept his hands at his sides, low and unthreatening, as he crept down the hallway. The men either failed to notice him or could not see far enough in the darkness until Grey had closed most of the distance. The guard on the left, the younger of the two, was dressed in jeans and a green-and-white sweat jacket. When he finally saw Grey, he drew back in surprise and yanked a gun out of the back of his jeans. Grey put his hands up and spoke quickly, not giving them time to process the oddity of the situation. "Excuse me," Grey said in English, with as much bewildered humility as he could muster. "I'm a bit lost. Is the restroom down here?"

As he spoke, Grey kept moving forward at a steady clip, closing the distance to fifteen and then ten yards. *C'mon guys. Don't get spooked. Just let me get within arm's reach.*

The younger guard jabbered angrily in Romanian while he waved his gun as if shooing Grey away. The older guard on the right, a muscular man with a tattooed neck, had the flat nose of a boxer and more presence about him. One of his hands slipped beneath his corduroy jacket, and he eyed Grey with a distrustful gaze, trying to figure out his deal. "Wrong way," the older guard said in broken English. "No restroom. Go back."

"Ah, my bad," Grey said, still walking forward with a slouch, trying to appear as unthreatening as possible, pretending not to notice the gun waving in the air.

The younger guard leveled the weapon at Grey's head. "*Opri!*"

Five yards to go. A thought flashed through Grey's mind as he judged their movements and eyed their mouths for signs of dagger-like teeth.

What if they're like Cezar?

Grey took a risk and kept walking. No one wanted to shoot an unarmed person, especially a lost American tourist, when they didn't have to. *Or almost no one.* "Hey guys, sorry about that. Can you *please* tell me where the restroom is?"

The older guard had seen enough. The muscles in his neck flexed as he took a step forward and jabbed a finger in Grey's face. "Get out! Go back! Not for public!"

Wrong move, Grey thought as the guard closed the gap for him. The guy must be pushing two-fifty, outweighing Grey by seventy pounds or more, and kept his weight balanced on his heels.

Grey still had his lock picking tools clenched in his left hand. Without breaking stride, he tossed them straight in the face of the younger guard, hoping it was enough to distract him so Grey did not get shot as he made his next move.

The older guard's eyes tightened when he realized Grey was a threat. The finger in Grey's face was on the guard's left hand, which Grey could tell by his movements was his jab hand. The guard grabbed Grey by the throat with that same hand and took a huge swing with his right.

Grey winced at the pain in his wounded throat, but the worst thing to do in a fight with a jujitsu expert was to hold on to him while leaving his hands free.

Thinking he had Grey under control, the brute's hard right cross never landed. As the swing came in, Grey twisted his body and jabbed forward like a snake with his own right hand, using the web between his thumb and pointer finger to strike the guard in the throat. Grey did not want to collapse his trachea, so he did not strike at full strength, but he followed it up with a left uppercut below the chin that snapped the guard's head back and caused his knees to buckle.

This happened so fast the younger guard had no time to intervene. When he did react, instead of retreating and pointing his gun at Grey, he chose to rush to his friend's side, holding his gun out in front of him. The older guard was still too dazed to fight, and as soon as Grey saw the younger guard closing in, Grey jerked the older guard toward him, using the incapacitated man's body as a shield. The older guard made an effort to resist but Grey gripped the front of his hoodie, swept both his feet, uncoiled like a spring, and threw him into the younger guard, who was right on top of them. The two guards collided in a heap and went down. Both guns clattered to the floor. Grey kicked the younger guard in the face like he was striking a soccer ball, knocking him senseless, then pounced on one of the guns. As the younger guard struggled to move, Grey swiped him in the back of the head with the gun. The younger Romanian collapsed on his face and didn't move.

The older guard had recovered enough to lunge for Grey's waist. Grey sidestepped the lunge with perfect footwork, as graceful as a ballet dancer, and smacked him in the side of the head with the gun. The guard staggered, somehow withstanding the blow, and Grey hit him again.

He stayed down this time.

Moving with cold precision, Grey stuck one of the black handguns in the pocket of his coat with the safety on, and held the other weapon in his right hand as he surveyed the intersection. Dusty brick passages extended into the darkness on his left and straight ahead. The corridor on the right, though similar in construction, looked swept and was lit by recessed ceiling lights. About a hundred feet away, the passage dead-ended at another wooden door.

An easy choice. Grey sprinted down the right hand corridor and tried the handle of the solid door. It opened onto a scene from his darkest nightmares, a scenario his subconscious mind had not allowed him to consider.

Designer red wallpaper inlaid with an intricate rose pattern covered the walls. A velvet chaise and three overstuffed chairs were arranged around a flickering gas fireplace. Recessed pseudo-archways on the sides of the room sheltered cabinets topped by standing candelabra full of lit candles. An elegant rug covered the floor, and a tiny kitchenette—sink, stainless steel mini-fridge, and wheeled Indonesian liquor cabinet—filled a larger alcove to Grey's right.

All this he absorbed at first glance, at the periphery of his awareness, along with a strong aroma of a clove-and-citrus perfume and the music of the opera playing softly in the parlor, streaming in through hidden speakers. The rest of his focus remained on Dumitra Speluncescu, lounging on the green velvet chaise with her back against the side near the fireplace, her long arms wrapped around a little girl of about ten lying prone in Dumitra's lap. The girl's head was lilting to the right, and Dumitra's head was buried in the side of her neck, a thin trail of blood seeping from the side of her mouth.

When Grey entered, Dumitra did not respond at first. She appeared so intent on her unholy task, latched onto her victim with such complete abandon, that Grey was not sure she had noticed him. For a moment, he could not react either, so appalled and shocked by what he was witnessing that his brain had trouble processing it.

This doesn't happen. This isn't real.

His inertia lasted but a moment, replaced by a white-hot rage that clouded his vision and made him tremble with emotion.

There was a little girl on that couch and a monster perched above her sucking her life force away. Whether or not Dumitra Speluncescu was a real vampire did not matter to Grey.

Because what she was doing to that child was very real.

Dumitra finally raised her head and looked up at Grey, her sculpted white face flush with pleasure, her stiletto-sharp fangs flecked with blood. Her tongue flicked out like a jungle cat's to lick the crimson spots off her teeth.

He took a step forward. "Get off her," he said in a voice so hoarse with emotion that it cracked.

With a flick of her hand, Dumitra rose off the chaise, pushing the little girl to the side as if she weighed nothing. The bloodlust drained from her face, replaced by contempt as she leveled an imperious stare at Grey. "How dare you disturb me."

A flood of hormones was normal at the beginning of a fight, but a warrior operating on pure adrenaline was far less dangerous than a calm and rational one. Through long years of experience, Grey had learned to channel his heightened emotions, but it took every ounce of self-control he possessed not to shoot Dumitra in the head right then and there. Instead he turned, locked the door to keep the guards away in case they woke up, and reached for his cell phone to call an ambulance.

No signal.

"I'm taking her out of here," he said. "If you get in the way, I'll put you down."

"My my," Dumitra purred, still clad in her black evening gown. "That sounds promising. I know who you are, Dominic Grey."

One of the straps of her gown had slid off her shoulder, revealing the top of a small breast that was the same milk-white color as her face, as if no part of her had ever seen the sun. Grey noticed she was barefoot. He glanced down and saw her petite toes curling into the carpet. For some reason it was a fascinating sight. He yanked his gaze up as she took a step forward, more of a glide than a walk, her gown clinging to her svelte body. The passage of decades had left almost no impression on her flawless skin.

Grey raised the gun. "Not another step. Where's Viktor?"

"Or what? You'll shoot an unarmed woman?"

Dumitra's lips curled upwards, a playful smirk, and all of a sudden Grey realized her fangs had disappeared, replaced by normal teeth. How was that possible? They must be implants she could manipulate with her tongue.

"An unarmed woman preying on a young girl? If I have to, yes."

"Relax," she said, gliding forward once again, now less than ten feet away. Her throaty Slavic accent was syrupy, seductive. "The girl will be fine. Let's play for a while, just the two of us."

The girl isn't fine at all, Grey thought as Dumitra inhaled seductively and arched her back, drawing his attention to the contours of her breasts beneath the gown. She was not wearing a bra and her nipples pushed erotically against the soft fabric. Grey's head felt fuzzy, as if he could not quite concentrate on the task he was supposed to perform. As Dumitra took another step forward, he bit down hard on his lip and glanced at the prone form of the girl and the twin holes in her neck. *The girl might never be fine again.* He grimaced and shook his head, then raised the gun and took a step back, remembering the preternatural speed of Cezar Speluncescu.

"You're right to fear me," she purred, still moving forward. "But I'm afraid you've awoken too late."

When Grey took another step back, he realized the door was right behind him, and he had nowhere left to go. He aimed the gun at her chest.

"You've let me get too close," she said, her mesmeric gaze locking onto his.

Grey still couldn't bring himself to shoot an unarmed woman, so he decided to use the gun to knock her unconscious. It was the fastest, simplest way to incapacitate her. As he prepared to close in, Dumitra's mouth opened wide, revealing her fangs once again. She snarled and made a sound in the back of her throat that could have come from a cornered animal, something between a hiss and a growl.

Where the hell did those fangs come from?

Startled, he reared back to hit her with the gun, but she leaped at him before he had a chance to use it, smacking it out of his hands. He could not believe how fast she closed the distance between them. She moved even faster than Cezar. Grey was always a step ahead of his opponents, but before he could react, she grabbed him by the hair, jerked his head back, and went for his throat with her fangs.

Grey had no time to bring up an arm to defend himself. But he had learned from the fight with Cezar. Instead of going on the defensive, he head-butted her as she moved in, catching her forehead just before the fangs sunk into his flesh. Dumitra drew back and hissed, then reached out with both arms, grabbed him by the chest, raised him in the air like a child, and shoved him against the door.

"I'll drink you dry and toss your corpse to the dogs," she said, her eyes gleaming with a feral light, their faces inches apart.

As she moved in for the kill again, fangs glistening, Grey did not bother using his free hands to try for a pressure point or a joint lock. No more underestimating this family. Instead he reached into the pocket of his coat, flicked off the safety of the second gun with a finger, and shot Dumitra in the heart at an upward angle.

Half-expecting her not to react to the bullet, Grey watched in grim satisfaction as she screamed and fell off him, blood pouring through the hole in her gown. She stumbled and fell, then curled into a ball and lay still on the rug, her eyes staring straight ahead and her breaths coming in short, shallow pants.

Shouts came from the corridor outside. Convinced no one could survive a shot to the heart like that, Grey ran to the girl on the chaise and checked her pulse. Still breathing. "Can you hear me?"

No answer. The girl had lost too much blood, or lapsed into a comatose state at the trauma, or both. He picked her up gently, placed her over his left shoulder, and kept the gun in his right hand. She weighed very little and smelled of damp wool. He wished he had time to search the parlor and do something to help Viktor, but he could hear footsteps pounding in the hall, and saving her life took priority. He did not see a cell phone anywhere, but on his way out, he noticed a tiny black handbag on the cabinet with the candelabra. He stuffed the handbag in his coat pocket and pushed through the door.

When he stepped into the hallway, he saw the older guard running towards him, and the other struggling to his knees in the intersection. The older guard was less than twenty feet away and had a knife in his hands. Grey shot him in the thigh and kept walking. The guard dropped the knife and fell writhing to the ground. "Stay down," Grey said, kicking the knife away as he passed.

By the time Grey had reached the intersection, the younger guard had thrown his hands up and backed against a brick wall. "No shoot," he said, his eyes wide as he looked at the girl slung over Grey's shoulder. "Please."

"You want to live?" Grey said. "Take me to a car *right damn now*."

With a nod, still woozy from his concussion, the guard led Grey down the tunnel opposite Dumitra's parlor. A hundred feet down, the passage dead-ended at a freight elevator. "You first," Grey said, waving him through the door. "If this is a trap, you'll die before its sprung."

The guard looked at the gun and then up at the barely controlled rage in Grey's eyes. "No trap. Please."

"Go!" Grey said.

The guard jabbed the elevator panel and took them up two floors to a small garage with a handful of late-model SUVs. The guard fumbled in his pocket for a set of keys and beeped open a Mercedes. Grey told him to drive, cradled the girl in his lap in the back seat, and pointed the gun at the guard as he sped through the garage. An automatic door opened, and the Bucharest night was a blur of traffic and neon lights as the guard drove to the nearest hospital.

Grey pressed the unconscious girl into the waiting hands of an emergency room nurse. The woman took one look at her and barked an order for the receptionist to call a doctor.

Budapest

-22-

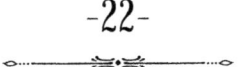

After using a swipe card to open a steel door in the subbasement of the National Library, Dr. Szekely led Viktor down a long flight of concrete steps that spilled into the caves and tunnels beneath Buda Castle. From previous visits to the city, Viktor was aware of the subterranean grottos that had sheltered humans from prehistoric times to the Middle Ages, and above which the Romans had founded the ancient city of Aquincum.

Dr. Szekely used her cell phone light to penetrate the darkness at the bottom of the stairs, illuminating the slimy, rough-hewn rock walls of an underground passage. The temperature had dropped twenty degrees, and the musty air carried the chalky tang of limestone walls honeycombed over the eons by thermal waters bubbling up from below.

Since leaving the Archives Room, Viktor had seen no sign of the pale woman in the library or the man in the shearling coat. Yet Viktor worried, as he and Dr. Szekely delved further into the natural rock tunnel, about the prospect of an unwelcome encounter in such a secluded place.

"Does anyone use these tunnels?" he asked, switching on his own cell phone light to help penetrate the gloom.

"This area? I doubt it. Part of the tunnels is a tourist attraction called the Labyrinth, as I'm sure you know, but we'll be passing through an abandoned exhibit. Except for a chance encounter with the urban explorers and homeless who come and go, we should be alone. Did I happen to mention that Vlad the Impaler was once imprisoned in a dungeon in these very tunnels, not far from this location?"

"You didn't," Viktor said with a smirk, knowing she was alluding to the pitch given to tourists. "And he was not. When Matthias took Vlad prisoner, he was held in Visegrad Royal Castle, miles from our present location. Vlad's imprisonment was more of a long vacation, since he was allowed to roam the castle grounds during most of his internment. Matthias was so concerned about the behavior of his infamous prisoner that he allowed him to marry his niece. But thank you for attempting to lighten the mood."

"You know your Hungarian history," she said with an approving smile as they walked.

"Falsehoods and misconceptions seem to follow Vlad the Impaler through history. Are there any true tales about these tunnels I should know about?" he asked, peering into the darkness that surrounded the tiny halo of light from their cell phones so completely that it felt tangible, alive.

"Let's see, there's the mysterious figure in the black cape said to haunt the Labyrinth, rumors of buried treasure and government experiments, and I'm sure you're aware the caves down here *did* serve as a prison and a torture chamber for centuries."

They entered a section of tunnels with ceilings so low Viktor had to duck. The feeling of oppression in the claustrophobic tunnels was getting to him. He did his best to ignore his atavistic fear of the dark, the rats skittering just out of sight, and thoughts of white-skinned figures creeping through the tunnels behind them.

"You mentioned something you had in mind about the chest," he said. "Care to expound?"

She continued walking confidently forward. "I know a bookseller and restorer who specializes in medieval manuscripts. He's seen almost as many heraldic emblems as I have. We consult each other on occasion, and I've found him to be an excellent resource. He seems to have an eidetic memory for his work. I'd like to consult him about the crossed spears."

"Where is he?"

"His shop is in Buda, not far from the Fisherman's Bastion. If we hurry, we can catch him before he closes."

Viktor checked his watch. Eight-thirty p.m. "Which is when?"

"Nine."

"I hope we're aboveground by then."

"That shouldn't be a problem. It's about half a mile walk from here."

Viktor pursed his lips and nodded. He had come this far and might as well see it through. "If we go, I want you to agree to let me conduct the research from here on out."

"I'll agree to nothing of the sort."

"You're an impossible woman."

"Thank you. Now, what is all this about?"

"I'll update you after we meet the bookseller. Trust me, this is not the place to hear this tale. I'd rather concentrate on getting aboveground as fast as possible."

"Fair enough."

After five minutes of walking, they encountered a rotting green hose in the center of the stone floor, stretching into the darkness like some slain chthonic serpent. "The original tourist attraction is abandoned," she said. "They used to turn off the gas lamps and let tourists navigate the darkness while holding onto this hose. The effect was quite spooky, I have to admit. The path leads through old prison cells they turned into exhibits."

"How inventive," Viktor muttered.

Every now and then, as they followed the hose for the next several minutes, Dr. Szekely would aim her cell phone into one of the eerie rock chambers on either side of the passage and illuminate shackles bolted to the wall, some very convincing skeletons attached to them, and rusting implements of torture. Near the end of the section was an old coffin covered in cobwebs.

"The alleged former residence of Vlad the Impaler," she said, "cast in blue light and with all the appropriate props. The children screamed every time."

As they walked past the decaying exhibit, clinging like lost pups to the feeble light from their phones, Viktor's mind wandered to the rumors about the Speluncescu family. He remembered the man in the shearling coat crossing the street to avoid the woman selling garlic, and the odd subtexts and congruences he kept encountering between his research for this case and Stoker's nineteenth-century novel.

Anomalies and coincidences, and nothing more. As I know better than most, the human mind longs for patterns and will ferret them out where none exist.

Something scrabbled in the passage just ahead of them, the sound of claws finding purchase on stone. Viktor jumped as Dr. Szekely swung her light back and forth.

"Just another rat, I'm sure," she said. "They grow to the size of small dogs down here."

Viktor did not think rats made sounds that loud, but he could not think of an alternative he wished to dwell on. He hurried forward, eager to escape the clammy air, Stygian darkness, low ceilings, and the feeling of someone skulking through the maze of tunnels behind them.

"Ah, here we are," she said, swinging the light around to illuminate a set of steep, rough-cut steps leading up through a long shaft of stone.

They climbed to the top and emerged through a removable iron grate near a birdbath in a ruined courtyard. Viktor breathed a sigh of relief. The weeds, broken glass, and pockmarked brick walls of the courtyard, most likely bombed during World War II, felt positively charming after the labyrinth.

She led him through a wooden door that opened onto a cobblestone alley that ran between the back sides of commercial buildings with iron-barred windows. The welcoming sounds of the city emanated from busier streets around them. At the end of the alley, Viktor stopped to peer down the street, seeing nothing out of place. Dr. Szekely led him through the hilly, lamplit streets of Buda, passing taverns and art galleries and cafes. On a particularly steep and scenic street, she approached a shop with a placard attached to the stone-walled exterior.

RARE BOOKS AND RESTORATIONS

Through the window, Viktor saw that the shop consisted of little more than a counter near the door and a single long corridor lined with overflowing bookshelves. They stepped inside. The store was empty except for a thickset man with a rambling white beard shelving books on a ladder near the door. A beige fedora was pulled low on his forehead, and his voluminous, wrinkled, short-sleeved dress shirt had brown stains on the collar. When he noticed Dr. Szekely, the man grunted, gave a nod of recognition, and continued shelving.

"Fair warning: he knows English but refuses to speak it," Dr. Szekely whispered to Viktor.

"Understood. I'll muddle through."

When the stack of books on the ladder had disappeared, the bookseller climbed down, huffing with exertion as he waddled towards them.

Dr. Szekely checked her watch and spoke in Hungarian. "If you prefer, we can wait until you close."

The bookseller walked to the front door and flipped the sign behind the window to *Closed*.

"Thank you," she said, and introduced Viktor as a professional colleague. "How are you, Tomaj?"

"Terrible," he answered in a voice like a growl. "Business was slow today, the weather is too warm for this time of year, and my arthritis will put me in an early grave."

Pleasant chap, Viktor thought.

"I'm sorry to hear that," Dr. Szekely said in a detached manner that suggested the bookseller's complaints were not an uncommon occurrence. "I know you love a good historical mystery, and I have a real puzzler on my hands. Maybe that will cheer you up."

"Talk," he said as he walked behind the register, reached down, and plopped a bottle of Hungarian fruit brandy and three shot glasses on the counter. He sloshed brandy into the glasses and pushed two of them towards his visitors. Viktor did not like pálinka, but he accepted the offer so as not to offend their cantankerous host. As the alcohol hit Viktor's system, he realized, after the events of the evening, the resulting warmth was quite welcome.

At Dr. Szekely's urging, Viktor showed Tomaj the photos of the book of poetry and the illustration of the carving on Dumitra's chest. The two of them gave a quick description of the dilemma. Dr. Szekely summarized her thoughts about the potential relation of the crossed spears to a heraldic crest belonging to one of the families involved with the Order of the Dragon. She named the three Transylvanian voivodes, Nicolaus de Chak in particular, though she left out the missing page in the library.

Tomaj thrust his ink-stained palms atop the wooden counter, his small eyes lost in his piggish face as he peered down at the images. He poured another shot of pálinka, downed it, and stroked the bottom of his beard. "Never heard of de Chak. Never seen a variation on the emblem of the Order." He looked up at Viktor. "You're not one of the Dracula crazies, are you?"

"I assure you I am not."

The bookseller grunted. "I wouldn't think Agnes would associate with the sort."

"Professor Radek is a renowned phenomenologist," she said.

Another grunt.

"Does anything stand out to you?" Dr. Szekely asked, after a period of silence.

The book restorer kept looking down at the images. "I've seen these spears once before, or something very much like them."

Viktor took a step closer to the counter. "You're certain? Where?"

"Yes, yes, that was it," Tomaj said rhetorically, as if talking to himself while he continued to stroke his beard. "It was an auction house in Prague, at least thirty years ago. The auction had some old codices I was keen to examine. Of course I couldn't afford them, but the purchasers allowed me to restore them the following year. I do a lot of business that way."

Prague again, Viktor thought. "What sort of codices?"

The bookseller waved a hand and finally looked up. "Irrelevant, but there were a couple of very rare items at this auction. One was a coat of arms, circa twelfth century, with a unique emblem: a pair of spears forming a cross above a dragon."

"You just said you'd never seen a variation on the Order's emblem," Dr. Szekely said.

"I didn't say *on* the dragon, I said above it. Nor was the dragon coiled into an ouroboros. It was more of a typical beast, claws extended, mouth gaping, you know the sort. That's not a variation in my eyes. The crossed spears," he said, wagging a finger, "those were unique. Especially fashioning a cross. Or unique until now."

"The tapered ends," Dr Szekely said eagerly. "You remember that as well? Suggesting an archaic type of spear?"

"Exactly so."

"Was it some sort of heraldry?" Viktor pressed. "A tapestry, a surcoat?"

"An actual shield."

"My God," Dr. Szekely said. "That should be in a museum."

"My thoughts as well."

Viktor worked to control his growing excitement. "Who was selling it?"

"I'll get to that in a moment. There was a piece from the same collection with a similar motif. An oil painting, one of the strangest I've ever seen. I couldn't even guess at the age, maybe as old as the shield. The painting was in dire shape. It depicted a moonlit path in a forest, and a cloaked figure on horseback holding a tapered spear just like the ones on your illustration. The cloaked figure was chasing a group of people in loincloths down the forest path, as if the figure was . . . well, *hunting* them."

"Strange indeed," Viktor murmured. His eyes strayed to the window, uneasy again. "Did you catch the provenance?"

Tomaj shook his head. "If I heard it then, I don't remember, and I've never seen anything like it before or since. Not until tonight."

"Do you have any idea what happened to the two pieces?"

"Some good-looking rich woman swept in and bought them both while I was there. You could tell by the way she bid that she wasn't giving them up."

"Do you remember her name?"

"No idea."

Viktor took out the photo of Dumitra Speluncescu and set it on the bookseller's counter. "Was it this woman?"

Tomaj peered down again and shrugged. "Could be, I suppose, if you account for the years. I can't say for sure. Sorry. I was paying attention to the collection more than the beautiful women in the room, I'm sorry to say. Story of my life. It was also winter, and the lady kept her coat and hat on indoors. Odd detail to remember, I know."

Viktor returned the photo to his pocket, ignoring Dr. Szekely's penetrating stare. "Do you remember the name of the auction house?"

"Fritsch and Schlessinger. The auction was the first Saturday in December, nineteen ninety-one I believe. I'll double-check that for you."

Viktor knew of the auction house. "I'd appreciate it. You have an impressive memory."

"Why do these crossed spears interest a phenomenologist?"

"Just a personal matter."

Tomaj poured a third shot of pálinka and glared at the two of them. Dr. Szekely gave an apologetic shrug.

"I really must be going," Viktor said, not wanting to linger in the bookseller's shop any longer than necessary. He drank out of politeness and pushed the shot glass across the counter. "Thank you for the hospitality. I hope to return it one day."

"I've got plenty of brandy. I'm much more interested in those spears."

"If I find anything, I'll be sure to pass it on."

Dr. Szekely followed Viktor out of the bookstore and to the nearest intersection. "You promised to let me know what this is all about."

"As soon as we catch a cab," he said, cursing as a taxi sped by them. The next one stopped, and he ushered her inside.

She gave the driver her address and turned to Viktor. "Well?"

He was hesitant to tell her anything, but he knew she was the sort of woman who would not take well to evasion. Fearing she would get herself in more trouble if she didn't understand the danger, he told her about Daryna's murder, which Agnes had seen on the news, and his limited involvement in the case.

"But I don't understand," she said. "How does this concern the illustration on the chest and the Order of the Dragon?"

"In brief, we believe a descendant of the family who owns this chest is involved with the murder, and has gone into hiding. We're trying to track them through . . . unconventional means."

Her eyes narrowed. "Tracing the family crest to modern day."

"Yes. I believe the name has changed at least once, making it difficult. But you've aided my progress, for which I'm very grateful."

"I take it this family does not want to be uncovered?"

"They're very dangerous. I'm sorry I involved you, I just wanted your opinion on the heraldry."

"Don't be sorry." She fell silent for a long moment, then said, "There are plenty of things you aren't telling me."

He confirmed with a nod.

"I probably don't want to know, do I?" she said.

"Probably not."

She turned towards the window, pensive until the taxi arrived at her townhome across the river. "I'll take another look at the de Chak genealogy."

"I'd prefer if you didn't."

"I'll do it from the safety of my office. It's within the ambit of my research, and I can do it better than you. If I find something of interest, I'll let you know."

He touched her arm as she was stepping out of the taxi, impressed by her pluck and bravery. "Thank you."

"A young woman was murdered. I'll help if I can."

Later that night, as Viktor sat in a velvet-lined chair facing the locked door of his hotel suite, he sank into his glass of absinthe, letting the wormwood both soothe and pique his mind as he pondered the case.

He had just sent an inquiry to the auction house in Prague. The event happened so long ago that Viktor did not have high hopes, but if Tomaj remembered it, maybe someone at the auction house did as well.

Regardless of the response, in the morning he would fly to Prague. Not only did the trail seem to have come full circle to his home city, but Viktor thought it prudent to return. Grey was due back in two days. While Viktor was not going to postpone the investigation until then, he would feel safer in more familiar surroundings. Unfortunately, he would have to send Mari home as soon as he returned. It was no longer safe for her to be in his presence, not until the case was resolved. He would buy her a ticket and make it up to her as soon as he could.

With those decisions made, all that remained was conjecture.

Who was the mysterious Speluncescu family?

What was their connection to the Order of the Dragon and the symbol of the crossed spears?

Why did the Speluncescus go to such great lengths to perpetuate the vampire mythology, including, if Florin's ex-girlfriend had told the truth about Cezar's visit to his brother's house in Cluj-Napoca, the internal affairs of the family?

A historical mystery Viktor could accept.

A vampire narrative he could not.

And yet . . . what if?

What if centuries and centuries of near universal belief in such creatures—nay, millennia—did in fact bear some truth? What if the . . . *thing* . . . from which the legend derived had eventually found its way to Eastern Europe? What if the deeply entrenched superstitions in Transylvania and Wallachia that had spurred Bram Stoker to write his novel were not as ridiculous as modern science liked to proclaim? What if Stoker himself, by the success of his book and the ensuing popularity, had played a part in driving the vampires, or whatever they were, away from Romania?

Bah, Viktor said with a snarl, sloshing his absinthe as he stood to pace the room, annoyed with himself for even harboring these thoughts.

And yet—since when do I ignore potential theories? Why am I so afraid to speculate on this case? Is it because I'm afraid to believe in the unbelievable, cogitate on the unthinkable?

I have stared down the impossible before today.

I have seen it with my own two eyes.

There is a word for the delusion that results when one ignores the facts and logic with which one is presented, and clings to the belief system in which one is mired so deeply that one cannot see outside it.

It is called superstition.

Something else on Viktor's mind was the tragic death of John Polidori, the English physician to Lord Byron and a minor writer whose short story, *The Vampyre*, Viktor had discussed with Dr. Fessler.

After leaving Romania, Viktor had done a little research. Unlike Bram Stoker, who had never traveled across the breadth of Europe, John Polidori had.

What if he had met someone on his travels, as Dr. Fessler had suggested? An aristocratic figure similar to the one described in his tale, who Polidori believed was a vampire? Perhaps, like the Speluncescus, this continental patrician sought to use the mythology to intimidate those around him and gain wealth or notoriety. Or perhaps he was just delusional. Viktor didn't know, and the truth was immaterial to the result.

What mattered was what John Polidori believed.

When *The Vampyre* first released, the publisher tried to pass it off as a work inspired by Lord Byron, and even put Bryon's name on the cover. Enraged by the stunt, Byron forced the publisher to remove his name, and publicly disavowed any connection to the story.

As for John Polidori, he committed suicide at the tender age of twenty-five, stunning all those who knew him.

What if *The Vampyre*, the story that had started the modern myth, was a roman à clef about someone John Polidori and Lord Byron had met on their travels, and of whom they were both terrified? What if Lord Byron sought to distance himself from the publication at all costs, and Polidori, equally frightened but desperate to make a name for himself, made something public he should not have? What if he was killed for this deed, or so terrified of reprisal he took his own life?

Could this enigmatic European aristocrat have been someone from the House of Drăculești, a forebear of the Speluncescus? Were the two families one and the same?

Large swaths of Polidori's diary had been mysteriously removed before they were published. Who did this, and what did they contain?

Did Bram Stoker know about any of this, or was he simply inspired by the tale?

Speculation. Pure speculation.

Forced to contend with his own principles, and analyze everything he had uncovered with a rational eye, Viktor gave his imagination free reign and let the absinthe spark his unconscious, as he often liked to do when baffled by a case. By the end of the night, he had made no further progress, but he could not deny that, in spite of the vehement protestation of his own rational mind, a small crack had appeared in his unshakeable conviction that vampires could not exist in this world.

-23-

Two nights after meeting with Erik Mittelman, Mari found herself alone in Viktor's kitchen, drinking wine as a coconut curry bubbled away. She had been working on her documentary, trying to distract herself as she tried to process the terrifying story she had heard about Dumitra Speluncescu.

While Mari did not believe in undead beings who stalked the night, cursed monstrosities forced to subsist on the blood of their victims, her conversations with Viktor about his work over the years kept replaying in her head.

There are things in the world, Dear Mari, which defy reason and logic and science as we know it. Phenomena of the human mind and the natural world which I believe will ultimately bear a rational explanation, but which human beings do not yet understand.

While Mari had a firm belief in the spiritual realm, and believed the universe harbored a great many mysteries, she had to admit she had never dwelled on the darker side of the paranormal, the yin to the yang, the toothed and fanged things that might lurk inside the fog or in an unexplored cave or deep within a primeval forest.

Where is Viktor? Why can't anyone find him?

She just could not bring herself to believe that something terrible might have befallen her towering uncle, a larger-than-life presence for as long as she could remember.

The wine glass retreated from Mari's lips, and she hung her head, overcome by sadness and a desperate frustration to do something proactive. The police had made no progress. Dominic Grey was chasing rumors across Eastern Europe, very dangerous rumors. She feared for his safety and did not see how one man could make progress where the police had failed.

As for herself, meeting with Erik had made her afraid to go out after dark, powerless to affect the course of events.

She *hated* how helpless she felt.

The curry was ready, but she had lost her appetite. She turned off the burner and stood in front of the stove, determined to do something, anything, to help her uncle. With a snarl, she left the kitchen and went to Viktor's library to research. If she had to, she would read every book on Eastern and Central European mythology cover to cover, searching for a clue.

It still bothered her that Viktor had returned to the house the night of his disappearance. Why had he done that? Was it the explanation which everyone, including herself, had accepted? That he simply had gone home to change clothes, use the restroom, return the car, or any number of mundane things?

But why not wake her to say hello or goodbye? Why leave so soon? The outside of the house was under video surveillance and had shown him leaving that night shortly after midnight. Not long after, he had shown up on another video feed outside Club Purgatory. Why had he done that? Was it just to leave a message, as Grey had speculated? Had her uncle gone anywhere else on his way?

This still did not explain his brief visit to the house. Yes, he might have gone out expecting to return. But what if he hadn't?

What if he had left a message for someone to find?

What if he had left it right here in the house?

She had thought of that before, but had never found anything.

Maybe she needed to look harder.

After pacing the room, thinking it through, she flipped through every single book in the library conceivably related to vampire mythology around the world. He had dozens of books on the topic, some with pages so brittle she feared they would crumble as she turned them. It took her some time, and she found no hidden notes or handwritten messages or anything else of interest. Her gaze roamed to the bay window and the beguiling glow of gaslight on the cobblestones.

Please come back to us, Uncle. There are so many things we need to discuss, so much life to live.

With a defeated sigh, she turned back to the handsome bookshelves and slowly paced the room, marveling at the sheer volume of the collection. An entire wall of philosophy and theology, from ancient times to the present. Maps of cities and countries long forgotten. The latest textbooks on quantum physics, astronomy, biology, and the other hard sciences. Shelves upon shelves filled with hardbound tomes on the occult, parapsychology, the history of magic, witchcraft, Druidism, cryptozoology, mysticism, every fascinating subject involving the unknown one could possibly imagine.

She returned to the section with the vampire books to ensure she had not missed anything. As her gaze roamed the periphery of the collection, she noticed something a bit odd. Right after *Vampires, Burial, and Death*, a book near the middle of the bookcase, there was a hardbound copy of *Alice in Wonderland*, followed by a handful of nonfiction titles relating to the purported symbolism and psychology underlying Lewis Carroll's famous creation. The section was bookended by four more works by the author: *The Hunting of the Snark*; *Sylvie and Bruno*; a softbound copy of *Alice's Adventures Under Ground*; and *Through the Looking-Glass, and What Alice Found There*.

The next shelf over harbored a collection of East Asian folklore. As she continued scanning the shelves, she realized there was nothing remotely resembling *Alice in Wonderland* anywhere near these sections. In fact, there was not another work of fiction in the entire library, as best as she could tell. Viktor kept his novels in other rooms of the house.

Mari's favorite book as a child was *Alice in Wonderland*. She remembered her uncle reading it to her in the same overstuffed leather chair that remained in the library to this day, beside the huge bay window on her right.

Mari plucked *Alice in Wonderland* off the shelf, flipped through it, and found nothing unusual. Same with the other Lewis Carroll books. She had loved the author's other works almost as much as *Alice*, though she had never heard of *Alice's Adventures Under Ground*. She picked up the paperback book again—one of the only softbacks in the whole library—read the back, and then skimmed the first three pages. She was confused. It appeared to be the same book as *Alice in Wonderland*. A quick search online revealed that it *was* the same book. *Alice's Adventures Under Ground* was the original title of the now-famous story that Lewis Carroll had first told to Alice Liddell, the daughter of a family friend, who had begged him to write it down. The rest was history.

As best as Mari could tell, the book in Viktor's library was a reproduction of the original manuscript and the illustrations Lewis Carroll had compiled before the publisher changed the name. The original title of the book, in the context of all that had happened, gave Mari a chill. It made her think of crypts and monsters and things that went bump in the night.

Viktor's grandfather clock chimed the hour, startling her. She took a deep breath, flipped through the book again, and came up short. Out of ideas, she started to replace it when she noticed a tiny switch, similar to a light switch but even smaller, set into the wall behind the book. She had almost missed it. All of Viktor's shelves were very deep, in order to accommodate the larger research tomes. There was almost a foot of space behind the tiny paperback.

The row with the Lewis Carroll books was set at chest-height and located in the middle of the wall. The switch could have been an old light switch, albeit a small one, that had been left in place during a remodel.

But that would be strange, and at odds with her uncle's attention to detail.

Mari flicked the switch and caught movement to her left, out of the corner of her eye. She whipped around and saw a door-size section of bookshelf swinging outward, revealing a patch of darkness behind it.

After recovering from her shock, Mari closed the blinds on the bay window and used her cell phone for illumination as she peered into the secret chamber behind the bookshelf. It had old stone walls and a steeply pitched ceiling, making her think it filled in the space behind the staircase. There was evidence of minor water intrusion, and the room had a musty odor. Except for another switch on the wall, which she assumed closed and opened the bookshelf from this side, there was nothing inside the chamber except for a steel door with a keypad lock set into the wall on the other side.

A door far newer than the rest of the hidden room.

Expecting the door to be locked, and the keypad code inaccessible, she was shocked once again when the handle turned and the door opened, revealing a set of finished concrete steps leading down into the depths of the house.

Bucharest, Romania

-24-

After Grey took the girl he had carried out of Dumitra's underground lair to the nearest hospital, the medics took one look at the wound on the girl's neck, blanched, and asked Grey what had happened. One of the women spoke good English, and Grey told her that he found the girl in an alley nearby. As they whisked her way, Grey pretended to use the restroom and hurried out of a side exit, still reeling from the abomination he had witnessed beneath the opera house.

He hated to leave the girl unprotected but didn't know what else to do. He couldn't even speak her language, and the doctors would no doubt call the police. Dumitra's associates would be hunting Grey as well, and he still had to find Viktor.

How many other children has Dumitra fed on?

After racing to the airport, returning his motorcycle, and buying the first ticket to Prague in the morning, he found a quiet corner where he could make a few calls. First up was a cute Irish doctor in Skopje.

"I didn't think I'd hear from you so soon," Cara O'Dwyer said sleepily, yawning through the phone. "Or at all."

"I'm sorry to wake you. I have a favor to ask."

"It's fine. I'm a doctor. I never get to sleep."

"I just dropped a little girl off at Central Hospital in Bucharest."

"You do get around."

"Remember that wound I came in with? The animal bite on my arm? She has one too. On her neck."

A long silence. "What . . . what was it?"

"Trust me, you don't want to know. Listen Cara, I can't stay here, and I'm worried about her. She lives at an orphanage, but she can't go back there under any circumstance, or leave with anyone. I don't know what the solution is, but for now, most of all, I want someone in the hospital watching out for her. Is Doctors Without Borders in Bucharest?"

"Yes."

"Do you know anyone who can help her?"

"I . . . I'll figure something out, if you tell me I need to."

"You need to."

"For how long?" she asked.

"I don't know. At least until she gets a transfusion and the immediate threat has passed. Ideally someone will watch over her at all times in the hospital."

"That will be tough."

"I know. Just do your best."

"Anything else?"

"Not for now. Thank you, Cara. It means a lot."

"My price for this favor is that one day we'll have a drink and talk about all this, and you'll tell me what's really going on."

"Deal. At least the first part."

"I had a feeling you'd say that."

After hanging up with Cara, Grey called Rick Laskin, a colleague of Grey's when he was a Diplomatic Security Special Agent. Last thing Grey knew, Rick was posted in Romania, and had helped Grey with a little off-the-books research during the Simon Azar case.

Rick answered on the fourth ring and sounded even sleepier than Cara. "Grey?"

"Hi Rick."

"You're one of the only people I answer the phone for this late."

"I'm sorry. I hope I didn't wake the family."

"The wife's out cold with a sedative, the daughter went off to college this year, and I have no doubt my son is still up playing video games. What's new? I assume this isn't a social call."

A former Navy Seal and high school quarterback, Rick was blond and crew-cut and as All-American as the Fourth of July. Though two very different people, he and Grey had bonded over their Special Forces backgrounds and their mutual loathing of bureaucracy. Unlike Grey, Rick had a family to feed, and harder choices when it came to paying the bills.

Grey knew integrity mattered to Rick as much as it did to him, and he was one of the few people on the planet who Grey trusted without question.

"I've got a situation," Grey said. "I can't get into it right now, but I'm on my way out of Bucharest. There's a little girl in a hospital who might need protection against some very bad people. I can't stay around to help her, and I thought I'd try you."

"You didn't know I moved to Vienna a year ago? I guess you wouldn't."

"Oh. Damn."

"I still have contacts in Romania. Is she one of ours?"

"She's Romanian. An orphan."

Rick sighed. "I'll be honest, I'm not sure what I can do. What's going on? Who is she?"

"You wouldn't believe me if I told you, and I don't even know her name. She's no one, just a little girl that needs help." Grey gave him the name of the hospital and described her injuries.

"Um, what the hell? A bite to the neck? Is this a joke?"

"I'm afraid not. Think child abuse and human trafficking on a mass scale. Some really sick people."

"My least favorite kind," Rick said grimly. "I'll do my best. Maybe I can pull some strings and get her moved to the top of the adoption list."

"I had the same thought. I'll send more details when I can, and I hope to have a doctor watching out for her also."

"If you have proof of the trafficking, I'll get the SRI involved."

Romanian intelligence, Grey knew. "I can help with that soon, but for now, put some pressure on a certain director of an orphanage in Bucharest. I'll text you his name and the details after we hang up. The Speluncescu crime family is involved as well."

"Never heard of them."

"No surprise. Oh, and there's a bus driver named Petru who works for the orphanage and hand delivers kids to traffickers."

"Good God. I'll try to take him off the board."

"I appreciate it, Rick. I've got to run now. Call me if you need anything."

"10-4, old buddy. Stay safe."

After hanging up, Grey debated calling the Romanian police to make a report, but he didn't know who to trust, nor did he want to tip off the wrong people. Better to make a full report to Rick and let him handle things through his channels.

Next Grey tried to call Jacques, but the Frenchman didn't pick up. Grey left a message, updating him on the case and asking about new developments.

Satisfied he had done everything he could to help the little girl, Grey moved to a secluded bench and sat with his back against the wall, where he could see anyone approaching. The last bit of adrenaline from the night's ordeal drained out of his system, leaving a hollow core inside.

If this vampire thing is a charade, the Speluncescus are taking it pretty damn far.

He checked his watch. 12:38 a.m.

His flight left at six in the morning, so he had a couple of hours to kill before boarding. As much as he wanted to sleep, he couldn't risk it before the plane. He shifted position to stretch his legs, and a bulge in his jacket pocket made him remember the handbag he had swiped from Dumitra. He pulled out the tiny purse made of supple black leather and undid the pearl clasp.

Inside he found a set of keys, tissues, breath freshener, five hundred dollars in cash, a jar of zinc oxide baby cream, a silver vial the size of his pinky, and another key ring, this one wooden with a large iron key and a strange stone tool.

He opened the vial, sniffed it, and poured a drop of liquid onto a discarded wrapper in the seat beside him.

Blood.

He replaced the stopper and picked up the iron key. The crude design resembled something that might open a dungeon in the Middle Ages. The stone tool it was paired with, a two-inch cylinder notched for most of its length, was even stranger. The notches suggested it was some type of key as well, though he had never seen one made of stone. Grey turned it over, felt along its smooth surface. A small hole in the top allowed the key ring to fit through. Intriguing, though he didn't know what to do with it.

Unfortunately, there was no ID in the purse, no credit cards or home address he might use to track down where Dumitra lived or a location where Viktor might be held.

Another dead end.

As exhaustion and hunger set in—even the airport cafes were closed at this hour—he started to dwell on the unfortunate byproduct of the night's events. Since he had shot and likely killed Dumitra, he had lost his chance to question another of the Speluncescus.

Grey put his head in his hands. Too much time had passed. The more he thought about it, the less of a reason he saw for the Speluncescus to keep Viktor alive. Yes, killing someone of Viktor's stature would cause major problems, but only if they got caught. Better to kill him and dump the body someplace it would never be found.

But that train of thought was useless, and Grey squashed it like he would a mosquito on his arm.

The night passed without incident. Unfortunately, the flight Grey had purchased had a long layover in Vienna, but he would rather linger in Austria than risk staying in Romania.

By the time Grey landed in Prague in the early evening, he had caught up on sleep and eaten a meal in Vienna. He had not told the lieutenant he was coming back. She didn't want him in the city, so better to stay anonymous until he decided on a course of action.

Which Grey was struggling to do. He felt deep in his bones that time was running out for Viktor, if it had not already. Cezar had disappeared, and Grey had no idea where he was. Dumitra was either dead or gravely wounded and under the protection of her organization. Grey had the strong feeling someone else knew where Viktor had been taken—the sole member of the Speluncescu family Grey did know how to reach.

Anton.

Grey was torn. The reason he had left Prague in the first place and chased the Speluncescus across Europe was because Anton was off limits. The middle Speluncescu brother had committed no crimes on record, had the ear of the city's elite, and had logged a police complaint against Grey.

Grey respected the rule of law, the absurd social contract needed to protect human nature from itself. But the law had its flaws and its limits. If he had to, Grey knew he would take whatever actions he deemed necessary to achieve justice. He had done it before and would do it again. He had done it in the last twenty-four hours, and saved a little girl's life.

But vigilante action was a slippery slope. One fraught with subjective belief and moral superiority and the elevation of individual needs over the group.

The more Grey thought about it, the more he wanted to stake out Anton's house and take him captive. It was the only immediate solution he could see. But two things deterred him. First, even apart from the moral concerns, torture of any kind was not a good way to obtain information. People would say anything under duress to make severe pain go away. Grey had used the *threat* of torture before to procure information, and occasionally gone further when innocent lives were in immediate danger, but he didn't like to do it. He supposed he could kidnap Anton and use him as bait to lure Cezar to Prague, but if Grey got caught, he would go to prison.

There were other risks as well. The risk of trying to fight people who moved like animals and had unexplainable strength and agility.

But those sort of risks Grey had long ago abandoned, if the need was great enough.

Viktor needed his help.

End of discussion.

In the safety and bright lights of Václav Havel airport, Grey paced back and forth, itching to take action, pawing at his stubble in frustration as he tried to think through the angles.

If there was no other choice, Grey would try to get some answers out of Anton one way or another. But if Grey botched the attempt and landed in jail or found himself deported, then Viktor's chances of returning alive went from slim to microscopic.

Instead Grey changed his mind and took a taxi to the police station near Viktor's house. Lieutenant Andrasko was filling out paperwork in her office and agreed to meet him. Thirty minutes later, he was sitting across from her desk with a cup of burnt coffee, watching her flinty gaze slowly widen as he gave her the rundown of events that had occurred since he had left Prague.

When he finished, she crossed herself, swore softly in Czech, and pressed a fist against her mouth. "Viktor, Viktor. I don't . . . I don't even know how to make a report on this."

"I'm not sure you should," Grey said. "Not until we know our next move."

"Those children. It's just so unbelievable. So . . . horrifying."

"I know," Grey said grimly. "Any developments on your end?"

The lieutenant looked off to the side. "Daryna's murder isn't my only case, and as much as I want to help Viktor . . ." She turned back at Grey. "At this point, I don't know where to turn. At least DNA results should come in this week. If no one in the criminal database matches the blood at the crime scene, which I suspect will be the case, I'll pressure Anton to give a sample. DNA can identify close relatives."

"You know he won't agree."

"There are other ways of obtaining DNA."

Grey waved a hand. "Which gets us nowhere. We already know it's the Speluncescus."

"It could help with the legal case," she muttered, though Grey could tell she was as unimpressed by the argument as he was.

"Let me know if you think of anything," he said as he stood.

"Where are you going?"

"I'm not sure." A feeling of helplessness overtook him, causing his hands to clench at his side.

"You know I can't protect you if you get in trouble."

"I'll be in touch."

After Grey left the police station, he hesitated when he got to the street, again debating where to go. Instead of heading for Viktor's townhome, he changed his mind and walked in the opposite direction. He had one last card to play before he considered drastic measures.

The sun started to descend on the spires and red rooftops of the city during Grey's short walk to Purgatory. The doors to the nightclub had not yet opened, but Grey pounded on them anyway. After a spell of hard knocking, he stopped and walked away, only to hear the door open behind him. Grey turned to see Anton Speluncescu exiting the club, flanked by two security guards.

Anton was wearing beige slacks, swanky brown loafers, a white turtleneck, sunglasses despite the late hour, and a wide-brimmed hat that accompanied the ensemble, but which elicited a whisper in the back of Grey's mind, asking whether the voluminous hat served another purpose.

Shielding Anton's skin from the last few rays of sunlight.

The flesh of the bar manager's hands was exposed, but Grey remembered the baby lotion he had found in Dumitra's purse. Zinc oxide, Grey knew, was also a heavy-duty sunblock.

The bodyguards waited by the door as Anton approached Grey on the street. The two men faced each other from a foot away.

"You seem surprised to see me," Anton mocked. "Perhaps because it's still daylight? You discovered a few things about my family while you were away, didn't you?" His eyes moved suggestively to the bandage on Grey's left arm from where Dumitra had bitten him.

Though fairly certain Anton would not attack him with people on the street, Grey's hands were tense at his sides, ready for anything. "I came to make a deal."

Anton opened a palm. "I'm a businessman. Speak your mind."

"What will it take to get Viktor back?"

"We've been over this before. What will it take for you to listen?"

Grey chuckled. "I thought you'd say that."

"Then why are you wasting my time?"

"To offer you the actual deal: let Viktor go, and I won't tear down everything you've built. So far, you're not a wanted criminal, at least in the public eye. This tells me you like your life here. You don't want to live on the run and give it all up."

"I find it highly amusing that you believe you understand my motives or those of my family. What I do not find amusing is your threats. You must know I've filed a police report to stop you from harassing me further with this nonsense. I'll have you arrested the next time it happens."

"Last chance," Grey said. "Viktor has Interpol contacts. We'll spare no effort to ensure your family's crimes are exposed."

Anton smiled as if for the cameras, then took a step forward, standing toe to toe with Grey, and spoke in a low, ominous voice. "You shot my mother in the heart last night. Do you think we'll let that go unpunished?"

"Do you think I'll let you keep Viktor?"

Anton's lips curled upwards in a slow, sinister smile. "His life has assumed a purpose he never knew he had."

"What the hell does that mean?"

"You'll know soon enough. I can see in your eyes that you already have suspicions, but there's so much more to discover. Are you ready to meet that which truly owns the night, feeds in the darkness?"

Grey snarled in order to mask the prickle of gooseflesh creeping down his arms. "I don't care what sort of twisted surgeries you and your family have had. Dumitra bled when I shot her, and I'll hunt the rest of you down too."

"For millennia, many have tried."

Grey was tired of the charade, sick of exchanging words, bristling with rage and frustration. Just before he turned away, Anton pulled back the sleeve on his left arm, exposing a swath of milky white skin. The dying rays of the sun caused the flesh to pinken almost at once and form little blisters, as if exposed to a hot iron.

As Grey stared down in shock, Anton gave a nasty laugh and replaced his sleeve. "Are you a believer yet, Dominic Grey?"

Prague

-25-

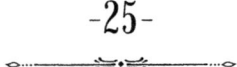

Mari stood very still at the top of the staircase in the secret chamber she had found behind the bookshelf in her uncle's library, listening for sounds from below. The library was on the ground floor, so the stairs must lead to a basement or an underground passage. She had no reason to think anyone was down there, but the clandestine nature of the chamber, and her general state of fear, contributed to the dryness of her mouth and her hesitation to take that first step.

She had the sudden irrational, terrifying thought that her uncle himself might be a vampire. *What if I find a crypt with an open coffin down here? What if* Alice's Adventures Under Ground *is a reference to something disturbing and otherworldly that I'm about to uncover?*

Using a breathing technique she had learned in yoga class, Mari brought her stress to a manageable level and found a light switch. She flicked it. Light from a pair of iron sconces flooded the staircase. There were no cobwebs and very little dust. Her uncle had kept the area clean. Nervous she might not be able to get back, she wedged a book at the base of the metal door.

As Mari crept down the stairs, berating herself for her fear of the unknown but unable to shake it, she noticed the smell of mildew in the secret chamber had started to dissipate, replaced by a faint odor of wood polish.

Thirteen stairs in total. The mark of a coven.

Stop it, Mari.

She supposed Viktor could be hiding out down here, though she found that unlikely. He would know everyone was worried sick about him. Another possibility, that he might be injured or unable to escape or . . . worse . . . caused her to grit her teeth and press forward.

Motion-sensor pendant lights flicked on as Mari stepped into the underground room at the bottom of the stairs. The sizeable space had a wood-beamed ceiling and old brick walls.

A wool rug covered the floor. More bookshelves lined the walls. Glancing at the collection, she noticed a more unruly collection of books, papers, and folders filling the shelves. Mari guessed this was an old wine cellar converted to a storage room for Viktor's overflow research.

Not just a storage room, she thought as she examined the contents of the alcoves between the bookshelves, noting the stacks of bottled water and absinthe, canned food, a full-size refrigerator, a toilet, fire extinguisher, first-aid kit, batteries, a laptop, device chargers, blankets, pillows, and a little kitchenette.

A safe room.

Near the staircase, Mari saw a smart home device mounted on the wall, as well as a monitor for a security camera. She peered into the monitor and started when she saw the street outside the front of the townhome. According to the time and date on the monitor, she was looking at the street in real time.

Two comfy chairs and a leather sofa were arranged around a marble coffee table on the rug in the center of the room. A black Moleskine notebook was lying atop the coffee table. Before she examined it, she paced the room to ensure there were no more surprises.

Her eyebrows rose when she found a bone-handled, wavy dagger and a handgun with spare ammunition in a drawer beneath the coffee table. She had no idea her uncle kept weapons, and wondered if he had ever used them. What kind of strange dagger was that?

She closed the drawer and picked up the notebook. The way it was sitting out in the open, in addition to the unlocked metal door in the chamber above, made her think her uncle had left the notebook for someone to find.

Was this why he returned to the house on the night of his disappearance? If so, why not just tell someone?

Maybe there was no one he could trust.

Or maybe he had stashed it here as emergency insurance, in case something happened to him.

There was only way to find out. Mari wasted no more time thinking about Viktor's motives, and took a seat on the leather sofa with her legs crossed under her. She opened the first page, drawing a sharp breath when she saw the note written in Viktor's handwriting just inside the cover.

Record of Inquiry into the Speluncescu Family

I have left this journal in case something befalls me this night, or before I can make a full report to the police. The house is being watched—I am being watched—and I cannot discount the possibility someone has gained control of my surveillance system. The library is the only room off camera, and I cannot risk a search by an intruder, so I've hidden the journal here. Mari, if you've deduced the location, I'm sorry it's come to this (I did not know how else to keep it safe in the limited time I had), and please give the journal straightaway to Dominic Grey (or, if he is not there, give it to Lieutenant Andrasko and ask her to summon Grey at once). As soon as you do this, I want you to go to the airport and immediately return to Los Angeles. Under no circumstances do I want you involved in any other way. There is grave danger to you as well. Please heed my wishes in this regard.

Love,
Uncle Viktor

Mari forgot all about the curry getting cold on the stove. She barely moved for the next two hours as she read Viktor's hastily penned summary of what he had done, and where he had gone, since the night he had left Prague for Cluj-Napoca. The last entry of the journal was dated the night of his disappearance. At the very end, she found a chilling paragraph which she read three times, both stunned and aghast by the implications.

I now know the ancient name of the family we seek, but I've yet to locate their true home in the Czech Republic. If I or someone else does, I believe we will find the answers to a great many questions. Not just the location and identity of Daryna's murderer, but—incredibly—perhaps a glimpse into the mystery of the true origins of the vampire myth.

Mari closed the journal and sat deep in thought, barely able to believe what she had read.

What has Viktor found?

Who are these people? What *are* they?

Most importantly, what have they done with him?

She was terrified of the answer to that question.

Mari had lost her appetite, but she had eaten very little all day, and needed to put something in her system while she decided what to do. She took the journal and headed for the stairs, but stopped when she noticed a flicker of movement on the security monitor. Peering closer, assuming it was a random passerby, she instead saw the silhouette of a lean figure wearing a dark jacket, his face concealed by a hooded sweatshirt worn beneath the outer layer, veering off the street and walking swiftly towards the entrance to the townhome.

Fear gripped her by the throat.

-26-

Though Viktor half-expected to be awakened by a billowing curtain and a mysterious figure climbing through the window of his hotel suite, the rest of his night in Budapest passed without incident. He hunkered down in his room and recorded everything he had witnessed during his investigation in a Moleskine journal.

The next day, by the time he flew to Prague and made it through customs, the sun had already begun to descend. As he walked through the familiar surroundings of Václav Havel Airport, he shouldered his traveling bag and dialed the number for the auction house the bookseller had mentioned. An older male voice answered on the third ring.

"Fritsch and Schlessinger."

"Good afternoon. This is Viktor Radek. I made an inquiry last night about two pieces that were sold at auction some time ago."

"Yes, we received your inquiry."

"I apologize for the inconvenience. It's a rather pressing matter. If there's any way you could expedite it, I'd be happy to compensate you."

"That won't be necessary, Professor. We know you've frequented our auctions over the years and appreciate your patronage. I did check the transaction log on the auction you mentioned. Not all buyers release their information, as I'm sure you know, but in this instance, the name and purchase price were smudged out on the ledger."

"Smudged out?"

"It's a little strange, there must have been an ink spill at some point. This auction occurred decades ago."

"Are you sure it's the right transaction?"

"A medieval shield and an oil painting were mentioned together. That's a rather unique occurrence."

"It seems odd those details escaped the ink spill."

"The items were mentioned in the auctioneer notes, which are kept in a separate location. We don't always keep those, so that was a stroke of luck."

"What else did the notes say?"

"They only mentioned the items."

"Who was the auctioneer?"

"Deceased, I'm afraid."

"Does anyone still work there who might remember the auction?"

"Current management bought the house five years ago but kept the name. *Pane* Fritsch is also deceased, and *Pane* Schlessinger has retired to his estate. I would not normally suggest this, but for someone such as yourself, if you desire I could make an inquiry—"

"I know the Schlessingers. I'll contact Jan myself."

After the call ended, Viktor debated asking Lieutenant Andrasko to accompany him to the Schlessinger family estate, then decided not to waste her time with an excursion that he doubted would provide much insight.

Instead he texted his private driver and requested an airport pickup.

The Schlessinger estate had seen better days.

Located in the Hanspaulka neighborhood of Prague 6, a favorite of diplomats and other wealthy residents desiring larger, more private estates than the city center offered, Viktor had once attended a dinner party at the Schlessinger house and remembered a cream-colored Georgian manor with manicured gardens. Now, as Viktor stepped out of the black town car and into the chilly evening air, he noticed the grass was overgrown and littered with fallen leaves, the once-gurgling fountains were silent and miasmic, the air had the faint whiff of a compost heap, and the exterior of the house was in desperate need of a new coat of paint.

Someone had planted a scarecrow in the front yard. As he navigated the moss and vines that had overtaken the walkway, a loose piece of cloth on the scarecrow flapped eerily in the breeze. A finch darted out of a hedge, and a crow cawed from a nearby tree.

The emaciated man with a crown of wispy white hair who opened the front door bore little resemblance to the lean, energetic businessman Viktor remembered from twenty years ago. In the heyday of his auction house, Jan Schlessinger was respected around the city for his discerning taste in art and wine, and for his lavish dinner parties.

Jan squinted at Viktor from behind his glasses. It was clear he did not remember him, even after Viktor introduced himself and the nature of his visit. Jan invited Viktor inside anyway.

"My wife died a few years ago, and my butler retired," Jan said as he led Viktor to a dusty sitting room that looked unused for months. A window overlooked a beech tree with barren limbs. "I don't entertain like I used to, but I can offer you something to drink."

"I'm sorry to hear that, and no thank you. I won't be long. I just have a few questions."

Jan flicked a switch, igniting the gas fireplace, and sat in an armchair opposite Viktor. "I'm sorry, what was it about again?"

Viktor repeated his initial inquiry, again asking whether Jan remembered an auction some time ago with a medieval shield and an oil painting, both bearing a similar motif of crossed spears.

At first Jan looked at him as blankly as before, but then something sparked in his eyes, a memory ignited.

"I remember her now . . . so tall and beautiful, so pale . . . she bought both pieces and some others as well, all from the same collection. In fact, she bought everything."

Relieved Jan's memory of the auction had survived, Viktor took out the photo of Dumitra Speluncescu and showed it to him.

Jan jabbed a gnarled finger at the photo. "Oh, that's her. A real dish, eh? I can't remember what I had for breakfast sometimes, but I can remember some of my auctions as if they were yesterday. And this one I'll never forget. One of the strangest sales we had."

"Why is that?"

"I didn't know her, for one. And I knew almost everyone that came in. I never saw her again, or the old man she came in with. Do you know who they are?"

"I believe the woman is Dumitra Speluncescu."

He squinted again. "Don't know the family."

"Neither do I," Viktor said. "This old man . . . you're sure they were together?"

"She came in on his arm. I thought maybe he was her father."

"Can you describe him?"

He shrugged as his eyes went distant. "Stooped, skin like sandpaper and even paler than hers, so pale I thought they must be albinos. He had a long hooked nose, a raspy voice . . . he had to be ninety years old. They spoke to each other in Romanian, which I recognize but don't speak. It happens a lot at auctions. Buyers discussing the sale in another language to keep the conversation private."

Viktor filed the information away, wondering about Dumitra's companion.

"Here's the thing about the pieces they bought," Jan continued. "They were all stolen."

"What do you mean? By Dumitra and the old man?"

"No, no. From their house, by someone else. They were there to retrieve them. I never did business again with *that* middleman, I'll tell you. I tried to tell the woman and the old man how to file a claim, but they didn't seem interested. They paid for their items and left without a word."

I bet that thief had a very short life span. "Do you remember what else they recovered?"

This time, Jan stared off to the side for so long Viktor thought he had lost him. "Just one more thing I can remember," Jan said finally. "It had an odor about it. It's the most powerful memory associative, you know. The smell of something. It's so odd how it sticks in the mind."

"What sort of smell?"

"Like something rotten. It was coming from a little chest with holes in the top. Nothing too strong, not like there was a dead animal inside, just something that was . . . off. A funky mushroom kind of smell. I paid a bulk price and the middleman dropped it off with the other items. The chest had a padlock, and I hadn't had a chance to have it opened. Because of the smell, I didn't think it had much value, and hadn't brought it out yet. The woman specifically asked about it."

Viktor leaned forward. "Did it have a carving on the side? Crossed spears on the back of a dragon?"

"Something like that, yes. It was an old wooden chest, very old, and there was a name on the bottom . . . I used to know what it was because I searched for it . . ." he held his palms up, sheepish, as he searched his memory.

Viktor held his breath while Jan tried to recall the name. So far, while it might have been a stroke of pure luck that a thief had picked the wrong house to rob, and drawn Dumitra out into the open, Viktor hadn't heard anything yet that would help him move forward.

"Devořchák," Jan said with a great sigh, as if relieved his memory still functioned. "E. Devořchák. Ever heard the name?"

"No," Viktor murmured, which was true, though his mind had quickly made an association.

Nicolaus de Chak.

De Chak.

De-voř-chák.

Dvořák was a common Czech name, and in Czech, a *vor* was a raft or flatboat. Viktor imagined that when the first de Chaks had migrated from Romania, they must have changed their name to make it sound more Czech, and inserted a word in the middle, perhaps to symbolize the journey. He further assumed the family had eventually changed their name to Speluncescu, imagining that when the world changed and technology took hold, making it far easier to trace backgrounds and names, the family had sought to protect its identity even further.

But why? What are they hiding?

What is in those strange chests?

Viktor probed for more details surrounding their visit but heard nothing else of interest. He stood and thanked Jan for his time, wondering if anyone was checking on him in that huge house during the week, hoping he had family members who were still alive.

When Viktor returned to the private car, buoyed by the new information, he got a text from Lieutenant Andrasko inquiring if they could meet first thing in the morning at the station. He replied in the affirmative. Now that they had a name, he felt confident she could help him trace the journey of the Devořchák-Speluncescu family in the Czech Republic.

"Where to, sir?" his driver asked.

"Home."

"Right away."

Viktor checked the time. Seven p.m.

Grey still had not responded, but Viktor decided it was time to contact Mari. She was not scheduled to arrive until ten p.m. from Kutna Hora. Perhaps they could have a late dinner together when she arrived, before he sent her off in the morning. As he started to place the call, a text arrived from an unlisted number. Odd. He almost never got spam on his phone. Before he deleted it, he realized a photo was attached.

A photo of Mari.

His breath caught in his throat as he realized someone had caught her walking out of Viktor's townhome, unaware of the camera trained on her. *Someone is watching my house. Watching my niece.* His distress spiked further when he read the text itself.

> Libeňský most. Midnight. Come alone and contact no one.

Do prdele, he swore.

Libeňský most was a bridge spanning the Vltava, one of the longest bridges in the city. Located about three miles downriver from Stare Mesto, the bridge connected the Holešovice quarter with Libeň, was closed to vehicles, and would be deserted at that time of night.

I should have sent her home sooner.

Before now, Viktor had not considered the fact Mari might be in imminent danger, especially since his investigation had taken him so far from home.

That promise of danger to his niece might never manifest—as long as he did as he was told.

Why wait until now? Why not come for me in Cluj or Budapest?

But he understood. The Speluncescus did not like exposure. They did not desire to eliminate anyone they did not have to, especially someone with Viktor's reputation. They had tried to warn him off—but he hadn't listened.

And now he had found them, picked his way carefully through the tangled strands of their web. Yet he knew—had known from the beginning—that when you plunge your hand into the home of the spider, waving blindly through the silken threads spun in dark and secret places, the fanged monster lurking in the center will always strike back.

When Viktor arrived home, he dismissed his driver and found the house empty. He felt relieved he did not have to pretend everything was fine. If she did come home early, what should he say? What should he do?

In the end, he knew he could do or say nothing.

At least nothing the Speluncescus would know about, because Viktor did not dare disobey their orders. If Grey was here, maybe he could come up with a tactical solution to shield Mari from harm, but Viktor did not know how to guarantee her safety. He could not refuse to go to the bridge and ask the police for help, because they couldn't watch her forever, and maybe not even for a night. He simply couldn't risk it. No, the more he dwelled on it, pacing back and forth in his kitchen, the only option he saw was to comply.

He was under no illusion what would happen when he did. At best, the Speluncescus would keep him alive for a short while, or take him somewhere far outside the city to kill him. If so, Grey or Lieutenant Andrasko might have a tiny window of opportunity to save him, and it was up to Viktor to keep himself alive until they did. If he couldn't be saved, then maybe his journal could help bring down the Speluncescus.

The only place in the townhome not under the Orwellian eye of his security system was his study. This was by design. He needed at least one place he knew was private. He supposed he could turn the cameras off, but if the Speluncescus broke in and checked the footage, he did not want to betray any evidence of his intentions.

In the study, Viktor closed the blinds and opened the secret bookshelf door. He descended to the basement and updated his journal of the investigation with the visit to the Schlessinger estate, plus all of his thoughts and suspicions that flowed from that meeting. He recommended a full trace and genealogy search for the Devořchák name, as well as all transactional documents connected to the house where Florin had been staying. He sensed the Speluncescus had not used the Prague house as their family home for some time, if ever. But somewhere, somehow, they must have left a record of where they had settled when they left Romania.

He set the journal on the coffee table in the basement and wrote Mari a note inside the front cover. He struggled with the decision, since it involved her further, however slight her role may be. But the Speluncescus needed to be stopped. More innocents would die if he did nothing. Mari could hand over the journal straightaway, the Speluncescus should never find out, and once Mari returned to Los Angeles, they would have no reason to pursue her.

Next he opened the bottom drawer and debated taking his kris and his handgun, the latter of which he almost never carried. In the end he left them both. *Even if I can defend myself successfully, which is highly doubtful, my resistance will just spur them to come for Mari.*

With a heavy heart, he studied the shelves in the basement and decided on the Lewis Carroll collection. He gathered the books, climbed the stairs to the library, closed the bookshelf door, and rearranged the shelf with the hidden switch. Mari was a very clever girl, and he felt sure she would notice. They had read *Alice in Wonderland* over and over together when she was a child. He would have preferred to leave a clue for Grey, but Grey might not arrive for some time. Nor could Viktor risk dropping the journal off with the police, or even in Lieutenant Andrasko's mailbox, since he didn't know who the Speluncescus were watching, or how they kept finding him. The risk to reward ratio, with Mari's life in the balance, was too great. He even debated leaving the journal out in the open in the library, but the Speluncescus might search the house and find it first.

He knew his plan was far from perfect, but it was the best he could do on short notice. He was just going to have to use his wits and stay alive.

Before leaving the library, Viktor took a moment to scan the titles in the section on Eastern and Central European folklore. A memory bubbling in his subconscious compelled his eyes to roam further, to the Byzantine, Achaemenid, and Central Asiatic empires.

Something clicked, and he pulled out a history of Sogdia, an ancient civilization roughly encompassing the modern territories of Uzbekistan, Tajikistan, Kazakhstan, and Kyrgyzstan. He flipped through the slender tome published a decade ago by Oxford University Press, scanning the tabbed pages until he found the reference he wanted. *Yes, that's the one.*

A little-known culture outside of academic circles, Sogdian history began deep in the Bronze Age, if not earlier, and had flourished until Cyrus the Great swept through with his vast army in the fifth century BCE. The city of Samarkand, a fabled stop on the Silk Road and one of the oldest continually inhabited cities in the world, was once the unofficial capital of the Sogdian city-states. Evidence of human activity in and around Samarkand dated back to Paleolithic times.

Viktor read the passage he had once marked, a footnote in a section on the prehistoric people of the region.

> Herodotus first noted a reference to tribes that hunted blood drinkers in the caves that lay beyond the northern steppes. The oral account was passed to an Athenian soldier during the Greco-Persian War. Recently, a cuneiform clay tablet found beneath the former Principality of Khuttal, a Sogdian city-state, also made reference to "those in the caves who crave blood."

Viktor had always found the passage odd. But he had assumed, in agreement with the scholar who wrote the book, that the "blood drinkers" were a barbaric tribe who imbibed the blood of animals or their vanquished enemies for ritualistic purposes. Or else the reference pertained to one of the many stories of blood-thirsty demons circulating in ancient Mesopotamia, neighbors of the Sogdians. In fact, Viktor might characterize the proliferation of such tales in Mesopotamia as rampant. The Mesopotamian civilization was among the oldest sources—if not the first—of legends tied to vampire mythology in some way. Pottery shards excavated in the region depicted creatures trying to drink the blood of men, and the Epic of Gilgamesh described phantomlike creatures called Ekimmu, wayward spirits returning from the grave to torment the living.

What if the Mesopotamian legends had originated a little further to the east, in the remote, unexplored mountains and cave systems of Central Asia?

What if the progenitor of the vampire had evolved deep inside the Earth, and the legendary pale skin and intolerance of sunlight was attributable not to a curse from God, but a genetic result of subsurface dwelling?

It was just a wild thought, and Viktor had no idea how the rest of the mythology aligned, but the possibilities unnerved him—especially when he considered the meaning of the Latin surname which had prompted him to search out the footnote mentioning the Herodotus account in the first place.

Speluncescu.

Ruler of the cave.

Just before ten p.m., Viktor decided to leave before Mari arrived. He had grown so jittery that, if she did return, she would know something was wrong. Better just to go.

With two hours remaining until his appointment, Viktor did not dwell on past mistakes or how much he wished he could change the future. Instead he stuck a set of lock picking tools Grey had given him in his pocket and pressed forward with the case. Doing his job. Remaining a professional.

And in this regard, he had two final stops to make.

First he took a risk and walked right by Purgatory, the club managed and owned by Anton Speluncescu. Viktor knew a city camera would catch him on CCTV just outside the club, passing the crowd of people waiting in line. He also knew the lieutenant and Grey would check the footage at some point in the near future. Before he passed another camera, Viktor stopped walking and hailed a taxi. He wanted Purgatory to be the last place he was seen, his final message before succumbing to whatever fate awaited him that night.

Investigate the family. They know where I am.

Inside the taxi, he checked the time again. Ten-thirty.

Ninety minutes until his appointment with destiny.

"Where to?" the driver asked.

"Olšany Cemetery."

The driver gave him a funny look—*who visits a cemetery this late?*—but did not argue.

Earlier, after leaving the journal in the hidden basement, Viktor had thought of another method to locate the Speluncescus. He had wondered if, after emigrating to Bohemia, the Devořchák name had ever appeared in a local paper. A birth, a death, a property notice, anything. Viktor had gone online, signed into his account with the Czech National Library, and conducted a thorough search of the archives. This included a microfiche scan that pulled up documents as far back as the turn of the twentieth century.

To his shock, he found a hit. Only a single one, but that was more than he expected. What he unearthed was a public notice in 1910 in a Sunday edition of a defunct Prague newspaper, *České slovo*, announcing the death and impending burial of *Pane* Evzen Devořchák. The entire edition of the paper was preserved in microfiche.

The burial notice shocked him more than the reference to the family itself, though on reflection, he did not know why. It was normal for a family wealthy enough to purchase an historic home in Stare Mesto to make use of a graveyard for the affluent. It should be more surprising he did not find *more* references, but he attributed that to the family obsession with secrecy. Maybe, at the time, they could not avoid public notice of the death of Evzen Devořchák. Or maybe they had used the burial as a way to appear normal and not attract attention. Or maybe in 1910 the Devořcháks *were* normal.

If he was honest with himself, what surprised him about the notice was the reference to death itself.

Because a vampire is an immortal creature, and an immortal creature should not die.

Yet what if the Speluncescu are not immortal? What if, like all myths, parts are true and parts are false?

Bah!

What are these thoughts in your head?

The Speluncescus have well and truly gotten under your skin, Viktor Radek, and beaten you at your own game.

After another bit of research, this time on a genealogy website dedicated to locating gravestones—truly, the Internet was a remarkable thing—he purchased a map and database of Olšany Cemetery that told him exactly where to find the tomb of Evzen Devořchák.

The cemetery was located in Vinohradská, a fifteen-minute drive. When the driver arrived at the cemetery, eying the closed gates with a dubious expression, he offered to wait. Viktor dismissed him. He did not know how long he would take, and he could find another taxi by walking a block away.

A light fog had arisen. As Viktor walked alongside the high wall beside the gate, searching for a place out of sight of the road to enter, he told himself he was searching for a family plot with additional names to research, or some other clue to locating the Speluncescus. But he knew the chances of such a thing were slim, and Viktor had written down the information about the gravesite in his journal.

So why was he out here, sneaking into a cemetery in the dead of night?

In his heart, he knew the reason.

Because if he was wrong, and the descendants of the de Chak family were indeed vampires, or something like it, then the body of Evzen Devořchák should not be in that tomb. Or if the body was there, then it should be *different*.

Silly, perhaps, but he had to conquer his fears.

He had to see for himself.

He had to know.

Feeling somewhat ridiculous, his knees creaking, Viktor heaved himself over the wall and landed heavily on the ground. He looked up, peering through the fog at the ivy-covered tombs and thick vegetation. Headstones tilted at odd angles and the breeze caused the spindly branches of the trees to scrape against the stone sides of mausoleums.

He used the light of his cell phone to consult the map of the cemetery he had printed. He knew he was in the general vicinity of the Devořchák grave. Once he had his bearings, he took the most direct route and began walking deeper into the overgrown section, tramping over the mossy ground, inhaling the dampness of the soil. He passed a freshly dug grave from which he half-expected a white hand to explode from the earth and drag its decomposing corpse out of the grave. *Do prdele, Viktor, you're as twitchy as a child.*

He checked his watch. 11:15 p.m. The Libeňský bridge was a ten-minute drive from the cemetery. He needed to hurry.

Less than five minutes later he found the footpath he needed. It twisted and turned deeper into an even more disheveled corner of the cemetery, a lightless area where the moonlight barely penetrated the thick canopy. Grimly he continued, the sound of his footsteps accompanying the constant rustle of branches and the distant hoot of an owl.

At last he found it. A moss-stained crypt of modest size—no larger than a master bedroom closet—with a wolf's head carved in counter-relief into the weathered stone above the door.

He stepped through the high grass to read the inscription on the side wall. Most of the words had eroded but he could read enough letters to deduce the name was *Evzen Devořchák*. He could not make out the birth date, but the date of death—1910—was intact.

Viktor did not have Grey's lock picking skills, but Viktor thought he could muddle through a hundred-year-old lock on a crypt. First he tried simply to push on the door—and was shocked when the door creaked inward, releasing a rush of stale air.

After looking over his shoulder, Viktor swept a spiderweb aside and stepped into the crypt. The only thing inside was a stone coffin with a set of crossed spears carved into the lid.

A motif of crossed spears that was very familiar by now.

If Viktor did not have a midnight deadline looming, he did not know how long he would have stood in front of the coffin, shivering in the cool air, staring at those tapered spears, gathering the courage to lift the lid. Disturbing a tomb felt wrong to him. Unnatural. After trying to steady his nerves and failing, he grimaced as he put his hands on the pitted gray stone, then tried to shove the lid aside. It moved a few inches. The groan of protest sounded like a thunderclap in the silence of the tomb.

Viktor planted his feet, lowered his weight, and shoved harder. The lid moved another foot, revealing the edges of a decaying cloth lining the inside of the coffin. With a mighty heave, he pushed the lid further back, enough to reveal the contents of the coffin.

It was empty.

As shock and horror surged through him, Viktor stumbled away, only to back into someone who had silently appeared behind him. Terrified, Viktor whirled and tried to scramble in the other direction, but the crypt was tiny and his back was stuck against the coffin. With nowhere to go, he looked up and saw Cezar Speluncescu standing in the entrance to the tomb, backlit by a shard of moonlight.

The corners of Cezar's lips upturned, revealing two glistening fangs stabbing downward from the top of his gumline. "Hello, Viktor. I believe we've let you discover quite enough."

-27-

As Grey reached for the door handle of Viktor's townhome, the door opened on its own, and someone tall and willowy flew into Grey's arms. Grey was so on edge from recent events that he barely caught himself from lashing out before he realized Mari had opened the door to greet him.

"That's quite a welcome," Grey said, as she disengaged from his arms, a trace of coconut shampoo lingering on her hair.

"Thank God it's you. For a moment, when I saw your hood, I thought . . . let's just go inside."

Grey glanced over his shoulder to scan the street before they entered the townhome and shut the heavy door. As he shrugged out of his jacket, Mari sagged against the wall, her head in her hands, trembling with emotion. "What's wrong?" he asked. "Did something happen?"

She closed her eyes, exhaled, and pushed off the wall. "I need a drink. Then I'll tell you everything."

They moved to the kitchen. Grey poured himself a glass of water as Mari sloshed red wine into a glass. She disappeared for a moment while Grey sat at the kitchen island, collecting himself after the long day and the disturbing meeting with Anton.

How did his skin react to the sun like that?

Easy answer: he knew I might come by, and set something up beforehand to unnerve me.

But if that was no trick, what the hell just happened?

As Grey hunched over his glass of water, the air in the kitchen seemed to grow warmer, flushing his cheeks and causing him to strip off the hoodie. Something Anton had said kept repeating in Grey's mind, a warning made all the more chilling by the confident manner in which it was delivered.

Viktor's life has assumed a purpose he never knew he had.

Did the Speluncescus mean to harvest Viktor's blood and organs for their criminal enterprise?

Or had Anton meant something else?

At least, Grey thought, he had used the present tense. At least Viktor could still be alive.

But for how long?

Mari came back in holding a black Moleskine journal. She set the journal on the island and proceeded to tell Grey the story of how she had found it, as well as a summary of what it contained.

"Rather incredible, isn't it?" she said quietly.

"I would have said *unbelievable*, if I hadn't just had some similar experiences."

"What happened?"

Grey hesitated. Viktor's note accompanying the journal was clear about what role he wished Mari to have: the one where she returned immediately to Los Angeles.

On the other hand, while Mari might be Viktor's niece, she was also a grown woman who had risked her safety by staying in Prague, seeking out the journalist, and finding her uncle's journal.

"Don't you dare hold anything back," she said, sensing his indecision.

He pursed his lips and nodded, then watched the blood slowly drain from Mari's face as he described the incident beneath the opera house.

"Oh my God," she said, sinking into one of the leather-backed swivel chairs at the kitchen island, struggling to accept what she had heard. "Who . . . who are these people? *What* are they?"

"I don't know. I know what they want us to believe, and . . ." Unable to make sense of what he had seen, Grey cupped his mouth with a hand and looked away. He moved to the library with the journal and sat unmoving in the leather chair by the window for the next hour while he finished reading Viktor's account, remaining deep in thought until Mari came into the room with a glass of wine and sat beside him.

"We have to get him back," she said softly.

Grey admired her courage in the face of what she had just heard. "Viktor was clear in his instructions. He told you to give me the journal and go back to Los Angeles. I agree whole-heartedly."

"That's nice," she said. "Would you like to dish out any other paternalistic commentary before we discuss what to do next?"

Grey crossed his arms. "If what you just heard doesn't deter you, I doubt anything will."

"You got that goddamn right. I'll leave the fighting to you, but I'm not going anywhere."

"Viktor might never forgive me."

"It's not your choice to make. Or his."

Grey looked out the bay window. "Okay then."

"Since that's settled, where do we go from here?"

"Before we worry about anything else, we need to find where the Speluncescus are, and hope Viktor is with them."

"He gave us a name, but what do we do with it?"

"To be honest, I think we need help. I have no idea how to research something like this here. I think we should call Lieutenant Andrasko."

"Do you think she'll help us?"

Grey shrugged. "I don't think she'll stand in our way. And from my brief interaction with her, I do think she'll want to help, even if it's off the books."

"What about Interpol?"

"Jacques is another story. I'll fill him in, but I wouldn't expect him to move as quickly. Anyway, Interpol would just make a local request for assistance, and we already have the lieutenant on board. So let's start with her."

"Viktor was worried about a mole. What if it's the lieutenant?"

"I'd be very surprised, and we're running out of options."

Mari thought about it. "Okay. Call her."

After an hour of voicemails and pestering text messages, the lieutenant finally called Grey back. He summarized the contents of Viktor's journal and the conversation he and Mari had just had."

"Vampires and ancient orders and . . . *do prdele*. I can't believe this is happening. If I tell anyone else about this, I'll be laughed out of the office. Maybe I should be laughing too."

"Trust me, you shouldn't."

She swore again. "I just got home, and I have a full schedule the rest of the week, starting at six a.m. tomorrow."

"Clear it. Viktor won't survive until the weekend. We both know this."

There was another long pause that caused Grey to tense. He wasn't sure where they would turn in the Czech Republic if the lieutenant didn't agree to help them. Finally she sighed and said, "I'll see what I can do tonight. I'll run a records search on the *Devořcháks* and go from there. Not much else to accomplish at this hour."

"Thank you," Grey said. "I'll call you first thing in the morning."

The lieutenant hung up.

The phone had been on speaker, so Mari had heard everything. "That's something, at least. What else can we do?"

He checked his watch. It was after midnight. "I'll try Jacques and see if he can help, then we'll do some research ourselves."

Three hours later, Jacques had still not gotten back to Grey, and they had not uncovered anything new about the Devořcháks. That did not surprise Grey. The lieutenant would have access to far better databases than a private citizen. Frustrated, he and Mari ended up in the kitchen again, nursing a nightcap as they brainstormed their options.

"If we don't find anything tomorrow," she said, "what then?"

"We don't have a lot of options, and I don't like the one we do have."

"Which is?"

"Persuade the only member of the Speluncescu family whose location we do know to tell us something useful."

"Persuade?" she echoed. When he didn't respond, she noticed the grim set to his mouth. "Oh," she said. "Persuade."

"It's not a good plan. I don't think we can touch Anton. But at this point, I don't have another one." His eyes felt gummy from staring at his phone. "We should get some rest. I have the feeling we'll need it."

Mari drained the last of her wine. "Do you think Dumitra survived?"

"I don't see how," he said. "You're wondering who we might have to deal with?"

"Just thinking about that little girl, and hoping the evil bitch who did that to her is dead."

"Yeah. Me too."

"Who do you think they are, Grey? I mean really?"

He took a sip of wine, staring straight ahead. "I don't think they're vampires, if that's what you're asking."

"Why not? I mean at this point, after all we've seen and heard, isn't that the more logical solution?"

"I don't think *vampires* is ever the logical solution."

"That's because your logic has confirmation bias," she said quietly. "Remember when I asked you what you believe in?"

"Yeah."

"How come you never asked me?"

"Hmm? Does it matter at this point?"

"Most people would have asked," she said.

"I'm not most people."

"Believe me, I've figured that one out. I'll tell you anyway. I believe in everything, Grey. If human beings can imagine something, then why can't it exist? Doesn't it sort of exist already, just by virtue of being in our heads, our dreams, our imagination? Is the possibility of a living creature that survives on blood any harder to accept than ones that survive on meat, or plants, or air, or other things you find in nature? If you spend half a second thinking about it, which most people don't, our universe is deeply, deeply strange. Take a step back and look at the world from ten thousand feet. The only reason we think any of this is halfway sane is because we're *used* to it. But what about the things we aren't used to, or simply haven't encountered yet?"

"Mari?"

"Yeah?"

"Get some sleep."

At seven a.m., Grey was making a pot of French press coffee in the kitchen, bleary-eyed from lack of sleep, when he got a call from Lieutenant Andrasko. Grey answered on the first ring.

"I found something," she said.

Grey put the lid on the pot and stepped away, gripping the phone. "What do you mean? The family?"

"When this all started, I traced the property records for the house where Florin was living. That was nothing but a dead-end road to a holding company. When I researched the name Viktor gave us, I found a fifty-year-old deed transfer from Evzen Devořchák—to the same holding company that owns the house in Prague."

"Why didn't you find that the first time?"

"It didn't come up when I researched the holding company. I saw it on a copy of the deed. Anyway, there was also a street address for Evzen Devořchák on the deed. The postal code is in a village called *Lovecký Odpočinek*. It's an hour north of Prague. The best I can tell, the land at this address was purchased a hundred and fifty years ago by Mihaly Devořchák. I don't know what, if anything, is there now. It doesn't show up on Google maps. Those are the only references to the Devořchák family I could find. I tried to search for a Mihaly or Mihai Devořchák leaving Romania, but public records from that time in a backwater like Transylvania are abominable."

A shiver of hope coursed through Grey. "That's great work. And the village isn't far."

"There's something else you should know. On a whim, I ran a check for criminal activity in and around the village."

"Did you sleep last night?"

"Barely. Though Lovecký Odpočinek is only an hour from Prague, it's on the edge of a huge wilderness. I've hiked nearby and it feels very remote. Nothing but a few other villages around. Anyway, an odd pattern appeared in the crime logs. About once every six months, going back at least thirty years, there's a report of a missing person, either an adult or a child, in roughly a twenty-mile radius around that village. That's definitely abnormal for settlements of that size."

Grey had a sudden mental image of Dumitra hunched like a spider over the little girl beneath the opera house, those long glistening fangs sinking into soft flesh. He plunged the stopper on the French press and poured a cup of coffee. "What do you plan to do about all this?"

"That's where it gets tricky. With time, your testimony could help Europol build a case around the Speluncescus and the red market. On the other hand, the . . . stranger things . . . you and Viktor have witnessed will not, shall we say, lead to an instant subpoena."

"Building the case could take weeks, months, years."

"That's right. We don't even know where Cezar is, nor do I have a prayer of getting a warrant for that address in the village. Not without more evidence than Viktor's wild theory about some ancient family changing its name."

"We don't have time for any of this. *Viktor* doesn't have time."

"Thus our dilemma. What I propose is that you and I conduct a little fact-finding mission to this village. It wouldn't be official police business, you understand. Just a trip to the country to follow up on a hunch in our spare time."

"It might even be better," Grey said as he took a long sip of coffee, now that it had cooled a fraction, "if no one knows about this but us. That way any ears that might be listening won't have anything to hear."

"We're on the same page. If we're lucky, we'll have the element of surprise, should we need to use it."

"When can you leave?"

"I have a report to finish this morning which I absolutely cannot put off. Can you meet me at one p.m. two blocks north of the station? Turn right and look for a flower seller on the little side street. I'll be waiting in a blue Škoda."

"I'll be there."

After the lieutenant rang off, Grey stood in place as he finished his coffee, thinking everything through, relieved the lieutenant was on board. He had a couple of errands to run before they left, items to procure in anticipation of his next meeting with the Speluncescus. Whether he believed in vampires or not, he had to deal with the reality of what he had seen.

Mari entered the kitchen wearing slippers and cinnamon-colored pajamas, her hair in a bun above her head, yawning as she sat at the island. She woke up quickly as Grey poured her a cup of coffee and filled her in on the conversation with the lieutenant.

"My uncle could be there," she said. "Do you think . . . do you think Cezar is with him?"

"There's no telling. Viktor got close to them, so even if they don't know we're coming, they'll be on their guard. Listen, Mari—"

"Don't bother. I'm going with you."

He looked her in the eye. "This isn't a dress rehearsal. Whether Viktor is there or not, if we run into the Speluncescus . . ."

"Then I'm counting on you to protect me."

"I couldn't even protect myself the last time I met Cezar."

"There's a gun in that room below the library. Maybe you could use it."

That's one thing I can check off the morning shopping list, Grey thought as he stared across the island at her, admiring her courage but knowing with a sinking heart that it was untested in battle.

And, if someone from the Speluncescu family was living at that address in the village, a test would most surely arise.

-28-

At a quarter past one, Grey found himself in the passenger seat of Lieutenant Andrasko's Škoda Octavia, leaving Prague on a blustery fall day. Not long before they left, Jacques had finally returned Grey's calls, listening in disbelief to Grey's summary of his attempts to find Viktor.

Grey couldn't blame the Interpol agent for his skepticism, even though Grey had left out some of the more incredible details. Unfortunately, without firm evidence of Viktor's whereabouts, or the commission of a crime at the address in the village, Jacques couldn't offer much help other than research from afar.

The lieutenant was driving. Mari was in the back seat, staring out the window with a solemn expression, her hair in a ponytail, dressed in jeans and a gray turtleneck sweater and knee-high leather boots. A lavender Windbreaker with a thick cotton lining was folded on the seat beside her. When Grey left the house wearing jeans and his motorcycle jacket, she had changed out of her own black leather jacket, declaring with a nervous laugh they looked too much like vampire hunters.

Viktor's eight-inch, wavy-bladed *kris* dagger lay in its sheath on top of Mari's Windbreaker, so she would not be defenseless. Grey had used duct tape to form a makeshift waist strap.

Lieutenant Andrasko had shown up in dark slacks, a fitted beige shirt, a *Slavia Praha* ball cap pulled low over her cropped blond hair, and a quilted jacket that gave her plenty of room to conceal her firearm. Like Grey, the lieutenant's sharp blue eyes underwent a constant journey from the rearview to the road as she drove through the city. He sensed she was a woman who missed very little.

As they left the outskirts of Prague and entered a long flat stretch of countryside, the sun poked through the moody cloud cover, causing the leaves in the forest to glitter like gemstones. Grey cracked his window, feeling warm from the turtleneck shirt clinging to his skin. He did not think he had ever worn a turtleneck before, but he and Mari had both worn them to cover up the steel collars Grey had picked up at a BDSM store in Prague. He had also purchased leather bracelets with metal studs to protect their wrists, the best he could do on short notice. The collar and the bracelets made him feel a little ridiculous, but if the Speluncescus decided to go for an artery again, they would be in for a nasty surprise. Mari was glad for the extra protection, but the lieutenant had declined to join them, shaking her head and muttering that she would shoot any lunatic who tried to bite her. Grey also had Viktor's CZ75 semi-automatic handgun—a serious weapon—tucked into a shoulder holster the lieutenant had lent Grey.

"What's in the bag?" Lieutenant Andrasko asked with her eyes still on the road, referring to the red Columbia backpack Grey had found in Viktor's garage, then stocked with items he had purchased in a quick shopping trip that morning.

"A first-aid kit, utility knife, bottled water, and granola bars. Just in case we have to hike somewhere."

"Good thinking."

"Then there's the other stuff," he said, pulling out a trio of necklaces strung with silver crosses, a canteen, a plastic bag full of garlic bulbs, a hammer, and a pair of solid wooden stakes. He set the items in his lap as the lieutenant glanced over with raised eyebrows. Mari gave a sharp intake of breath as she leaned in from the back seat.

Grey slipped on one of the necklaces and tucked it under his turtleneck. He offered one to Mari, which she quickly accepted, and one to Lieutenant Andrasko as well.

"You're serious?" the lieutenant said, glancing over at him.

"I wish I wasn't. I call it hedging our bets."

With a frown, the lieutenant took the cross necklace and slipped it on as she drove.

"What's in the canteen?" Mari asked.

"Holy water," Grey said. "Blessed by a priest at the Catholic Church near Viktor's house. He charged me five dollars and didn't even ask me what it was for."

Mari fingered the necklace at her throat. "Silver is for werewolves, not vampires."

"I couldn't remember."

The lieutenant chuckled. "What are you going to do, peel some garlic and toss it at them?"

Grey started replacing the items in the backpack. "It took a lot for me to go this far. I read what Viktor wrote in his journal about the Bram Stoker connection, and the guy in the shearling coat who avoided the woman selling garlic. With all the other stuff that's happened . . . I decided to take some basic precautions, even though yeah, I feel silly. Just in case . . ." he trailed off as he zipped up the backpack. "Well, just in case."

"I feel better having it with us," Mari said.

The lieutenant snorted. "I can't believe we're having this conversation."

Grey's hand strayed to the wound on his shoulder from where Dumitra had bitten him. Cezar's bites still pained him as well, but so far, Grey had not felt any . . . stranger . . . effects.

"Don't forget sunlight," Mari said. "Maybe what Anton did to show off in front of you wasn't too smart."

"Maybe it's a serious weakness," Grey said, "or just a minor inconvenience. Or maybe, like everything else, it's all a calculated ploy designed to chip away at our sanity and confidence and reinforce the family legend."

"Of course it's a trick," the lieutenant said. "Human beings don't blister that quickly in the sun. Not even people with skin conditions. And vampires," she said with a set to her jaw, "aren't real."

A long silence followed her comment. Grey's eyes roamed to the window. They had just entered a semi-mountainous region of thick forests and ridges and giant eroded rock pillars jutting out of the ground like gnarled stone fingers. Though beautiful, the high ridgelines and karsts gave the landscape an impregnable feel, as if something ancient could have survived in the inaccessible nooks and crannies of the rocky landscape for millennia untold.

"One thing bothers me," the lieutenant said as she gripped the wheel. "The garlic, the fangs, the skin trick, all that scary Halloween nonsense . . . that I get. It all serves a purpose and can easily be manufactured. Well maybe not easily, but goddammit, I'll believe in a twisted crime family with high-tech fang implants ages before I'll believe in actual vampires actually walking the streets of goddamn Prague." She glanced at Grey. "But what about Cezar's superhuman strength and speed? You seem like a guy who'd be a pretty good judge of that. Maybe it was dark, and late, and you weren't sure what you saw? Did you have a couple of beers that night?"

Grey took a long moment to answer, for some reason dwelling on Dumitra's strangely hypnotic eyes as he tried to marshal the thoughts he had entertained on this very subject. "Cezar could be some kind of uber-athlete, I suppose. But even then, and his mother . . ." Grey shook his head. "No one is born that fast. I've fought someone like them before, though. Someone with enhanced physical capabilities that came from a cocktail of drugs and bio-enhancers."

"You mean like a super soldier. A government experiment."

"Something along those lines."

She pursed her lips and nodded, firmly back on the *terra firma* of a rational explanation. "I know stuff like that is out there now. It doesn't ever surprise me that much."

"Yeah," Grey said again, more slowly this time. "Maybe Cezar takes something just before he's about to fight. He knew I was coming to the bridge that night." *Sure, but that doesn't explain Dumitra. She had no idea I would be at the opera.* "Whatever the source, if you come up against one of them, be extremely careful. He took me by surprise, and that's hard to do."

The lieutenant glanced over at him, as if to judge whether or not he was boasting, then returned to watching the road.

"Does either of you have a plan?" Mari asked. "For when we get there?"

"Not until we know the lay of the land," the lieutenant said, which elicited a nod from Grey. "But that might come sooner rather than later," she said as she veered onto an exit marked with the name of the village they were seeking.

Four miles later they pulled into a small settlement scattered along a broad slope that rose to a towering rock formation high above their present location. On either side of the main road, small and irregular tracts of land interspersed with white farmhouses, some of it cultivated and some of it overgrown, lent the village a chaotic feel. Grey found that unusual. Usually these country hamlets were laid out in a tidy grid.

As they rolled through, he guessed the village housed a few hundred souls at most. The little settlement with its thatch-roofed houses and lack of infrastructure seemed lost in time, stuck in a different century. The only commercial establishments Grey saw were a pub and a post office.

As the lieutenant drove down the potholed road bisecting the town, Grey kept a sharp eye out, but never saw the street listed on the old Devořchák deed. Most of the houses did not even have visible numbers. The lieutenant tried driving down the handful of dirt roads leading out of the village, none of which had a street sign, but each time the road led back into the forest or dead-ended at a remote homestead.

"We're going to have to ask someone," the lieutenant said as they cruised through the center of town again. We could drive around all day."

"There's something off about this place," Mari said. "It's too quiet, and I haven't seen a single cemetery. Not even at the church. Is that normal here?"

"I noticed the same thing," the lieutenant said grimly. "And no, it's not."

When Grey glanced back, he saw Mari sitting with her arms hugging her chest in the back seat, staring out the driver's side window.

The lieutenant slowed to a stop alongside a man walking down the side of the road in a straw hat. His creased eyes narrowed with suspicion when he saw the lieutenant waving him over. She spoke to him in Czech, and, for a long moment, Grey didn't think the man was going to respond. When the lieutenant repeated herself, the man spat on the ground and said something in return. By the set of his jaw and the tone of his voice, it was obvious he did not appreciate the question.

After a brief conversation, the man shuffled off. The lieutenant watched him leave and said, "He claims he's never heard of that street, or the Speluncescus, or the Devořcháks. I think he was lying."

"So what, the whole village is in league with them?" Grey asked.

"That or terrified." The lieutenant snarled as she clutched the wheel, threw the gearshift into reverse, and whipped the car around. "I've had about enough of this."

"What are you doing?" Grey asked.

"Going to that pub so we can discuss what to do. I haven't had a bite to eat all day, we're wasting petrol at this point, and bartenders are good sources of information. Somebody in this damn village is going to tell us where this street is."

They returned to the only pub or restaurant they had seen, a two-story tavern made of white brick at the edge of the village. Weeds had sprouted through the pavement in the parking lot. A sign hung from a wooden post jutting out from beneath the overhang of the thatch roof. *The Village Arms*, Mari translated.

As the lieutenant parked the car, Grey checked his watch.

Three-fifteen p.m.

Judging by the position of the sun, they had less than two hours of daylight left. Some primeval, irrational part of his psyche told him they did not want to be caught in the village after dark. He grimaced and forced the thought away.

That's exactly what the Speluncescus want you to think.

As they approached the entrance to the pub, Grey's boots crunched on a thin layer of debris. Assuming it was fall leaves, he glanced down and realized the brick path leading to the front door was covered with brown, desiccated thorn branches, as if someone had trimmed a rose bush and scattered the clippings on the path. When they reached the battered wooden door to the pub, he noticed a faded mural painted in the center: the Czech-double-tailed lion surrounded by a quartet of white crosses.

The lieutenant caught up to him and stood with a tightened jaw in front of the door. "Thorns across the threshold and crosses on the door. Classic wards against vampires."

In the corner of his eye, Grey saw Mari crossing herself. He opened the door and saw a dimly lit interior filled with people, all of whom ceased talking to stare at the newcomers. Grey had seen so few residents along the way that it seemed like half the town was inside. It was odd to see the pub so full at such an early hour, and he wondered with a scowl—annoyed at his own train of thought—if the villagers came early so they could leave before dark. He did not see any children and noticed most of the people looked well over forty years old, all of them bearing the weathered, plain-spoken look of people who work the land.

Grey walked beneath looping strands of garlic strung above the door. The villagers seemed tense as he did this, then relaxed a fraction. The pub was a simple affair: tables in the center and a line of booths on the long wall to Grey's left. All of the furniture was dark wood and rustic. To his right was the bar. At the far end, a fire crackled in a stone hearth. On the wall opposite the booths hung an assortment of rusty farm implements such as pitchforks and axes. With a start, Grey realized they all looked very sharp and could be used, if the need arose, as weapons.

They took the only seat remaining, a booth near a dartboard in the back. The bar smelled of good beer and dumplings. A waitress with graying hair and a checkered apron came over to take their order. The lieutenant asked for a medium pub burger and a Diet Coke. Grey opted for a coffee, Mari a water with lemon, and they all decided to share a loaf of fresh bread with butter and jam.

"I can't believe this place," Mari said in a low voice. "It reminds me of the Petre Toma case the journalist mentioned. Have you read about that?"

As the lieutenant nodded with compressed lips, Grey said, "Who?"

Mari glanced side to side before she spoke. The chatter in the pub had resumed, loud enough to cover their conversation. "A group of Romanian men in some remote village that looked a bit like this one dug up the remains of a laborer who had died not long before—Petre Toma—from a cemetery. The people in the village thought he had become a vampire. After digging up the corpse, the men cut out the heart, burnt it, and drank the ashes in a glass of water."

"Good god," Grey said, drawing back in his seat. "When did this happen? The 1700s?"

"About twenty years ago. It's right there on the Internet."

Grey looked from Mari to the lieutenant. "Is this for real?"

"I wish I could say it wasn't," the lieutenant said. "Local customs vary, but similar incidents have popped up in Central and Eastern Europe since the Toma case, and long before it. The local police prosecuted the men, but they never served time, because no one besides the police thought they should. Here we laugh at the superstitions of the Romanians, but the people in this pub seem to have kept the traditions alive and well."

Mari set her palms on the table and let out a deep breath. By the pain in her eyes, even more evident than her fear, Grey knew she was thinking about her uncle.

As they waited on the food, the lieutenant sidled up to the bar, mingling with the customers. Since Grey did not speak Czech, he was forced to watch as person after person shook their heads at the lieutenant's questions, and gave her sidelong, mistrustful glances as she moved away.

"No luck?" he asked quietly when she returned.

"Not a damn thing. Apparently this address doesn't exist."

They ate in silence, paid quickly, and returned to the lieutenant's car, frustrated by the lack of progress and unsure where to turn. Before they pulled away, a gray-haired woman with a slight limp left the pub, glanced around to see if anyone was watching, then hurried to their car.

The lieutenant rolled down the window and had a quick conversation while the woman wrung her hands and pointed nervously towards a line of sword-like karsts in the distance. When the lieutenant produced her badge, the woman's eyes flicked to the solid door of the tavern. Once they finished talking, she scurried to an old pickup truck, started the coughing engine, and drove away in a cloud of dust.

Grey could tell by the way Mari had paled that she had understood the conversation. "Well? Grey said as the lieutenant pulled out of the dirt lot and sped down the road in the direction the woman had pointed. "What'd she say?"

"First she asked who I was and why I was asking about that address. I showed her my badge, told her I was investigating a murder, and promised her she wouldn't be in any trouble. Then she told me about a stone manor on a hill outside town that might be the place we're looking for. And *then* she told me not to go there if I valued my life."

"If she's so scared, why did she tell you?"

The lieutenant gripped the wheel. "She's not from this village but lives nearby. She came in today to mail some things at the post office. Her cousin disappeared from her village three years ago, and so have other people over the years. According to her, everyone around here believes the family living in that manor is responsible."

"Because the family almost never comes out," Mari added, "and if they do, it's always at night, driving out of the village. People think they're *upíri*. Vampires."

"Superstitious peasants," the lieutenant muttered.

"The Speluncescus have done a number on this place," Grey said grimly. "How far is the house?"

"Ten minutes outside town," the lieutenant said as she turned onto a narrow side road they had driven down earlier in the day, only to turn around when it did not look promising.

Within minutes they had entered the wild and rugged landscape surrounding the village, thickly forested valleys and hillsides punctuated by jagged limestone ridges jutting up like the spiked backs of great saurian beasts. Many of the ridges and karsts were pockmarked by the yawning mouths of caves.

"Did she say what the house looks like?" Grey asked, just as they rounded a bend and saw a dirt drive winding up one of the long limestone ridges, ending at a stone manor perched at the crest like a gargoyle squatting atop a rampart.

"About like that," the lieutenant said.

-29-

The enormous three-story manor atop the ridge was as isolated and inaccessible as any residence Grey had ever seen. Dense forest extended to the horizon in every direction, most of it pine and spruce, evergreens that would keep the property shielded from view in the winter months. The little Skoda bounced and rattled as it navigated the rough road, and Grey had to imagine the Speluncescus drove 4x4 SUVs to access the property. For most of the circuitous drive up the ridge, the manor disappeared from view, only to re-emerge as the road evened out near the narrow limestone crest. Once they reached the top of the ridge, they slowed to a stop as they approached the entrance to the manor, which was protected on two sides by a sheer plunge to the forest floor. The crest of the ridge continued on behind the manor for another quarter mile or so, but the terrain looked rocky, heavily forested, and unnavigable.

As Grey stepped out of the car, his hands tense at his sides, he got a better look at the stone manor in the failing light of dusk. The beige stone walls, stained black in places by age or moisture, had no windows except for a handful of constricted apertures that looked more like arrow slits, and were concealed by red drapes. Turrets, multiple chimneys, and a tall weathervane rose from a pitched roof that rose and fell at irregular angles. Creeping ivy covered the base of the manor and snaked up the walls. Two slender towers carved in bas-relief from the stonework on either side of the front door, an unusual feature, jutted upwards and tapered to a point like upright spears standing sentinel at the front entrance. Other than the ivy and the strange spears, he saw no adornment on the walls or landscaping of any kind. The manor seemed a natural inhabitant of the craggy ridgeline, a wild and barren thing that had formed over the centuries.

The dirt lane had turned into a paved driveway that fronted the manor and continued behind it on the left side, hugging the precipice. The smell of pine infused the air, and a preternatural stillness seemed to encase the ridge, at odds with the chatter of animal life in the forest below.

"What now?" Mari said, peering around the empty grounds. "Do we knock on the door?"

Grey and the lieutenant exchanged a glance. He knew what Zuzana was thinking: that she was a police officer and should not be breaking into houses, but knocking on the front door could be a very bad idea.

"There's not much daylight left," Mari said nervously.

Grey looked around. The sun had sunk beneath the trees, casting deep shadows on the face of the manor. He did not like the isolation of this place. He looked up and noticed, oddly, that all of the windows were on the second and third stories. After compressing his lips, he glanced at the drawn curtains, searching for a sign of life, before approaching the nine-foot-tall front door. He noted the clover-shaped iron knocker and gently turned the handle.

Locked.

Remembering the odd key ring he had found in Dumitra's purse, Grey took it out and tried the large iron key. It didn't fit.

The lieutenant glanced at the pewter sliver of moon that had appeared above the western horizon. "Maybe we should come back in the morning."

"We're going in now," Grey said. "Or at least I am. If we have any element of surprise from driving all the way out here, it will be gone by morning. And so will Viktor, if he's here." As the lieutenant shuffled in place, still looking uncertain, he said, "Let me do some reconnaissance and see if I can get inside. I'll let you in the front door so you technically don't have to break in."

"It doesn't work that way."

"Maybe not, but Viktor's life is at stake. You have to make a decision."

The lieutenant mashed her lips together, took a long look at the house, and let her gaze roam to the surrounding forest. "Fine. Do your thing. If you see someone inside, don't take any risks. Come back for me, and we'll decide what to do. We'll have to give them the chance to talk."

Grey gave a half-hearted nod. He had serious doubts as to whether any meaningful conversation would occur that night. As he started to walk away, he reached into the car and shrugged on the backpack he had brought.

"Be careful," Mari said, gripping his arm just before he hurried around the side of the manor on the paved drive.

The rear of the estate looked similar to the front: high stone walls, windows on the upper stories obscured by drapes, and an imposing door. The rocky ground narrowed to a precipitous point not far behind the manor. The paved drive ended at a little roundabout with two black Mercedes GL SUVs parked side by side. Grey wrote down the plates but did not try the doors, fearing he would set off an alarm.

As he approached the back entrance, a raven cawed and flew out of one of the trees on the stony ridge, startling him. He took a moment to compose himself and lifted the handgun out of the shoulder holster. The door, while it looked just as solid as the one in front, did not have a fancy knocker. He tried the handle. Also locked, and Dumitra's key still didn't work.

The stone blocks forming the manor walls were large and irregular but still too smooth to climb. Even if he could, he doubted the windows were unlocked, and he would be in a vulnerable position. To cover all his bases, Grey circled the entire manor but did not find another means of ingress. Strange for such a large property not to have a side door or first floor windows, but it fit with his general feeling that the manor was more of a fortification than a residence.

He held up a finger to Mari and the lieutenant, asking for patience, then returned to the rear of the property and stood in front of the back door. It had a double deadbolt and a very solid lock that took him ten minutes to pick. Surely, if anyone was home, they had noticed Grey and the others by now. He glanced up at the rapidly darkening sky and felt a shiver whisk through him. After standing in place for a long moment, listening for sounds of occupation from inside the manor, Grey eased the safety off of the handgun and cracked the door open.

No light escaped from inside the house. No sounds or smells other than a faint musty odor. Keeping his gun trained on the inky interior, Grey reached into his pocket with his other hand and took out his cell phone. He flicked on the light, aimed it at the wooden floor in the entryway, and eased the door further open, wary of rusty hinges. After staring into the blackness of the house, letting his eyes adjust, he stepped inside—only to be tackled by someone rushing him from inside the house.

Reacting with instincts honed by a lifetime of martial arts training, Grey fell to his back, dropping both the gun and the cell phone as he grabbed onto what felt like a thick wad of animal fur. He managed to insert a foot into the stomach of whoever had rushed him. Using the attacker's own momentum, Grey used his foot to propel his assailant past him in one smooth motion. Grey leaped to his feet, spun, and saw that he had thrown a man in a shearling jacket out of the doorway and into the deep shadows behind the house. The man rose to his feet almost as fast as Grey, opened his mouth, and bared two sharpened fangs that, while unnerving, were nubs compared to the fearsome length of Cezar and Dumitra's.

A low growl issued from the back of the man's throat. He went right back at Grey, reaching for his neck with both hands. While the man moved fast, he did not move with nearly the speed of the Speluncescus Grey had faced. Grey managed to brush-block the man's outstretched hands away, step to the side, and catch him square on the side of the chin with a straight right. The tip of the jaw is a bullseye. A direct blow like that, snapping the man's head to the side, should have led to vasovagal syncope and unconsciousness.

The man in the shearling coat reeled but did not fall down or cry out. Before he could recover, Grey kept moving forward, throwing a flurry of blows in rapid succession. He landed four more punches, followed by a dropping side elbow that finally made the light go out in the man's eyes. After he fell, Grey kicked him in the head for good measure, then checked his eyes and his pulse.

Unconscious but very much alive.

Footsteps from the side of the house. Grey whirled and saw the lieutenant running over holding her gun. "Where's Mari?" Grey said. "Why'd you leave her?"

"I heard commotion." The lieutenant slowed as she saw the man on the ground. "Who's this?"

"No idea." Grey peeled back the man's upper lip to reveal his fangs. "But he's going in the trunk of the car."

The lieutenant's eyes widened. "Maybe we should stake his heart and cut off his head instead."

"Maybe we should," he said grimly.

She looked as if she wasn't sure if Grey was serious or not. "It doesn't seem like you had much trouble with him."

"He was no Cezar or Dumitra."

"Why do you think that is?"

"No idea," Grey said, though he did in fact have a suspicion gnawing at him, one he was too embarrassed to give voice to.

Maybe the smaller fangs and slower reactions means he's a new vampire. One who's just gaining his powers, speed, and strength.

Except there's no such thing as vampires.

As Grey hoisted the larger man on his shoulders, the lieutenant eased the door shut and followed Grey around the side of the house. When they reached the front, Mari ran over to meet them as the lieutenant opened the trunk and Grey tossed the limp form inside.

"Are you okay?" Mari asked, her voice trailing off as she noticed the same thing Grey had noticed: a weak ray of sunlight, perhaps the last of the day, had snuck through the trees on the western side of the ridge and fallen on the outstretched right arm of their captive. The arm had flopped over the side of the trunk as Grey tossed him inside, and the portion of the flesh on the forearm exposed to the sunlight had started to redden and fester. The blistering effect was much less pronounced than on Anton's arm, but it defied explanation nonetheless.

Or at least rational explanation.

Mari's next comment came out as a croak. "What . . . what is that?"

Grey shoved the arm inside the trunk and shut the lid. "Nothing we can do anything about right now." He took a deep breath and turned to face them. "I should do this alone. Take the car and go back to town. I'll call you if I need you."

"Not a chance," the lieutenant said quietly. She was still staring at the closed trunk. "Whatever this is, you're going to need help."

"My uncle's in that house," Mari said in a small voice. "I know it. So I'm going with you." When Grey started to protest, she said, "Do you really think I'm better off on my own after sunset? Either here or in that creepy town?"

"You can go back to Prague."

"So can you."

"If the Speluncescus are inside, they might leave or call for reinforcements or move Viktor. Or they might just kill him. I'm not taking that chance. I'm going in now, and I'm searching that house."

"Can you call for backup now?" Mari asked. "Since that guy attacked Grey?"

The lieutenant shook her head. "We broke into the house, and even if I could get a warrant, it wouldn't be tonight. No way. Besides," the lieutenant said, holding up her phone, "we haven't had a signal for miles."

Grey had heard enough. Viktor wasn't going to be saved by bureaucracy or playing by the rules. Grey had the strong feeling that, if the professor could still be helped, they had a small window to reach him.

That window being tonight.

Right now.

As Grey spun and walked towards the rear of the manor, Mari and the lieutenant stayed on his heels without a word. When they reached the back door, Grey saw that Mari had taken Viktor's knife out of its sheath and was holding it awkwardly in her right hand. Grey eased open the door with Mari pressed tight against his back and the lieutenant on his left, aiming her gun with both hands at whoever—or whatever—they might find inside.

-30-

The back door to the great manor creaked as it fully opened. Wary of another attack, Grey and the lieutenant stepped into the doorway with their firearms raised, while Mari hovered behind them gripping Viktor's wavy-bladed kris.

No one else rushed them. Grey took the lead, taking a cautious step forward on wide-planked floorboards that had long since lost their sheen. An eerie silence encased the old manor, the anthropomorphic stillness of shadowy nooks and secrets lurking behind closed doors. Motes of dust danced in the minutiae of twilight seeping into the room.

Grey could tell they were in a large spherical foyer with mahogany paneling. The odor of mildew had increased but was not overpowering. After ensuring they were alone, or at least alone in the room, Grey signaled for Mari to close the door.

"No sign of cameras," the lieutenant whispered, waving a small flashlight around the room, all the way up to the twelve-foot coffered ceiling.

"I think the Speluncescus are the security system," Grey said grimly.

"And that guy who bum-rushed you?"

"The doorman. I'd like to save time by spreading out but it's too dangerous. There are two SUVs in the driveway, and I have the feeling someone's home. I don't know where the hell everyone is, but we need to watch each other's backs."

The lieutenant tipped her head towards the arched opening on the far side of the foyer. "Want to take the lead, and put Mari between us?"

Grey nodded and continued towards the archway with his gun at chest level. The opening led to a broad hallway that seemed to stretch on forever. A number of doors branched off the corridor. About halfway down, Grey spied a grand staircase. He moved carefully forward, checking each door as he went, revealing a series of rooms with period furniture. He saw a pair of dark-paneled parlors, a billiards room, and a dining room with a table large enough for a king's banquet. The antique furniture was exquisite but coated with a thick layer of dust. Grey did not see any family portraits on the walls or notice any of the usual bric-a-brac that people collected, such as curios on the shelves or coats hanging on hooks by the doors. The tapestries and paintings felt like museum pieces rather than family heirlooms.

They did not see a soul and did not stop to explore the rooms. When they reached the staircase, a beautiful piece of carpentry with elaborately carved spindles and red velvet handrails, Grey stopped to consider their choices. The staircase curved gently to the upper stories and down to the basement.

"That's odd," Mari said, looking back and forth between the symmetrical set of stairs. "Basement stairs are usually in a separate location, and never this nice."

"It is strange," Grey murmured as the lieutenant shone her light up the stairs, failing to expose anything other than high walls and a hint of silent corridors. The stairs leading down continued much longer than the stairs to the upper floors, perhaps to a cellar deep underground.

Yet as Mari had said, why build such an elaborate staircase for a basement or a cellar?

The lieutenant pointed the light at the floor, leaving their faces in shadow. "Which way?"

"Let's clear this level first," Grey said. "Quickly."

As the night continued to deepen—which Grey could acutely feel, despite the absence of windows and the sense they were walking through an abandoned tomb of a house—they continued down the hall, passing through a series of rooms in rapid succession, poking their heads in long enough to ensure no one was inside. The kitchen on the far side of the hallway was as big as a small house. Remembering the vials of blood in Anton's bedroom, Grey peered into the vintage fridge but found only some hard cheese and a shelf full of bottled water.

He made a mental map of the layout as they proceeded. They did not see any more staircases or means of egress other than the front door and the back, which the lieutenant left unlocked in case they needed to make a hasty retreat. Satisfied the ground floor was unoccupied, they returned to the main staircase and cast the light up and down, straining to hear a sound. The house was so quiet Grey could discern the faint thud of his own pulse, though he wondered if he was not imagining it, a trick of a tell-tale mind to fill the silence.

"What now?" Mari said in a voice so low and throaty he could barely make it out.

Grey pointed up the stairs. The lieutenant did not object. He had the strong feeling they needed to visit the lower level, but first he wanted to know if anyone was upstairs and foreclose any surprises.

They moved through the living quarters on the second floor even faster. The period furniture continued. Like the rooms on the ground floor, the bedrooms and bathrooms had a showroom feel and did not seem lived in. The windows had crimson drapes so thick not a trickle of light passed through. Grey peered behind one of them and saw the ridgeline wrapped in the purple cloak of dusk. A shiver passed through him.

The third floor held more of the same: long lightless hallways, bedrooms that looked as if no one had ever slept in the beds, sitting rooms with no bottles in the liquor cabinets.

"This is just spooky," Mari said as they finished the walk-through.

Grey did not disagree. He led the way to the ground floor and stood beside the staircase, peering down into the depths of the house.

"We can still come back in the morning," the lieutenant said quietly.

"Just be ready," Grey replied, holding the gun in both hands as he took the stairs one by one, creeping down as quietly as he could. The brocaded silk runner softened their footfalls, and the stairs did not creak. He counted eighty-eight steps until the staircase ended at a stone-floored landing with a bronze-studded wooden door on the far side that had not been in their line of sight from the top.

"Why do the stairs go so far down?" Mari said uneasily.

Grey shook his head and put a finger to his lips. The door was almost as massive as the one at the front entrance to the house, and had a beautiful wolf's head handle as big as a bowling ball. He had the feeling this elaborate door at the bottom of the steps was the true entrance to the house.

He gently tried the handle.

Unlocked.

Grey glanced back at his companions before pushing on the door. It opened without a sound.

On the other side, they stepped into a vast room with stone-block walls and an arched ceiling so far overhead Grey had to crane his neck to see the top of it. Thick wooden pillars rose from the floor of the room and connected to a matrix of support beams high above them. The air was ten degrees cooler than on the upper stories. A pleasant earthy aroma with undertones of cinnamon and wet limestone had replaced the smell of mildew.

Dark leather furniture dotted the room, sofas and chairs arranged in seating areas, along with display cases full of jewelry, oil paintings and tapestries, huge rugs with intricate patterns, and a fleet of standing iron candle holders, some of them lit. There were even two metal knights in full plate mail armor on display in the center of the room.

The lit candles put Grey even more on his guard than before. The dim illumination revealed three wide hallways branching off of the great room, each on a separate side.

Grey took a moment to digest the contents of the room, which looked far more personal than the upper levels. Hanging on each wall, he saw a pair of full-size crossed spears with wooden handles and tapered ends that reminded him of the description in Viktor's journal, as well as the stone carvings framing the front entrance. The oil paintings depicted stern men with flowing moustaches and Slavic profiles, their hands resting on the hilts of swords, as well as paintings of both genders astride horses in elaborate equestrian costumes, all holding one of the tapered spears like lances at their sides. The object of the largest portrait of all was a tall, broad-shouldered man with a high forehead and long nose staring imperiously outward, dressed in regal clothing, his palms resting on the silver hilt of a broadsword. The women bearing arms in the portraits seemed uncharacteristic of the time period, which Grey estimated were at least a few centuries old.

One thing it did not take an art historian to deduce was the theme of the portraits.

Whoever these people are, they're a family of warriors.

At first glance, one of the tapestries depicted a scene from a nobleman's hunt, except the canines were enormous, and the lone hunter marshaling the pack on foot—an odd thing to do—carried one of the tapered spears in his left hand. On closer inspection, two things about the tapestry disturbed Grey. The quarry of the hunt was not a grouse or a deer, but a human male clad in a loincloth, running for his life through the forest. At the rear of the pack, the lone hunter's mouth was open as if shouting a command to the dogs, and a pair of sharpened fangs thrust wickedly out of the hunter's gumline.

"These jewels must be worth a fortune," the lieutenant murmured from Grey's left, breaking his morbid fascination with the scene. "Look at this diamond tiara."

Mari snapped her fingers in the air, calling them over. Grey found her standing by a massive hearth edged with mosaic tilework. If functional, the chimney must be over a hundred feet high. Above the hearth, a massive, wooden, almond-shaped shield hung on the wall bearing a familiar motif: a pair of spears forming a cross above a dragon. Unlike the Order of the Dragon emblem, a sickle moon occupied each of the four corners, and the dragon in the center of the coat of arms was emerging from the mouth of a cave surrounded by an artfully carved forest. The muscular claws of the dragon's forelegs were planted into the earth.

"This must be the de Chak coat of arms," Mari said. "I've never seen a cave on one before. I wonder where it came from."

I'm not sure I want to know, Grey thought. The bizarre underground room bothered him more than he cared to admit. He tried to convince himself the Speluncescus were a family afflicted with porphyria or some other rare disease that had caused others to condemn them as monsters over the centuries, provoking the family to carry the vampire ruse further than anyone could have dreamed.

With a grimace, he pushed his thoughts away and focused on his task.

I'm here to find Viktor and bring him home. He can sort out the mystery later.

Grey eyed the open corridors leading out of the room. They were unlit and looked the same to him, stone-walled and rectangular. He chose the one closest to the hearth and waved the others over.

As the lieutenant flicked on her flashlight again, Mari stayed so close to Grey he could feel her hand pressing against the small of his back. The lieutenant's light revealed a door set into the wall on the other side of a stately stone hallway that extended into the darkness on both sides. A sweep of the flashlight revealed unlit candles resting in iron sconces high on the walls, and more doors further down.

The lieutenant covered Grey with her gun as he tried the door across from them. Unlocked. He eased it open and took a quick step back. No one emerged. The lieutenant stepped forward to shine her light inside, revealing a large bedroom with a writing desk, a clawfoot tub, a pair of settees, a wooden armoire, a powder room in an alcove, and a four-poster bed with a midnight blue bedspread that looked rumpled. Sitting at the foot of the bed was a larger version of the medieval iron-banded chest with tiny holes on the side that Grey had seen in Anton's bedroom.

More living quarters far from the light of the sun.

As Grey started forward, determined to force open the chest, he heard a deep male voice calling out behind them.

"Were you expecting to find a coffin in the bedroom?"

Grey whipped around and shined the light across the hallway and into the great room, where he saw Cezar Speluncescu standing beside one of the hulking support pillars near the middle of the room, his strong jaw and close-cropped beard cast in candlelight. The eldest Speluncescu brother was dressed in dark slacks, calf-high boots, and a fitted beige sweater. Rings glittered on his fingers, and a thick silver necklace was draped over his chest.

"Or perhaps you've read one too many Gothic novels?" Cezar continued. "I assure you they provide very little insight into the life of a true vampire."

"Let me know when you find one," Grey said, stepping in front of Mari and the lieutenant, gripping his handgun at his side as he advanced slowly out of the hallway and into the room.

"The curse of this age is disbelief, though I admit it makes our existence in the modern world far easier to hide."

Grey glanced back and noticed the lieutenant taking up a defensive position near the entrance to the hallway, her gun pointed at Cezar. Mari stayed with her, the knife held awkwardly in her hands, looking terrified but determined.

Satisfied they were out of harm's way, or at least immediate harm, Grey took a step forward, his eyes sweeping the room and then Cezar himself, seeing no sign of a weapon. "Where's Viktor?"

"It's poor manners to bring violent intentions into someone else's home."

"Unless the host tried to kill you the last time you met. Now where is he?"

A slow, arrogant smile crept onto Cezar's handsome face. "I believe my brother answered that question last night."

Grey took aim with both hands and leveled his handgun at Cezar's heart. "You may be fast, but you're not faster than a bullet. I won't ask again."

"You'd shoot someone in cold blood?" Cezar mocked.

Grey felt with utter certainty that his adversary would make a move before Grey had to decide on the answer to that question. Keeping his eyes trained on the eldest Speluncescu, Grey stalked forward, aiming to force Cezar's hand, banking his trigger finger could twitch and fire faster than Cezar could lunge.

Instead of attacking, Cezar took a step back. That surprised Grey, unless Cezar was planning to duck behind the wooden pillar. Twenty feet separated them. Grey kept moving forward, keeping Cezar away from Mari and the lieutenant, his eyes focused on the center of his enemy's chest—his center of gravity—as Grey's peripheral vision absorbed a much larger area.

Cezar took another step back, in line with the pillar. Not wanting to lose sight of him, Grey kept moving forward—right until a piercing scream from behind shattered the silence of the room.

Another scream quickly followed the first. Female screams, from two different people. *Mari and the lieutenant.*

Grey did not want to turn his back to Cezar, but he had no choice. Cursing his own stupidity, scuttling backward to create some distance, Grey spun around and saw a sight that chilled him to his core. Next to one of the standing candles, the flickering light illuminating the scene in macabre detail, Dumitra Speluncescu had the lieutenant pressed against the wall, her face buried in the lieutenant's neck, tearing at her throat like a wild animal. Blood was everywhere, covering the stone floor at their feet, drenching their clothes, gushing out of the lieutenant's ruined flesh. Grey did not see her gun anywhere. Dumitra must have rushed out of the hallway and caught her by surprise.

Mari was standing five feet away, paralyzed with fear, Viktor's knife hanging loosely in her hand. She took a step towards Dumitra and raised the knife higher as if summoning the courage to use it.

"No!" Grey shouted. Mari would be torn apart by these people. He stepped forward and pointed his gun at Dumitra, forced to shoot at her legs to avoid sending a bullet through her back and into the lieutenant.

As Grey pulled the trigger, he sensed a looming presence behind him, just before two strong hands grabbed him by the shirt and a powerful force struck him in the side of the neck, right on top of the steel collar Grey had put on before he left Prague.

Cezar roared in pain and backed away. His attack had knocked Grey's shot off target, but Grey recovered quickly and raced towards Dumitra, screaming to distract her. She dropped the lieutenant and turned, blood coating her face as she bared her fangs at Grey like an angry feline, her eyes wild with bloodlust. Grey had the unnerving impression her instincts were urging her forward, like a predator compelled to chase its prey.

You shouldn't have dropped the lieutenant, Grey thought as he pulled the trigger twice in rapid succession, both shots catching Dumitra in the chest. He did not know how she had recovered from their last encounter so quickly—or survived at all—but the bullets ripped through her, causing her to shriek in pain, driving her back and to the ground. She tried to get up but slipped in a pool of blood and fell on her side.

Grey wanted to finish her off but had to spin and find Cezar. The eldest Speluncescu was standing by another of the stone pillars fifteen feet away from Grey, hunched over and pulling at his blood-flecked mouth. As Grey aimed his gun, Cezar flung something away, leaving the jagged stump of a broken fang poking out of the top of his mouth. Grey fired twice, but Cezar ducked behind the pillar to avoid the bullets.

"Clever," Cezar said. "The collar was very clever. But oh, you'll scream for that."

Grey held his gun up as he backed away and to the side, creating a triangular line of vision between him, Cezar, and Dumitra, who had managed to move beside a pillar but seemed shaky on her feet. *How is she still alive, much less standing?* He took a shot at her but she ducked behind the pillar. "Get out of here, Mari! Lock yourself in the bedroom! I can't fight them and watch you at the same time!"

To Grey's relief, Mari did the smart thing and listened to him. With the knife still in her left hand, her other hand gripping the cross necklace he had given her, she sprinted into the hallway and disappeared. Grey heard a door slam behind her and hoped it had a lock that would hold if someone went after her.

The lieutenant was lying motionless on the ground in a pool of blood. He could hear the shallow rasp of her breathing but knew she would not be of any help to him.

He gritted his teeth and shrugged out of his backpack. The Speluncescus were foes unlike any he had ever faced, but Grey was a warrior too.

A warrior who had dedicated his life to his art from a very young age.

A warrior who would give no quarter and ask for none in return.

In the corner of his eye, Grey spied Cezar walking swiftly to the closest candle holder and snuffing the wick. Grey fired but was too slow. Across the room, Dumitra did the same, evading his shot by ducking behind another pillar. As Grey swiveled, trying to keep them in his sights while deciding on a course of action, Cezar extinguished two more candles, moving too swiftly in the failing light for Grey to hit.

"Be careful, Mother," Cezar called out. "The human has protection for his vitals."

Dumitra hissed in reply as she darted out to extinguish another candle, limping but still incredibly swift. Grey missed her by inches this time.

Two candles remained, one of them beside a pillar thirty feet to Grey's left, the other close to Dumitra.

"It's almost a new moon," Dumitra mocked in her hypnotic voice. "Then however shall our visitor see?"

Grey shrugged off the weirdly narcotic effect of Dumitra's voice by summoning his anger and focusing on the fight. Watching the room carefully, he used one hand to remove the canteen from the backpack and unscrew the lid. He slipped on the backpack again. Both Speluncescus had disappeared into the darkness. He knew they were going to try for the remaining candelabras, and given that knowledge, he decided to act. The candelabra behind Grey was close to the wall and easier to defend, but also closest to Cezar, who was mostly unharmed and, at this point, the more dangerous opponent.

Grey's eyes moved back and forth in a constant pattern, waiting for them to make their move. Seconds later, both Speluncescus darted out, racing forward so fast Grey could hardly believe it, moving like shadows whisking across a wall. As Cezar went for the candelabra to Grey's left, Grey put his disbelief aside and sprinted across the room towards the second one. Dumitra closed in on the light source. Grey fired six shots in rapid succession. Instead of trying to hit her slender form racing through the darkness, he aimed at the candelabra instead, knowing she would reach for it, hoping she would be unable to stop her forward momentum in time.

His ploy worked. Just as Dumitra reached the candle and snuffed it with her hand, two of Grey's shots found their home and slammed into her chest, spinning her around. He was less than ten feet away now, still racing forward, and shot her in the chest again. She stumbled and fell, crying out as she did, her hands reaching up, grasping for air. He ran right up to her and shot her in the head, the powerful caliber weapon exploding her skull, spraying blood and gray matter as her lifeless body collapsed on the floor.

"*Mother!*" Cezar roared from across the room—right as the final light went out, casting the underground chamber into absolute darkness.

-31-

Footsteps racing across the floor. Grey gripped the gun and stepped back, wanting to reach for the light on his cell phone but not daring to take the time. He fired off another round—he knew he did not have many left in the magazine—but heard the bullet thump against the stone wall. Before Grey could back up again, two red eyes appeared in the darkness right in front of him, and then Cezar was on top of him, swiping the gun away and clutching Grey by his jacket in both hands, hissing as he leaned over to bite Grey's face.

Grey did not have time to do anything except fall backwards, let his back hit the floor, and throw up his hands to ward off the attack. Cezar bit down onto the leather wristband, causing him to howl in fury but not shattering his fang as he had on the iron collar. In a rage, he used his superior weight and strength to keep Grey on his back, gripping the front of his motorcycle jacket while he bit even harder, piercing Grey's skin through the bracelet. Grey jerked his arm away and got it loose. His opponent snarled and went for his face again. Again Grey stopped him with the thick leather band on his right arm, but this time Cezar reached up to pull Grey's hand away.

A heavy smell of cologne and Dumitra's spilled blood washed over Grey. He tried to resist but Cezar was much stronger. Once he moved Grey's arm, he would have a clear path to his face, and the fight would end in a very ugly way.

Grey's other arm was still free and holding the canteen of holy water. Hoping for a miracle, he dumped the canteen on Cezar's head. The water had no effect. Not even a twitch. Next Grey jerked the silver cross off his neck with his free hand and shoved it against Cezar's face, hoping the contact with his flesh would deter him.

Still nothing.

Cezar's weight was crushing him. Grey went for Cezar's eyes, but the larger man lowered his head and shook off the attempt. Sweat stung Grey's own eyes as Cezar kept forcing his arm away from his face. Grey resisted with all his might, but it was a losing battle. He felt his arm slipping down, and knew Cezar would overcome him in moments. Desperate, Grey groped the floor with his other hand, brushing against Dumitra's limp black hair before feeling something long and metal in his fingers. *The candelabra.* With a sharp intake of breath, Grey used all the strength in his forearm to heave the heavy object in the air and bring it crashing against the back of Cezar's head.

The blow stunned the eldest Speluncescu. Grey felt the weight on his chest and arm slacken, allowing Grey to execute a sweep from his back and throw Cezar off him. In an instant Grey had scrambled away, reaching for his cell phone as he raced across the room, putting as much distance between them as he could.

"Run, prey," Cezar said in the darkness. "The hunt is the best part."

Grey did not have the option of trying to flee the manor because of Mari and the lieutenant. He had lost his gun, the cross and holy water had failed, and Cezar could see in the dark and knew the outlay of the house. This left Grey with no weapons or options against a deadly foe whose strength and powers seemed supernatural.

"You killed mother. For that you'll die a thousand deaths on a thousand torture racks."

Grey backed into one of the wooden posts and saw, across the room, a pair of red eyes moving towards him in the darkness.

Working to suppress the shudder rolling through him, telling himself that Dumitra had fallen and Cezar was just as mortal, Grey tried furiously to think of a way to defend himself.

The red eyes moved closer. Grey could sense the fury radiating out of Cezar as if from a furnace.

Wishing he could reach one of the spears high on the wall, Grey stepped out from the post to give himself room to maneuver, readying his hands for a fight he did not think he could win.

All of a sudden, he realized there was another weapon in the room he could use.

A weapon in the gauntleted hands of a knight.

Grey flicked on the light on his cell phone. The small halo of illumination allowed him to see Cezar's shadowy form advancing on him from across the room. Grey glanced quickly around to orient himself. The two suits of armor in the center of the room were spaced ten feet apart. Grey was about thirty feet away from the nearest one. When Cezar gave chase, it would be a close call.

In another flash of motivation, remembering the barely controlled bloodlust in Dumitra's eyes, Grey realized Cezar's predatory instincts might work against him. If Grey dashed across the room as if going for the door to the stairs, passing right by the knight on his way, Cezar might chase him without thinking too hard that his fleeing prey might turn and fight.

Grey did not want to admit that Cezar and Dumitra were not fully human, but if they were indeed some sort of superhuman predator, then those instincts he had sensed when Dumitra had stared hungrily at Mari's fleeing back, as if she were something to be chased down and killed, might give Grey an edge he could use.

Cezar and his burning red eyes drew closer. Grey had to act now or he would lose his chance. Gripping the cell phone in his left hand, he feinted one way and then turned and dashed across the room, in a direct line to the door to the stairs. Behind him, he heard Cezar's footsteps pounding on the stone as he gave chase, approaching shockingly fast. As Grey neared the first armored knight, Cezar had drawn so close Grey could hear his harsh breathing.

The elbows of the knight were bent, holding the sword hilt at waist level. The tip of the sword was pointing downward into a pedestal at the base of the figure, hopefully into a slot from which the blade could be extracted. If the sword was affixed to the base and did not easily slide out, Grey would have no defense when Cezar pounced on him from behind.

Grey drew level with the knight. Cezar was right on his heels. Grey had the sudden visceral awareness—a primal, subconscious certainty—that Cezar was a predator and Grey was his prey. He knew it deep down inside, as if this knowledge were imprinted there by events occurring deep in the prehistory of the human race, instilling an instinctual reaction in both pursuer and pursued.

As Grey reached out to grab the hilt of the sword, he threw the cell phone behind him without looking, hoping to hit Cezar in the face and divert his attention from Grey's actions, even if just for a moment. Grey did not hear a reaction, but to his great relief, the knight's sword slid out and came into his hands in one smooth motion. Grey didn't even have to break his stride. The weapon was much heavier than he expected, but Grey had trained extensively in Kenjutsu, the art of the sword, and he could adjust. He knew exactly how to move his feet and wield the blade.

Throwing the phone had cost Grey his light source, but there wasn't time to use it anyway. Grey had only one shot at ending this fight, and, with Cezar so close on his heels, he did not need vision to try it. Sensing his enemy was inches behind him, knowing he was about to pounce, Grey spun and thrust upward with the weapon, feeling sweet satisfaction as the blade caught Cezar in the stomach and pierced his flesh. Cezar's momentum carried him right into Grey, and Grey stepped into the thrust and drove the blade upward, impaling Cezar's internal organs as the sword ripped through his guts and came out of his back.

Not even Cezar, whatever he was, could withstand such a blow. He dropped to his knees with his hands clasped around the edge of the sword in vain, as if trying to force it out, cutting his hands in the process. Grey thrust the blade even deeper, shoving Cezar to his back on the floor. Wary of removing the blade in case Cezar might recover, Grey kept a foot on his chest in the darkness to ensure he knew where he was and could not get away. Grey let go of the sword, jerked off his backpack again, took out the utility knife, and drew it deeply across Cezar's throat.

The big man gurgled and choked and eventually lay still. As his life blood poured out of him, Grey could not help but wonder at the origin of that blood. Was it gained from his victims over the years? Enhanced by some bizarre cocktail of Mother Nature or science? He held his enemy down until he could no longer feel a pulse, and waited another minute to be sure. Flush with adrenaline, Grey spied the glow of his cell phone and retrieved the device. He shone the light into Cezar's eyes and saw no flicker of life.

What if he can regenerate those wounds? Should I pierce his heart with the wooden stake?

After all that had happened, Grey still had no idea how to separate myth from reality. But he was taking no chances. He had shot Dumitra in the heart at point-blank range in Budapest, only to see her make a full recovery within days. Wary of the unexplained powers of the Speluncescus, Grey pulled the sword out of Cezar's body and, with a few heavy swings, hacked through his neck. When he finished, he pushed on the severed head with his toe, watching it roll across the floor like the denouement of a Greek tragedy. With grim satisfaction, Grey carried the sword to Dumitra's body, relieved to see it was still in the same place, and repeated the gruesome task.

Grey stood over her headless corpse, breathing heavy, then rushed through the shadows of the great room to check on the lieutenant, his stomach clenched with dread. He found her sitting with her back against the wall in the same place he had left her. She had taken off her blood-soaked jacket and tied the sleeves around her neck as a tourniquet. The bleeding had stopped but she must have lost a ton of blood.

Thrilled she was alive, he tempered his relief when he heard her labored breathing and saw how dull her eyes looked. *I should have prepared her better against these monsters. I should have insisted she wear the collar.*

"We have to get you out of here," he said.

She pushed her words out with great effort. "No. Find Viktor. I'll survive."

He wasn't so sure about that.

"Go," she said, sensing his indecision. "I wasn't asking."

"Okay," he said finally. "I'll hurry."

She didn't respond, and he realized he might not be out of danger either. Anton Speluncescu was still out there somewhere, possibly in the manor. With a start, he realized that Florin, too, was still missing.

Grey rose, moving swiftly to the bedroom door just inside the hallway, and knocked on the door.

"Mari," he said in a low voice. "It's me."

The door flung open. Mari stood in the room with a wild look in her eyes. "Thank God you're alive. Where's Zuzana?"

"Alive. Barely. We have to hurry."

"My uncle?"

"I killed Cezar and Dumitra, but I have no idea where Viktor is. And Anton and Florin are unaccounted for. They could still be inside."

Mari's eyes swam with fear, but she absorbed the information with a determined nod. "I'm not leaving until I know my uncle isn't here."

Grey set the backpack down and reloaded the magazine in Viktor's pistol. "Agreed. We need to search the rest of this basement. But first—" Grey approached the chest and placed the tip of the sword against the padlock—" We have to know what's inside this thing.

A heavy blow from the sword sufficed to break the clasp securing the chest. Sensing the chest contained some secret important to the Speluncescus, Grey toed open the splintered lid with his boot, inhaling the same foul stench of rotting meat that had wafted out of the chest in Anton's house.

Inside, Grey saw a mushroom growing in a pile of moist soil that filled half the chest. The stalk of the mushroom was grub-white and thick enough to support a two-inch cap that shone with a pale green phosphorescence. The cap was unusual, inverted like a hollow bowl instead of the typical bulbous head Grey was used to seeing. Tiny thorn-like protrusions covered the inside of the cap, toothy little protuberances that reminded him of a carnivorous plant like a Venus flytrap. The comparison strengthened when Grey picked up one of the splinters from the chest and poked the center of the hollow cap, causing the entire head to clamp down on the intruding object.

Mari gripped his arm and peered over his shoulder. "What *is* that?"

Grey eased her away, put a foot inside the chest, and ground the mushroom into the dirt with his heel. "Something that shouldn't survive," he said grimly, shouldering the backpack again. "C'mon. We need to hurry."

Before they searched the rest of the level, Grey used his cell phone light to wade through the darkness cloaking the great room. After taking another look at the headless corpses of the Speluncescus, reassuring himself they were still in fact dead, he retrieved both handguns and the lieutenant's flashlight. Debating whether or not to drop the sword, he decided to keep it, and returned Viktor's handgun to the shoulder holster. He handed the lieutenant's gun to Mari and gave her a quick tutorial on how to use it.

Searching the rest of the basement revealed three more bedrooms, all with dirt-filled chests supporting a single mushroom that looked identical to the first. Grey crushed them all. They also found a refrigerator full of bottled blood, a lounge with a television and leather furniture, and a well-appointed office with desktops, cables and routers, and file cabinets full of papers. He found a glass in the lounge, filled it with water from the sink, and brought it to the lieutenant.

"Thanks," she said, still very pale and struggling to speak.

"Do you want to move to the bedroom?" he said. "It might be safer."

"No. Better to . . . stay here."

Mari held out the gun. "Take it."

"I'm too weak. Keep it. Now go."

They hurried away, and Grey's hopes soared when they found another staircase, much narrower than the main one, that led up through an unlit stairwell. Thinking it might lead to a hidden room, he was disappointed when they pushed through a concealed door into a sitting room on the first-floor library.

Mari put her hands against the sides of her head. "My uncle has to be here somewhere."

Grey didn't want to voice the alternative out loud.

Unless they killed him and buried the body.

Not sure where to look next, they returned to the great room, searching for incongruities. Finding the hidden door to the sitting room made him think the house might contain more secrets. He tried moving the pedestals beneath the sets of armor but they wouldn't budge. There were no rotating stones or hidden levers near the hearth, nor did any of the jewelry cases respond to manipulation. After thinking through everything he had seen that night, he crossed through the deep shadows filling the room to stand in front of the large tapestry depicting the creepy hunt. The wall hanging was made of a material that felt like reinforced silk and looked very old, perhaps medieval. Though the weight of the tapestry kept it hanging tight to the wall, it was not secured at the bottom. When Grey took one of the edges of the tapestry and peered behind it, he saw a cavity in the wall. He assumed there was some mechanism to raise the tapestry but didn't have time to search for it. After calling Mari over to help hold the edge, he squeezed behind the embroidery to investigate the opening, and found a set of rough-hewn stone steps leading down into an even deeper darkness.

-32-

Mari joined Grey at the top of the hidden stairwell as he peered down the twisting stone steps that wound into the bowels of the earth beneath the manor.

"Whatever's down there," Grey said, "I'd feel a lot better if you let me investigate."

Mari held the gun awkwardly against her chest, as if she were cradling a baby bird. "We're wasting time. My uncle could be down there."

With a grim nod, Grey took the lead and crept quietly down the primitive steps, pausing every few feet to listen, straining to peer into the darkness. The stairwell seemed carved straight from the limestone and bore no ornamentation.

Grey counted one hundred steps until they arrived at a small landing with a stone door built right into the bedrock. The door had no apparent lock or handle other than a square hole two fingers in width, right in the center of the door. Grey tried pushing on the door to no avail. It felt as solid as the earth. He shone his light into the opening but saw only a notched hollow space about two inches deep.

"How do we get inside?" Mari said in frustration.

Grey stared at the strange opening, his memory sparked by the odd shape. "I think I might know," he said, digging in his pocket again for the key ring he had found in Dumitra's purse. In addition to the large iron key, there was a two-inch granite object with notches along both sides.

He tried sticking the unusual granite object into the opening in the door.

A perfect fit.

Grey turned the stone tool clockwise, resulting in a series of clicks that caused a palm-sized window around the cavity to swing open, revealing another keyhole behind it. Grey tried using the iron key on Dumitra's keyring, and felt a tingle of satisfaction as the key began to turn and another lock clicked open.

Grey pushed. The heavy stone door made a faint protest as it swung inward to reveal three final steps leading down to a dirt-floored passage that disappeared into the darkness. A stench wafted down the tight corridor, similar to the foul odor in the Speluncescu's chests, and this time the darkness was not absolute: in the distance, a faint green glow emanated from an unseen source.

Grey turned to Mari and pressed a finger to his lips. She swallowed and gave a single nod in return. Stepping quietly in front of her, he gave her the flashlight, then gripped the sword and eased the gun out of the holster with his other hand.

The passage was five feet wide and rose a foot above his head. The eerie green glow increased as they walked, enough for him to see on his own. The source was revealed when the path dead-ended into a limestone wall at a T-junction.

A much wider dirt-floored passage ran on either side of the T-junction, bisected in the center by an underground stream spanning about three feet in width. The water was still and clear, glistening eerily in the dim green light. In the soil along both sides of the stream, a little forest of bioluminescent mushrooms had sprung up, identical in appearance to the ones in the wooden chests, except they ranged in size from mere nubs to specimens over two feet in height, with caps as large as a garbage can lid. The protrusions lining the inside of the inverted caps resembled fangs more than thorns, and Grey had the distinct impression the organism was waiting for something to pass by so it could snap shut on the unfortunate creature.

"Christ," Mari said with a shiver. "There's hundreds of them. Have you ever seen a corpse flower? That awful smell is similar. This looks like a fungus, though."

Grey did not know what they were, nor did he care. He just wanted to stamp out every single one of the monstrous things. With a grimace, he asked Mari to shine the light up and down the pebble-bottomed stream, but they detected no movement. Though the underground nursery of carnivorous plants posed no real threat, it gave Grey the shivers, a cradle of unnatural life in a place devoid of sound and light except for that alien green glow.

Both passageways looked identical. Grey chose the left one at random. With Mari close to his side, he pressed forward, unsure what to expect or how deep the passages would go, harboring very little hope of finding Viktor alive.

About fifty yards later the stream spilled into a larger pool of water sheltered by a cavern with stalactites clinging to the twenty-foot ceiling. More of the glowing fungi ringed the pool, a scene of otherworldly beauty despite the stench.

Mari touched his arm as she shone the light towards the far-left corner of the cavern. He turned and saw a small cluster of knee-high stones that resembled grave markers. Grey did not want to waste more time, but he walked over for a quick glance, catching his breath as he looked for Viktor's name.

His first instinct had been correct; the collection of upright stones were indeed headstones. They were carved with the name and date of the deceased, but only two family names were represented: de Chak and Drăculeşti.

On the right side of the creepy little graveyard—who puts the family cemetery in an underground cave?—was a mound of freshly dug earth. He shone the flashlight at the headstone to illuminate the name.

Florin Drăculeşti.

"That solves that mystery," he muttered as Mari stood by his side, joining him as they stared in silence at the headstone. He could tell by her small release of breath that she harbored a similar fear of finding her uncle.

"They killed him," she said. "Because he wouldn't stay quiet."

"I suppose so," Grey replied, though he could sense her thoughts. *If they murdered their own family member, what would they do to Viktor?* "Let's go," he said in a rough voice.

They swept the cavern with the flashlight and saw no other exits. After retracing their steps along the underground stream back to the T-junction, they followed the passage for a similar length on the other side before it spilled into another cavern much larger than the first. The stream widened as it ran through the grotto before flowing through an opening in the opposite wall, a waterway bored through the porous limestone over the eons.

When Grey saw what else occupied the cavern, the two gargantuan fungi sprouting from the soil on either side of the subterranean river, chills swept down his arms, and the sour taste of bile rose in his throat.

Mari gasped and put a hand to her mouth. "Uncle," she said with a sob, crossing herself as she absorbed the awful sight.

For a moment, Grey found himself frozen with inaction, fixated on the terrible sight of Professor Radek imprisoned inside the bowl-shaped cap of a seven-foot-tall fungus, or whatever the thing was, with a stalk as thick as a telephone pole. Grey could not see all the way inside the massive cap from his vantage point—it was too tall— but he could see the sinister thorn-like protrusions lining the edges. The inverted cap had such a wide diameter that Viktor was secured inside it with his limbs spread-eagled. His hands and feet were manacled and kept in place with wire cables that draped over the side of the thing, then attached to steel hooks mounted in the floor. A thick iron chain extended from the cavern ceiling to a harness wrapped around the professor's waist, keeping him suspended inside the giant maw.

Grey could not see Viktor's eyes or tell if he was alive, but he was unmoving and had not responded to his niece's voice.

"Uncle!" Mari cried again.

As she started to dart towards the base, Grey held her back. "I'll go," he said, raising the sword in preparation to chop down the stalk of the vile thing. He did not know if the fungi could snap closed or had other defense mechanisms, but if so, he wanted to be in the line of fire.

The stench of rotting meat was overwhelming, almost causing him to gag as he advanced with his eyes trained on the sinister thorn-like protrusions. When he drew to within ten feet, a scream from Mari diverted his attention.

"Grey! The other one!"

Confused at first, Grey spied movement in the corner of his eye. He whipped to his left to see a bald, deathly pale man clad only in a pair of brown pants climbing out of the inverted cap of the other giant fungus. The man placed his hands on the lip of the bowl and vaulted over the top with the agility of a gymnast, landing catlike on the ground. Grey was stunned when he saw the man's aged face and sagging white skin. He must be a hundred years old. His face bore a distinct resemblance to the other male Speluncescus, while his long nose, high forehead, and imperious brow matched the oil painting hanging in the great room of the manor.

Good God, is this the family patriarch? Evzen Speluncescu?

Belying the display of agility, the elder Speluncescu had a sleepy look to his eyes, as if he had just awakened from a deep slumber. Blood trickled from fresh wounds all over his body, and Grey sensed he had disturbed Evzen from some ritual or state of symbiosis with the horrid host creature.

Evzen had two-inch long fingernails and toenails that tapered to sharpened points at the ends. Half of his face was disfigured with the sort of wrinkled, pinkish scar tissue that signifies a burn, giving Grey the distinct impression that someone—perhaps a group of angry villagers—had once dragged him into the sunlight.

As the old man released a bestial roar, Grey saw that he did not have any teeth except for two knife-sharp fangs that sprang out of his upper gums as his mouth opened, the fangs extending halfway to his chin and curved like a sabre-tooth tiger's. He realized by now they could retract their fangs as they wished, and that was the last thought Grey had before Evzen sprang across the ten-foot-wide stream in one bound, moving even faster than Cezar, so fast Grey would not have thought it possible.

"Stop!" Grey shouted as Evzen came at him with his terrifying fangs bared.

The old man kept coming, forcing Grey to shoot him in the chest. The bullet barely had an effect. Evzen twitched and then leaped on Grey before he had a chance to shoot him again or use the sword. Evzen swiped the gun out of Grey's hand and shoved him to the ground with superhuman strength, the old man's face stretched like a ghoul as he bent down to bite Grey's neck, his red eyes glowing like hot coals in the semi-darkness. Grey dropped the sword and threw his hands up in defense. Evzen bit down, the knifelike fangs impaling the center of Grey's palms.

Pain seared through Grey as the monstrous old man pulled his head back, straddled Grey, and gripped him by the throat with both hands, his long fingers curling around the steel collar. Grey realized he should have let Evzen bite his neck and break his fangs on the collar, but the shock of his appearance and the speed of the attack had caused Grey's instincts to take over.

Grey tried everything he could to worm out from underneath his opponent or throw him off, but the old man had the strength of a giant. Realizing Grey's throat was protected, Evzen held Grey down by the neck as he sank his fangs into Grey's right arm, cutting through muscle and tendon, causing Grey to arch in agony and drop his weapon.

A gunshot interrupted the fight, followed by another. At the sound, Evzen reared up and cocked his head like a dog or a wolf. Grey saw bloodlust drenching his eyes, a look even more crazed than Grey had seen with the other Speluncescus. At first Grey feared Mari was shooting at Evzen's back, not understanding the bullets would rip through him and hit Grey. But as Evzen clambered off him, Grey saw that she had turned the weapon on the giant organism from which the elder Speluncescu had emerged. Mari was gripping the gun in both hands and wading through the stream as she advanced, firing the gun over and over, ripping bullets into the cap and thick trunk.

While the thing gave no sign of distress, Evzen uttered a strangled cry, jumped up, and ran towards Mari with his fangs bared.

"Mari!" Grey yelled. Pushing through the intense pain in his right arm and palms, he leaped to his feet in one smooth motion, grabbed the sword off the ground with his left hand, and ran after them.

Mari turned to shoot Evzen before he reached her, but she was too late. He surged towards her and backhanded her with such force that her head snapped back, and she dropped the weapon. Grey could tell the blow had knocked her unconscious by the way her body sagged before she hit the ground. Whether consumed by bloodlust or unconcerned with Grey, Evzen pounced on Mari, yanked the turtleneck down, and sank his teeth deep into her neck above the collar. Aghast and enraged, Grey raced forward and drove the sword into Evzen's back, feeling a rush of satisfaction as the blade cut deep into his flesh, stopping his thrust before he impaled Mari as well.

Evzen roared and whipped around, leaving Mari bloody and unconscious on the ground. Grey lost his grip on the sword and watched in terrible fascination as Evzen reached back, grabbed the hilt, and slid the blade out of his body. Grey knew he should never back up in a fight, but the aberrant nature of his foe caused him to take a step back as Evzen flung the sword aside and advanced in a crouch, fangs glistening and hands spread wide, the tips of his elongated fingernails extended like daggers. Weaponless, Grey tried to think of something, anything, that might affect this monster and turn the tide of the fight. He tried a snap kick to the groin as Evzen rushed him, but Evzen pushed through the blow, grabbed Grey by the lapels of his jacket, and threw him against the cavern wall ten feet away.

Dazed, Grey thought he might lose consciousness for a moment, but he blinked his eyes over and over, willing himself to stay awake.

Evzen roared again and stalked towards him, slowed from the pain of the sword thrust but looking more than capable of finishing the fight. Grey's eyes swept the room, desperate. He saw the sword lying on the floor beside Mari, but Evzen stood between Grey and the weapon. Even further away, barely visible in the faint green light limning the cavern, he caught a glint of steel from his gun.

Grey knew he could not outrun this monster and reach his weapons. Even if he could, he wasn't sure it would matter. He had just impaled Evzen and watched him pull the sword out of his body. The only option Grey had left was his bare hands and the pack still on his back. Grey mentally ran through the contents as he dropped the backpack to the ground and thrust a hand inside. *Wooden stakes, a hammer, a utility knife, and garlic.* The knife or the hammer seemed to be the obvious choice. The other Speluncescus had not reacted to the cross necklaces or the holy water, making Grey think most of the lore surrounding vampires was fictional, and the items in the backpack would be equally useless. *Whatever these things are, they were made by Mother Nature and not the Devil.*

Grey heard Evzen's bare feet slapping on the cavern floor as Grey's fingers closed on the utility knife and the hammer. He jerked them out just in time to turn and thrust the knife into his enemy's stomach, and swing the hammer at his head.

Evzen threw up a clawed hand to block the hammer, but the razorlike utility knife bit deep. A groan of pain escaped his lips, but he still managed to knock the hammer away, jerk out the knife and toss it to the side, grab Grey again, and shove him down. As blood poured out of Evzen's body from the stab wounds, Grey attacked with a flurry of blows, hands and knees and headbutts, but they barely seemed to affect his opponent.

Evzen had both hands on Grey's collar again, holding him down at arm's length, his clawed fingernails digging into Grey like thorns around the metal collar. The monster raised his head and opened his mouth wide, his fangs gleaming and his foul breath washing over Grey. Squirming like a trapped snake, Grey tried every move he knew from the ground but could not get free. His hammer blows against the backs of Evzen's elbows, hard enough to shatter the bones of a normal man, did not even distract him.

Desperate, Grey felt around with his hands, trying to find the knife so he could plunge it into one of Evzen's eyes. Instead his left hand closed on the open top of the backpack. Evzen bent down for another bite attack, forcing Grey to throw up his injured right arm. Enraged, Evzen clamped down on Grey's arm again, then jerked his fangs out and grabbed Grey's arm to force it away from his face.

Almost swooning with pain, Grey kept his focus and used the distraction to dig into the backpack. Hoping to grab the stake, his left hand closed instead on a handful of garlic in the bottom of the pack. The stake must have fallen out of the bag during the chaos. Left with no choice, Grey grabbed as much garlic as he could and pulled out his hand.

Evzen reared back in preparation for another attack. Holding Grey down by the collar and wrist, straddling his chest in a secure position, the wrinkled head thrust down once again, the wicked fangs arcing towards the center of Grey's face. Just before those awful teeth sank in, Grey raised his left hand and thrust it into Evzen's mouth, shoving it as far down his throat as he could.

Grey roared in pain as the fangs sliced like knives into his arm. He released the garlic and jerked his hand out of Evzen's mouth, hoping he had bought himself an instant of time to roll away. Yet instead of fighting for his life, Grey found himself pushing to his feet, watching the old man's eyes bulge as he gagged and grasped at his neck. His grub-white face twisted in agony and he began choking violently. Evzen tried to shove one of his clawed fingers into his throat, desperate to pull out the offending objects. The length of his claws seemed to deter him, and he gave up the effort, jerking to his feet and stumbling away. He began to shake uncontrollably as his skin turned bluish-purple and veins popped all over his body.

Grey was shocked by the reaction but did not wait around to ponder it. Instead he flew to his feet, hesitated for an instant with indecision, then sprinted to the sword instead of the gun. Quick as a cat, he snatched the blade by the hilt and changed direction in an instant, fighting through the pain in his palms and his numerous bite wounds, gripping the sword in his left hand as he raced towards Evzen, who was hunched over as he tried to dig the garlic out of his throat, shaking even more violently. Blood gurgled out of his mouth from where his clawed fingernails had pierced his flesh trying to extract the garlic.

Grey adjusted his grip as he approached, placing his hand just under the hilt with the thumb pointing forward, guiding the blade. Rearing back with his elbows, tensing his core and legs for power, Grey drew even with his opponent and swung the sword as hard as he could. At the last moment, Evzen saw him coming and tried to back away, but Grey was too close. He struck his neck in stride and at the perfect angle.

The monstrous patriarch's head fell away from his torso and thudded onto the floor.

Consumed in his own bloodlust, Grey kicked the head away like a soccer ball, raised the sword again, and impaled his enemy through the heart. He drove the blade all the way through until it hit stone on the other side, then stood and watched as blood and ichor spurted from the neck of the headless body. Satisfied there would be no unholy resurrection, Grey took the first-aid kit out of the backpack and sprinted to Mari's side. She was bleeding from the bite wound in her neck, but not as heavily as if an artery had been severed. As he bound the wound with gauze and medical tape, her eyes fluttered open.

"I'm okay," she said weakly. "Help Viktor."

With a nod, Grey left her and grabbed the sword again. He cut through the cables bolted to the floor which were keeping Viktor's hands and feet attached to the side of the giant organism. The professor's body sagged as his limbs were released, though he did not react in any way, and he was still held in place by the harness around his torso, connected to the chain hanging from the ceiling.

Grey started to chop down the stalk of the abomination when he realized he would not have a way to reach Viktor. Instead Grey dropped the sword and reached up to hoist himself onto the seven-foot-high edge of the inverted cap. With a grimace, both from the pain of his wounds and the grotesque sensation of placing his hands on the firm, rubbery flesh, he grabbed the lip of the cap and lifted himself up. The surface held, allowing Grey to throw a leg over and scramble onto the edge. His right arm screamed in pain and for a moment, he thought he might pass out. He took a few breaths to steady himself and looked down, grimacing when he saw the four-inch-long thorn-like protrusions covering the surface of the bowl-shaped depression like the back of an iron maiden. There were fresh puncture wounds covering Viktor's hands and feet, and minute trails of blood on the sides of the fungus. Grey shivered, knowing the Speluncescus had fed Viktor to the disgusting thing, and it was slowly consuming him.

After surveying the situation—Grey did not want to free Viktor from the harness only to see him fall onto a bed of spikes—Grey realized the leather harness holding Viktor in place could be unstrapped without having to cut through the chain attaching it to the ceiling. He called out to Mari, "I want you to chop this thing down. Are you recovered enough to do that?"

"I can do it," she said, in a firmer voice than before.

When Mari called out that she had the sword in her hands, Grey vaulted across the cap to the chain keeping Viktor suspended in the center of the fungus. Grey clamped onto the chain above Viktor's inert form, wincing at the gray pallor of his friend's skin and how frail he looked.

Most of all, Grey shuddered when he saw the miniature fangs growing out of Viktor's gums, and the way his fingernails had lengthened and begun to taper into sharpened points.

"Cut it down," he said grimly.

It did not take her long. As she chopped through the stalk, the weight of the giant cap caused the thing to collapse on itself. Mari kept swinging until the cavern floor was covered in thick white chunks. As Grey started unlatching the clips of the leather harness, Mari cleverly chopped off the thornlike protrusions from the largest pieces, forming a safe cushion for Grey and Viktor to land on. When she had finished, Grey held Viktor in his arms, undid the final clip, and the two of them plunged to the cavern floor, landing unharmed atop the rubbery sections.

Mari gasped and clapped a hand over her mouth when she saw the tiny fangs protruding from Viktor's gums. Grey rolled him onto the cavern floor and bent down to check for a pulse on the side of his neck.

A faint throb pushed against Grey's fingers. Grey closed his eyes and exhaled. "He's alive."

"Thank God," Mari said, gripping her uncle's hand.

With a grunt of effort, his wounds dripping with blood and the nerve endings in his palms and right arm screaming with pain, Grey managed to hoist Viktor's huge body to his shoulders in a fireman's carry. "Chop down that other abomination," he said to Mari as he started walking towards the passage leading to the underground stairs, "and bring the sword and gun."

When he returned to the great room, he quickly told the lieutenant what had happened. Shocked, she managed to stand and walk slowly up the stairs beside him. Mari caught up to them as they reached the ground floor, Grey carrying Viktor on his back and reaching for the sword with his free hand, the fiery glint in his eyes daring the shadows to come to life.

-33-

After leaving the manor, they were surprised and unsettled to find the trunk of the Maruit had been opened, and the man they had stashed inside was gone.

Grey noted dents and scratched paint along the rim of the trunk. "Someone pried this open. From the outside."

"Anton?" Mari asked.

"Maybe. Though I would have expected him to stick around and join the party."

Together they eased Viktor into the back seat. He was breathing fine but still unconscious. Mari sat beside him and helped prop him up. The lieutenant gave the keys to Grey and eased into the front seat, stumbling on the way. Using the cord on a phone charger, Grey tied the trunk down as best he could. By the time he returned to the front seat, the lieutenant was barely conscious, her breathing shallow and unsteady. "Prague hospital," she said. "Not here."

Grey grimly thrust the key into the ignition. On the drive back, he noticed fresh tire tracks on the dirt road, as if someone else had just come from the manor. As they drove through the village, Grey's eyes narrowed when they passed the *Village Arms*, where a few dozen people had congregated in the parking lot with shotguns and other firearms. They were also carrying axes, pitchforks, and dangerous-looking farm implements which Grey guessed they had taken off the walls of the pub. A long row of gasoline containers were lined up on the brick path leading to the pub, and a blood-spattered shearling coat was hanging from the front door, on top of the double-tailed lion and in the center of the four white crosses.

"I think we just found out what happened to our prisoner," Grey said.

Mari was staring in shock at the villagers. As Grey drove by them, one of them pointed out their car to the crowd. Grey tensed, ready for anything, but instead of trying to block the car, the villager who had noticed them raised a closed fist in the air as they passed.

Grey assumed one or more of the villagers had followed them to the manor earlier in the night. Maybe they knew the Speluncescus were dead already, and maybe not. Either way, he knew they had decided not to be victims any longer. He gave them a nod in return and kept driving.

Grey drove straight to a hospital in central Prague. After dropping off Viktor and the lieutenant with the emergency medics, he and Mari tended to their own wounds. Before they left, a doctor told them both the lieutenant and Viktor had lost an alarming amount of blood. Both were set to receive a massive transfusion.

After walking to grab some fast food nearby, Grey and Mari crashed overnight in the waiting room of the hospital, sick with worry. In the morning, they woke to the excellent news that Viktor and the lieutenant had stabilized, as well as a local news report about a large estate that had burned to the ground during the night near the village of Lovecký Odpočinek. They stared at the smoking remains of the Speluncescu manor on the television in the waiting room, stunned by the sight.

Mari translated the news report for Grey, describing how the local firefighters claimed the blaze had been sparked by gunfire striking canisters of gasoline. They guessed a gunfight had occurred inside the manor sometime during the evening. There was no mention of any headless corpses, underground caverns, medieval chests with foul odors, or strange mushroom-like organisms growing in the dark.

Grey had still not decided what to tell the police. Thankfully, Lieutenant Andrasko managed to dictate a report before Grey was questioned. The report described how Viktor and the lieutenant had worked together to investigate the red market allegations, and how the Speluncescus had kidnapped the professor in retaliation. Acting on a tip the lieutenant did not think warranted backup—she would have some explaining to do on this—the lieutenant had gone to the manor and found Viktor imprisoned in the basement. On their way out, she was attacked by Cezar Speluncescu and his dogs. She had shot Cezar, but one of the dogs had bitten her on the neck. Barely conscious himself from deprivation and torture, Viktor had carried her out, hidden in the woods, and called Grey and Mari for help. They had arrived, fended off another dog attack, and driven straight to the hospital.

"Necessary lies," the lieutenant had told Grey, "unless you've figured out how to convince everyone what truly happened."

Viktor regained consciousness later that afternoon. Though groggy and out of sorts, he stunned the doctors with his strength and vitality in relation to his blood loss. Viktor asked for food and water and demanded to know the full story at once. Staring uneasily at his teeth and pale skin and long fingernails, Grey and Mari gave him a lengthy recap of the events that had transpired since he had disappeared. Viktor listened intently and peppered them with questions, but did not offer any thoughts of his own. They also briefed him on the lieutenant's story.

By the second day, the professor was of sound mind enough to file a formal complaint against the Speluncescus concerning his kidnapping, including the potential role of Anton. The complaint mirrored the lieutenant's report, and the two together, combined with Europol's own file on the Speluncescu family, was enough to spark an investigation and issue search warrants for Anton's residence and the nightclub.

"Everyone believes the Speluncescus were protecting their criminal empire," the lieutenant said over lunch. "Which in fact they were. There will be questions, some of which we can't answer, but we police tend not to worry too much about the death or disappearance of human traffickers."

On the evening of the third day after the nightmare at the manor, Grey and Mari joined Viktor in the study of his Prague townhome. The professor had checked out of the hospital and asked to see them.

Outside the bay window, the sun had set, but the cobblestone street was aglow with warm pools of golden light cast by the gas lamps. Grey and Mari knew Viktor could not yet tolerate direct sunlight. It did not burn him like it had the Speluncescus, but it made him very uncomfortable, though his condition did seem to be improving. When he first awoke in the hospital, and a nurse opened the blinds in his room, he had bellowed in protest and retreated under the covers like a child.

"I have a theory or two," Viktor said, peering into the glass of absinthe he had prepared despite the doctor's orders.

Grey gave a small smile. His neck, hands, and right arm were still bandaged from his wounds. "I bet you do."

The professor was sitting in his overstuffed chair by the window, one leg crossed, freshly shaven but wan and malnourished from his captivity. He had asked the lieutenant to come over, but she was busy with work.

"How are you feeling?" Mari asked, walking over to lay a hand on Viktor's shoulder. "Are your vitals still good?"

"Surprisingly so. I believe the strange properties of the organism allowed me to survive the ordeal as long as I did, and recover much faster than normal. The blood loss would have eventually killed me, but whatever symbiotic properties the thing imparted gave me strength as well." He studied his fingernails, which Mari had clipped for him in the hospital. "And, of course, initiated a few changes."

Grey took a seat in an armchair across from Viktor. "I don't quite follow. I get that the Speluncescus were using those things to turn themselves into . . . vampires." He still felt ridiculous saying the word. "But how?"

"I don't exactly know," Viktor said slowly, "except that I *felt* it. On my second day in the hospital, I still felt better than I ever had in my life. Stronger. Faster. My senses were sharp like an animal's. I could hear whispered conversations from across the room, smell subtle odors from down the hall. It's fading, though. Just as my tolerance of sunlight is slowly returning, I feel as if these extraordinary abilities have diminished." He wiggled his fingers and bared his teeth, which looked normal again. "My nails have stopped growing in that absurd manner, and the new fangs I had pulled have shown no sign of returning."

As soon as Viktor woke up and realized he had two sharpened fangs growing out of his gums above his upper canines, he had called in his startled dentist to remove them at once. Grey had not heard the exchange between Viktor and his dentist or the doctors concerning the baby fangs, but no one had mentioned them again. Viktor had a way of cowing people into silence when he desired.

"Thank God for that," Mari said, taking a seat as well. "I'd prefer to see my favorite uncle without little pointies in his mouth."

Viktor patted her hand. "Thank you my dear. I as well."

"So you were a vampire for a while," Grey mused, "and now you're not."

The hint of a smile lifted the corners of Viktor's mouth. "That's a debatable conclusion, though not unwarranted. I'm certain prolonged exposure is key to the advancement of the . . . condition."

"That's why Evzen was the strongest of all," Grey said. "He'd been letting that thing feed off of him for decades. So what's the grand theory? How is such a thing possible?"

Viktor spread his hands, contemplative. "In the same way that parasitic wasps employ a form of mind control over their hosts, or countless other examples of extraordinary, belief-defying abilities imparted by Mother Nature. She is strange beyond all reckoning, even more so than I had grasped." Viktor shifted in his chair, uncrossing his legs as he glanced out the window. "Who knows when or where it started, how far back in history human beings discovered the creature. I believe that Nicholas de Chak—the oldest of the line I could trace—brought something back from his travels to the East. He was a trader on the Silk Road, and after one of his ventures, his family had a sudden explosion of wealth and power that lasted, well, until about three days ago. I can only surmise that what he brought back from some faraway land was a progenitor of the things growing beneath the Speluncescu manor. We should appoint a proper name for the species, should we not? Our very own discovery? Perhaps something along the lines of *Dracofungila*?"

As he chuckled, Mari rolled her eyes. "Let's stick with *the organism* for now."

"As you wish, dear. In any event, I further surmise that Nicholas de Chak was given instructions by someone on how and where to grow it and ensure its survival. The lineage of this mysterious 'benefactor' is a fascinating mystery I plan to explore. Was there once a tribe or even a race of hominids who once cultivated the organism in mass quantities? Did this occur in multiple locations around the world, or only in a singular cave system? Did diverse species or genera of the creature in prehistory account for the proliferation and variations in the vampire legend around the world? There are untold numbers of unexplored cave systems. Do more strains exist in lightless places we have yet to explore?"

"Let's hope not," Mari said with a shiver. "But what *is* it? A fungus, a plant?"

Viktor shrugged. "It does appear to be a fungi, though perhaps it's some new kingdom of living thing altogether. A carnivorous one that, I have to surmise, evolved to survive on the blood it was able to capture from other primitive life forms deep inside the earth."

"What a disgusting thing."

"So are ticks, mosquitos, and vampire bats. The more remarkable trait is how prolonged exposure results in such extraordinary symbiotic changes to the physiology of human beings. A cocktail of heretofore unknown chemicals must surely be involved. One can only imagine this was revealed by chance—like a great number of miraculous scientific advances—and expanded by trial and error. Perhaps in the dawn of history this discovery even changed the course of evolution, and allowed two species—the organism and the hominids who discovered it—to adapt together in some remote location. I doubt we shall ever know for sure."

"So that's why sunlight had such a powerful effect," Grey mused. "Growing underground made it vulnerable to any exposure to the sun."

"And garlic is toxic to many living things," Mari said. "It's even used as an antifungal. It must be poison to those things."

"And to those who use them," Grey said. "If not, I'd be dead right now."

"We all would be," Mari murmured.

That sobering thought induced a spell of silence. Eventually Viktor said, "Some snakes have retractable fangs. As Grey and I have seen before, engorged muscles and dagger-like growths on fingernails, which are formed of keratin, have names in science: hypertrophic myopathy and keratinopathy. In addition, two very real medical conditions, cutaneous porphyria and xeroderma pigmentosum, can result in severe, blistering burns after minimal exposure to sunlight. I'm sure that with the proper study, all of the bizarre powers imbued by regular exposure to the organisms can be explained by science."

"So you don't think they're immortal?" Mari said.

"Apart from Bram Stoker's infamous count, there's no evidence that any member of the family lived beyond the natural human life span. Evzen was obviously quite ancient, but I believe the protracted exposure allowed him to survive into very old age with extraordinary health and strength, and probably a heightened immunity to disease. The ultimate quality of life boost. But do they survive beyond 120 years or so? Again, we've seen no evidence."

"Maybe their ancestors are deeper underground," Mari muttered. "Locked away with those horrid things."

"What about Dumitra's weird charisma?" Grey asked. "Whenever I looked at her, it almost felt like she was casting a spell on me."

"Perhaps she was," the professor said softly. "The spell of a woman secure in her control over men, a heightened charisma born of natural beauty, money, power, and the knowledge that she was in effect a supra-human creature. We have seen this type of *spell* before, have we not?"

Grey looked away, thinking of a masked priest in Zimbabwe with a highly persuasive baritone voice, and a line of blood on the floor which Grey convinced himself he could not cross.

"It's hard to think of the Speluncescus as human beings and not monsters," Mari said with another shudder. She had a long leg thrown over the side of her chair. "But they were only people. Florin was just a confused kid. He wanted to live the romantic side of the myth and his own family killed him for it."

"Yes," Viktor agreed. "I do not believe he killed Daryna. Both their deaths were tragic. I've a feeling the Speluncescus had a custom of gifting one of the creatures to their children when they turn eighteen, or perhaps after college. Such a tradition would preserve the normalcy of the family in the eyes of society. Perhaps there are other considerations as well, such as exposing children at too young an age. I also suspect prolonged contact results in more than just physical changes. It might even change the brain chemistry, engender a lack of compassion."

"A lack of love as a child or a life of crime do the same thing," Grey said. "Human beings don't need to swap spit with a giant mushroom to start killing each other. So where does it go from here? If the secret gets out, what will people do? How will they react? There are plenty of those monsters growing beneath that manor, and some people will do anything to get them. Governments, corporations, criminals, biotechs who could mass manufacture the stuff."

"Which is exactly why I've taken steps to ensure the secret remains with us," Viktor said. "Science might benefit from studying the organism, but as you say, the knowledge would get out, and the results would be unpredictable. I called my lawyer from the hospital. She has already started the paperwork"

"For what?"

Viktor flashed a grim smile. "Once the fire cooled and the police were able to search the property, they found a collapsed tunnel in the great room at the bottom of the long staircase."

Grey's eyebrows lifted. "The villagers. They must have sealed it off."

"I assume so as well. Let's hope one of them was not tempted to take home a souvenir. In any event, I'll soon be the proud owner of the land housing the former Speluncescu manor. Once I take possession, I'll clear the rubble, make sure the life forms in the caverns are destroyed, and reseal the entrances for good."

Mari's brow knitted. "Are you sure that's the right thing to do? If it could cure even one disease . . ."

"I'm sure," Grey said, forcing away a mental image of Evzen's scimitar-like fangs clamping down on his arm and trying to bite his face. "We don't need something like that on sale at the garden store."

"I have to agree," Viktor said to Mari. "Normally I applaud science and progress, but the temptation for evil is too great, as the Speluncescus have proven."

"But they're just one family."

"Are they? In all the many manifestations of the vampire legend that have arisen around the world, I do not recall a single positive association. Instead there is death, fear, evil, and superstition."

"Maybe that would change if people knew the truth."

"And maybe it would get worse."

She looked away and did not seem convinced.

"History might judge us harshly," he said gently, "but so be it. I've made my decision."

"What if there's a will? Or some other family member steps forward?"

"Someone like Anton," Grey added. Ever since their return from the manor, he had kept a wary eye out for an appearance from the middle Speluncescu brother.

"Thus far," Viktor said, "my attorney has uncovered neither a will nor competing claims to the estate. He believes the property will go to auction, and, well, let's just say I will not be outbid. As for Anton . . ." Viktor took a long sip of absinthe and let it linger in his mouth. "Yes, he would have a claim to the manor. But I heard from the precinct just before you arrived tonight. The captain informed me that Anton has fled the city and left his possessions behind. None of his associates claim to know his whereabouts. He has been formally charged as an accessory to my kidnapping and the nightclub is closed for the time being. I specifically asked about vials of blood or an antique chest, but nothing of the sort was found in either the nightclub or his house. Nor did the police spot any unusual houseplants."

"He took it and left," Mari said in a whisper. "He'll start again someplace new."

Viktor fixed Grey with a level stare. "Anton was last seen leaving his nightclub with Pavla Čapek."

"Who?"

"The woman I interviewed at the Parlor, and who seemed quite taken with the vampire mystique."

Grey took this as a warning for the future. He leaned forward in his chair and gave the professor a hard stare of his own. "What about you? Will you really destroy every last one of those abominations in your new basement, or let one live in case you change your mind?"

Viktor absently ran his tongue over his gumline just beneath his upper lip, a movement that seemed habitual but which Grey had never seen before.

"I'll do what I must," the professor said.

"See that you do."

The professor compressed his lips and gave a solemn nod. "Thank you both again, by the way. For everything."

Mari walked over and flung her arms around her uncle. After she disengaged, Grey rose and put a hand on his shoulder. "I'm glad you're back, old friend."

"I'm glad that I'm lucky enough to have you watching out for me."

Later that evening, after Mari ordered Indian takeout and the three of them enjoyed a light dinner conversation that did not involve vampires or bizarre organisms or ancient mysteries, Grey opted for a night walk to help digest the tandoori chicken. Mari saw him to the door and said, "What time is your flight?"

Grey shrugged into the new motorcycle jacket he had purchased. He had loved the worn leather of the old one, but the fangs and claws of the Spelunscescus had shredded the sleeves beyond repair. "Nine in the morning."

"Back to New York?"

Grey hesitated. "Two days in Athens, and then yeah, back home."

"Athens?"

"I'm meeting someone for the weekend. A doctor who helped me out in Skopje."

Mari's eyes twinkled. "Oh, I see. *That* kind of weekend. You definitely deserve it. Is she brilliant and beautiful and worldly?"

"More or less."

Mari reached up to straighten the collar of his jacket. "Try to be a little more presentable, okay? Buy some luxury soap, see a stylist, wear something besides jeans and a black shirt every now and then."

"None of those things will ever happen."

She patted his cheek. "A girl has to try." As he opened the door to leave, her eyes slid into the darkness outside as if wary of what she might find. "You don't think Anton . . ."

"Will try to take revenge?"

She swallowed and nodded.

"I think Anton Speluncescu is a coward at heart," he said. "Long gone from the city, and never to return."

"I hope you're right."

Grey pointed at a dark blue sedan parked halfway down the block. "Viktor hired a private security firm to watch the house for the remainder of your visit. They have very explicit instructions on how to deal with Anton if he does appear. Viktor has a top-notch security system as well."

Mari stared at the sedan for a long moment. "Remember what I told you when we met? That I believe in everything?"

He chuckled. "I accept your *I told you so*. Want to walk with me?"

She blinked as if awakening from a daydream. "I think I'll stick around here, catch up on my yoga and work on the doc. I have some scenes swimming in my head I need to type up."

"Good luck with that. For the record, I think it's a brave topic."

"Thanks," she murmured. "When it's finished, maybe I'll tag along with you two for inspiration on my next one."

Grey zipped up his jacket, the movement causing a twinge of pain in his palms and right arm, and didn't answer. He did not know what the future held, and was not in the line of work conducive to someone *tagging along*, but he thought he knew Mari well enough to know that if she set her mind on something, there was probably little that Grey, Viktor, or anyone else could do about it.

After she closed and locked the door behind him, Grey thrust his hands into the pockets of his coat and set off on his walk, his boot knife in place and his hands brushing against the bulbs of garlic he had brought with him, just in case he was wrong about Anton.

As the cobblestones fell away beneath his feet, Grey's eyes searched the darkness with habitual caution as his mind roamed elsewhere, from the mysteries of the endless night sky to the whispered secrets embedded in the old stone walls of Prague.

To stay up to date on future Dominic Grey novels, as well as other new releases, please join Layton Green's VIP Reader's Group at:

www.subscribepage.com/laytongreen

Until the next adventure,
Layton

ACKNOWLEDGMENTS

In recent months, my dear friend and literary confidante, Russell Dalferes, passed away unexpectedly. Rusty read and edited every single one of my novels, including this one, and had an indelible hand on my work. Thanks for a lifetime of memories and collaboration, old friend. You will be dearly missed.

My amazing wife provided invaluable commentary on this book, as did early readers John Strout and Lisa Weinberg. A special thanks to Miloš Jovanović, historian and urban studies scholar at UCLA, for his insight into Matthias Corvinus and the Order of the Dragon. I consulted too many books on vampire mythology to list, but much of my knowledge about the red market stemmed from journalist and bestselling author Scott Carney's nail-biting and bravely researched book *The Red Market: On the Trail of the World's Organ Brokers, Bone Thieves, Blood Farmers, and Child Traffickers*.

LAYTON GREEN is a bestselling author who writes across multiple genres, including mystery, thriller, suspense, horror, and fantasy. He is the author of the Dominic Grey series, the Genesis Trilogy, the Blackwood Saga, and other works of fiction. His novels have been optioned for film, translated into multiple languages, and nominated for awards (including a rare three-time finalist for an International Thriller Writers award).

Word of mouth is crucial to the success of any author. If you enjoyed the book, please consider leaving an honest review on Amazon, Goodreads, or another book site, even if it's only a line or two.

Finally, if you are new to the world of Layton Green, please visit him on Goodreads, Facebook, Author Central, or at www.laytongreen.com for additional information on the author, his works, and more.

Books by Layton Green

THE DOMINIC GREY SERIES
The Summoner
The Egyptian
The Diabolist
The Shadow Cartel
The Resurrector
The Family
The Reaper's Game (Novella)

THE BLACKWOOD SAGA
Book I: *The Brothers Three*
Book II: *The Spirit Mage*
Book III: *The Last Cleric*
Book IV: *Return of the Paladin*
Book V: *A War of Wizards*

THE GENESIS TRILOGY
Genesis
Revelation
Ascension (forthcoming)

OTHER WORKS
Written in Blood
A Shattered Lens
The Metaxy Project
The Letterbox

Printed in Great Britain
by Amazon